# COMPASS SOUTH

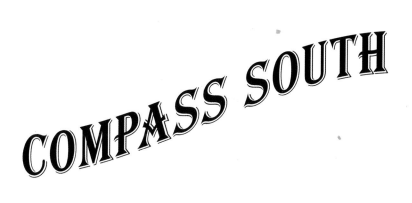

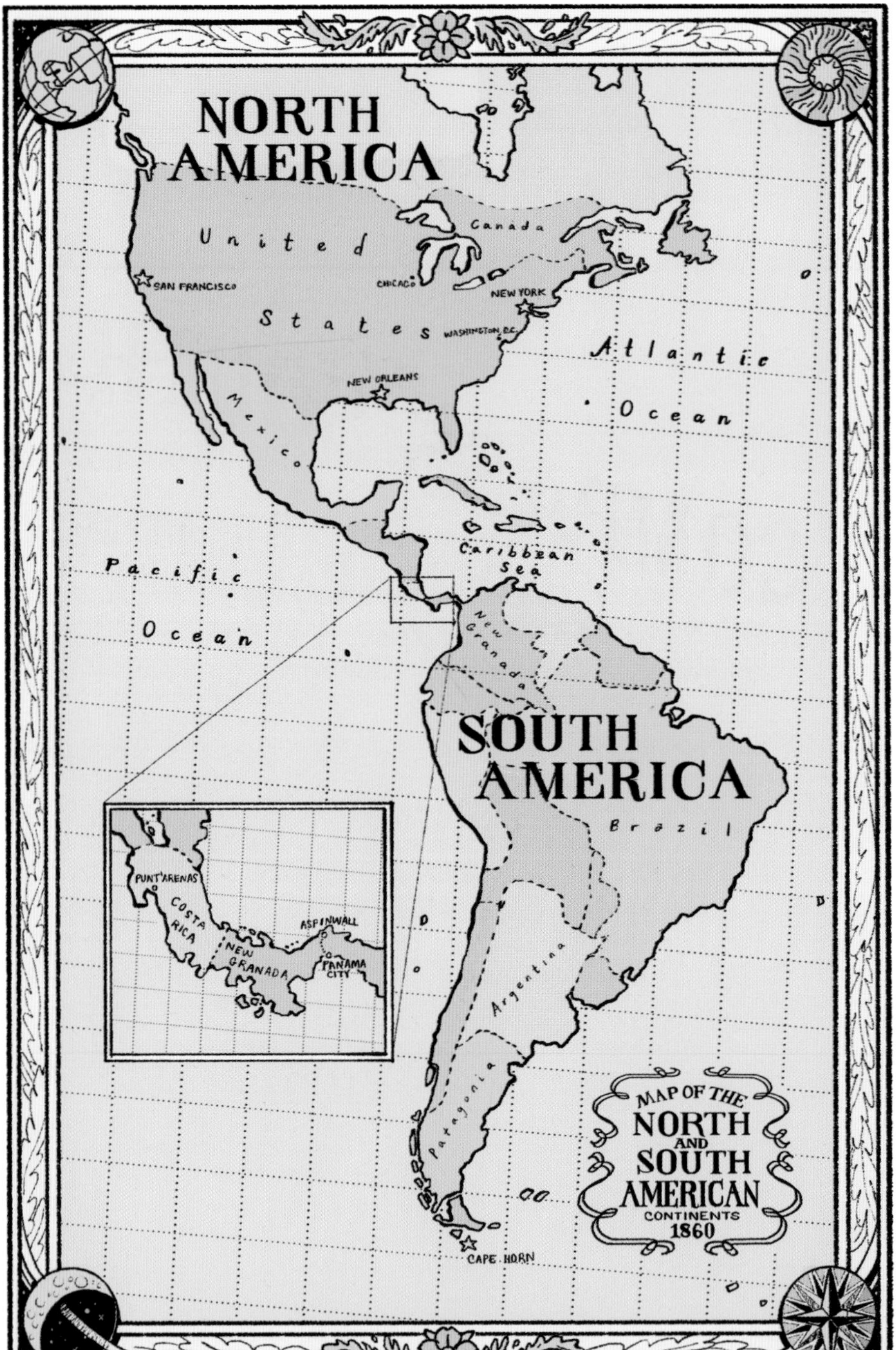

NORTH AMERICA
United States
Canada
SAN FRANCISCO
CHICAGO
NEW YORK
WASHINGTON, D.C.
NEW ORLEANS
Mexico
Atlantic Ocean
Pacific Ocean
Caribbean Sea
New Granada
SOUTH AMERICA
Brazil
Argentina
Patagonia
CAPE HORN
PUNT'ARENAS
COSTA RICA
NEW GRANADA
ASPINWALL
PANAMA CITY
MAP OF THE NORTH AND SOUTH AMERICAN CONTINENTS 1860

# HOPE LARSON

COMPASS SOUTH

BOOK 1

FOUR POINTS

*Illustrations by*

# REBECCA MOCK

SQUARE
FISH

MARGARET FERGUSON BOOKS
**FARRAR STRAUS GIROUX**
New York

*To Will, the original red-haired brother*
—H.L.

*To John and Kelly, my Alex and Cleo*
—R.M.

An imprint of Macmillan Publishing Group, LLC
120 Broadway,
New York, NY 10271
mackids.com

Square Fish and the Square Fish logo are trademarks of Macmillan and
are used by Farrar Straus Giroux under license from Macmillan.

Our books may be purchased in bulk for promotional, educational,
or business use. Please contact your local bookseller or the Macmillan Corporate
and Premium Sales Department at (800) 221-7945 ext. 5442
or by e-mail at MacmillanSpecialMarkets@macmillan.com.

Library of Congress Control Number: 2015039907

ISBN 978-0-374-30043-2 (Farrar Straus Giroux hardcover)
3   5   7   9   8   6   4

ISBN 978-1-250-12184-4 (Square Fish paperback)
7   9   10   8

Originally published in the United States by Farrar Straus Giroux
First Square Fish Edition: 2017
Square Fish logo designed by Filomena Tuosto

AR: 2.4 / LEXILE: GN290L

# TABLE OF CONTENTS

# PROLOGUE

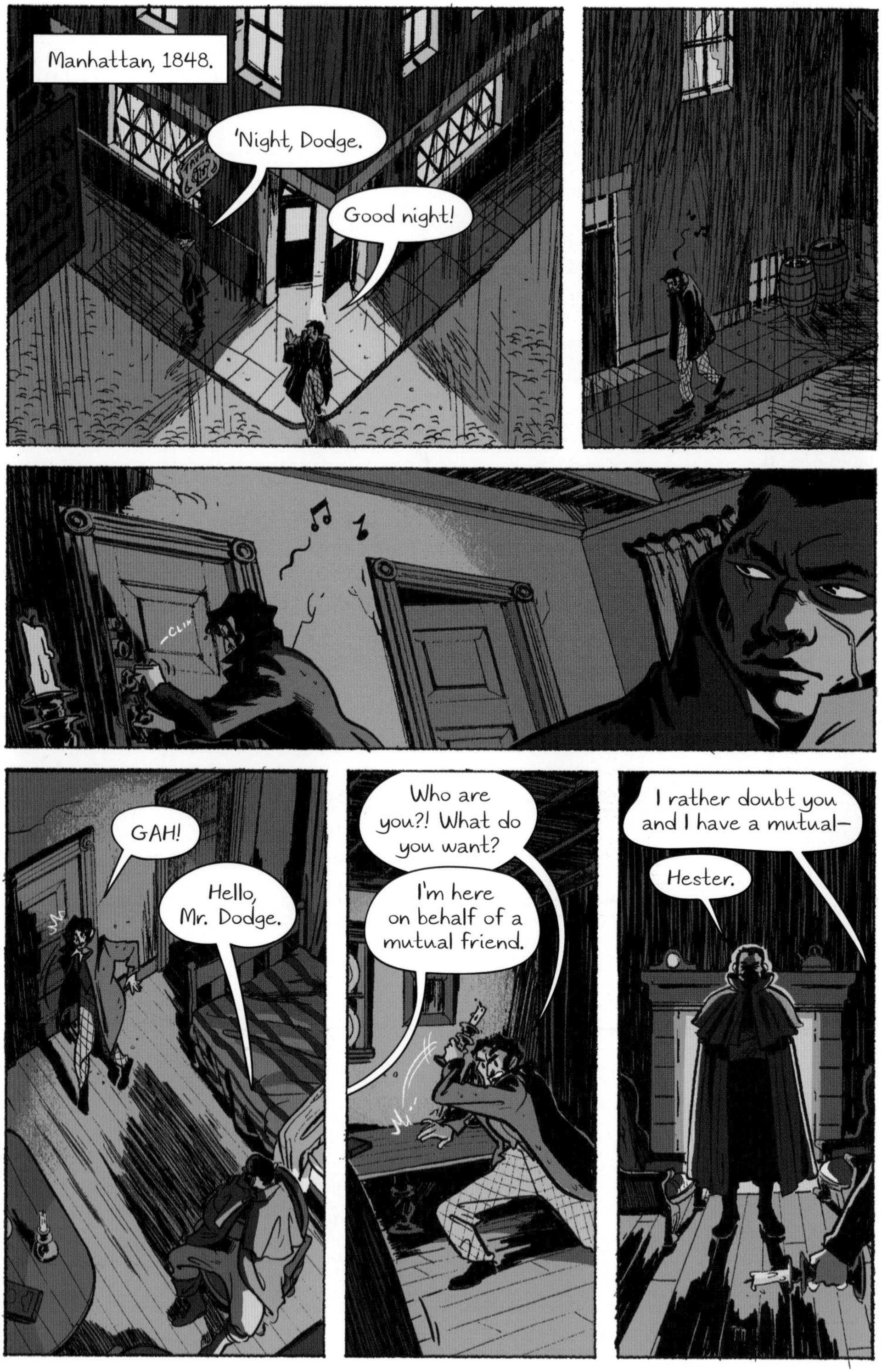
Manhattan, 1848.
'Night, Dodge.
Good night!
CLIK
GAH!
Hello, Mr. Dodge.
Who are you?! What do you want?
I'm here on behalf of a mutual friend.
I rather doubt you and I have a mutual—
Hester.

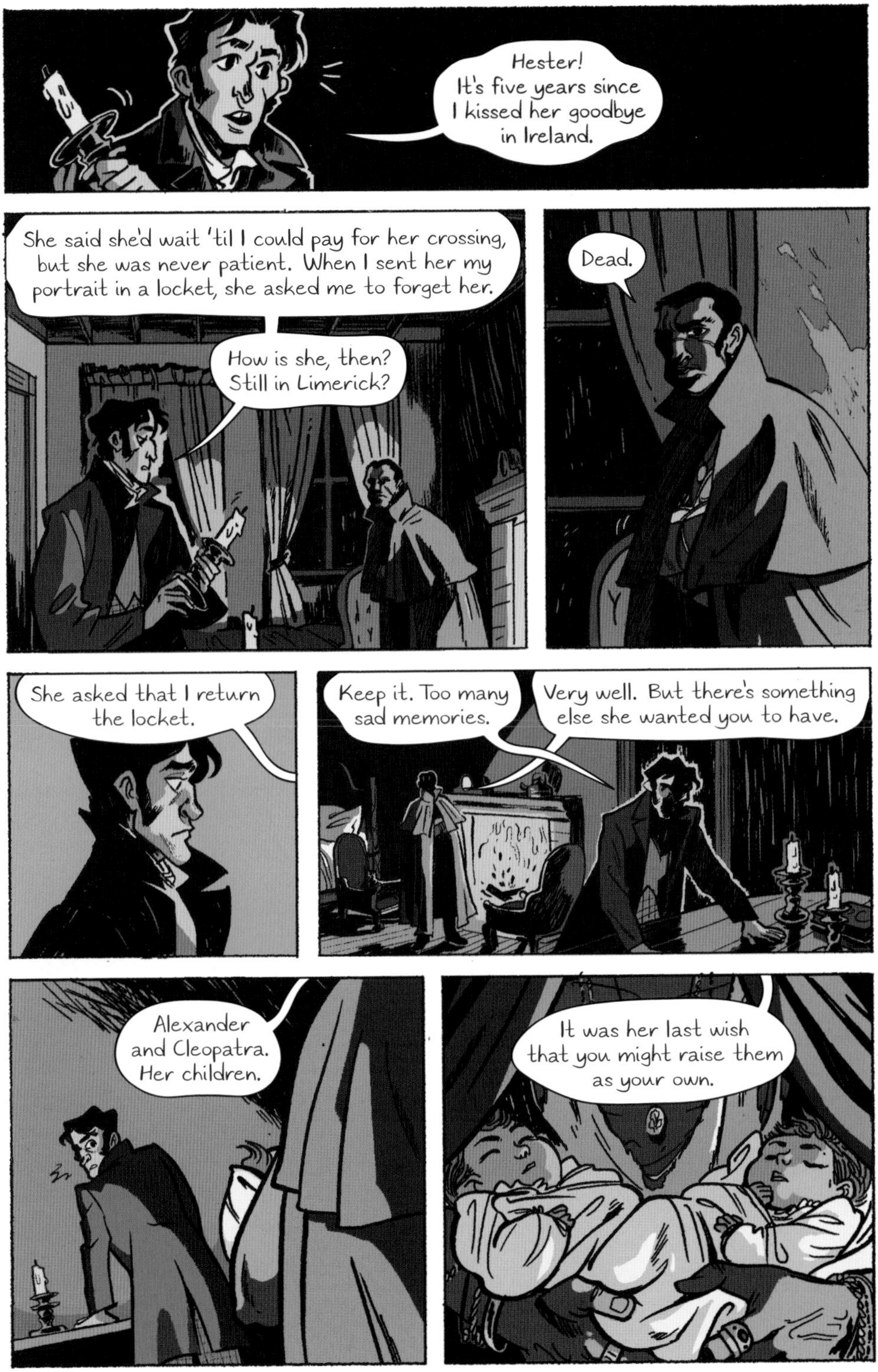
Hester!
It's five years since I kissed her goodbye in Ireland.
She said she'd wait 'til I could pay for her crossing, but she was never patient. When I sent her my portrait in a locket, she asked me to forget her.
How is she, then? Still in Limerick?
Dead.
She asked that I return the locket.
Keep it. Too many sad memories.
Very well. But there's something else she wanted you to have.
Alexander and Cleopatra. Her children.
It was her last wish that you might raise them as your own.

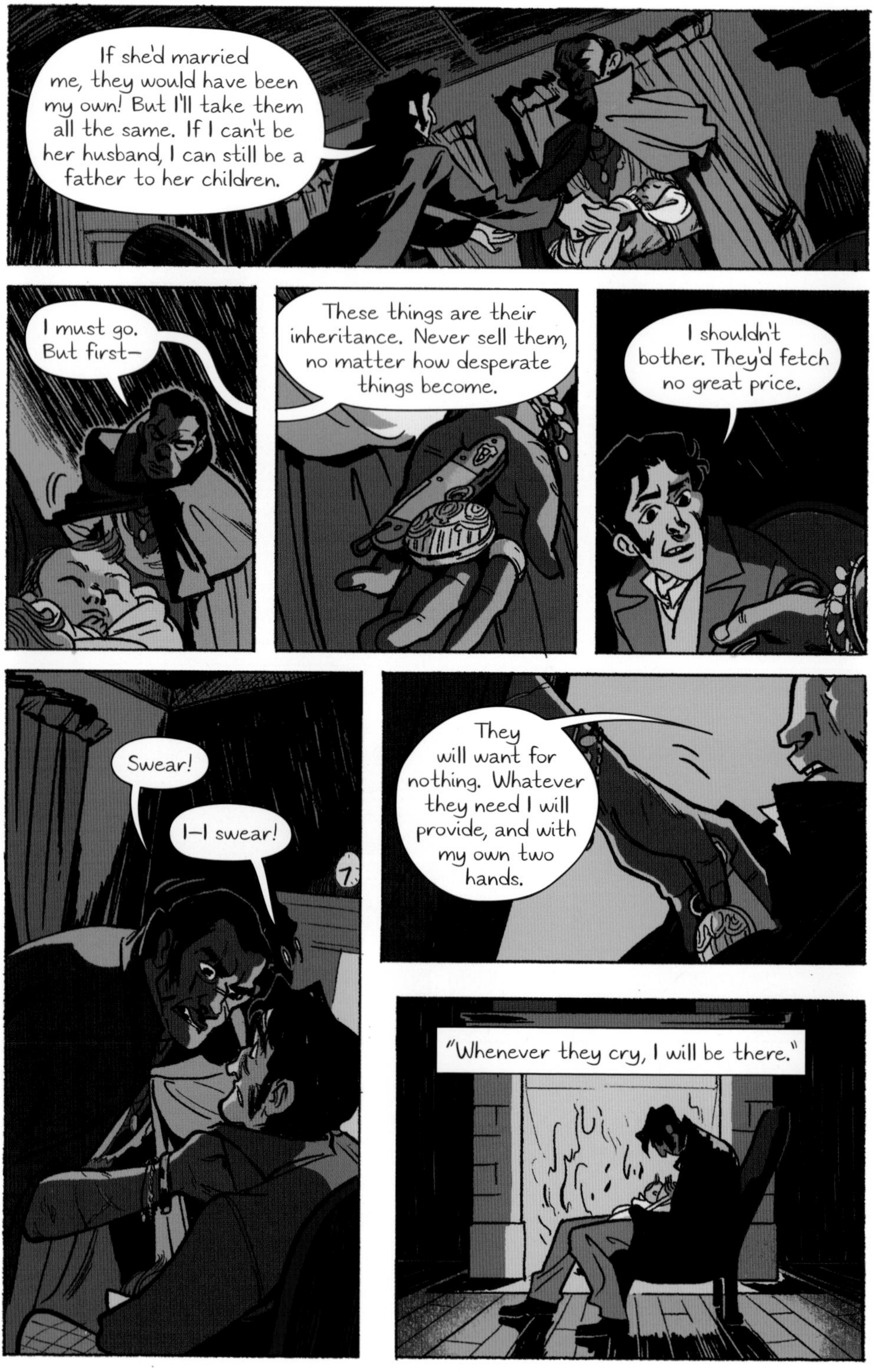
If she'd married me, they would have been my own! But I'll take them all the same. If I can't be her husband, I can still be a father to her children.
I must go. But first—
These things are their inheritance. Never sell them, no matter how desperate things become.
I shouldn't bother. They'd fetch no great price.
Swear!
I—I swear!
They will want for nothing. Whatever they need I will provide, and with my own two hands.
"Whenever they cry, I will be there."

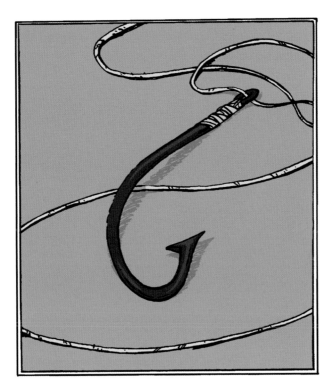

## CHAPTER ONE
# THE BLACK HOOK GANG

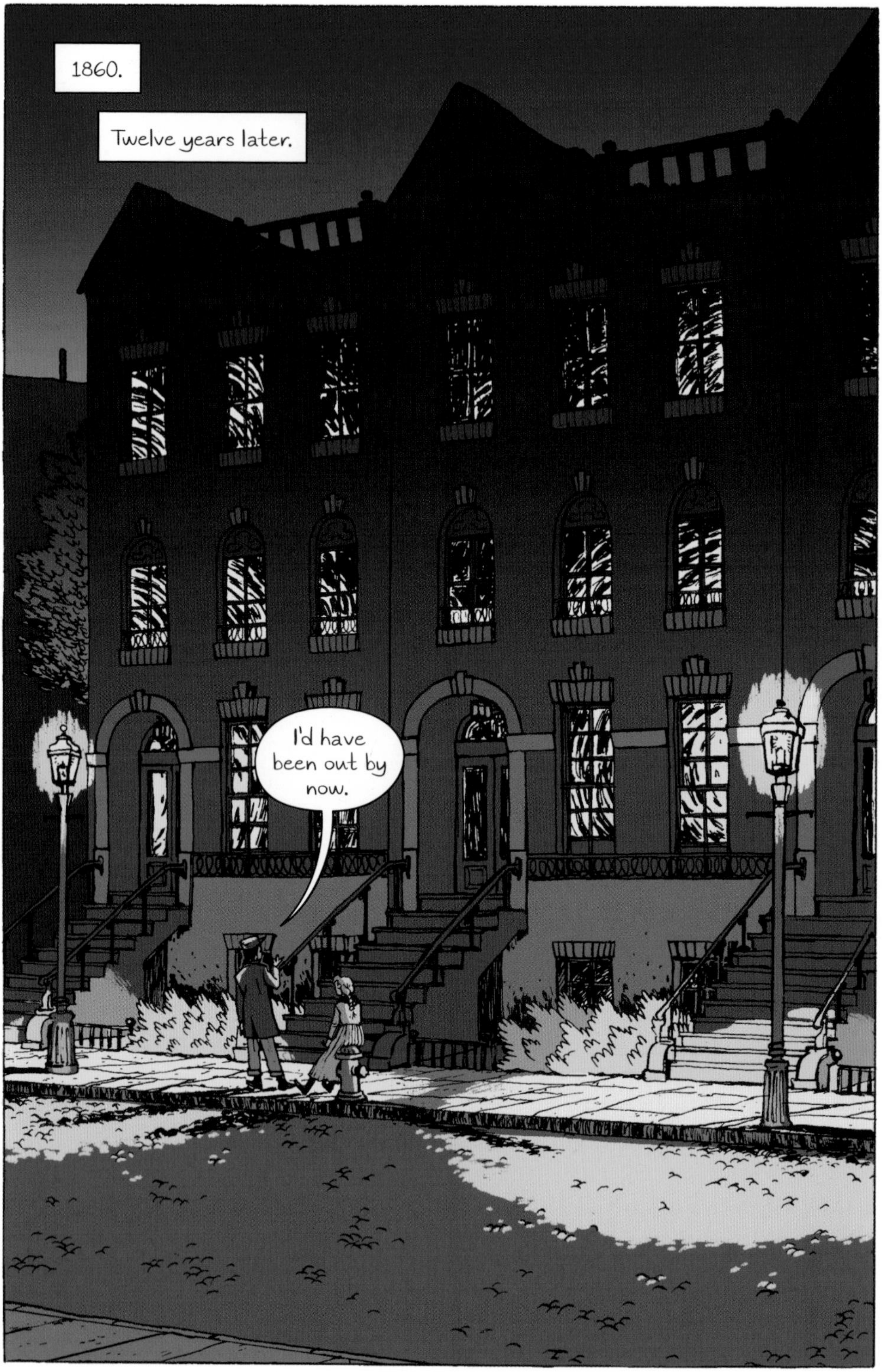
1860.
Twelve years later.
I'd have been out by now.

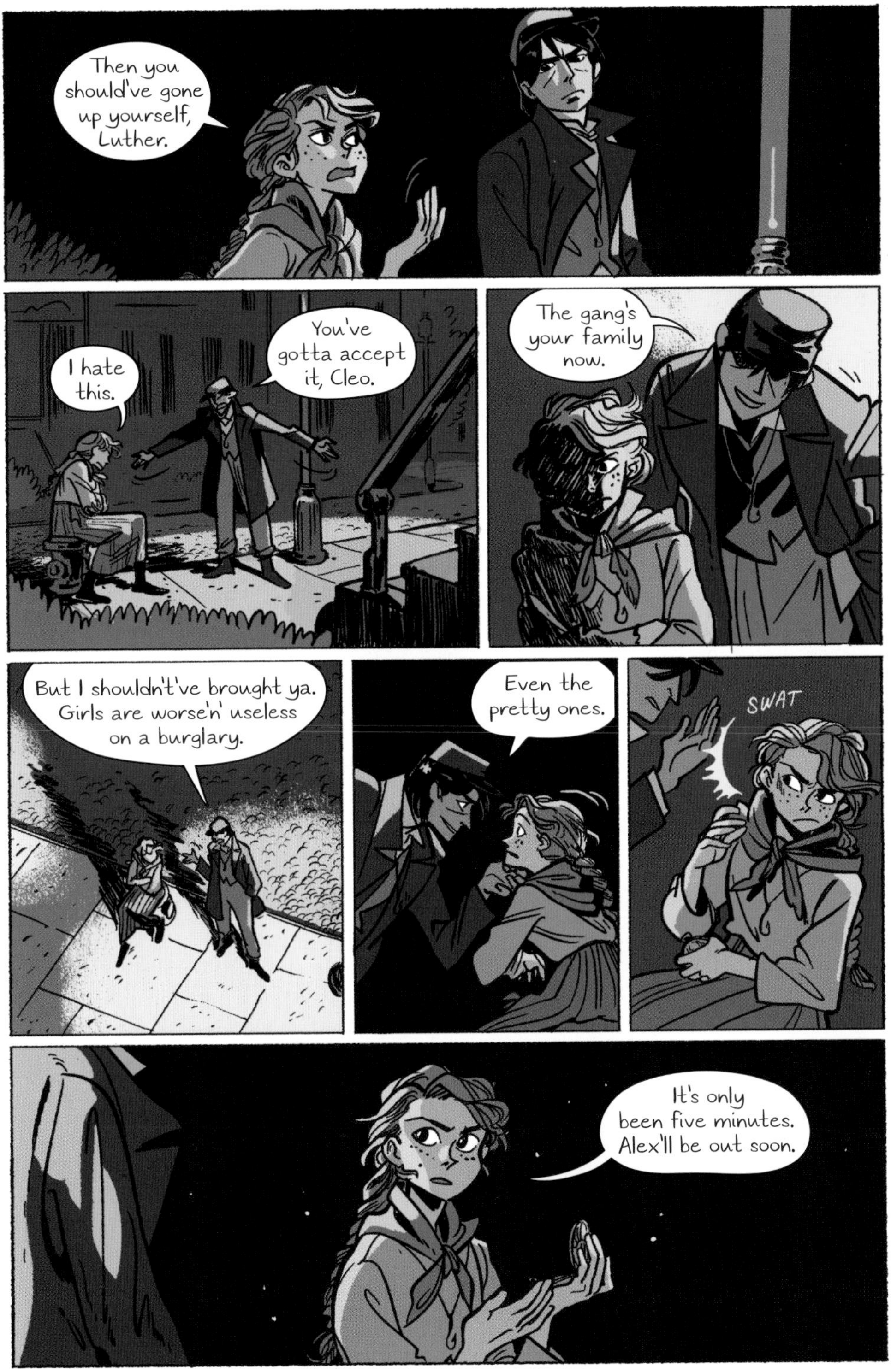
Then you should've gone up yourself, Luther.
I hate this.
You've gotta accept it, Cleo.
The gang's your family now.
But I shouldn't've brought ya. Girls are worse'n' useless on a burglary.
Even the pretty ones.
SWAT
It's only been five minutes. Alex'll be out soon.

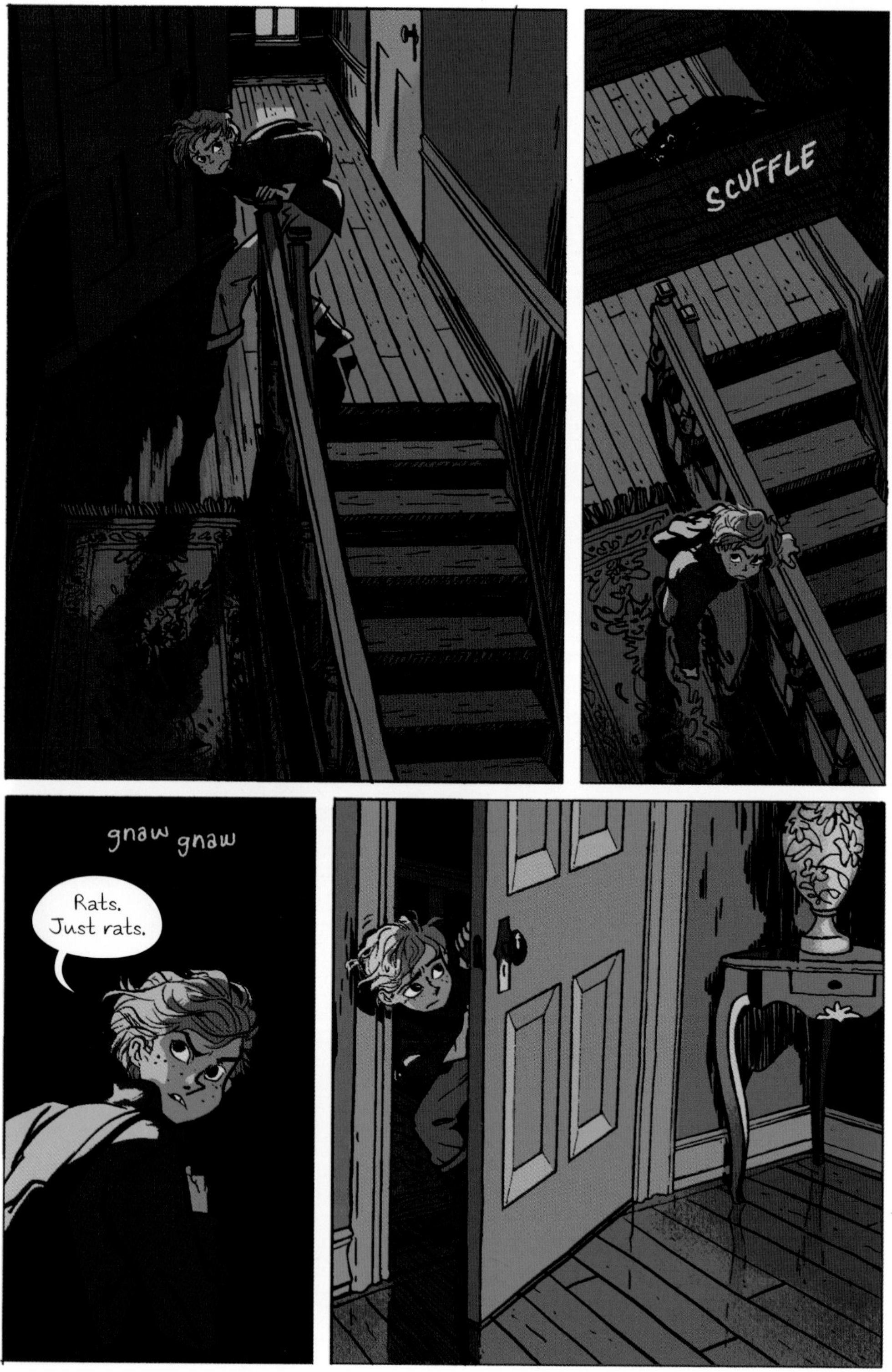
SCUFFLE
gnaw gnaw
Rats. Just rats.

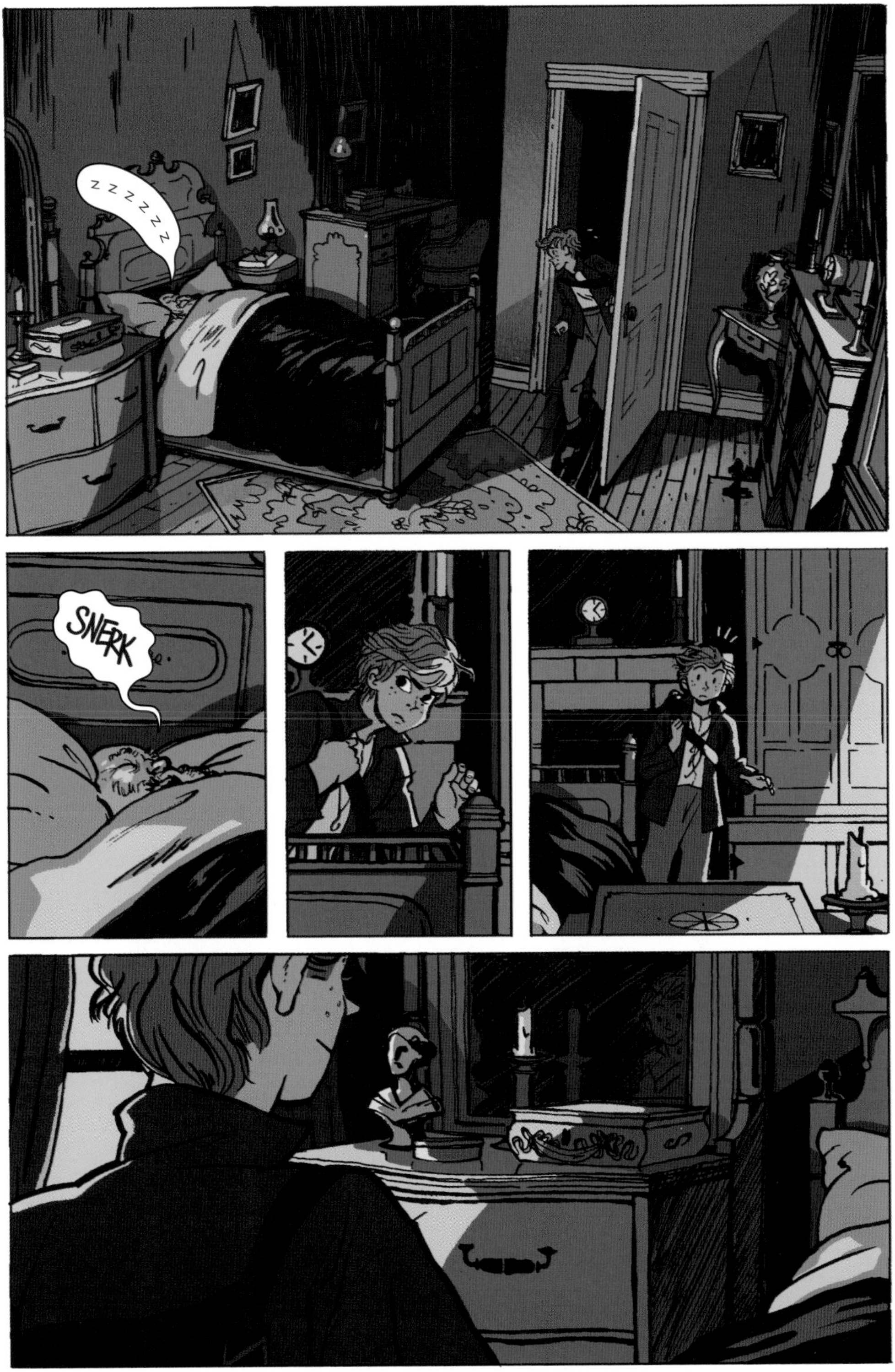
Z Z Z Z Z Z Z
SNERK

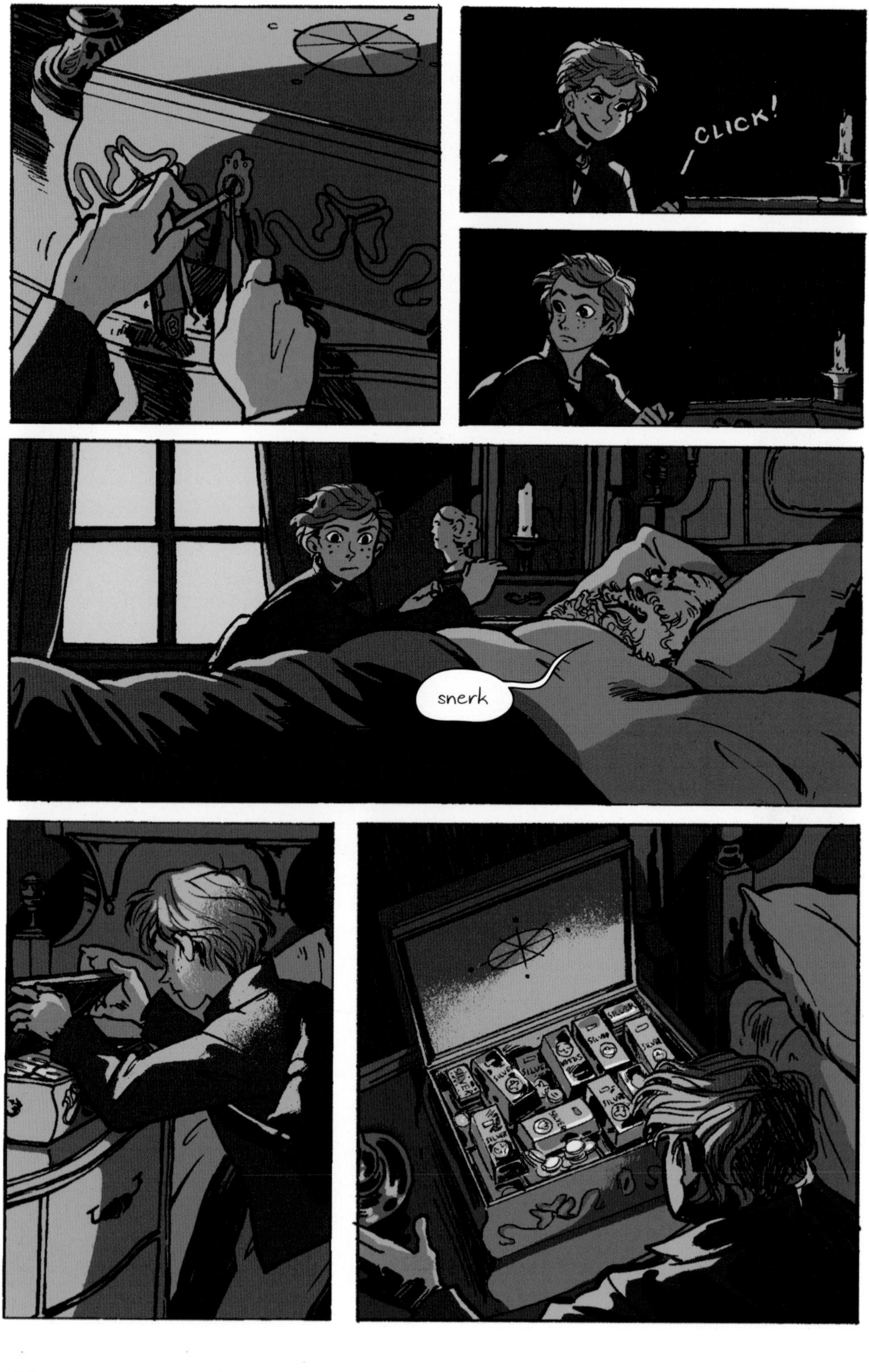
CLICK!
snerk

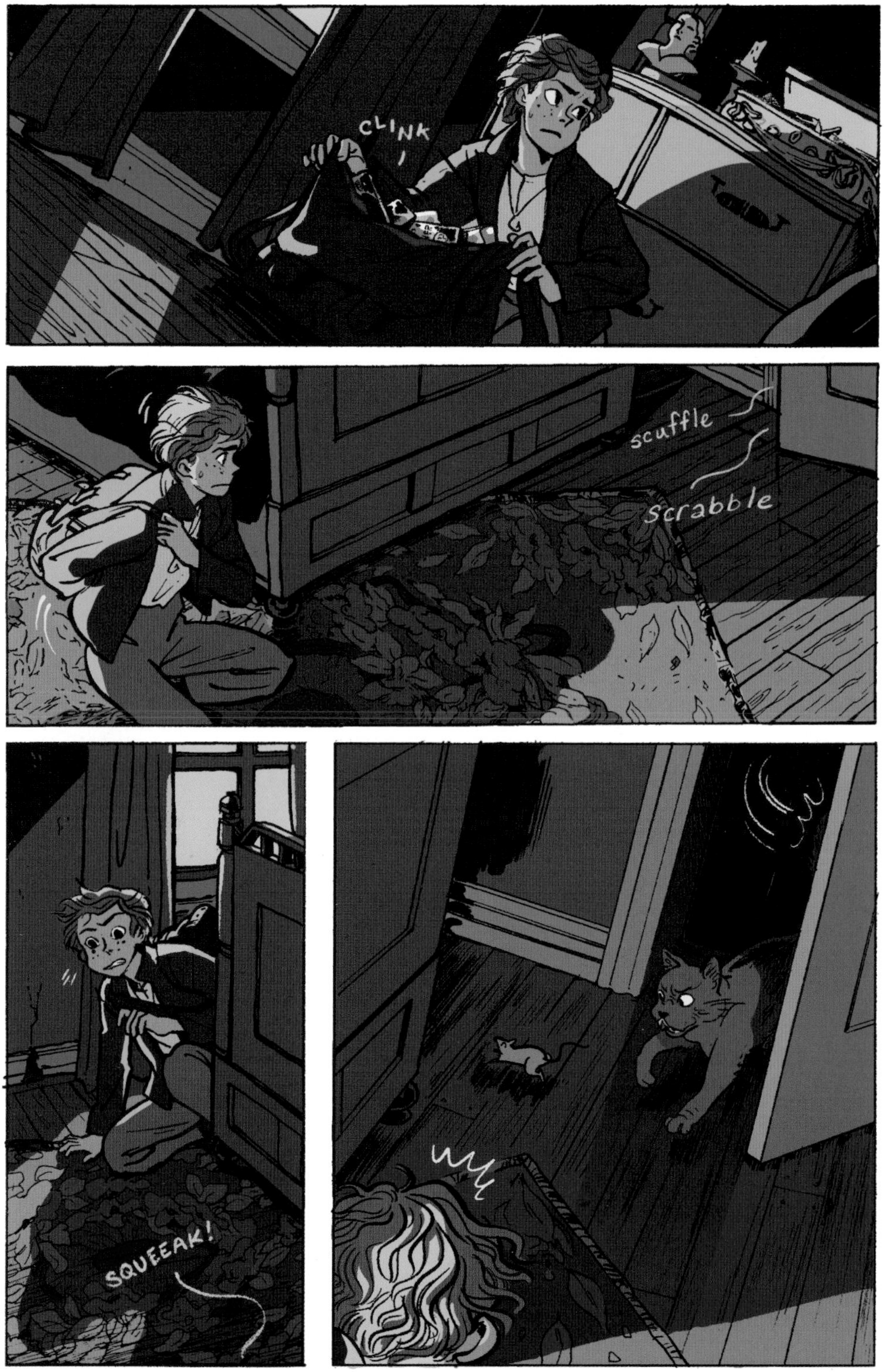
CLINK
scuffle
scrabble
SQUEEAK!

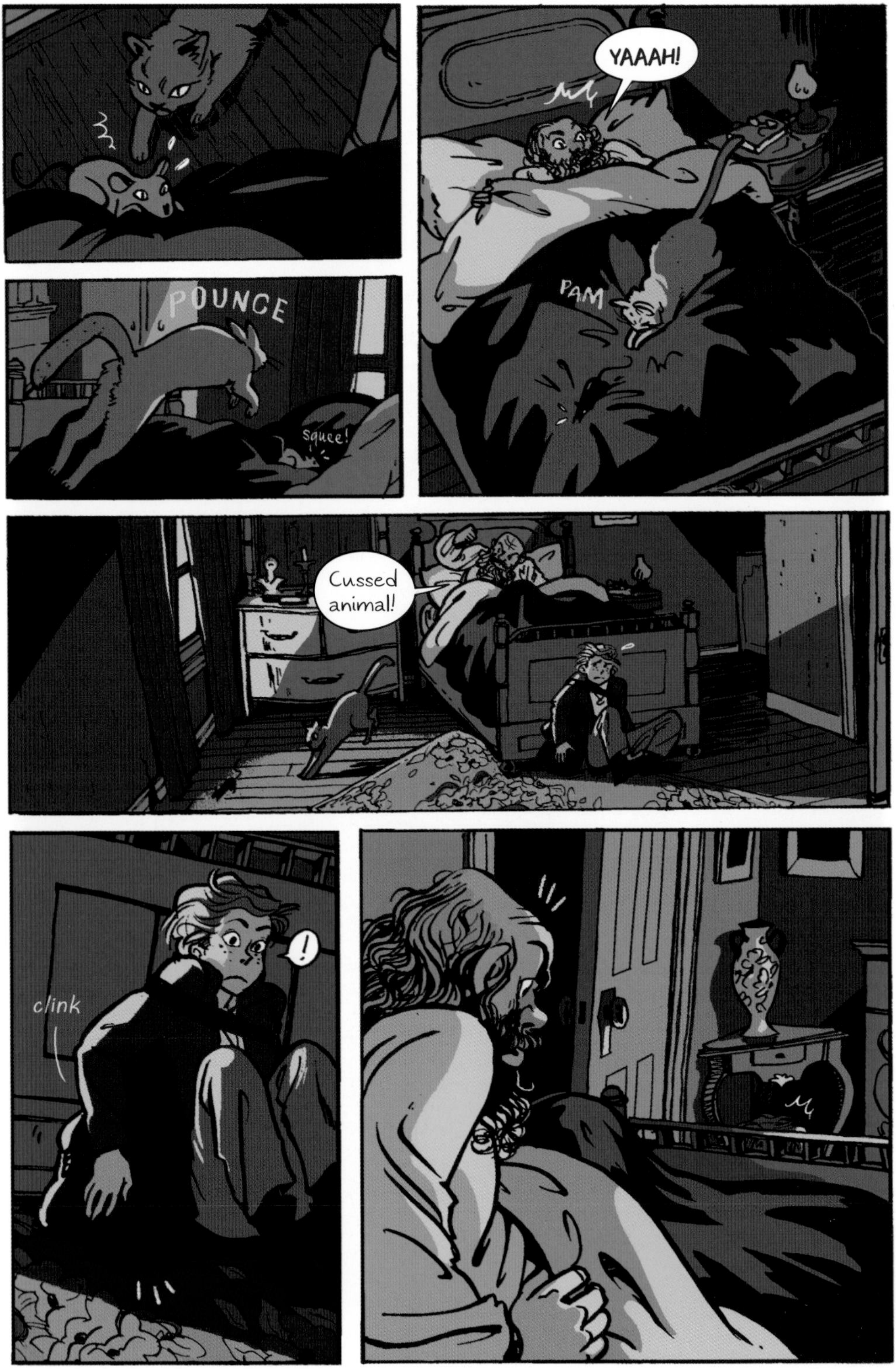

YAAAH!
POUNCE
squee!
PAM
Cussed animal!
!
clink

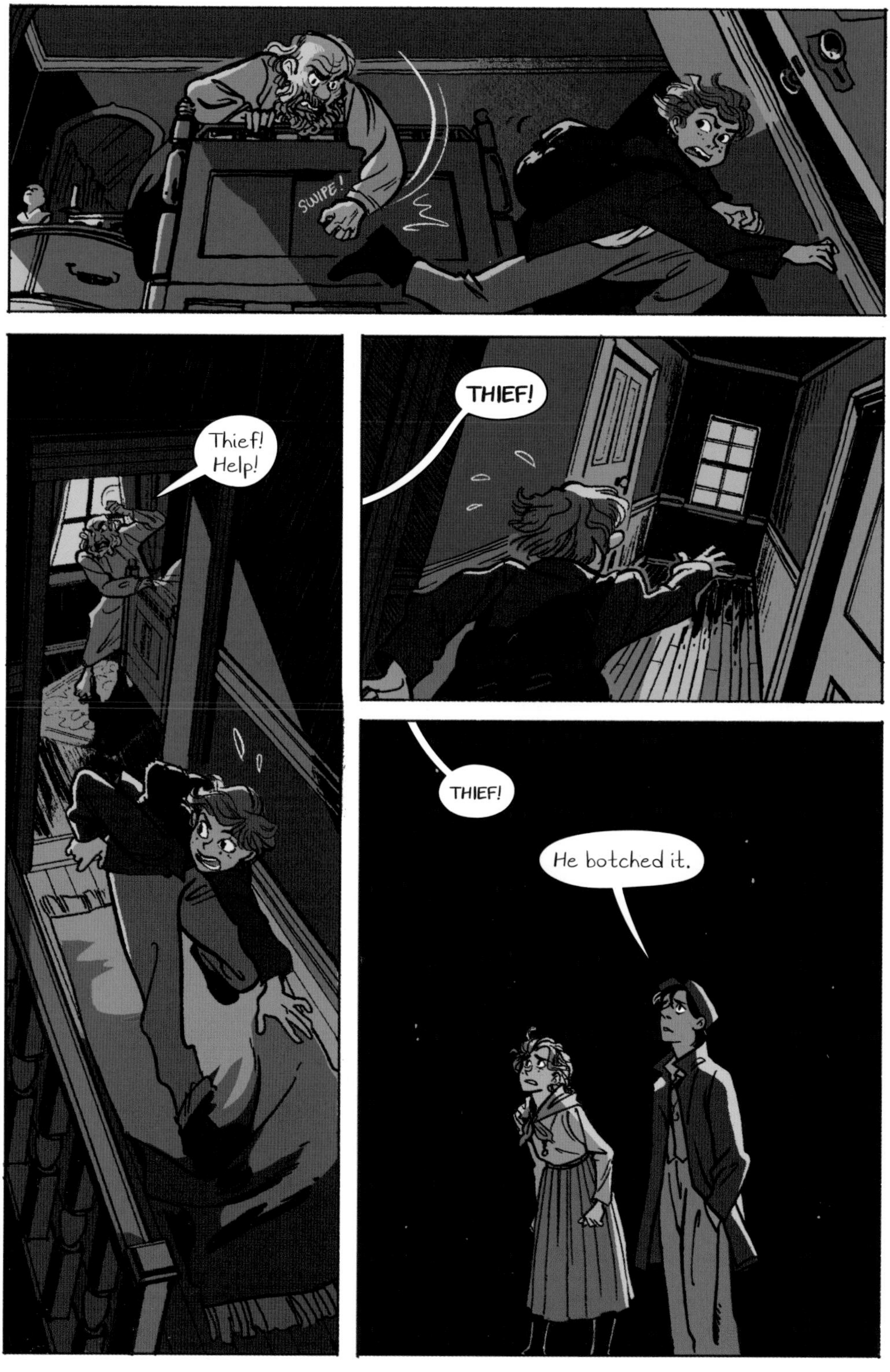
SWIPE!
Thief! Help!
THIEF!
THIEF!
He botched it.

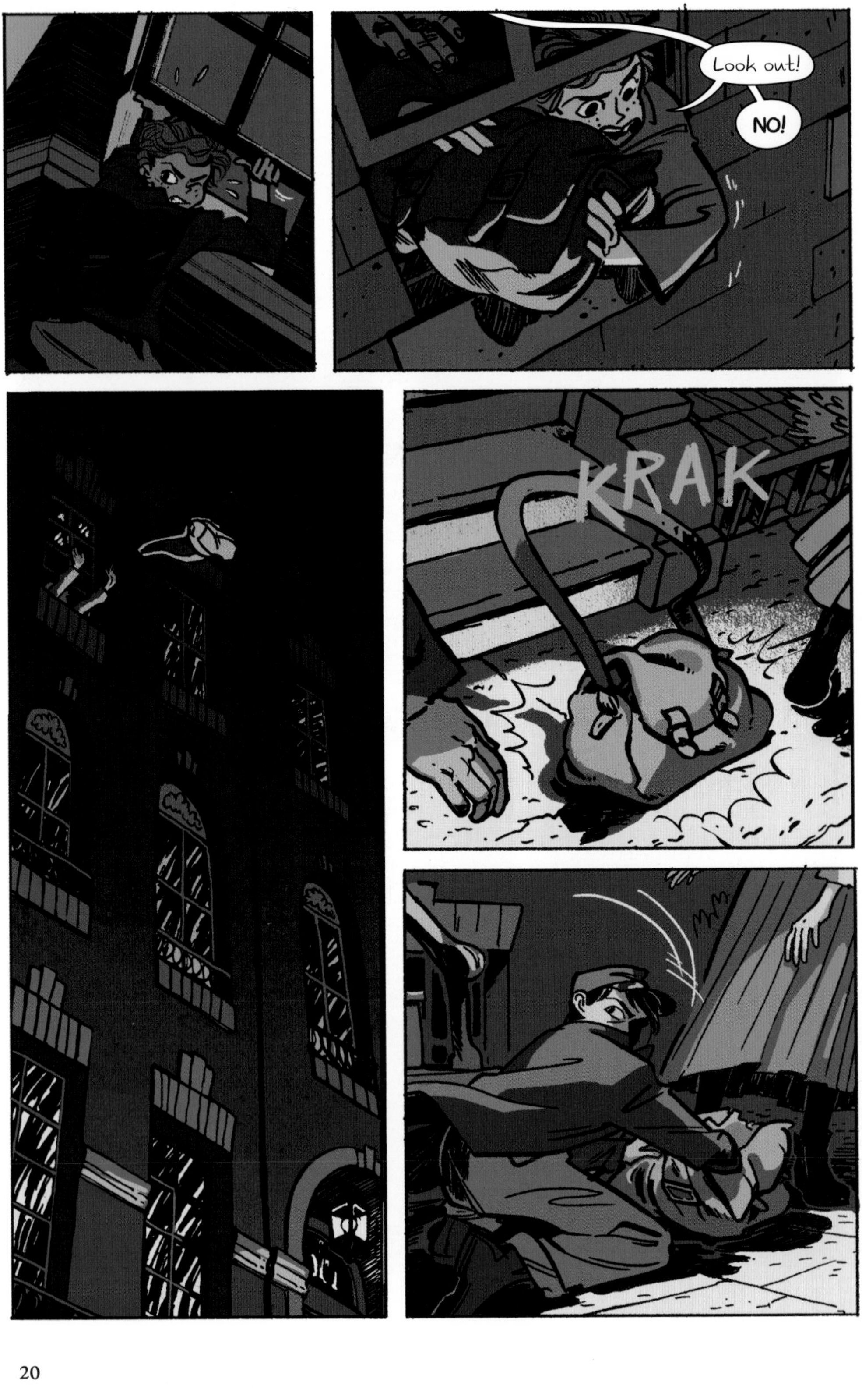
Look out!
NO!
KRAK

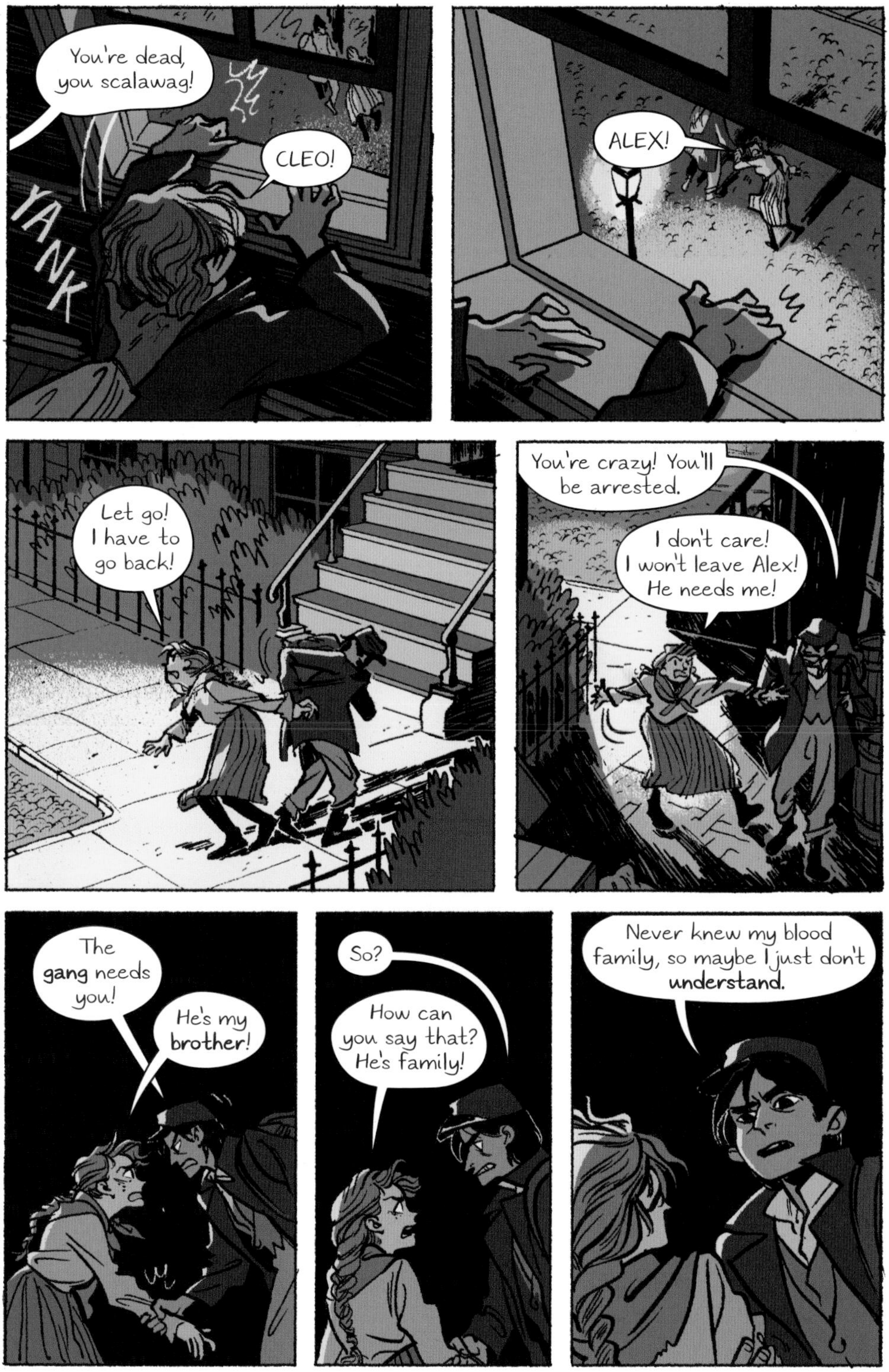
You're dead, you scalawag!
CLEO!
YANK
ALEX!
Let go! I have to go back!
You're crazy! You'll be arrested.
I don't care! I won't leave Alex! He needs me!
The **gang** needs you!
He's my **brother**!
So?
How can you say that? He's family!
Never knew my blood family, so maybe I just don't **understand**.

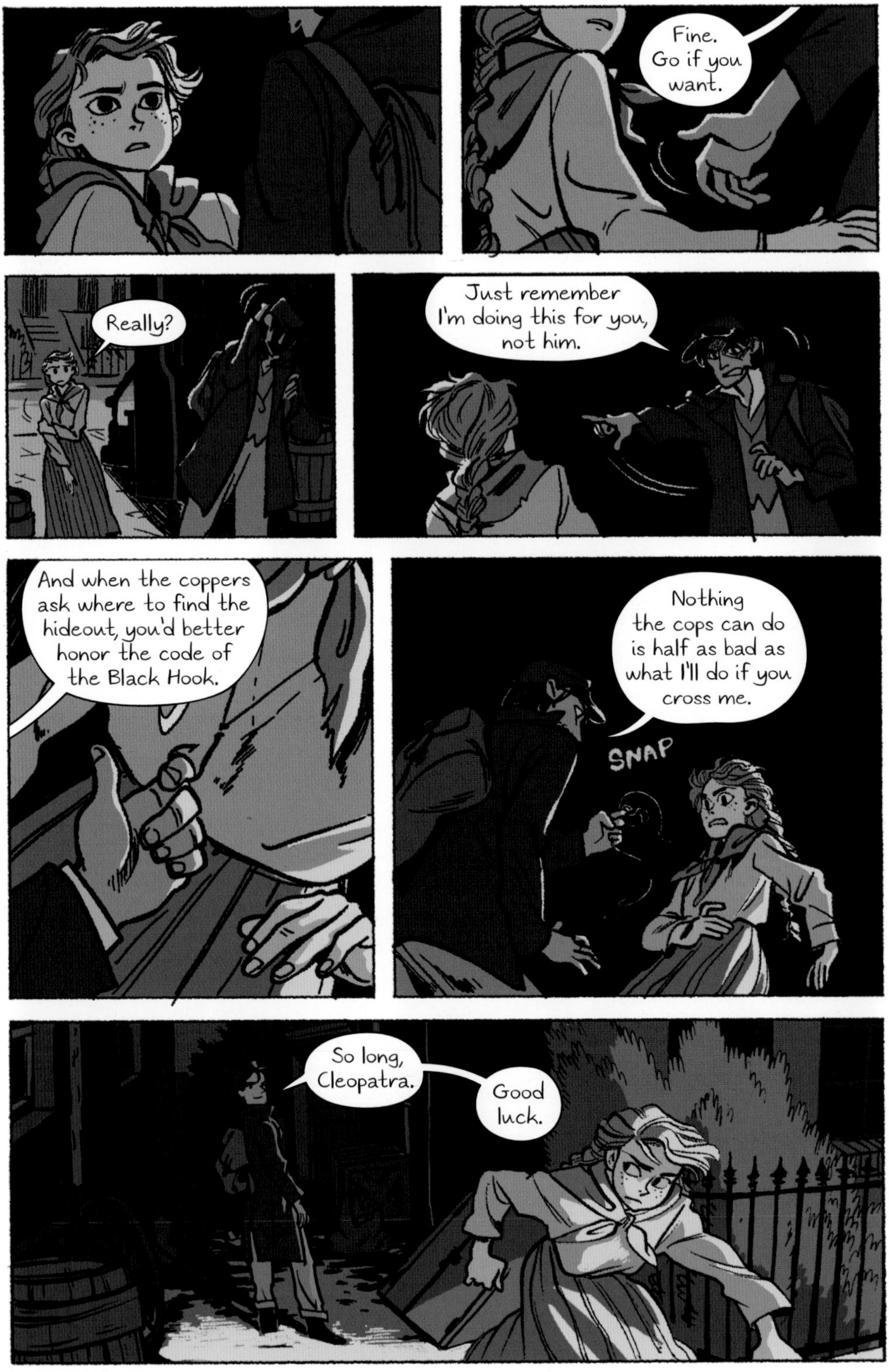
Fine. Go if you want.
Really?
Just remember I'm doing this for you, not him.
And when the coppers ask where to find the hideout, you'd better honor the code of the Black Hook.
Nothing the cops can do is half as bad as what I'll do if you cross me.
SNAP
So long, Cleopatra.
Good luck.

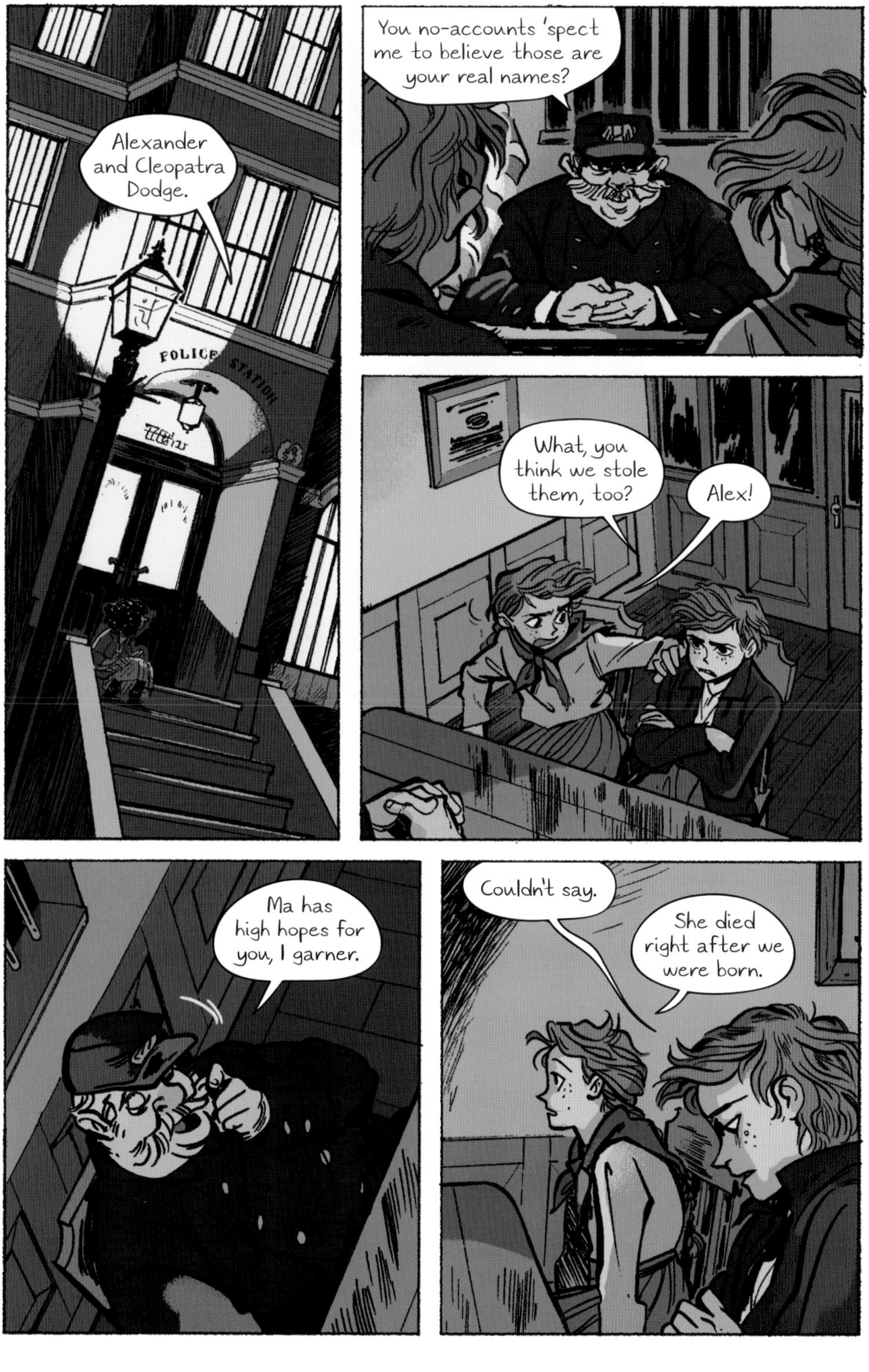
Alexander and Cleopatra Dodge.
POLICE STATION
You no-accounts 'spect me to believe those are your real names?
What, you think we stole them, too?
Alex!
Ma has high hopes for you, I garner.
Couldn't say.
She died right after we were born.

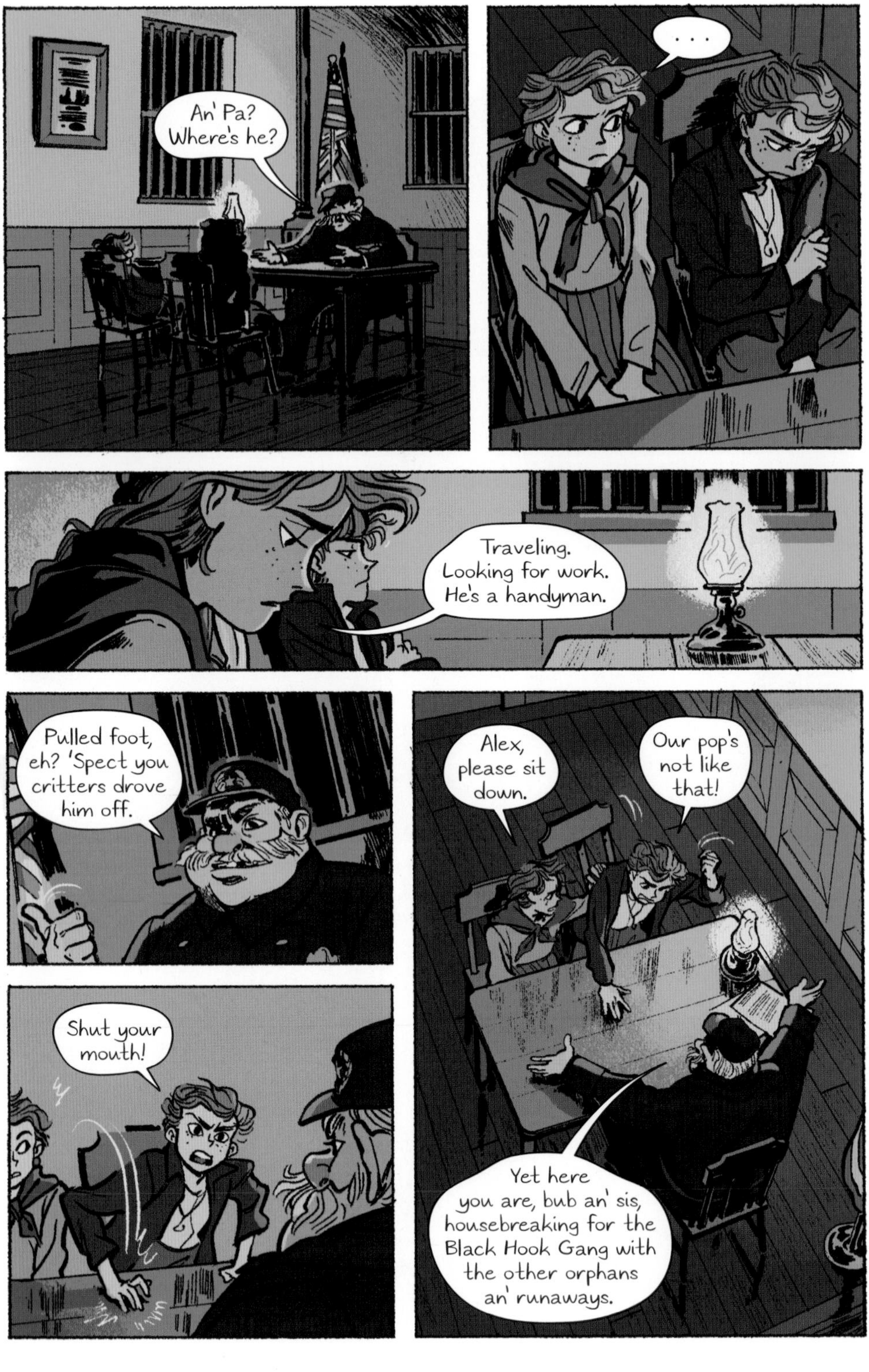
An' Pa? Where's he?
. . .
Traveling. Looking for work. He's a handyman.
Pulled foot, eh? 'Spect you critters drove him off.
Shut your mouth!
Alex, please sit down.
Our pop's not like that!
Yet here you are, bub an' sis, housebreaking for the Black Hook Gang with the other orphans an' runaways.

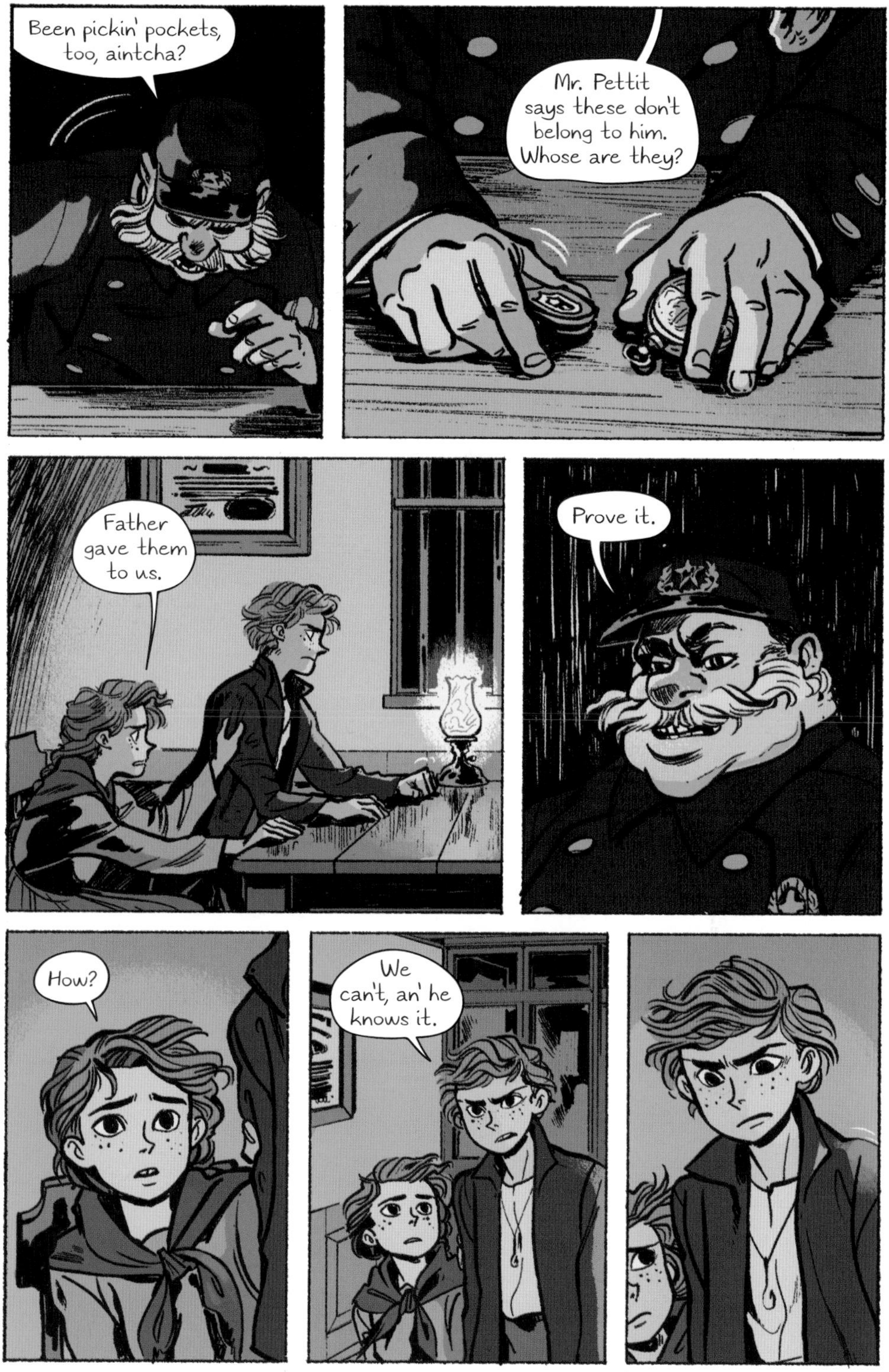
Been pickin' pockets, too, aintcha?
Mr. Pettit says these don't belong to him. Whose are they?
Father gave them to us.
Prove it.
How?
We can't, an' he knows it.

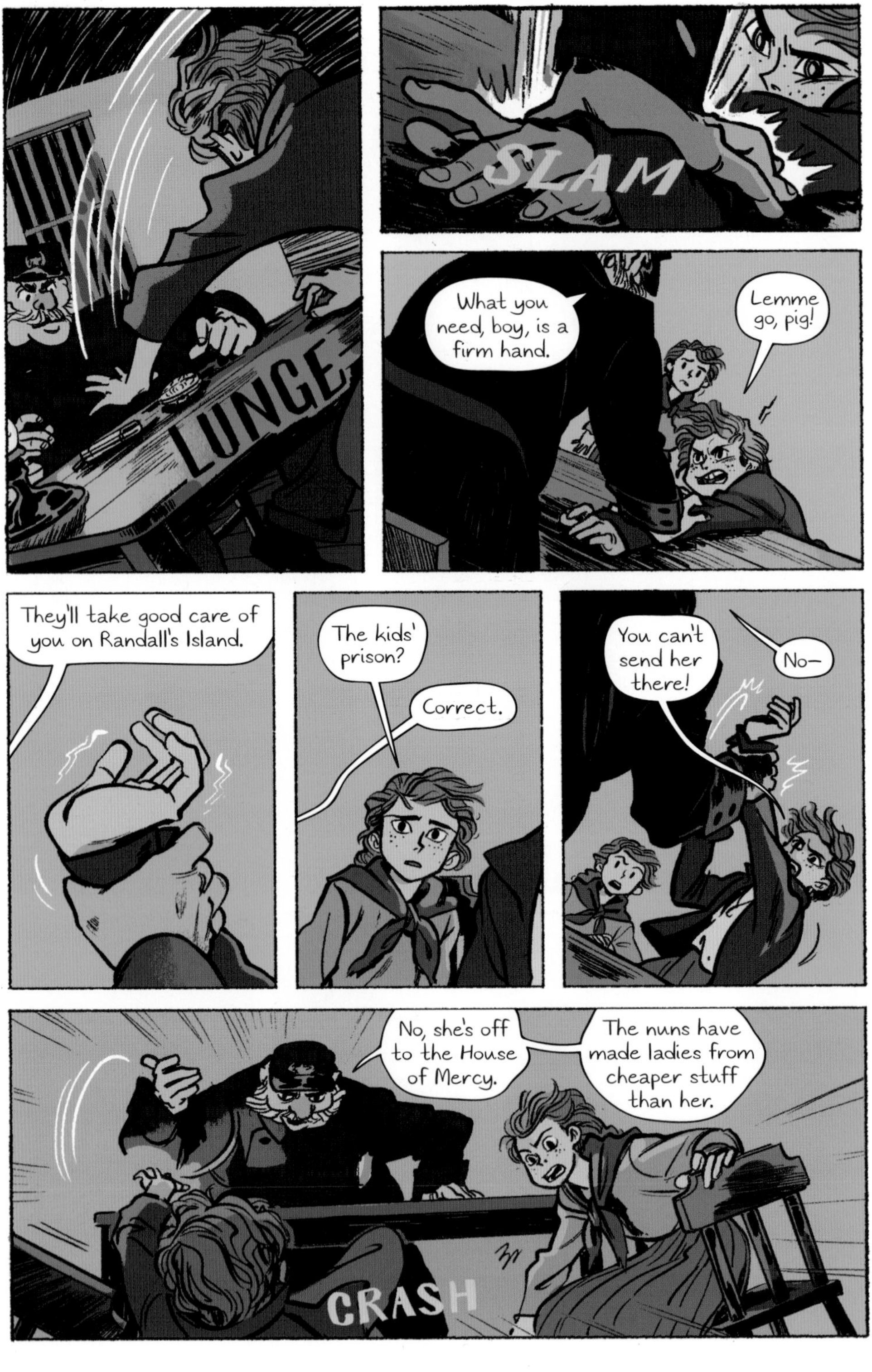
LUNGE
SLAM
What you need, boy, is a firm hand.
Lemme go, pig!
They'll take good care of you on Randall's Island.
The kids' prison?
Correct.
You can't send her there!
No—
No, she's off to the House of Mercy.
The nuns have made ladies from cheaper stuff than her.
CRASH

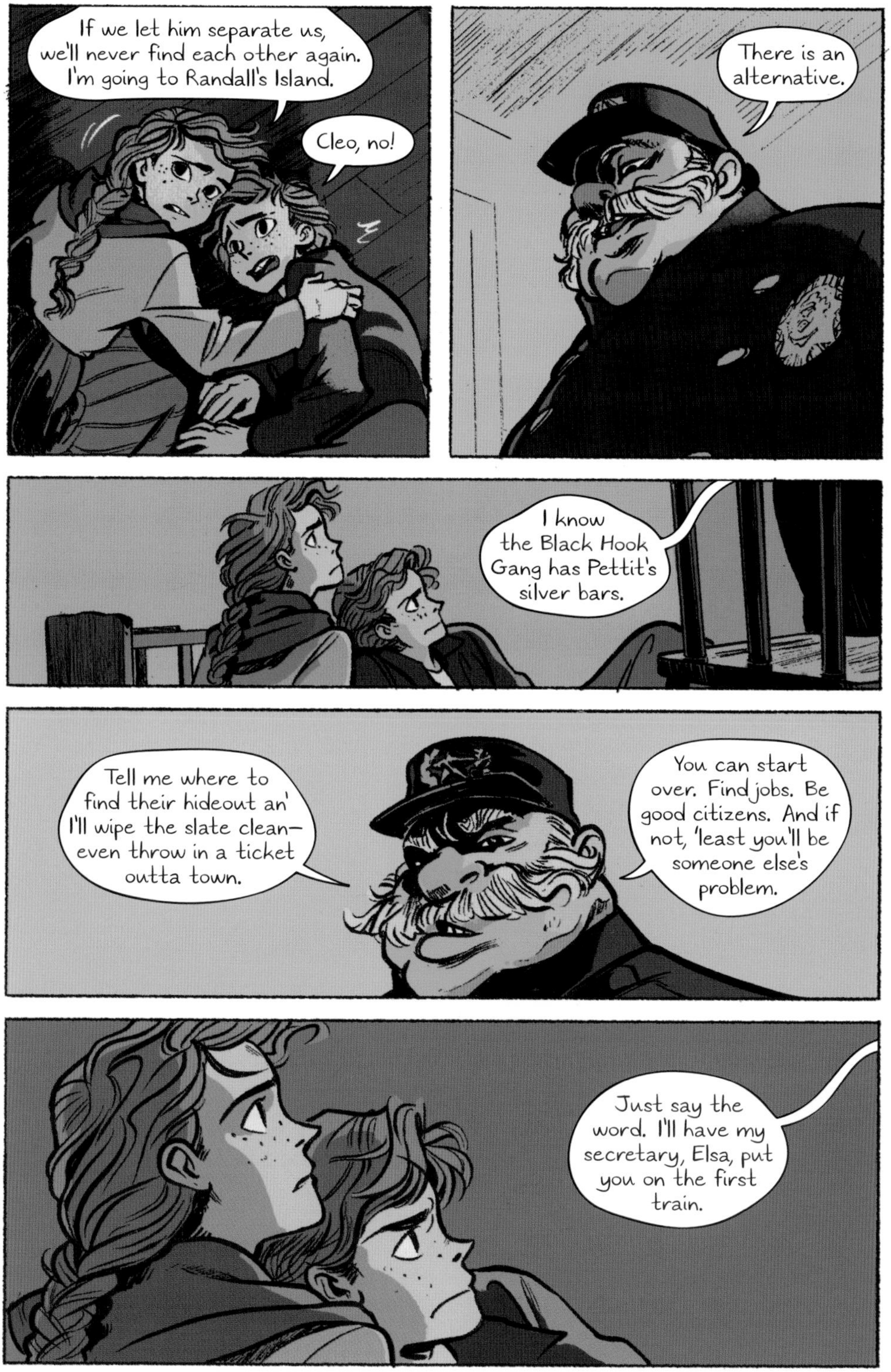
If we let him separate us, we'll never find each other again. I'm going to Randall's Island.
Cleo, no!
There is an alternative.
I know the Black Hook Gang has Pettit's silver bars.
Tell me where to find their hideout an' I'll wipe the slate clean— even throw in a ticket outta town.
You can start over. Find jobs. Be good citizens. And if not, 'least you'll be someone else's problem.
Just say the word. I'll have my secretary, Elsa, put you on the first train.

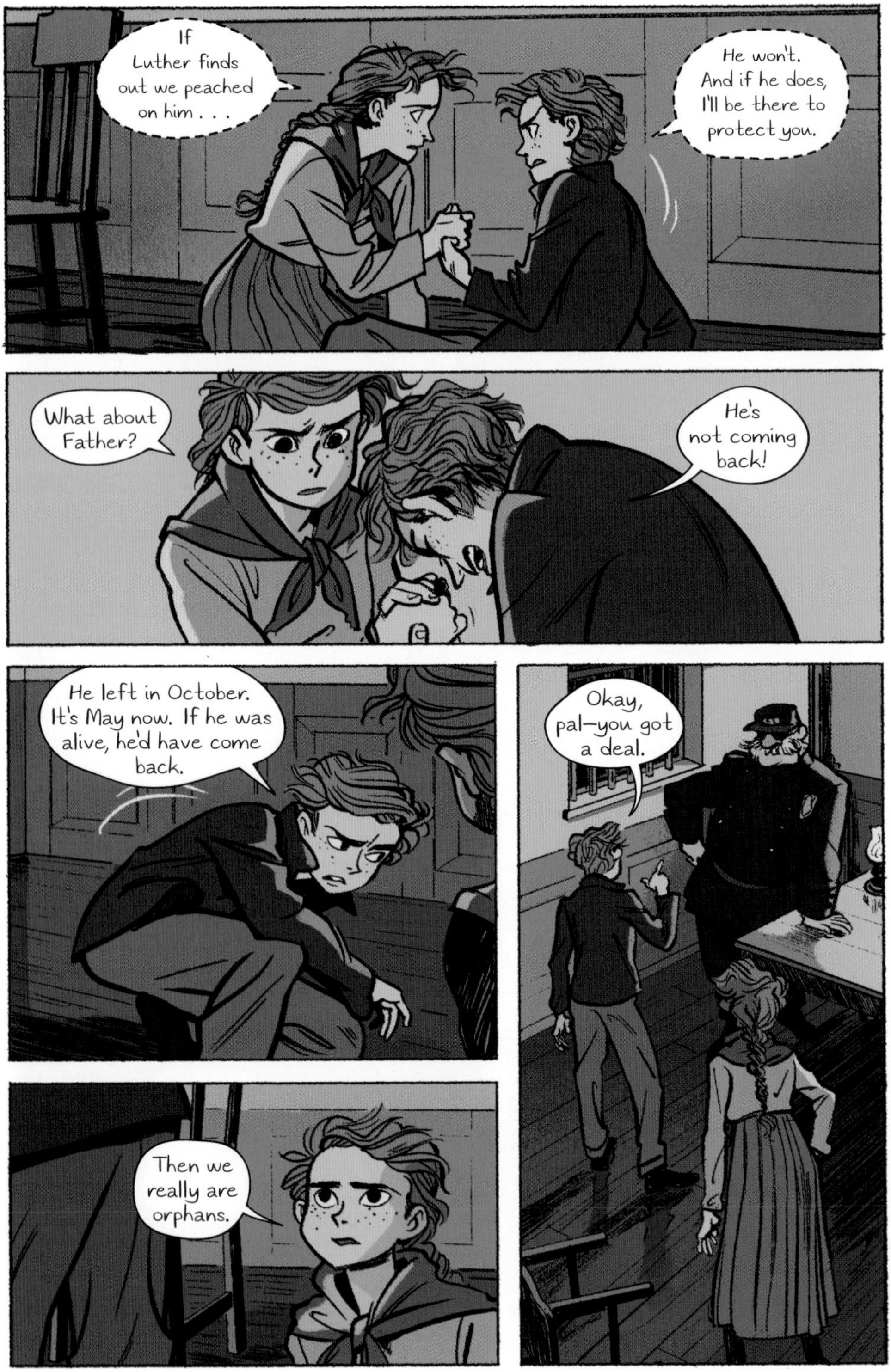
If Luther finds out we peached on him . . .
He won't. And if he does, I'll be there to protect you.
What about Father?
He's not coming back!
He left in October. It's May now. If he was alive, he'd have come back.
Then we really are orphans.
Okay, pal—you got a deal.

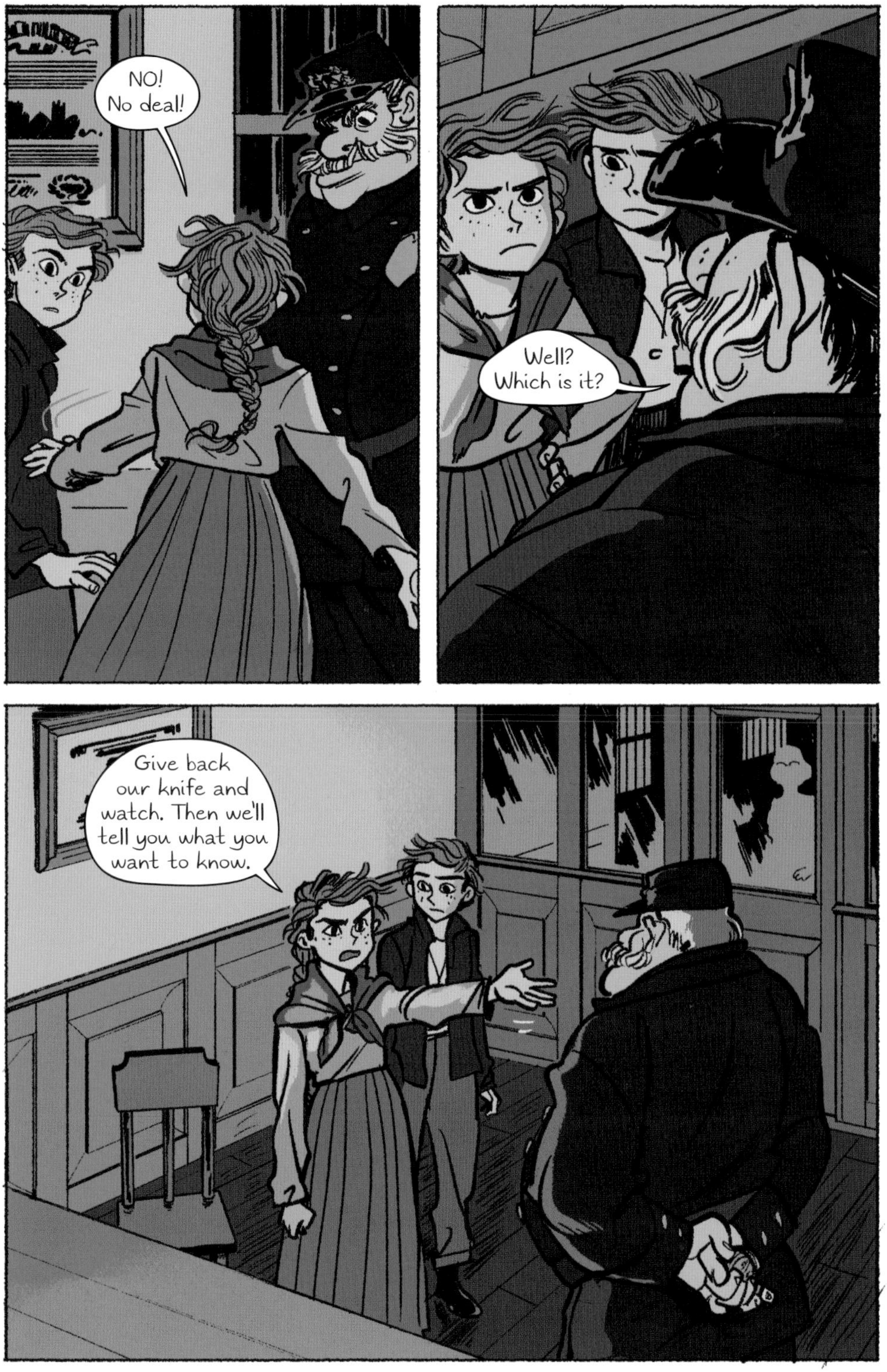
NO! No deal!
Well? Which is it?
Give back our knife and watch. Then we'll tell you what you want to know.

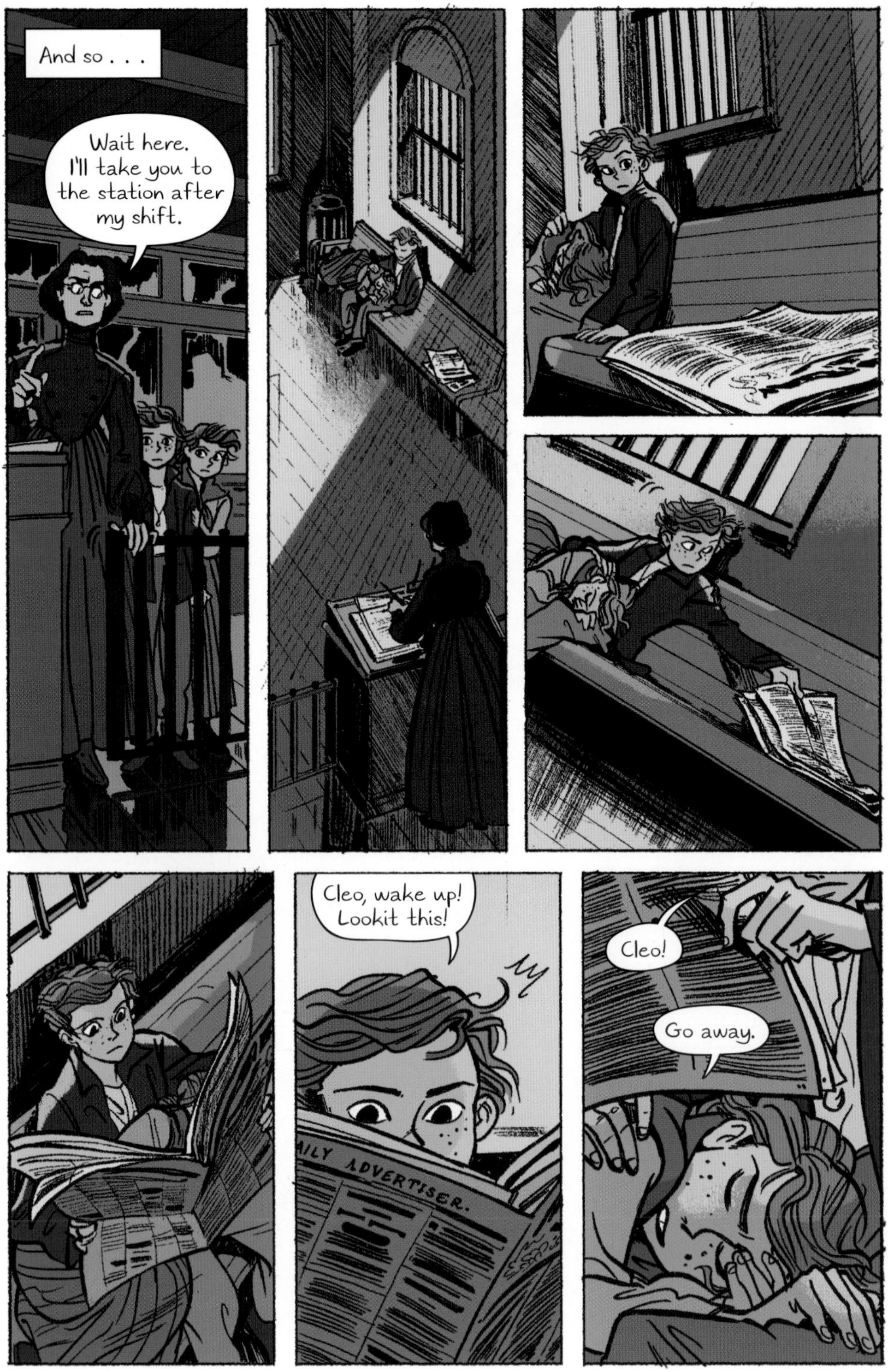

And so . . .
Wait here. I'll take you to the station after my shift.
Cleo, wake up! Lookit this!
AILY ADVERTISER.
Cleo!
Go away.

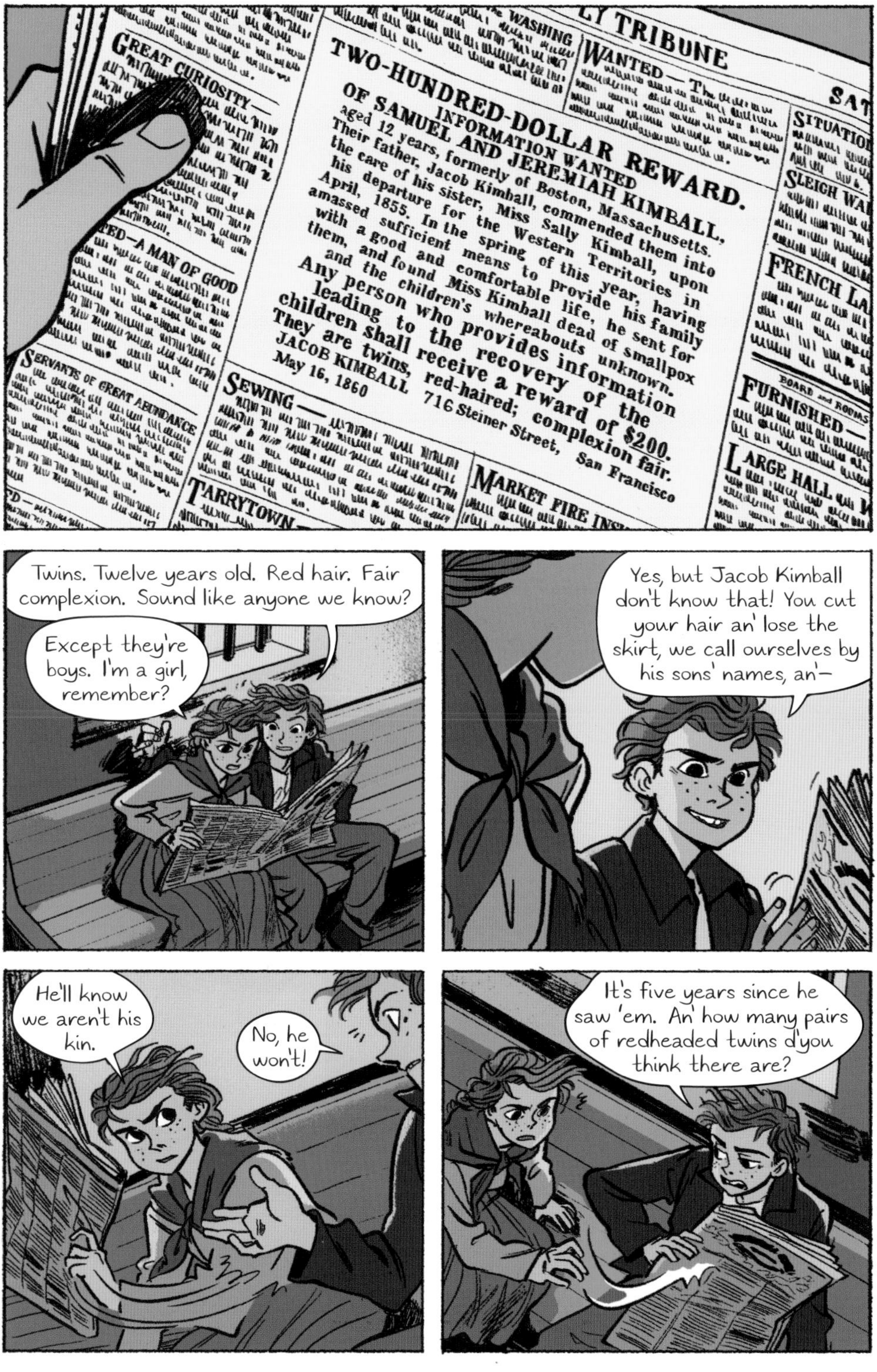
TRIBUNE
WANTED
GREAT CURIOSITY
TWO-HUNDRED-DOLLAR REWARD.
INFORMATION WANTED
OF SAMUEL AND JEREMIAH KIMBALL,
aged 12 years, formerly of Boston, Massachusetts. Their father, Jacob Kimball, commended them into the care of his sister, Miss Sally Kimball, upon his departure for the Western Territories in April, 1855. In the spring of this year, having amassed sufficient means to provide his family with a good and comfortable life, he sent for them, and found Miss Kimball dead of smallpox and the children's whereabouts unknown.
Any person who provides information leading to the recovery of the children shall receive a reward of $200.
They are twins, red-haired; complexion fair.
JACOB KIMBALL 716 Steiner Street, San Francisco
May 16, 1860
SEWING
TARRYTOWN
FURNISHED
Twins. Twelve years old. Red hair. Fair complexion. Sound like anyone we know?
Except they're boys. I'm a girl, remember?
Yes, but Jacob Kimball don't know that! You cut your hair an' lose the skirt, we call ourselves by his sons' names, an'—
He'll know we aren't his kin.
No, he won't!
It's five years since he saw 'em. An' how many pairs of redheaded twins d'you think there are?

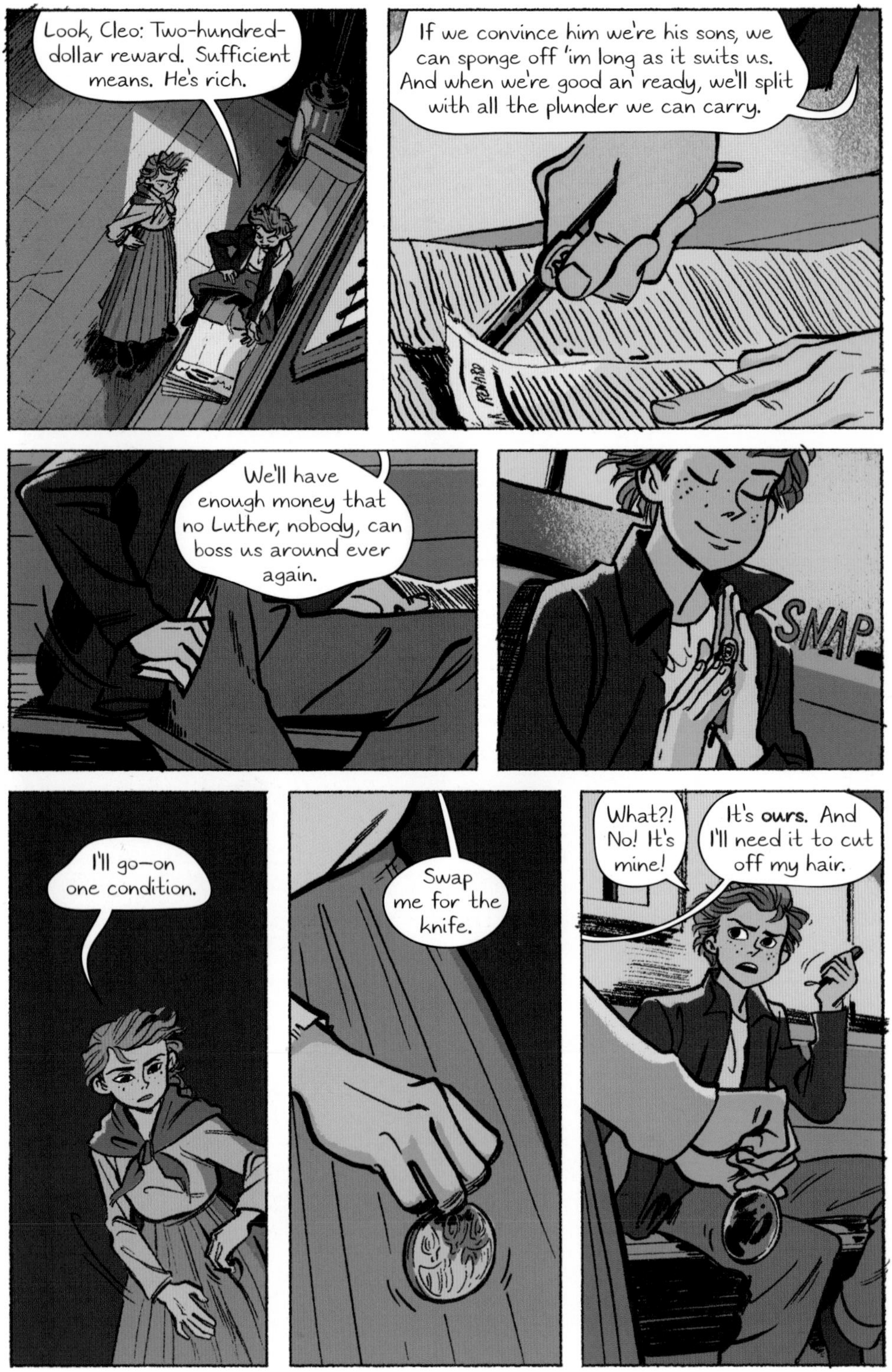
Look, Cleo: Two-hundred-dollar reward. Sufficient means. He's rich.
If we convince him we're his sons, we can sponge off 'im long as it suits us. And when we're good an' ready, we'll split with all the plunder we can carry.
We'll have enough money that no Luther, nobody, can boss us around ever again.
SNAP
I'll go—on one condition.
Swap me for the knife.
What?! No! It's mine!
It's **ours.** And I'll need it to cut off my hair.

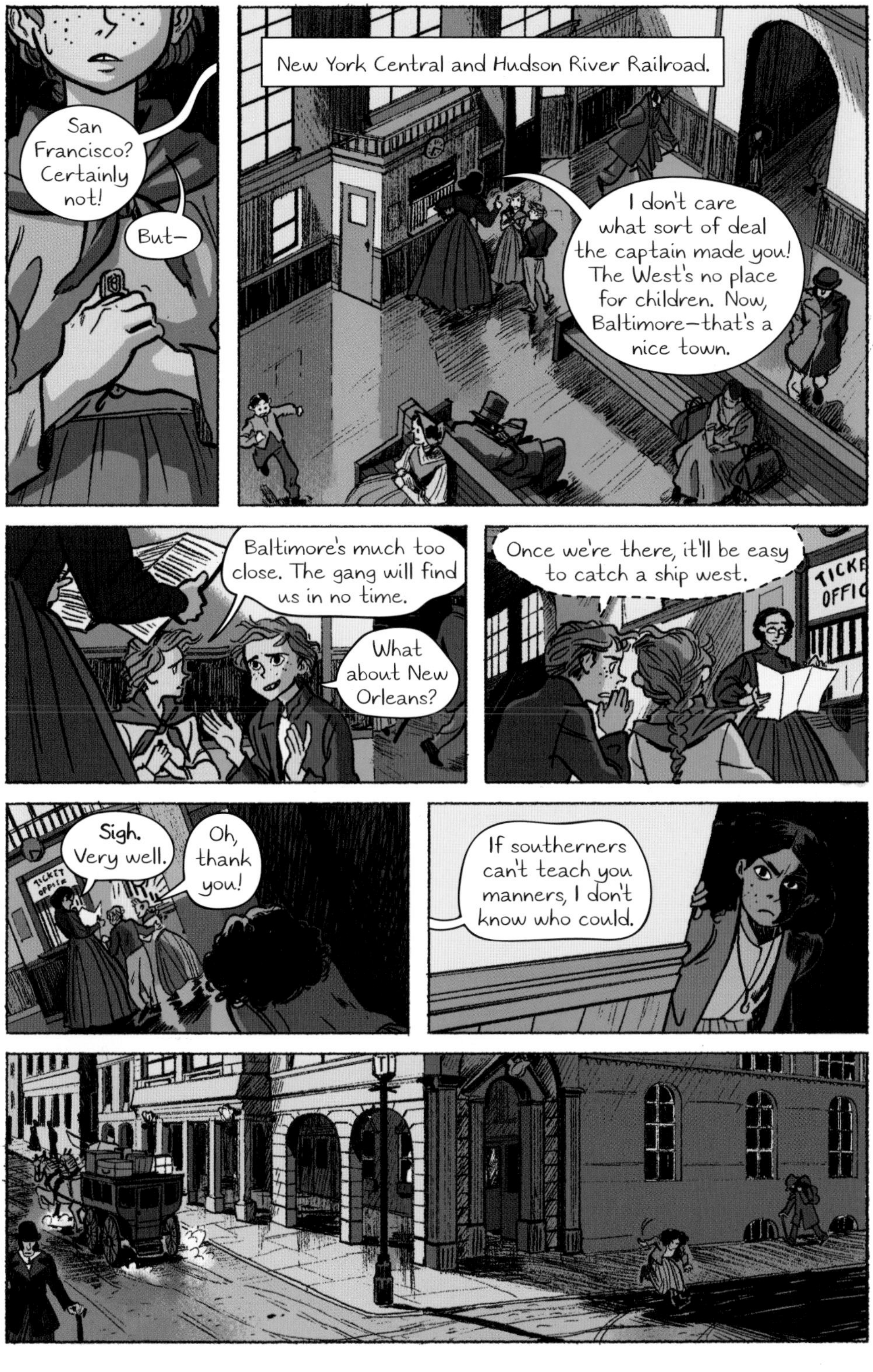
San Francisco? Certainly not!
But—
New York Central and Hudson River Railroad.
I don't care what sort of deal the captain made you! The West's no place for children. Now, Baltimore—that's a nice town.
Baltimore's much too close. The gang will find us in no time.
What about New Orleans?
Once we're there, it'll be easy to catch a ship west.
TICKET OFFICE
Sigh. Very well.
Oh, thank you!
If southerners can't teach you manners, I don't know who could.

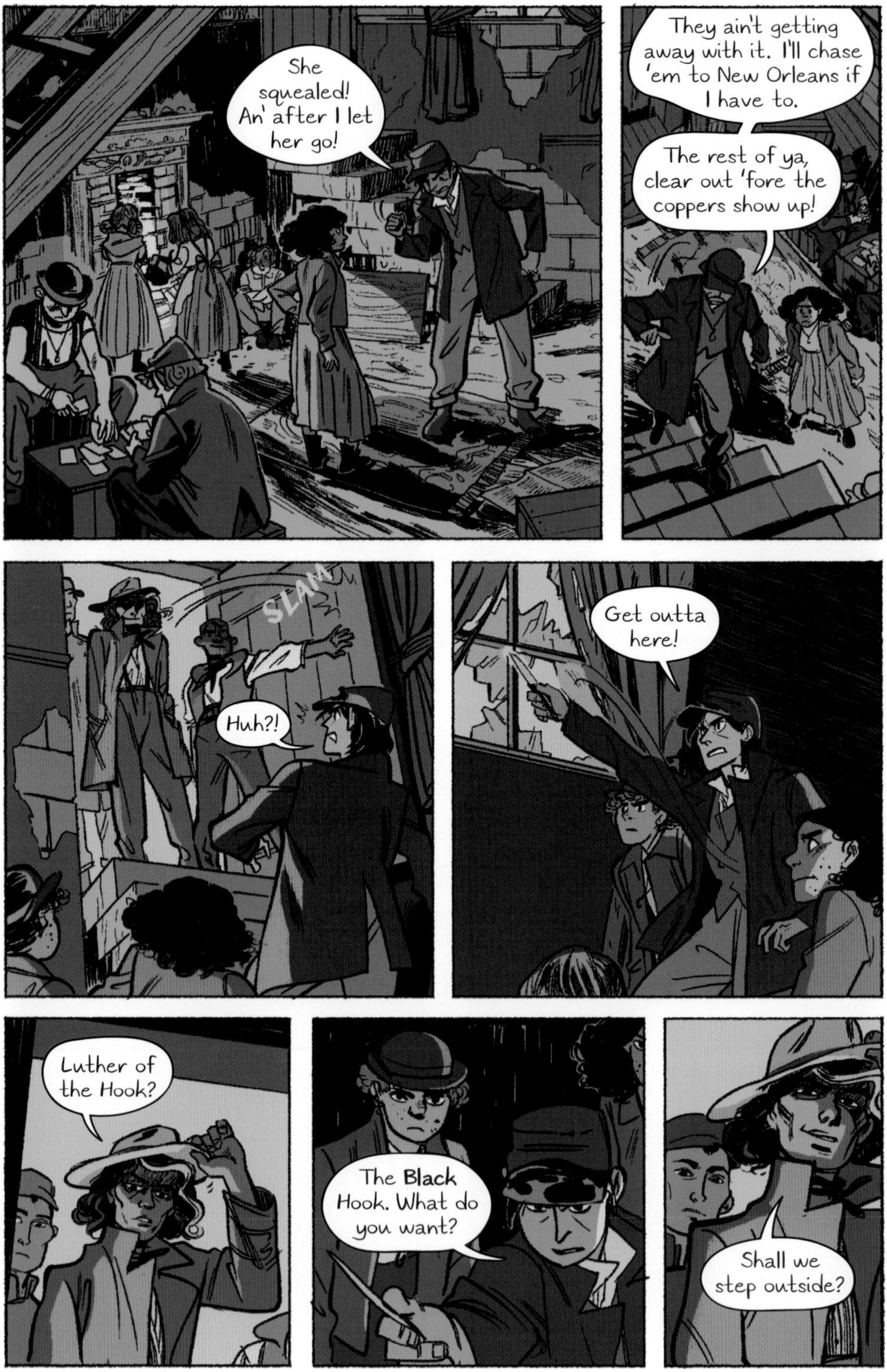
She squealed! An' after I let her go!
They ain't getting away with it. I'll chase 'em to New Orleans if I have to.
The rest of ya, clear out 'fore the coppers show up!
SLAM
Huh?!
Get outta here!
Luther of the Hook?
The **Black** Hook. What do you want?
Shall we step outside?

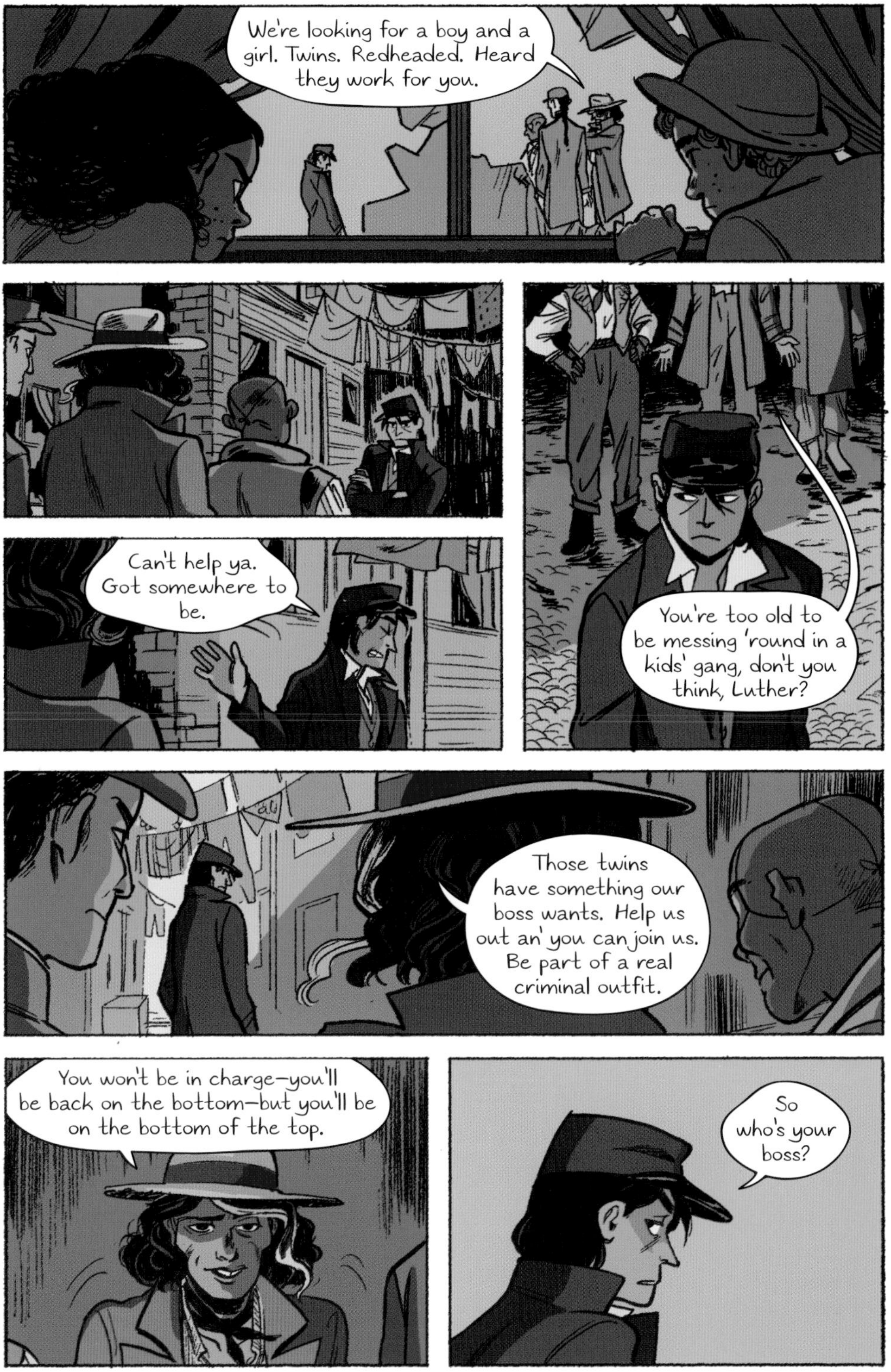
We're looking for a boy and a girl. Twins. Redheaded. Heard they work for you.
Can't help ya. Got somewhere to be.
You're too old to be messing 'round in a kids' gang, don't you think, Luther?
Those twins have something our boss wants. Help us out an' you can join us. Be part of a real criminal outfit.
You won't be in charge—you'll be back on the bottom—but you'll be on the bottom of the top.
So who's your boss?

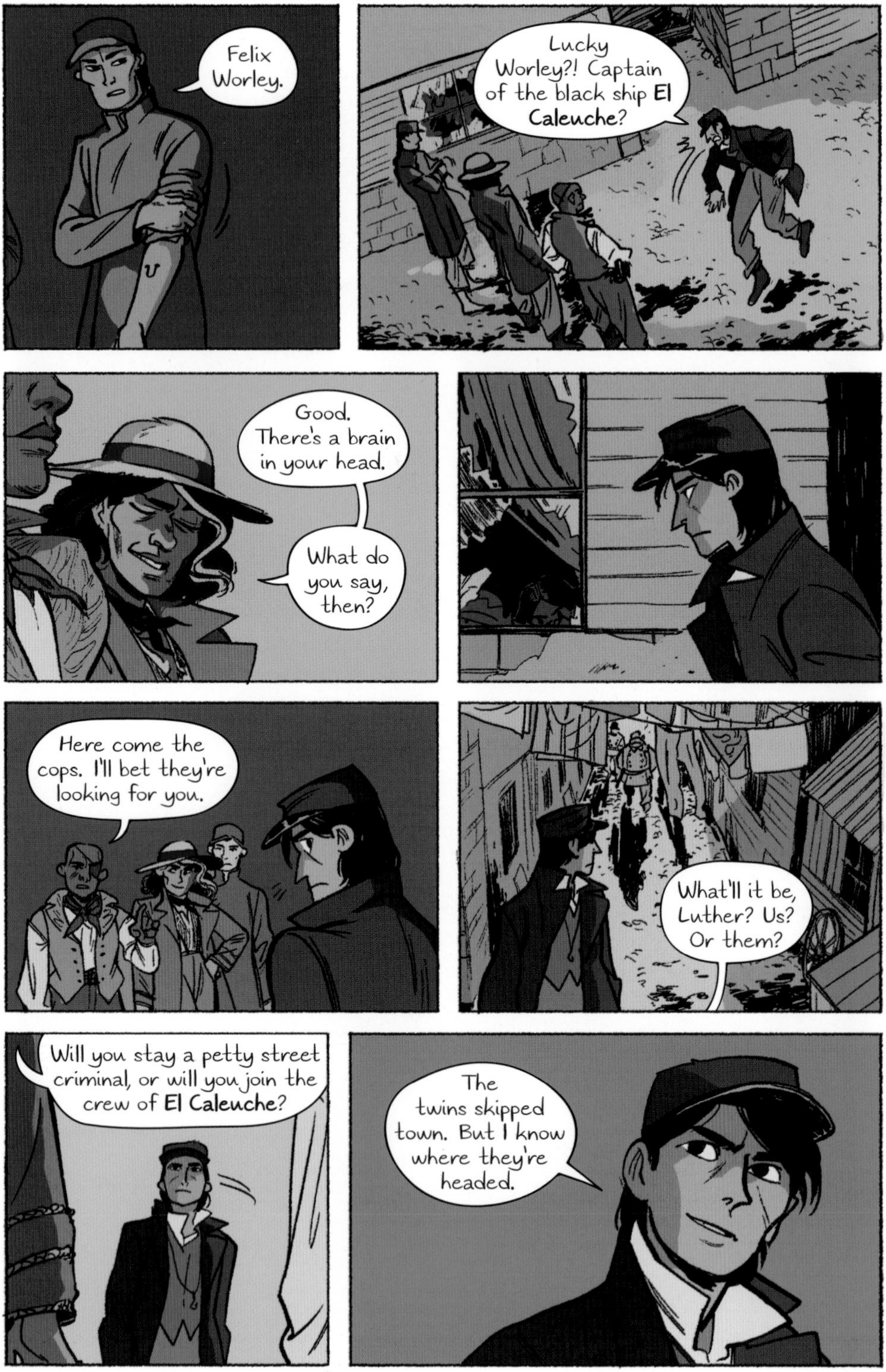
Felix Worley.
Lucky Worley?! Captain of the black ship **El Caleuche**?
Good. There's a brain in your head.
What do you say, then?
Here come the cops. I'll bet they're looking for you.
What'll it be, Luther? Us? Or them?
Will you stay a petty street criminal, or will you join the crew of **El Caleuche**?
The twins skipped town. But I know where they're headed.

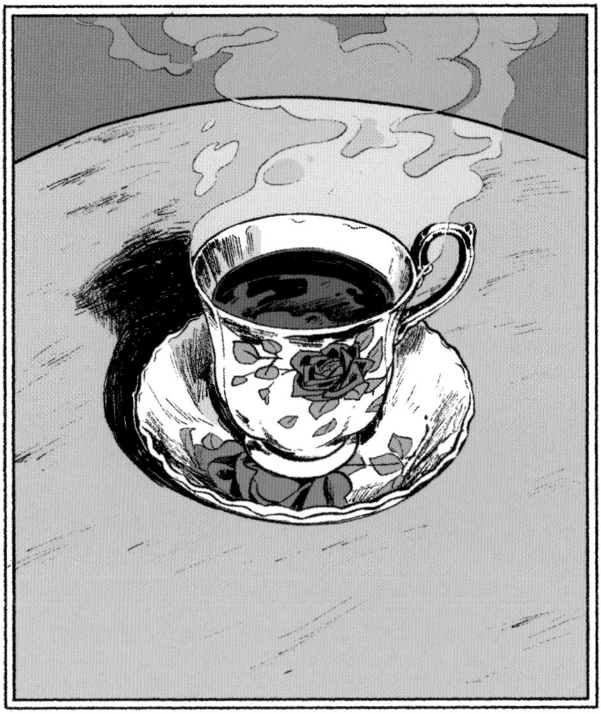

CHAPTER TWO

# IMPOSTERS

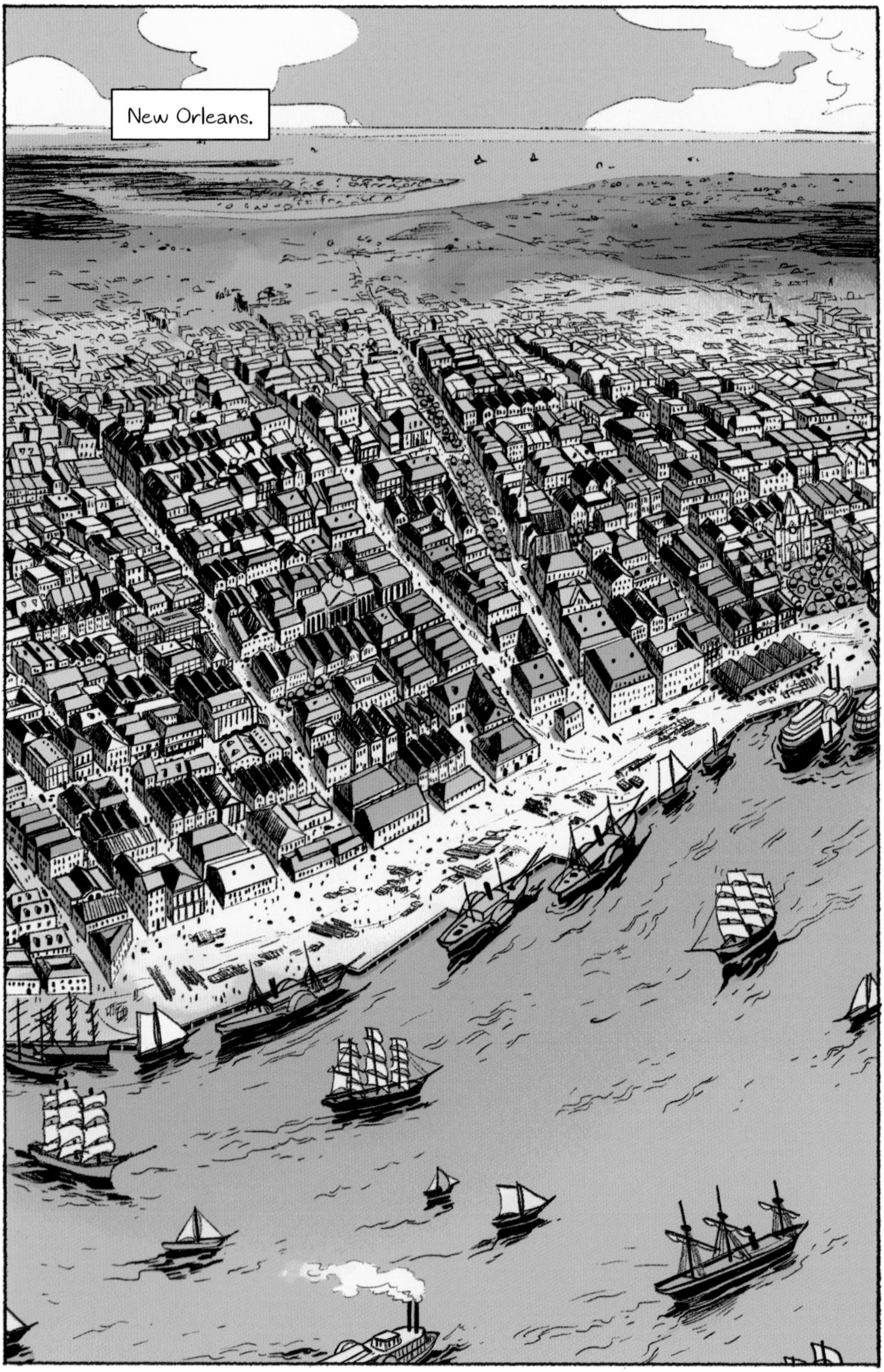
New Orleans.

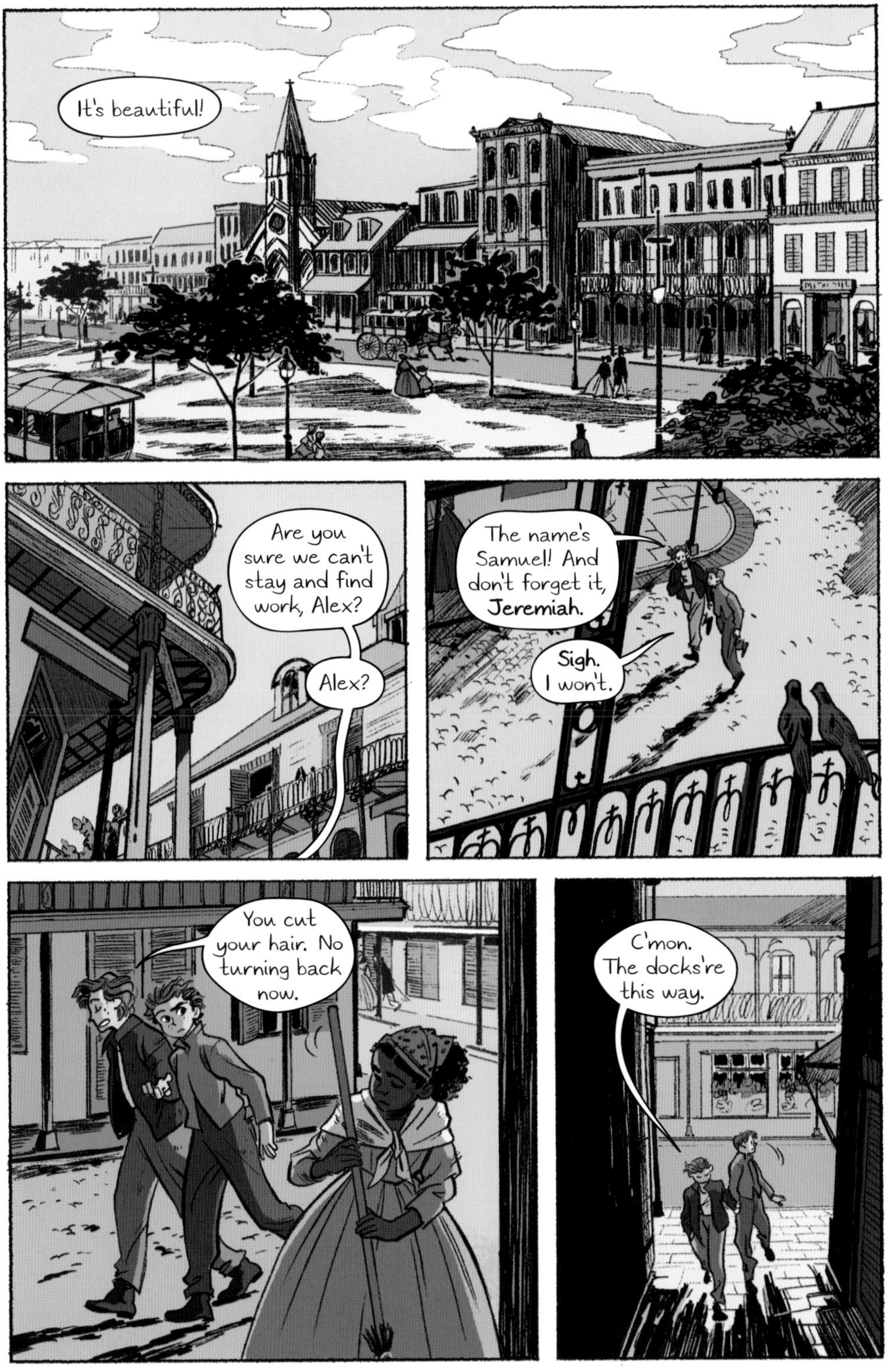
It's beautiful!
Are you sure we can't stay and find work, Alex?
Alex?
The name's Samuel! And don't forget it, **Jeremiah.**
Sigh. I won't.
You cut your hair. No turning back now.
C'mon. The docks're this way.

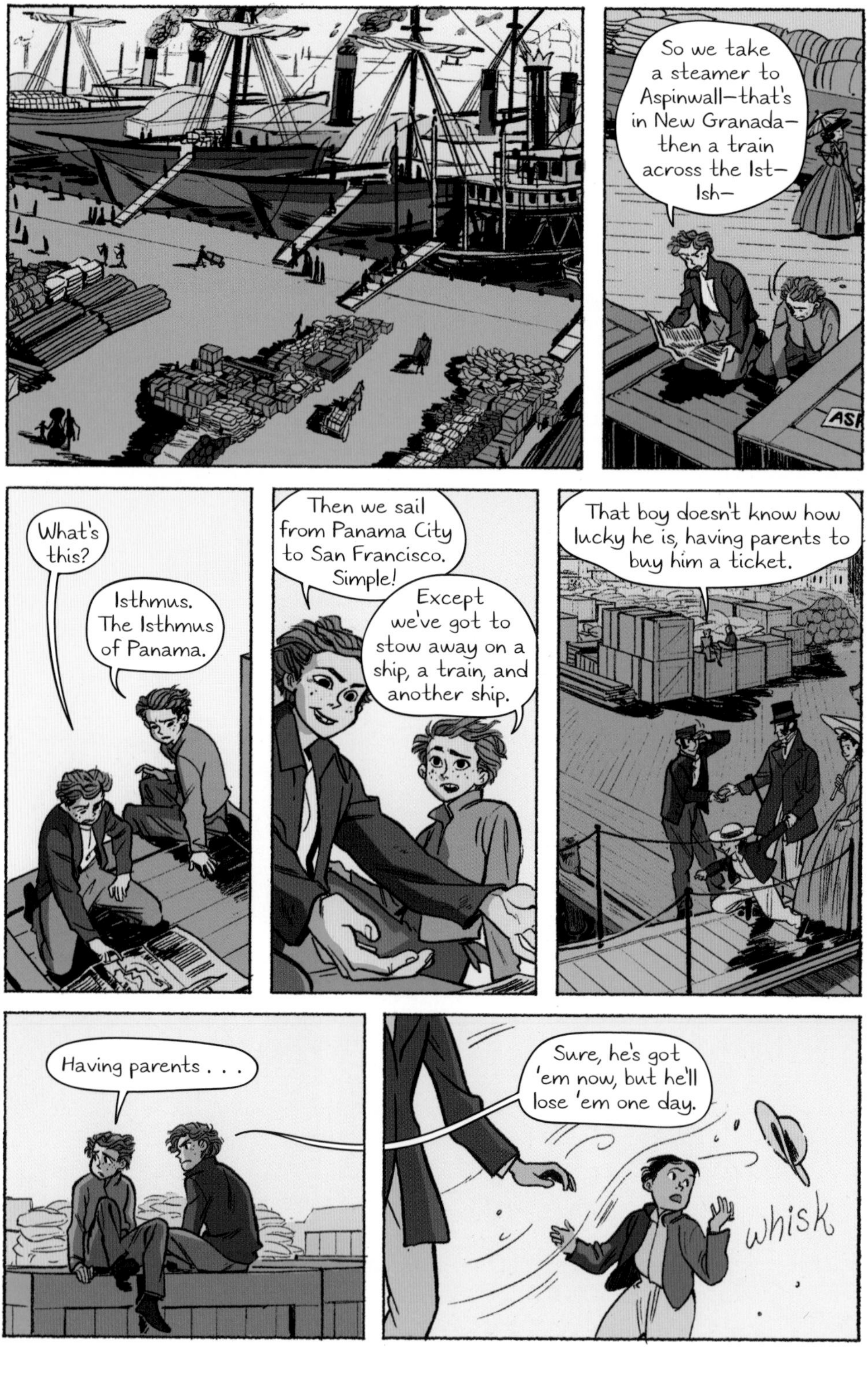
So we take a steamer to Aspinwall—that's in New Granada—then a train across the Ist—Ish—
ASP
What's this?
Isthmus. The Isthmus of Panama.
Then we sail from Panama City to San Francisco. Simple!
Except we've got to stow away on a ship, a train, and another ship.
That boy doesn't know how lucky he is, having parents to buy him a ticket.
Having parents . . .
Sure, he's got 'em now, but he'll lose 'em one day.
whisk

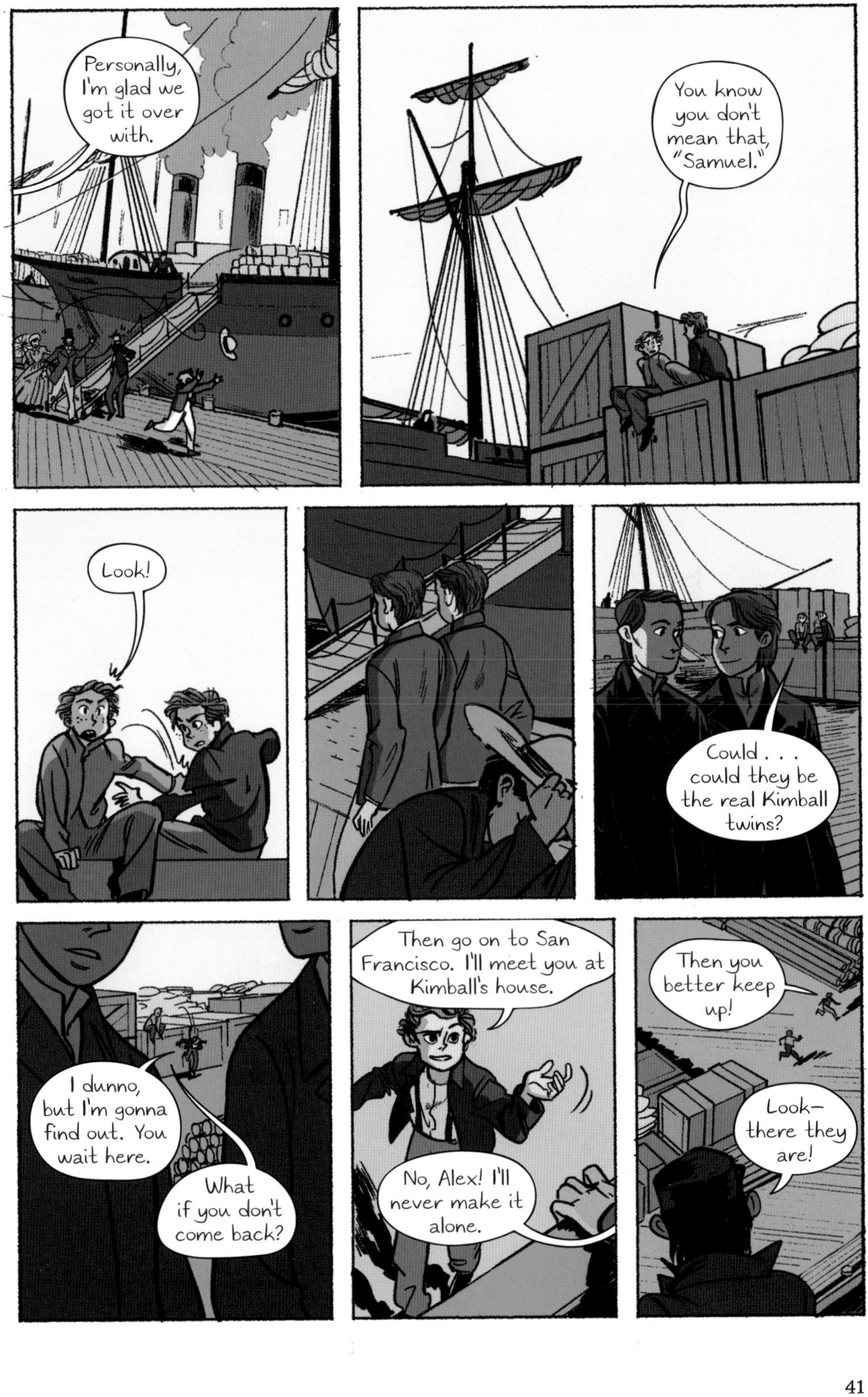
Personally, I'm glad we got it over with.
You know you don't mean that, "Samuel."
Look!
Could . . . could they be the real Kimball twins?
I dunno, but I'm gonna find out. You wait here.
What if you don't come back?
Then go on to San Francisco. I'll meet you at Kimball's house.
No, Alex! I'll never make it alone.
Then you better keep up!
Look— there they are!

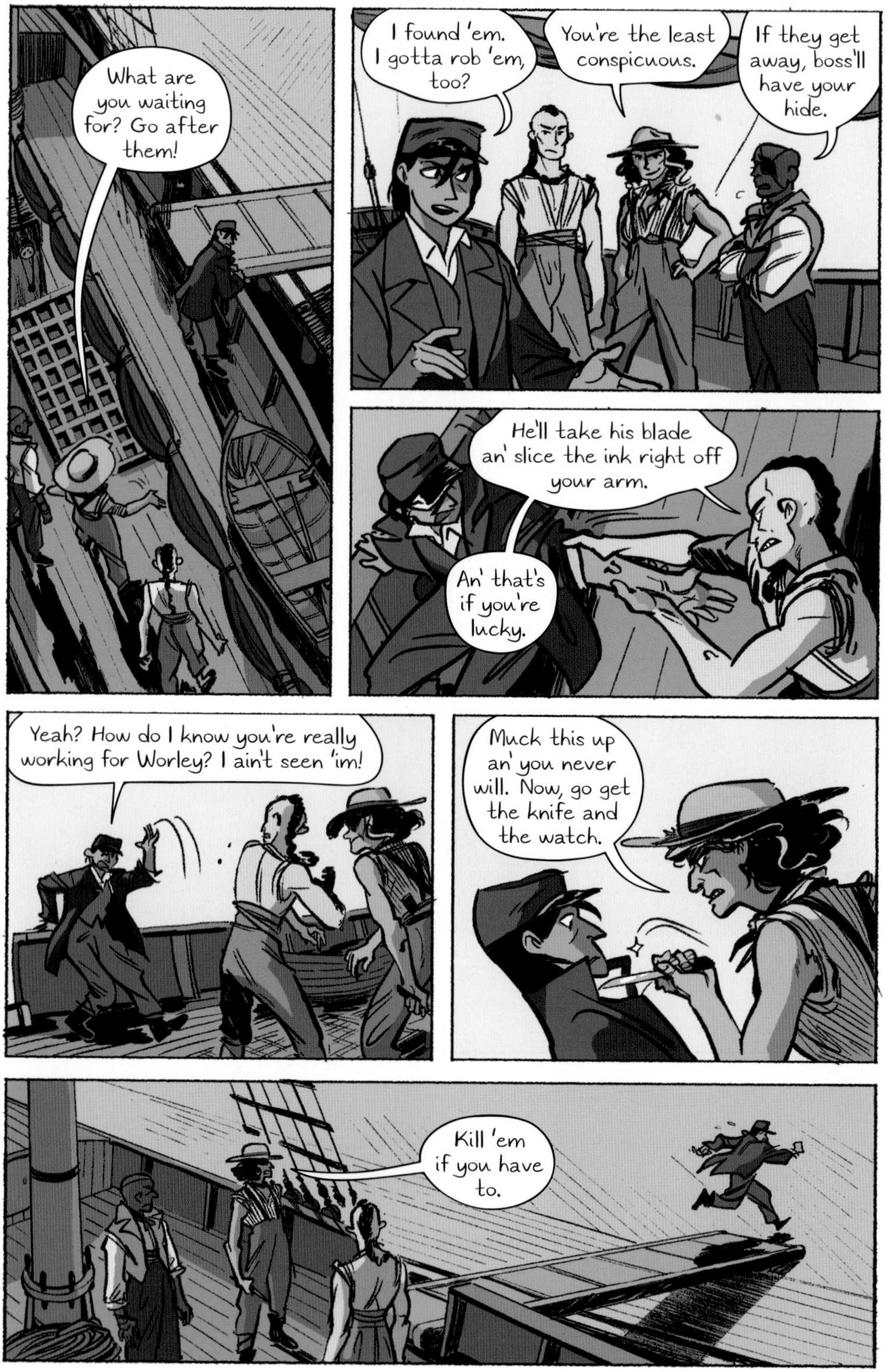
What are you waiting for? Go after them!
I found 'em. I gotta rob 'em, too?
You're the least conspicuous.
If they get away, boss'll have your hide.
He'll take his blade an' slice the ink right off your arm.
An' that's if you're lucky.
Yeah? How do I know you're really working for Worley? I ain't seen 'im!
Muck this up an' you never will. Now, go get the knife and the watch.
Kill 'em if you have to.

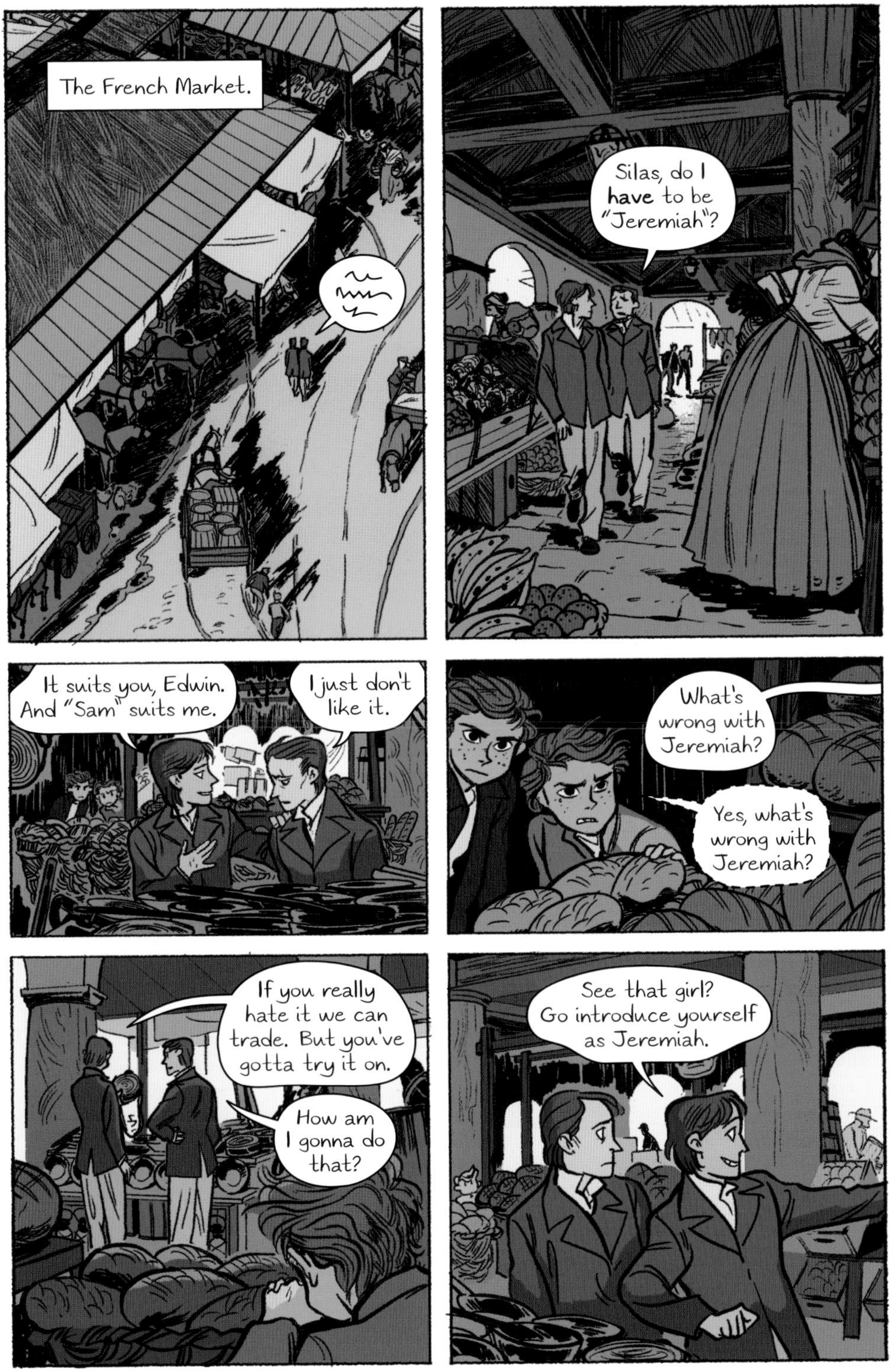
The French Market.
Silas, do I **have** to be "Jeremiah"?
It suits you, Edwin. And "Sam" suits me.
I just don't like it.
What's wrong with Jeremiah?
Yes, what's wrong with Jeremiah?
If you really hate it we can trade. But you've gotta try it on.
How am I gonna do that?
See that girl? Go introduce yourself as Jeremiah.

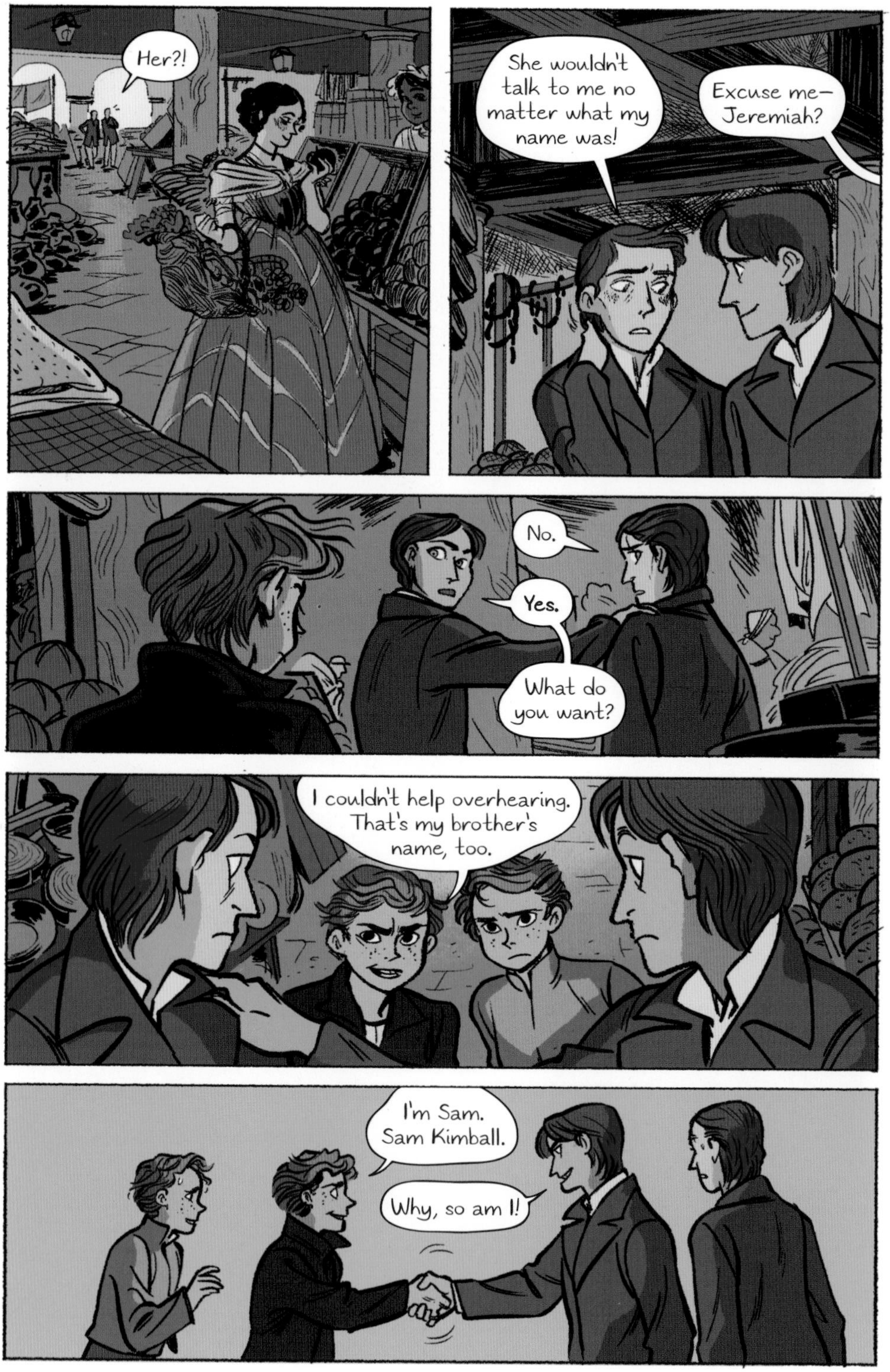
Her?!
She wouldn't talk to me no matter what my name was!
Excuse me– Jeremiah?
No.
Yes.
What do you want?
I couldn't help overhearing. That's my brother's name, too.
I'm Sam. Sam Kimball.
Why, so am I!

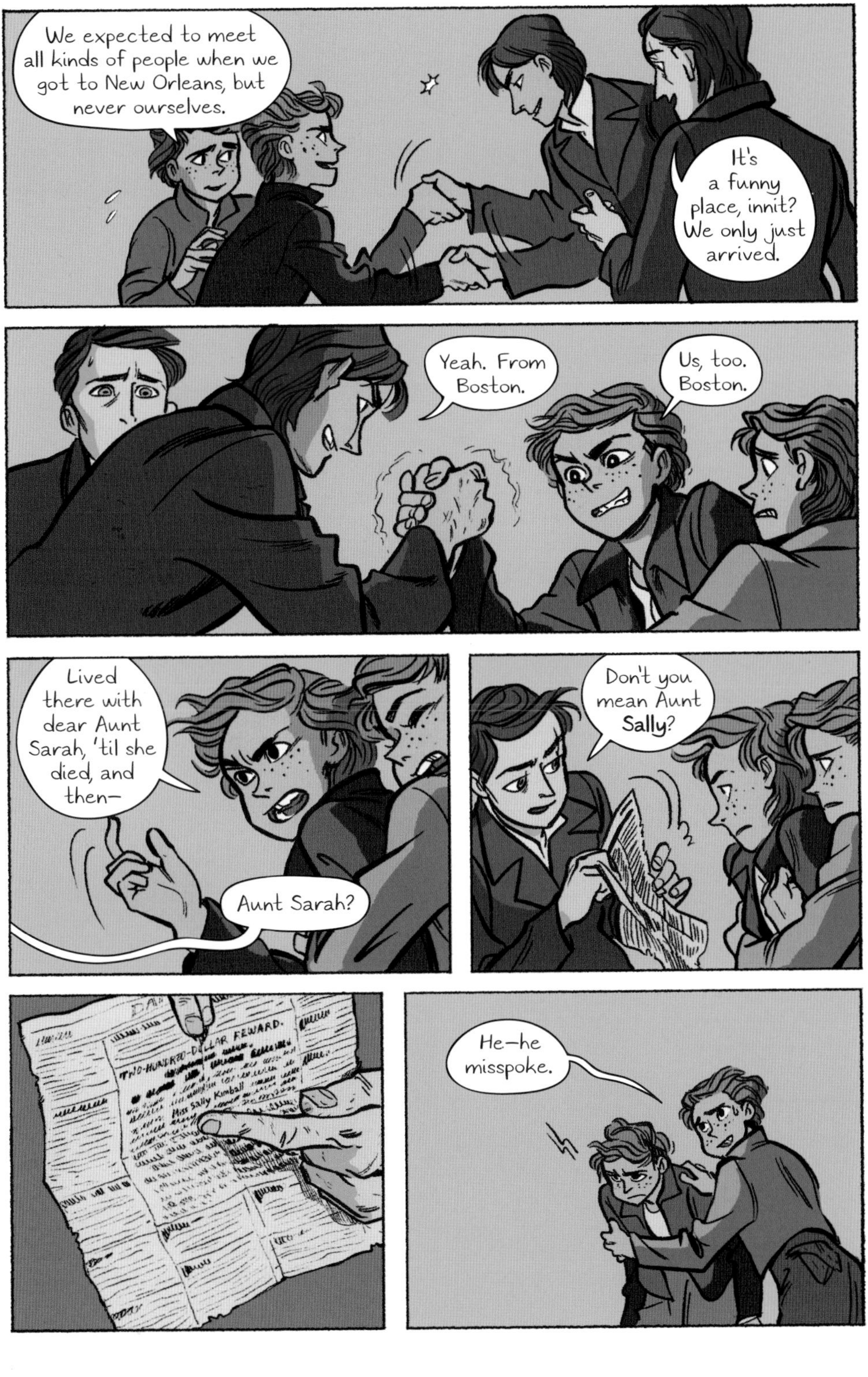

We expected to meet all kinds of people when we got to New Orleans, but never ourselves.
It's a funny place, innit? We only just arrived.
Yeah. From Boston.
Us, too. Boston.
Lived there with dear Aunt Sarah, 'til she died, and then—
Aunt Sarah?
Don't you mean Aunt **Sally**?
TWO-HUNDRED-DOLLAR REWARD.
Miss Sally Kimball
He—he misspoke.

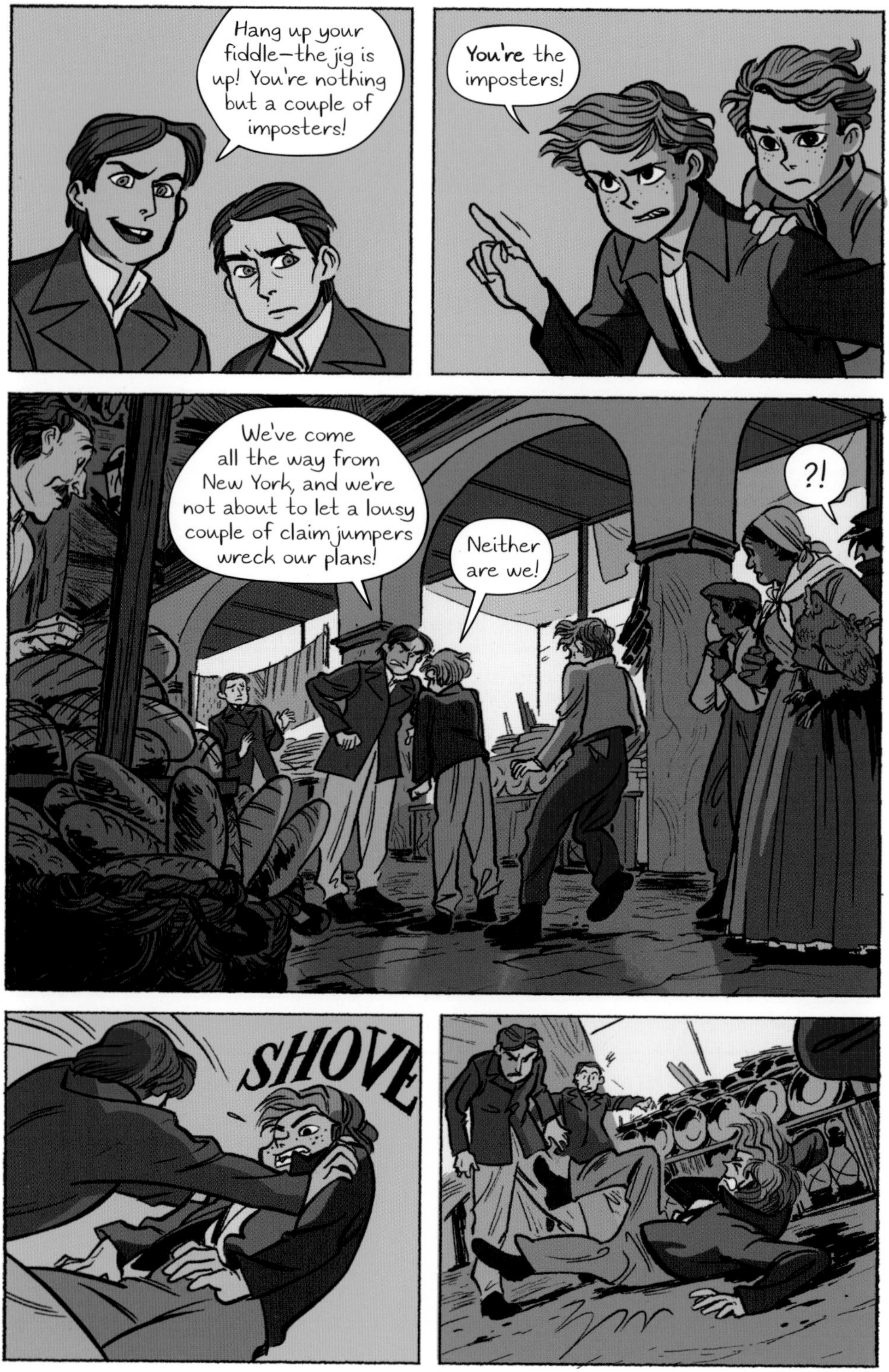
Hang up your fiddle—the jig is up! You're nothing but a couple of imposters!
**You're** the imposters!
We've come all the way from New York, and we're not about to let a lousy couple of claim jumpers wreck our plans!
Neither are we!
?!
SHOVE

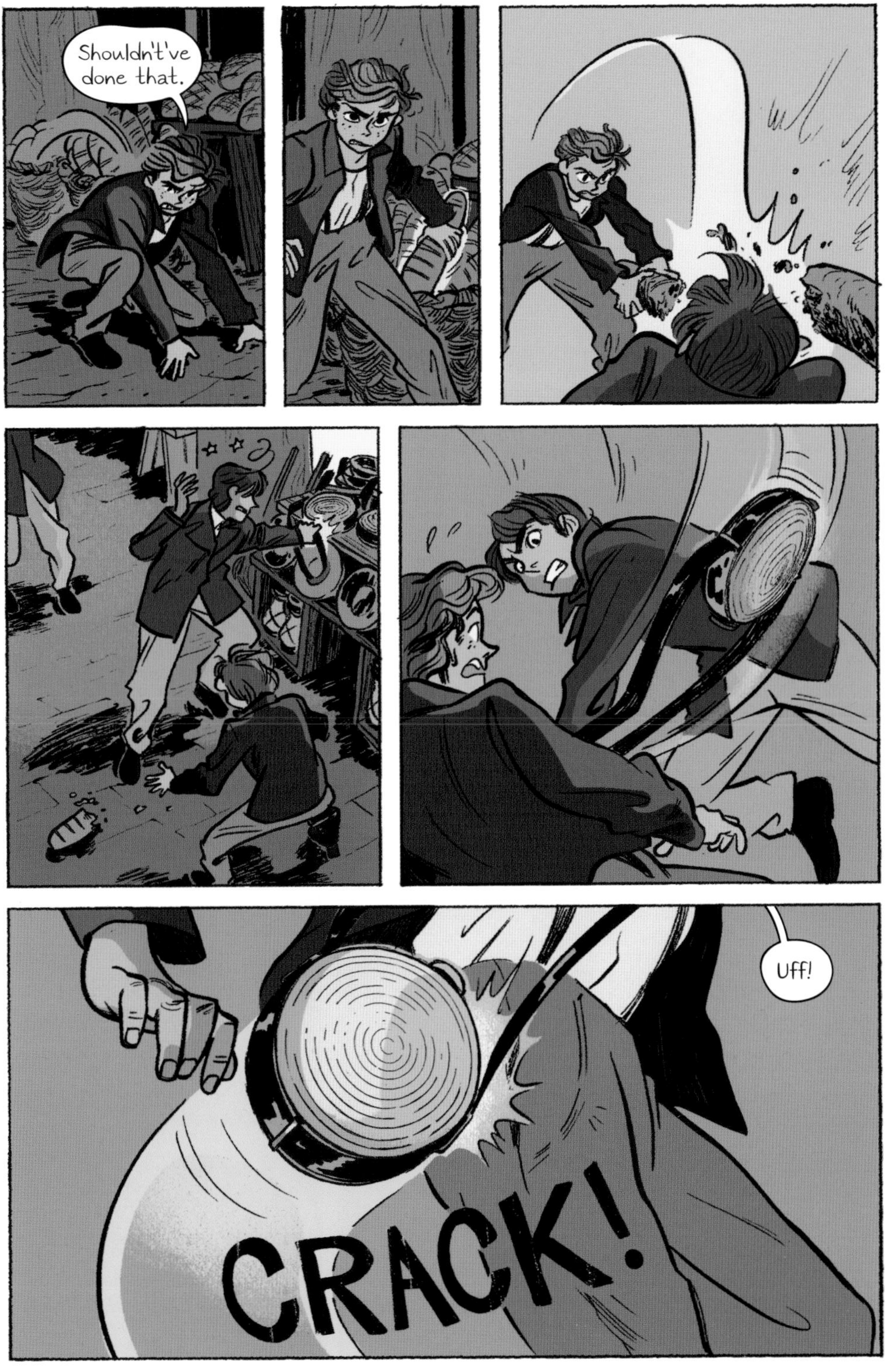
Shouldn't've done that.
Uff!
CRACK!

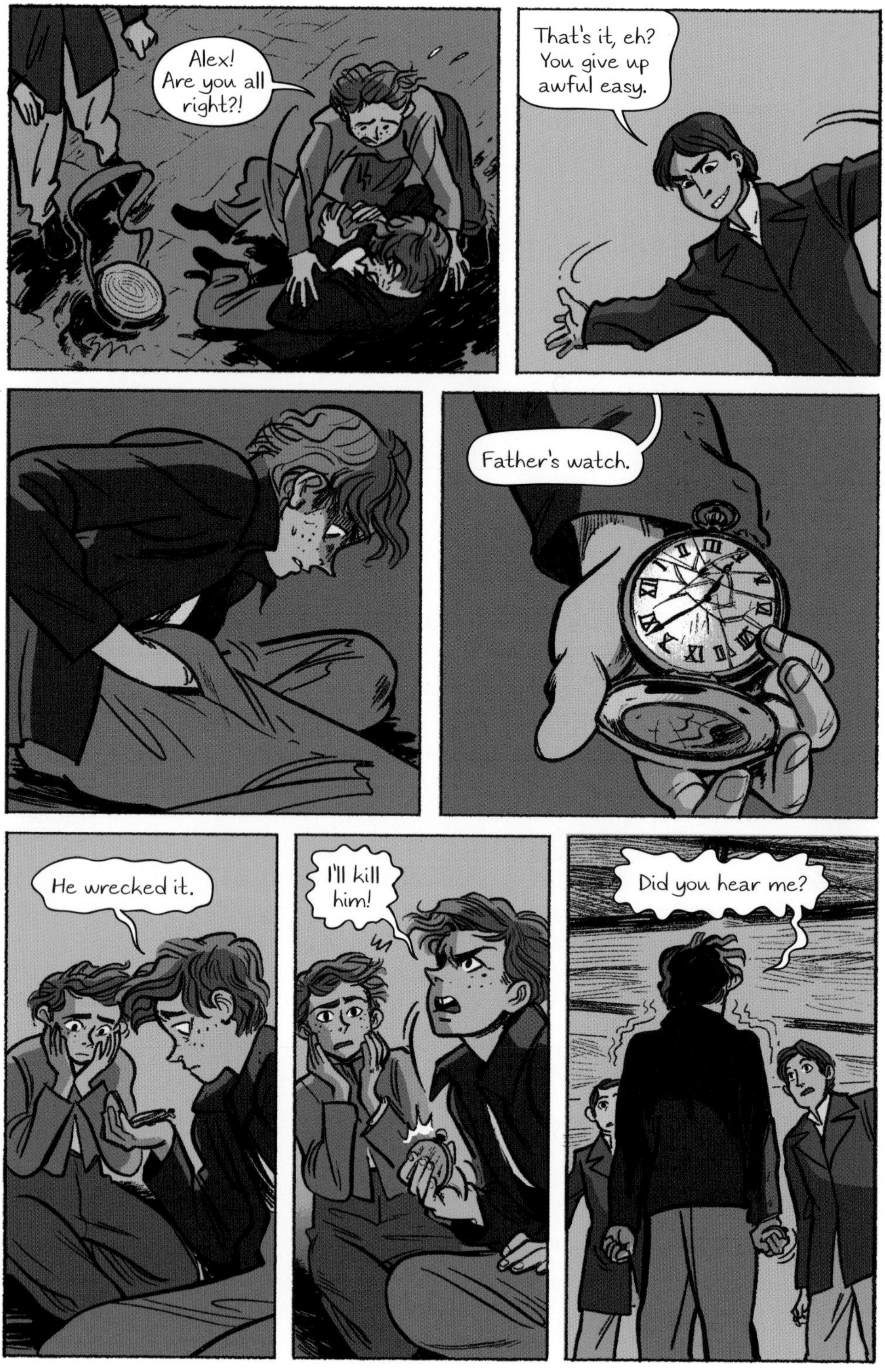
Alex!
Are you all right?!
That's it, eh? You give up awful easy.
Father's watch.
He wrecked it.
I'll kill him!
Did you hear me?

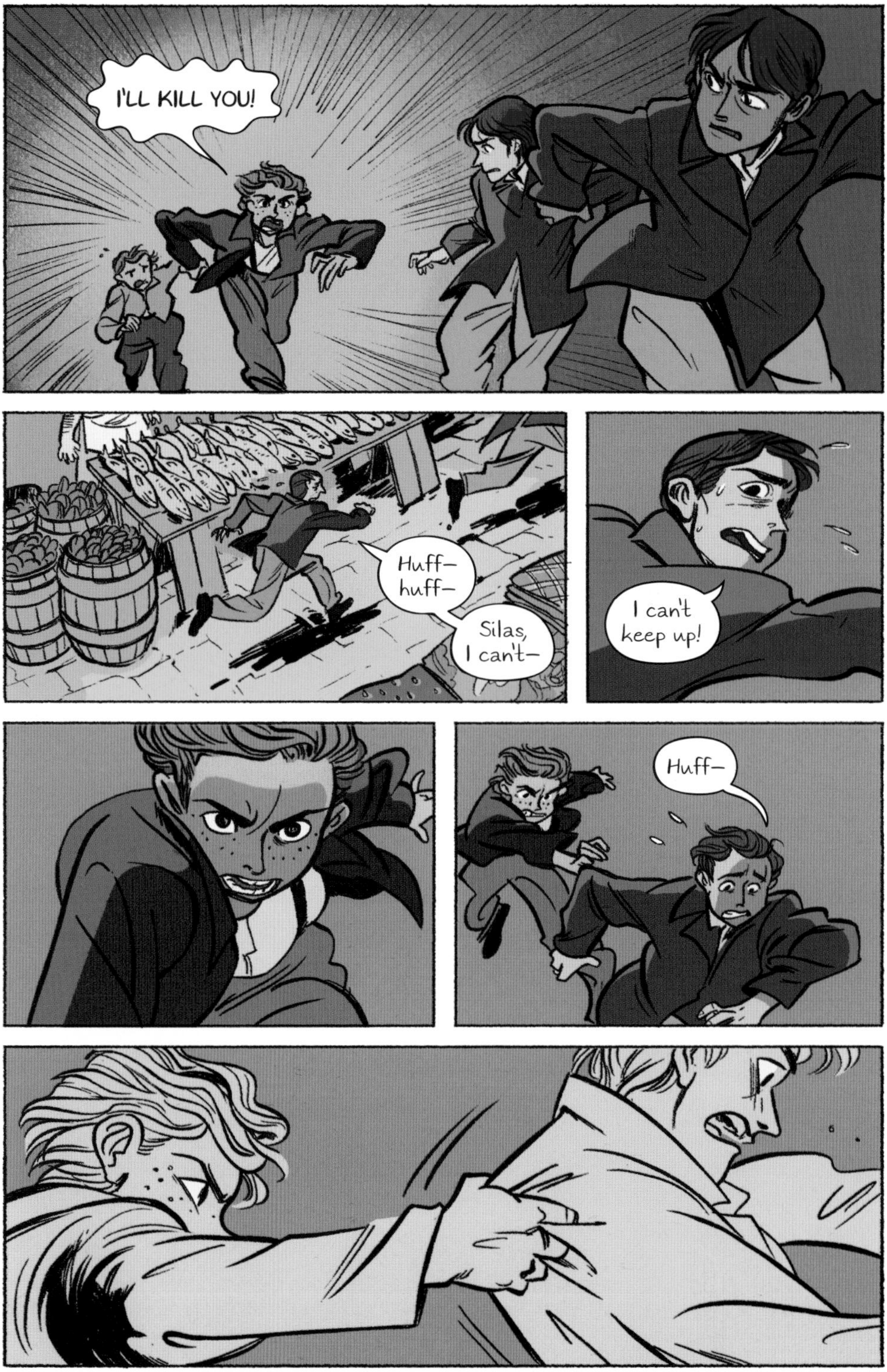
I'LL KILL YOU!
Huff— huff—
Silas, I can't—
I can't keep up!
Huff—

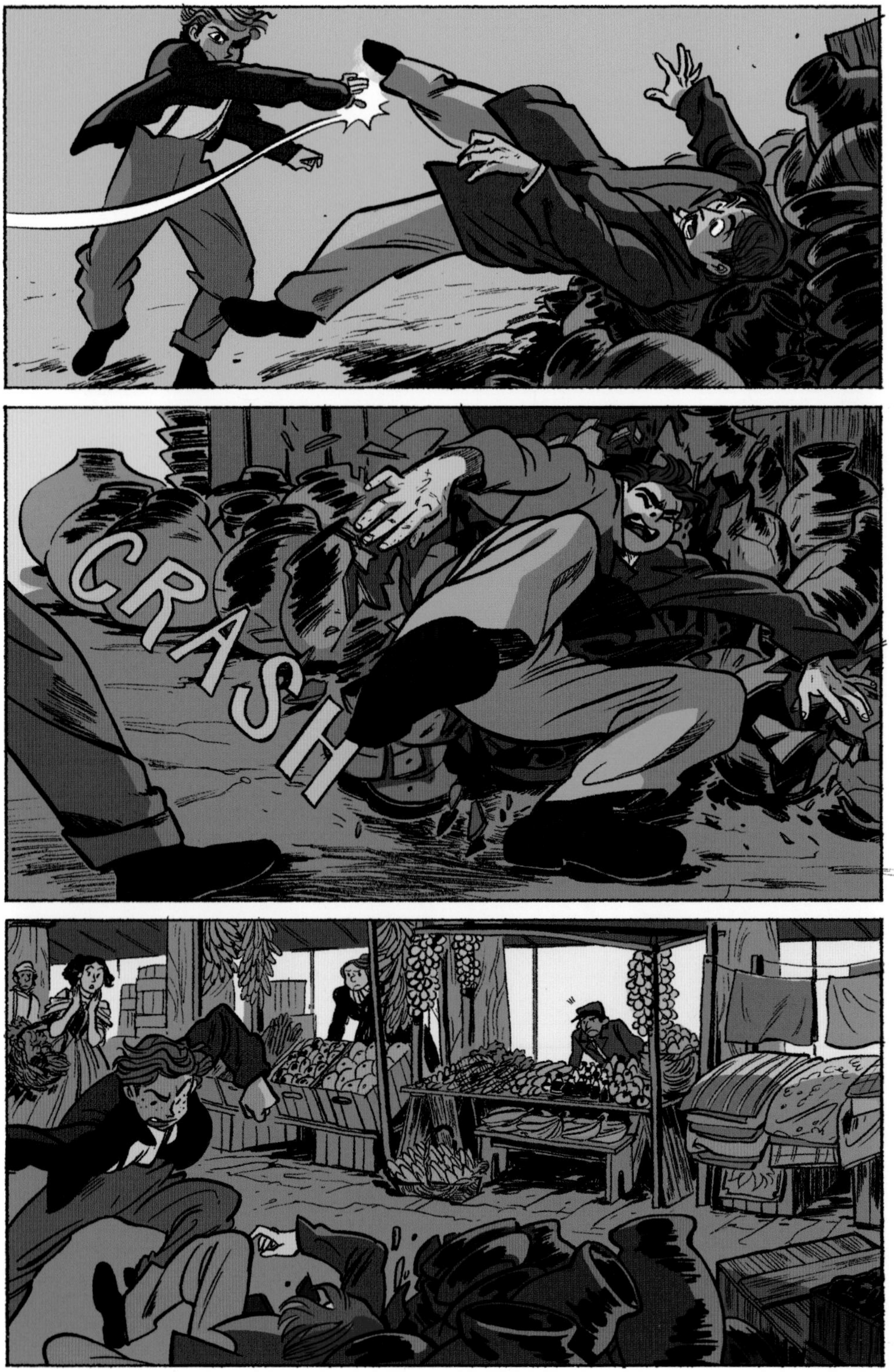
CRASH

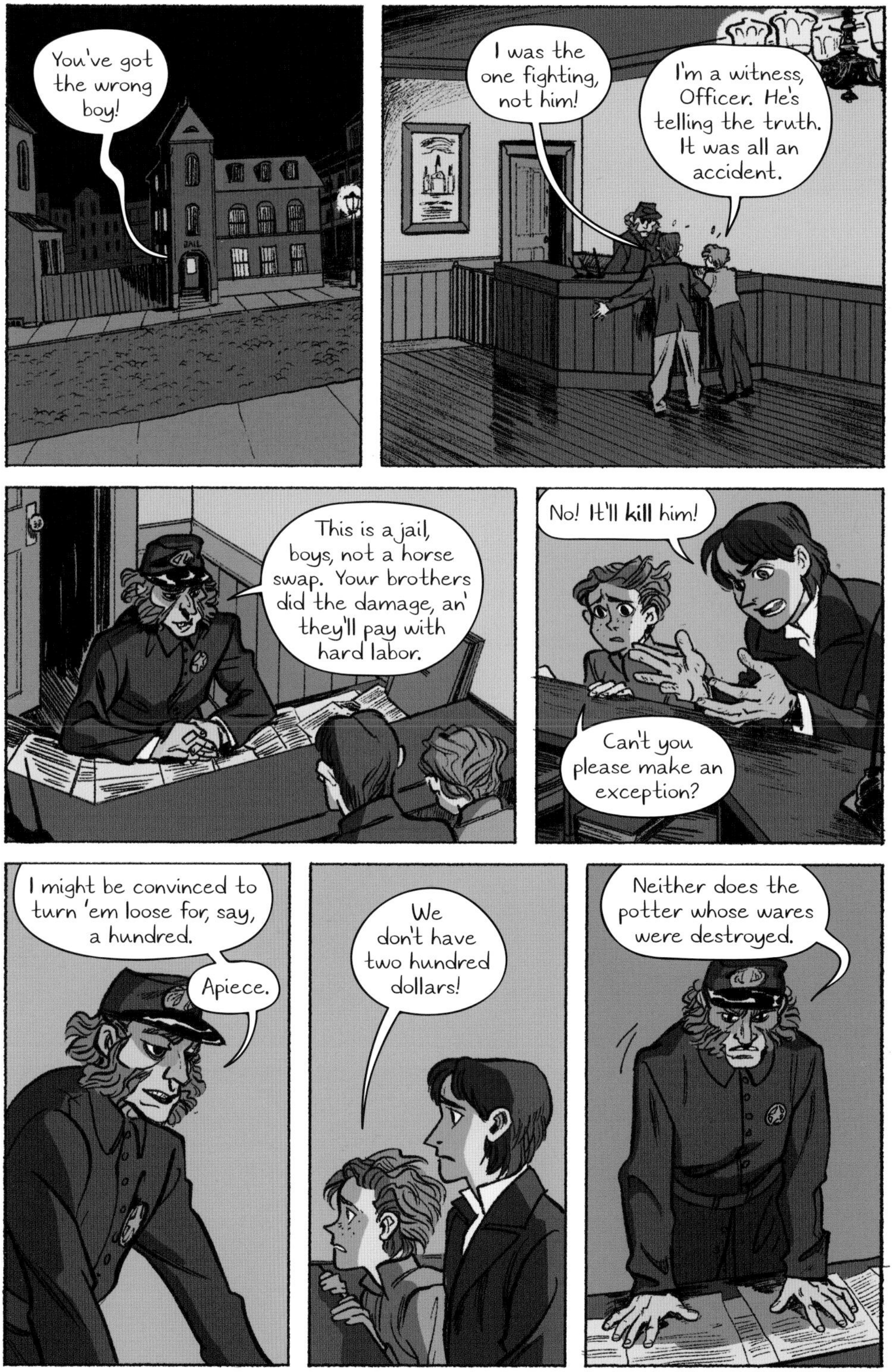
You've got the wrong boy!
JAIL
I was the one fighting, not him!
I'm a witness, Officer. He's telling the truth. It was all an accident.
This is a jail, boys, not a horse swap. Your brothers did the damage, an' they'll pay with hard labor.
No! It'll **kill** him!
Can't you please make an exception?
I might be convinced to turn 'em loose for, say, a hundred.
Apiece.
We don't have two hundred dollars!
Neither does the potter whose wares were destroyed.

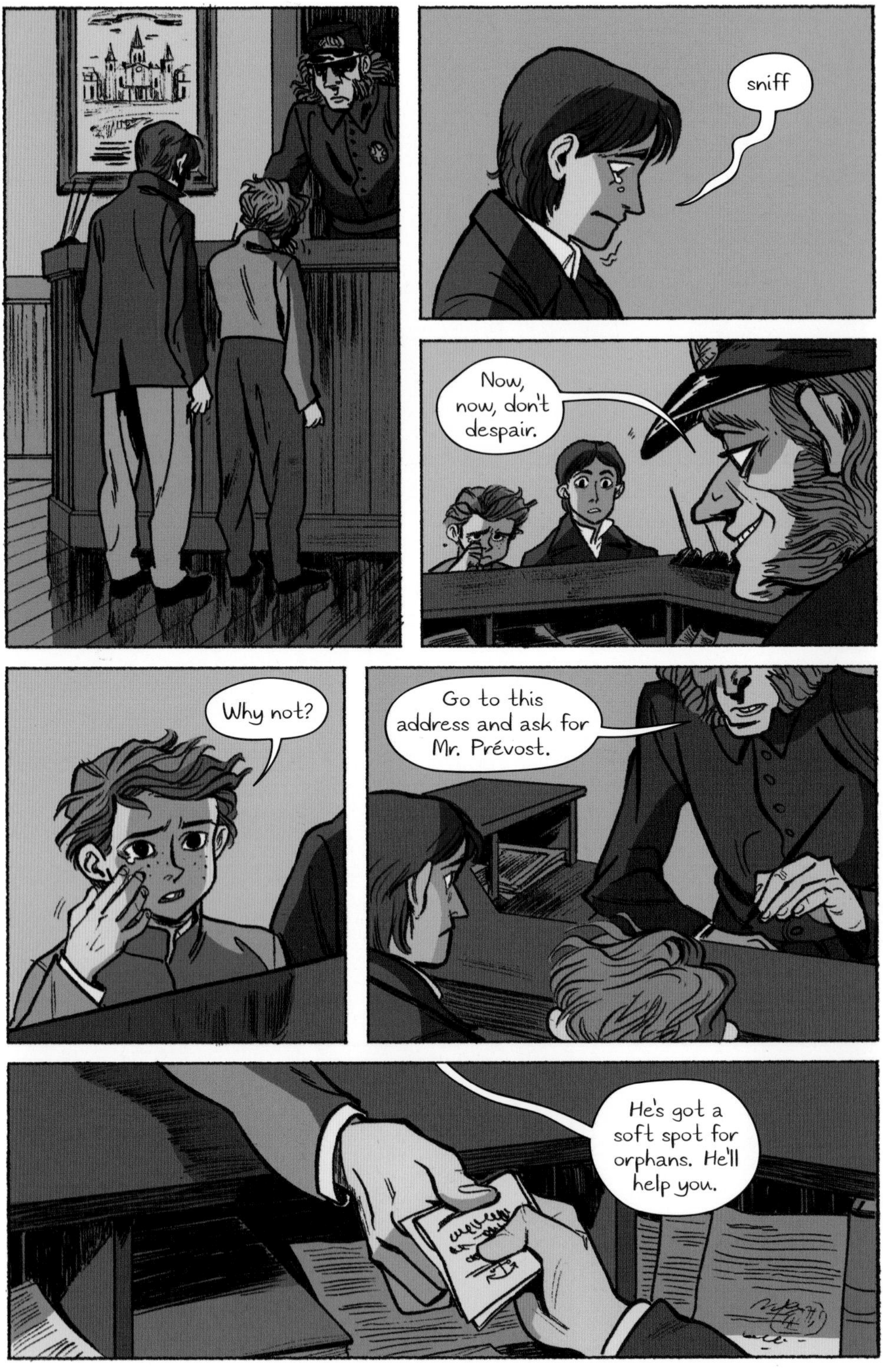
sniff
Now, now, don't despair.
Why not?
Go to this address and ask for Mr. Prévost.
He's got a soft spot for orphans. He'll help you.

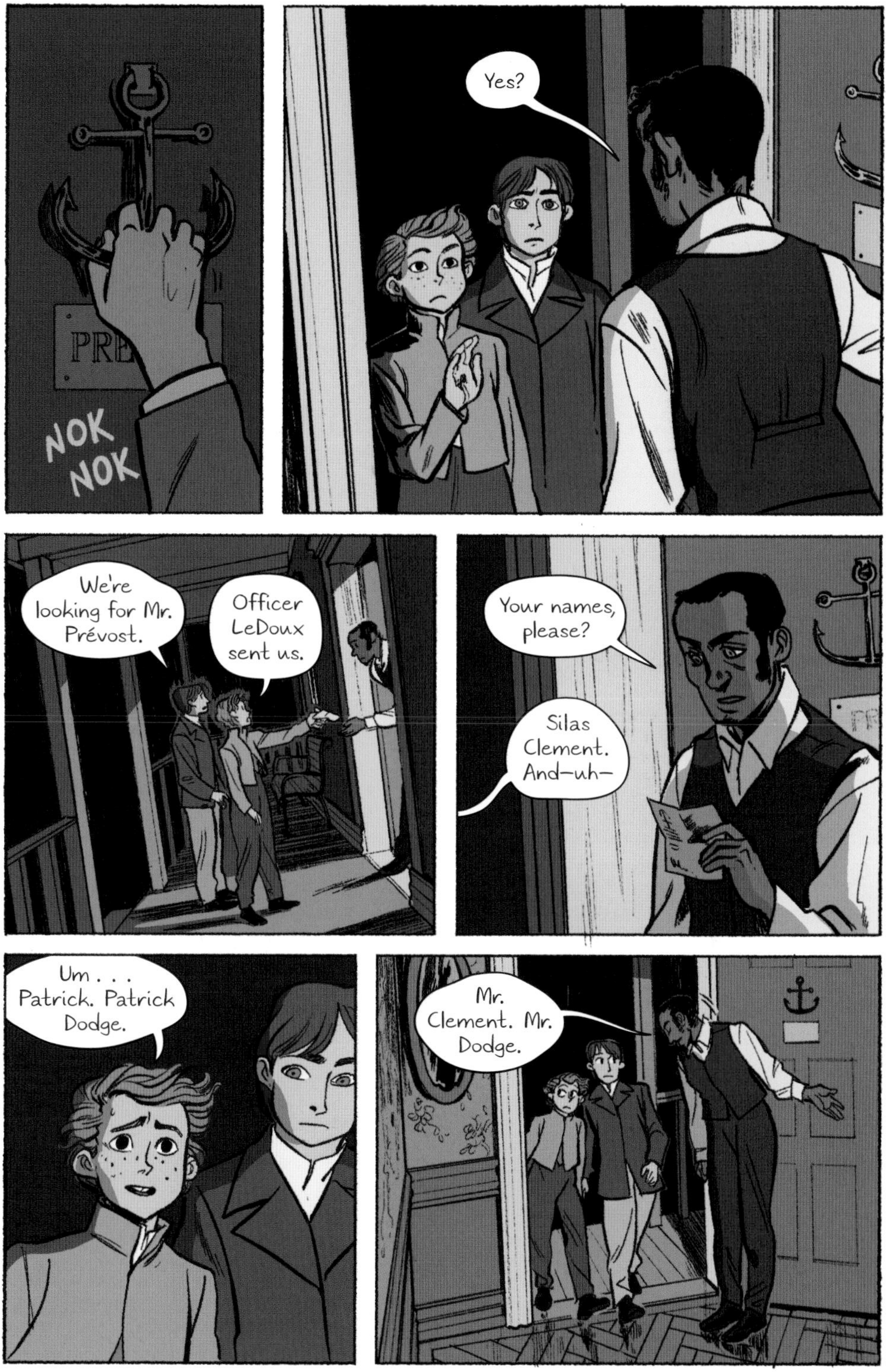
PRE
NOK NOK
Yes?
We're looking for Mr. Prévost.
Officer LeDoux sent us.
Your names, please?
Silas Clement. And—uh—
Um . . . Patrick. Patrick Dodge.
Mr. Clement. Mr. Dodge.

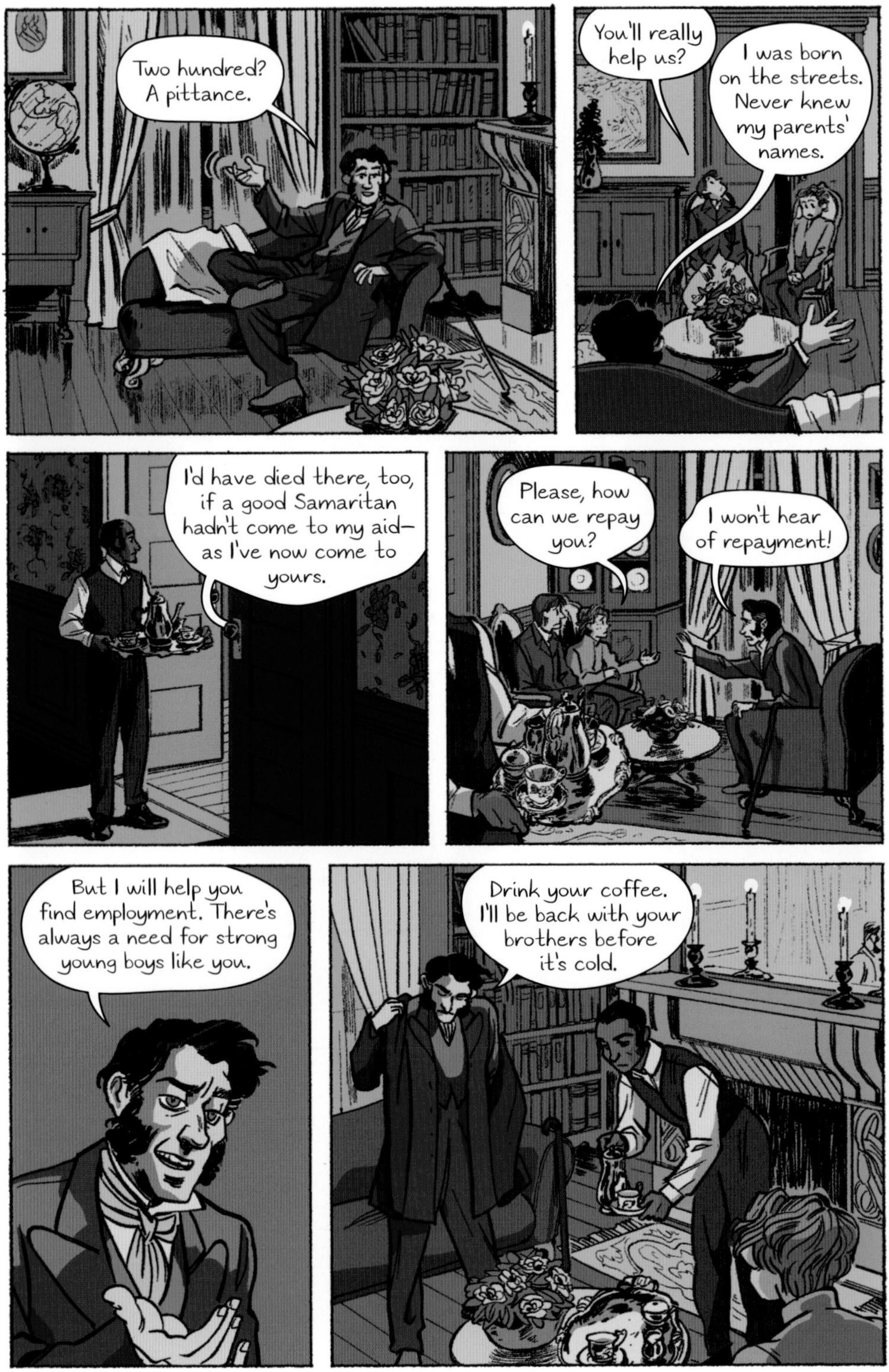
Two hundred? A pittance.
You'll really help us?
I was born on the streets. Never knew my parents' names.
I'd have died there, too, if a good Samaritan hadn't come to my aid—as I've now come to yours.
Please, how can we repay you?
I won't hear of repayment!
But I will help you find employment. There's always a need for strong young boys like you.
Drink your coffee. I'll be back with your brothers before it's cold.

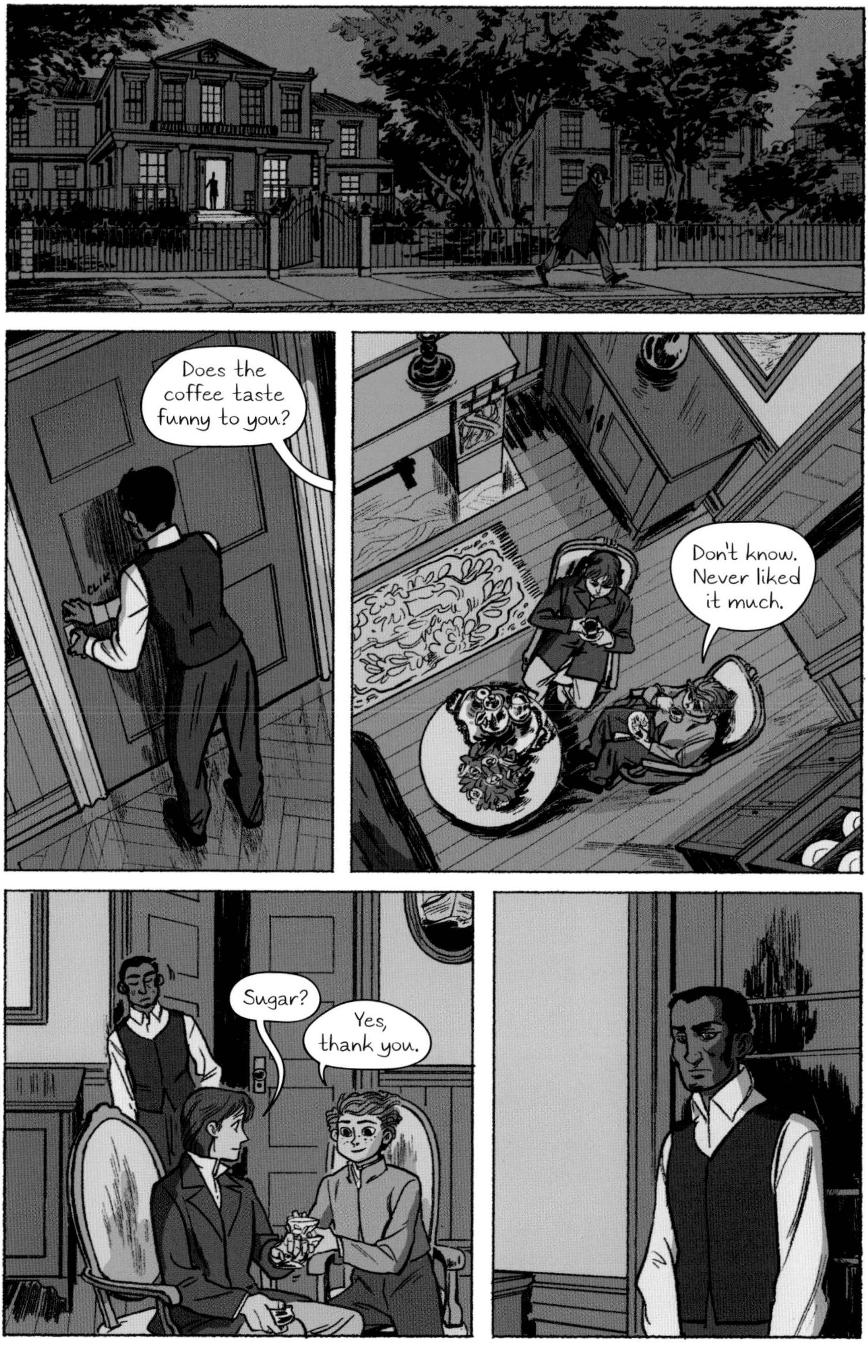
Does the coffee taste funny to you?
CLIK
Don't know. Never liked it much.
Sugar?
Yes, thank you.

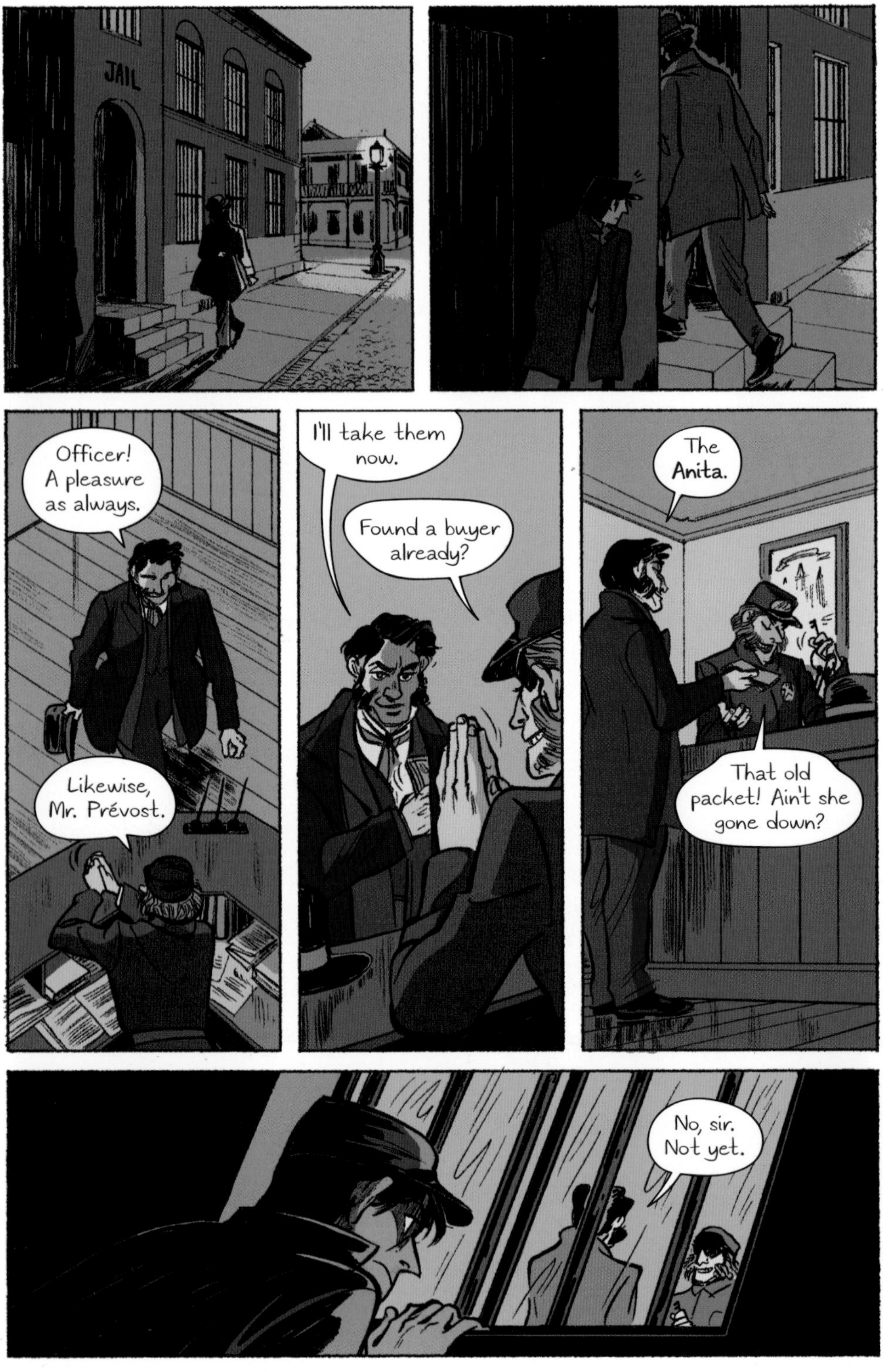
JAIL
Officer! A pleasure as always.
Likewise, Mr. Prévost.
I'll take them now.
Found a buyer already?
The Anita.
That old packet! Ain't she gone down?
No, sir. Not yet.

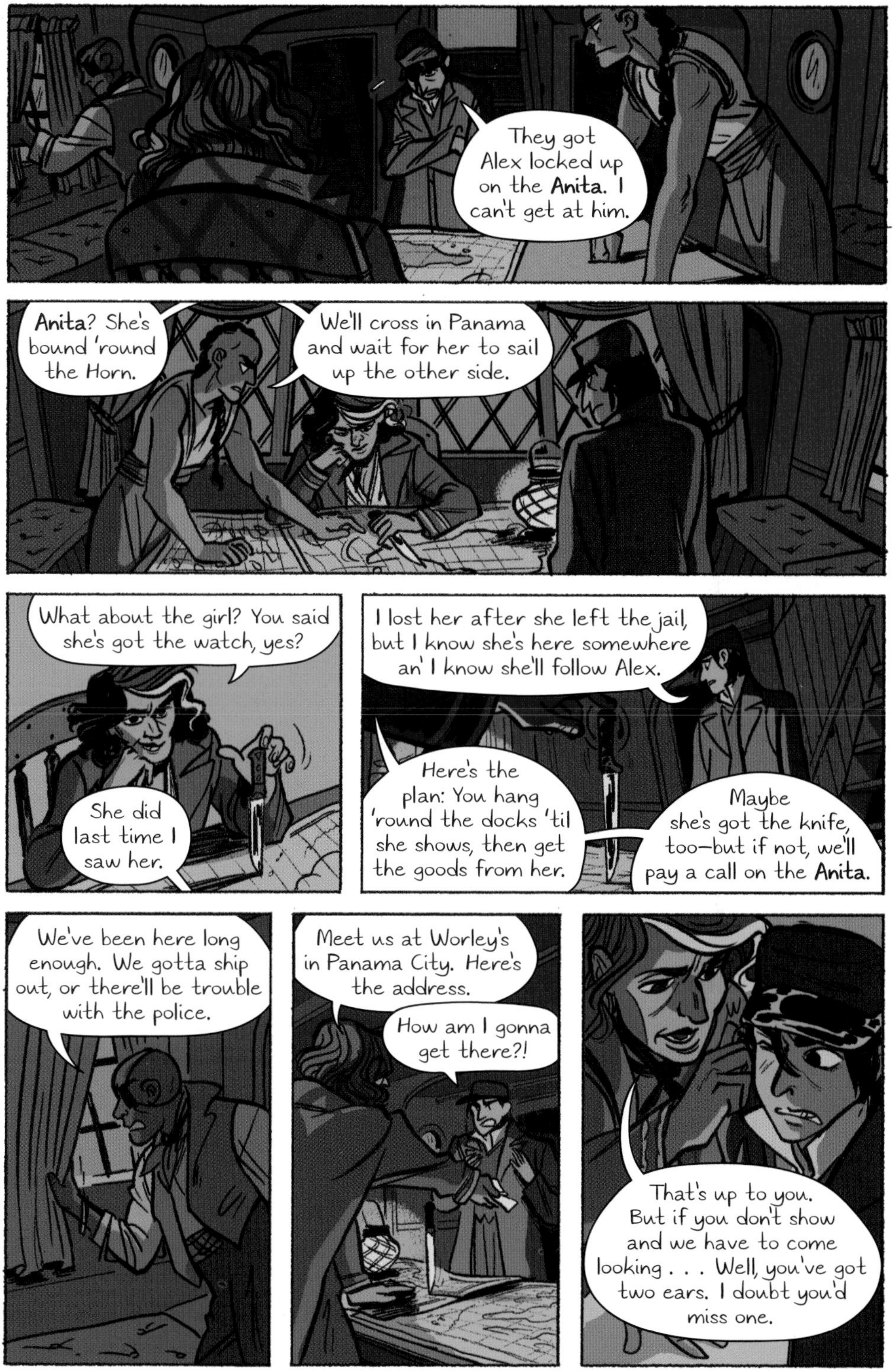
They got Alex locked up on the **Anita.** I can't get at him.
**Anita**? She's bound 'round the Horn.
We'll cross in Panama and wait for her to sail up the other side.
What about the girl? You said she's got the watch, yes?
She did last time I saw her.
I lost her after she left the jail, but I know she's here somewhere an' I know she'll follow Alex.
Here's the plan: You hang 'round the docks 'til she shows, then get the goods from her.
Maybe she's got the knife, too—but if not, we'll pay a call on the **Anita.**
We've been here long enough. We gotta ship out, or there'll be trouble with the police.
Meet us at Worley's in Panama City. Here's the address.
How am I gonna get there?!
That's up to you. But if you don't show and we have to come looking . . . Well, you've got two ears. I doubt you'd miss one.

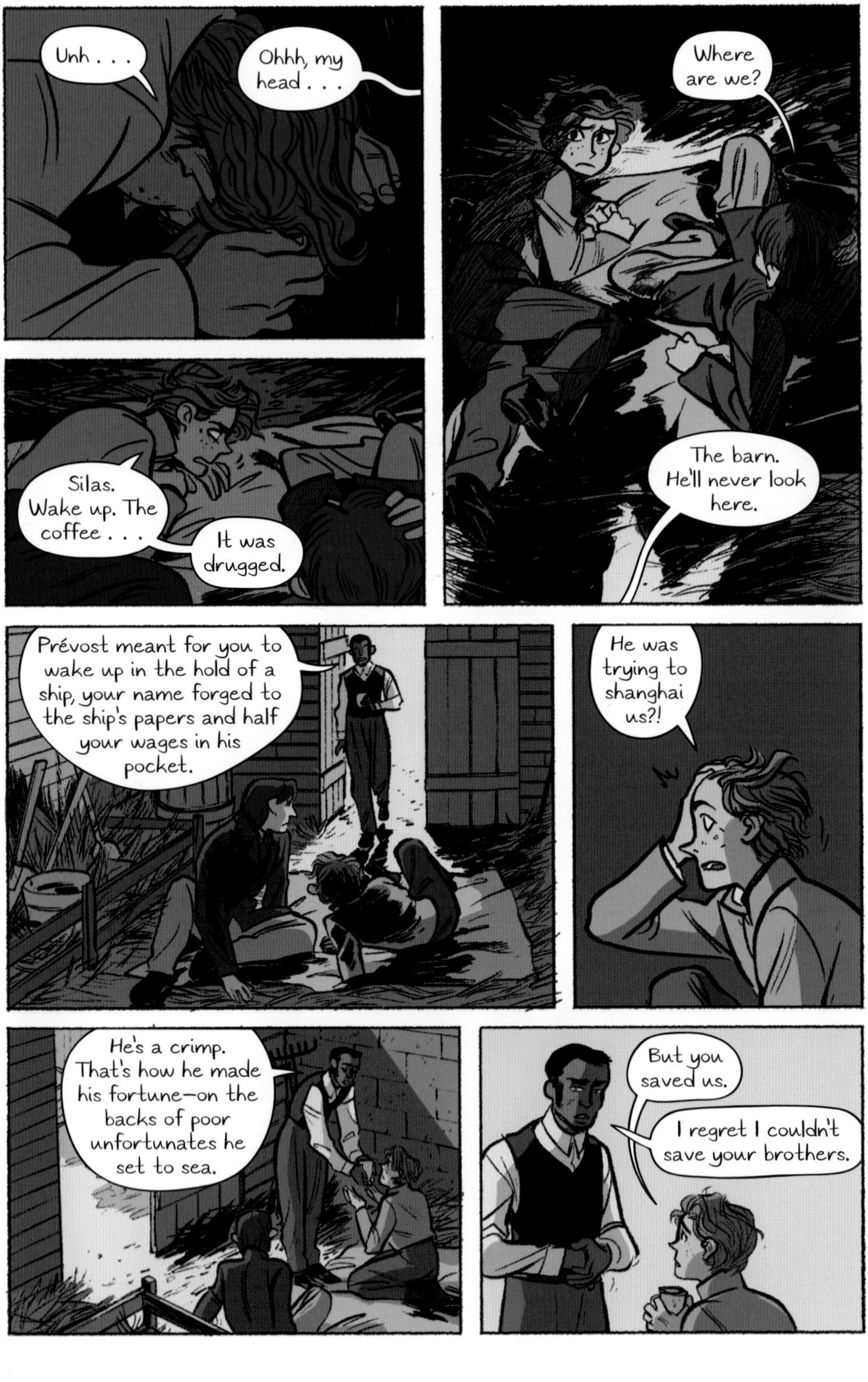
Unh . . .
Ohhh, my head . . .
Where are we?
Silas. Wake up. The coffee . . .
It was drugged.
The barn. He'll never look here.
Prévost meant for you to wake up in the hold of a ship, your name forged to the ship's papers and half your wages in his pocket.
He was trying to shanghai us?!
He's a crimp. That's how he made his fortune—on the backs of poor unfortunates he set to sea.
But you saved us.
I regret I couldn't save your brothers.

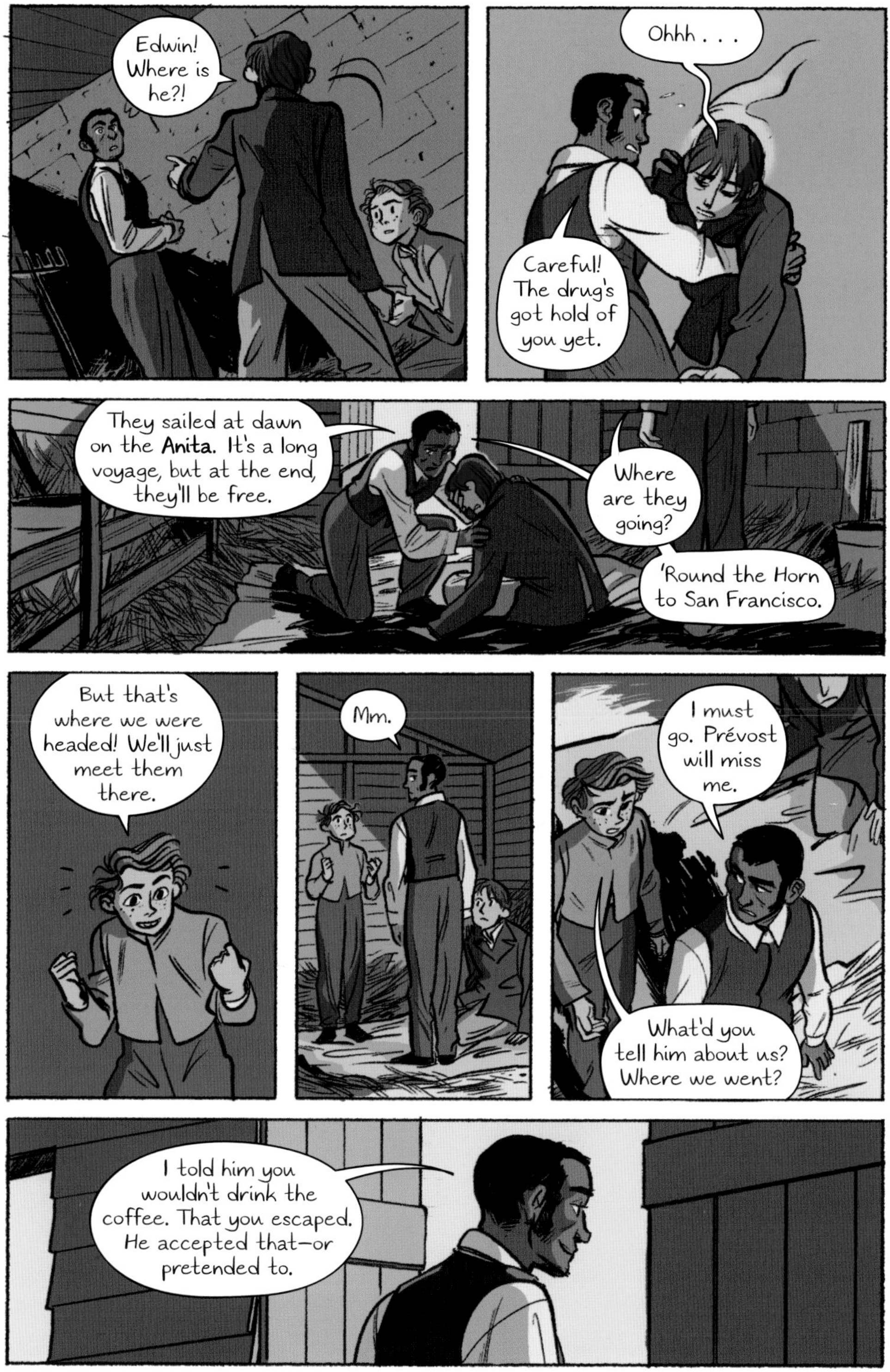
Edwin! Where is he?!
Ohhh . . .
Careful! The drug's got hold of you yet.
They sailed at dawn on the Anita. It's a long voyage, but at the end, they'll be free.
Where are they going?
'Round the Horn to San Francisco.
But that's where we were headed! We'll just meet them there.
Mm.
I must go. Prévost will miss me.
What'd you tell him about us? Where we went?
I told him you wouldn't drink the coffee. That you escaped. He accepted that—or pretended to.

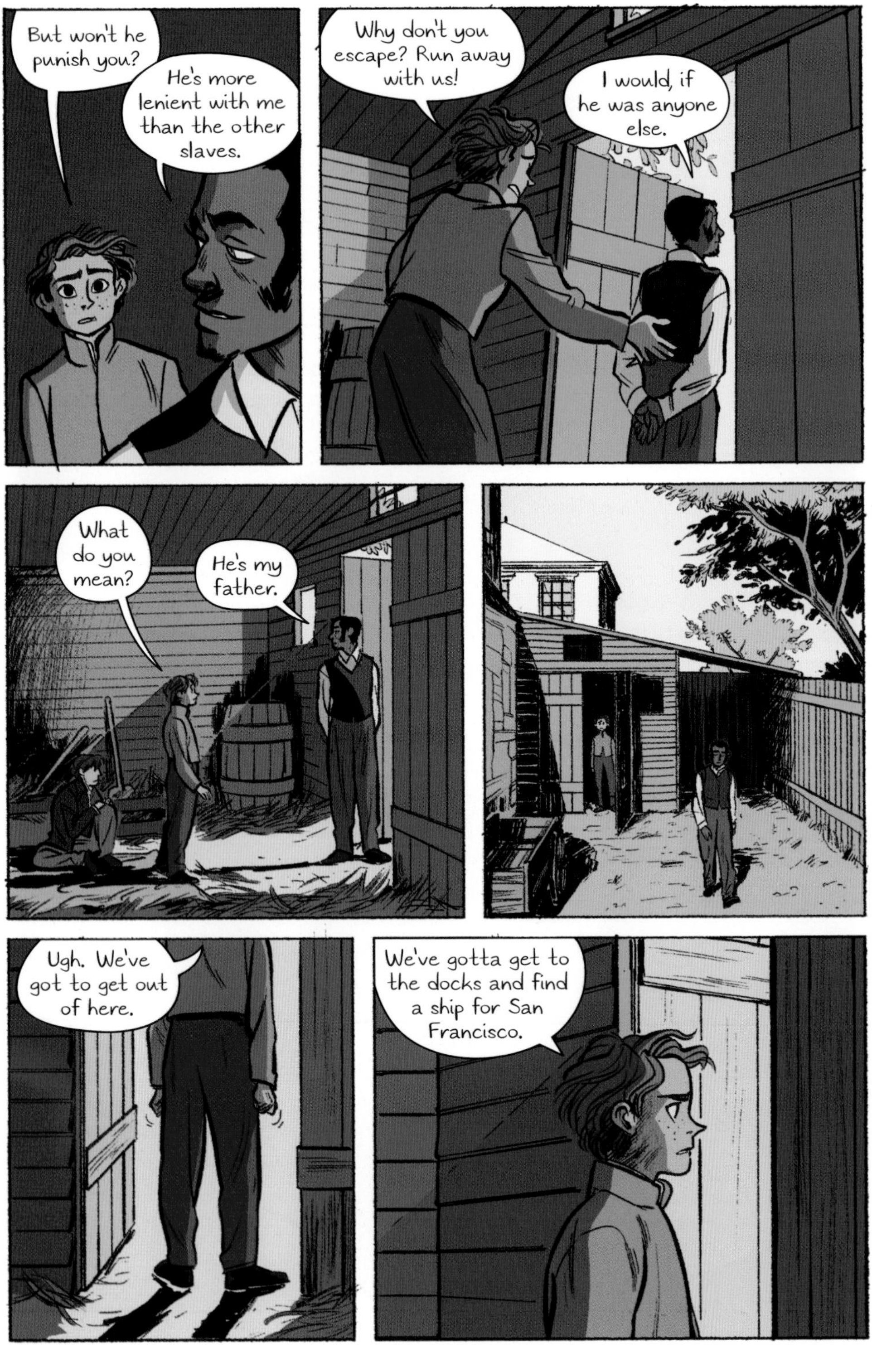
But won't he punish you?
He's more lenient with me than the other slaves.
Why don't you escape? Run away with us!
I would, if he was anyone else.
What do you mean?
He's my father.
Ugh. We've got to get out of here.
We've gotta get to the docks and find a ship for San Francisco.

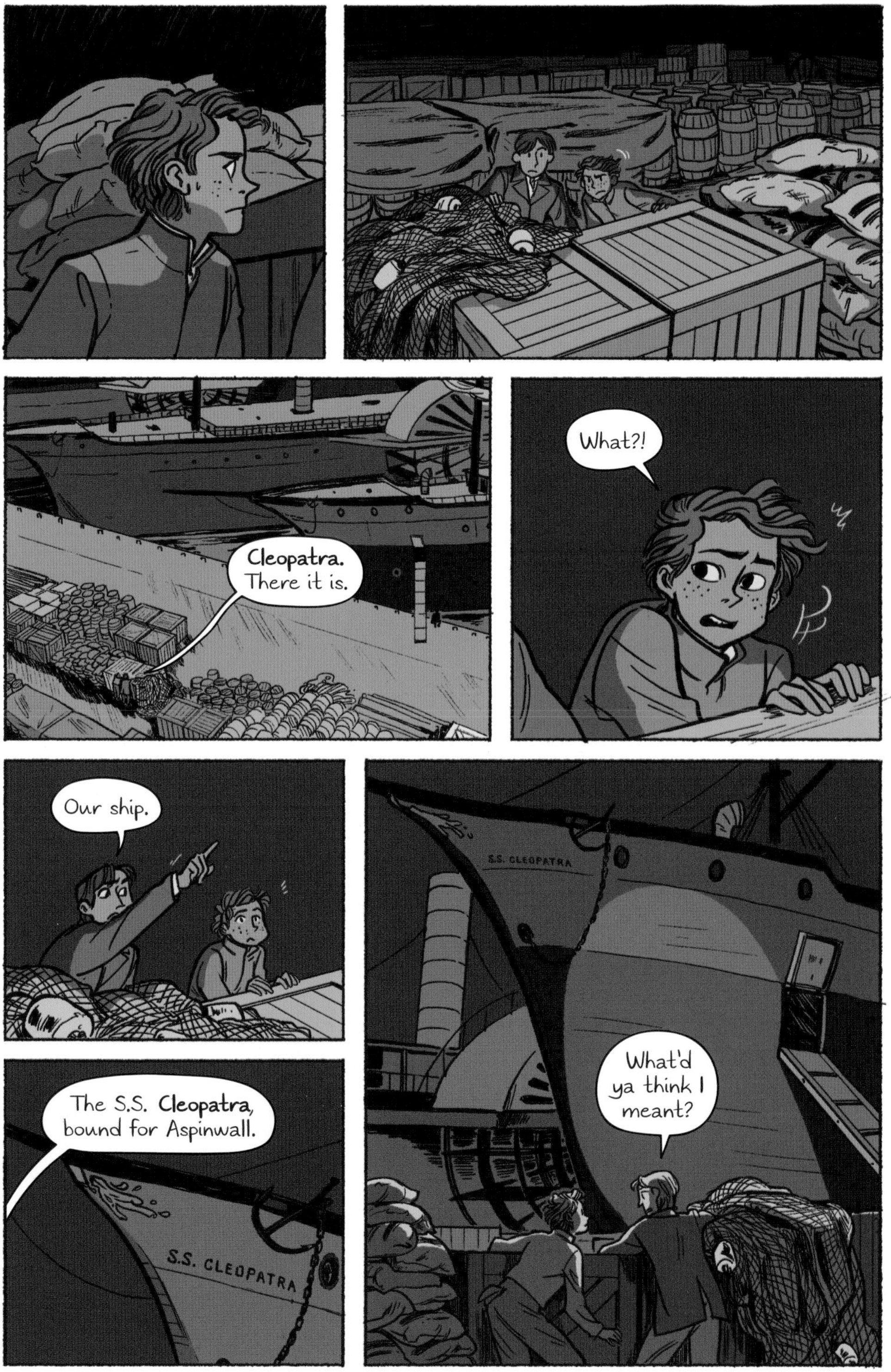
Cleopatra. There it is.
What?!
Our ship.
The S.S. Cleopatra, bound for Aspinwall.
What'd ya think I meant?
S.S. CLEOPATRA

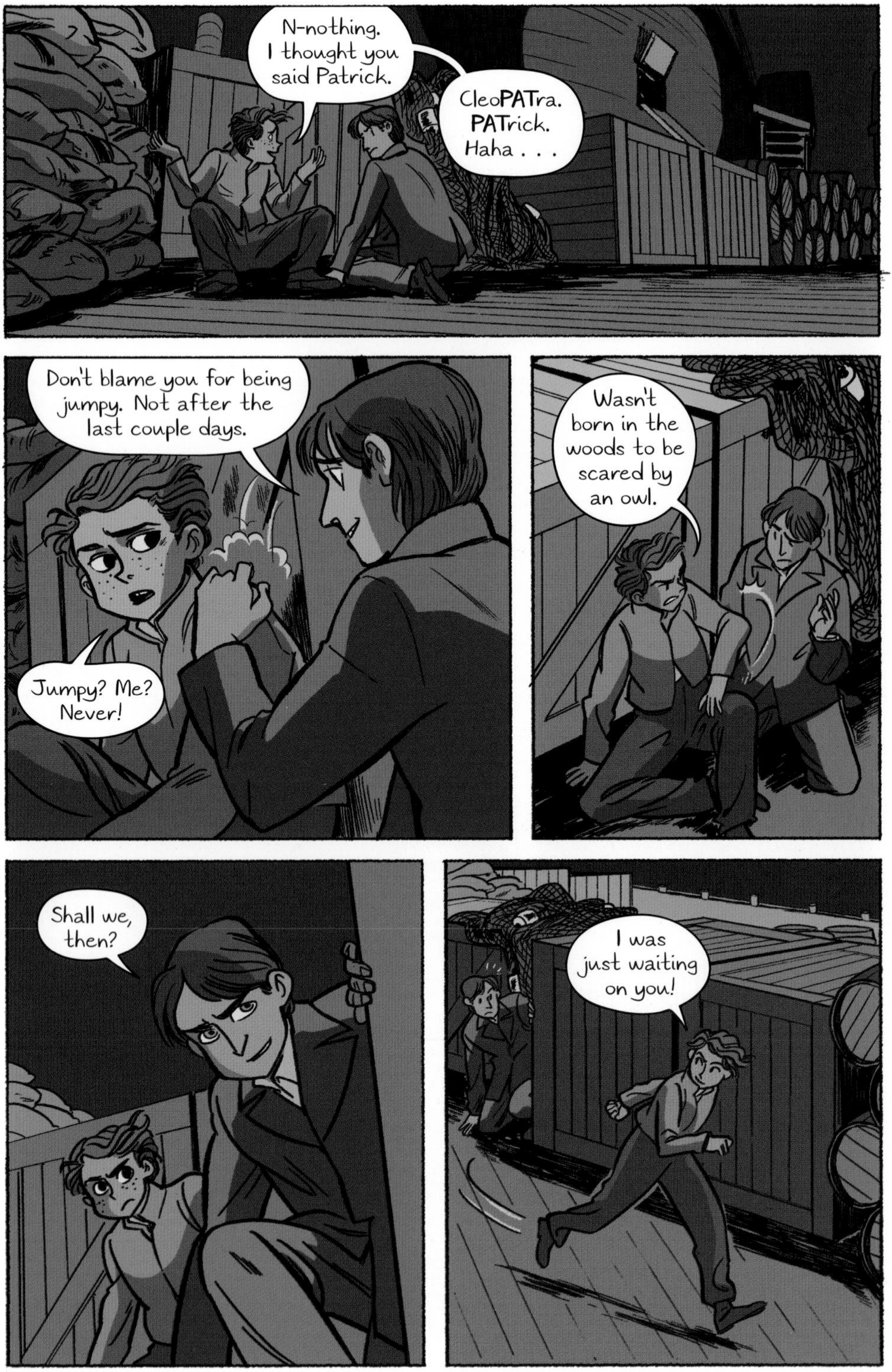
N-nothing. I thought you said Patrick.
CleoPATra. PATrick. Haha . . .
Don't blame you for being jumpy. Not after the last couple days.
Jumpy? Me? Never!
Wasn't born in the woods to be scared by an owl.
Shall we, then?
I was just waiting on you!

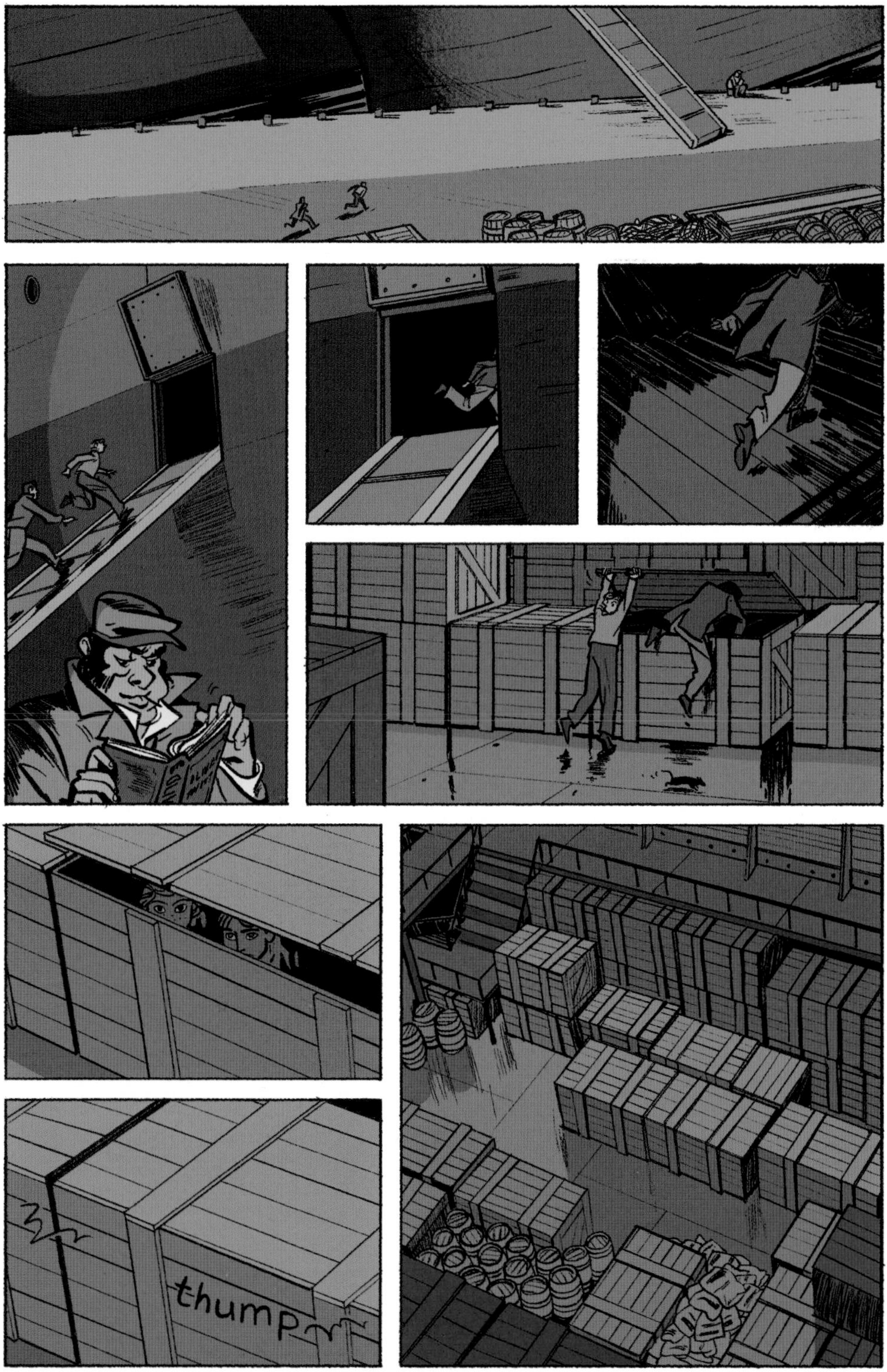
thump

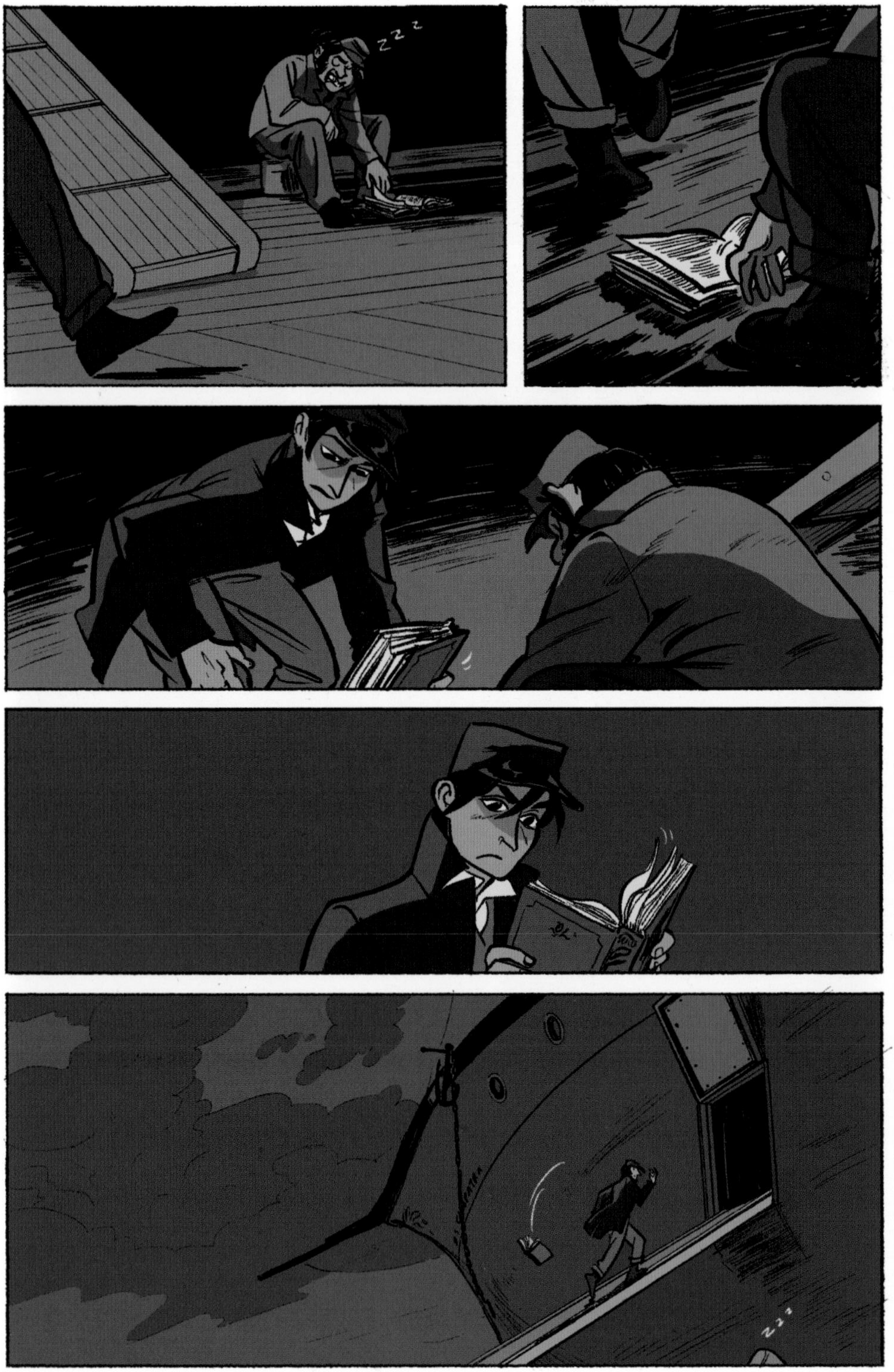
Z Z Z

# CHAPTER THREE
# **TO SEA**

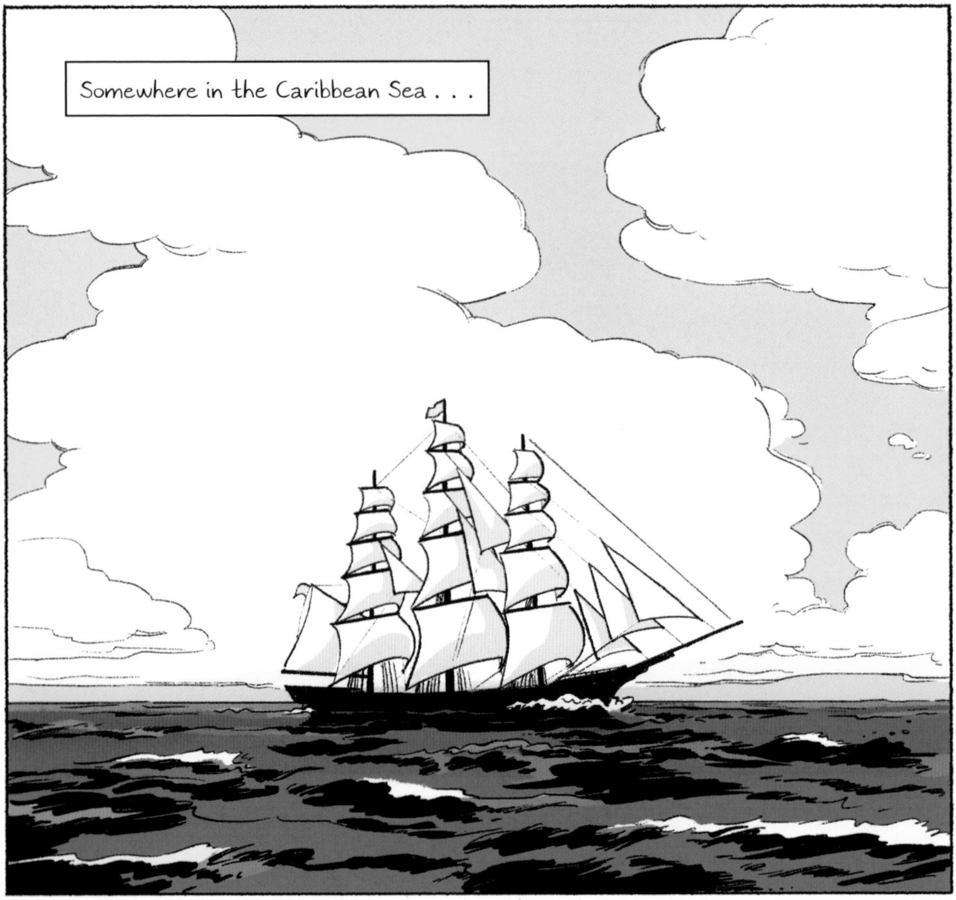
Somewhere in the Caribbean Sea . . .

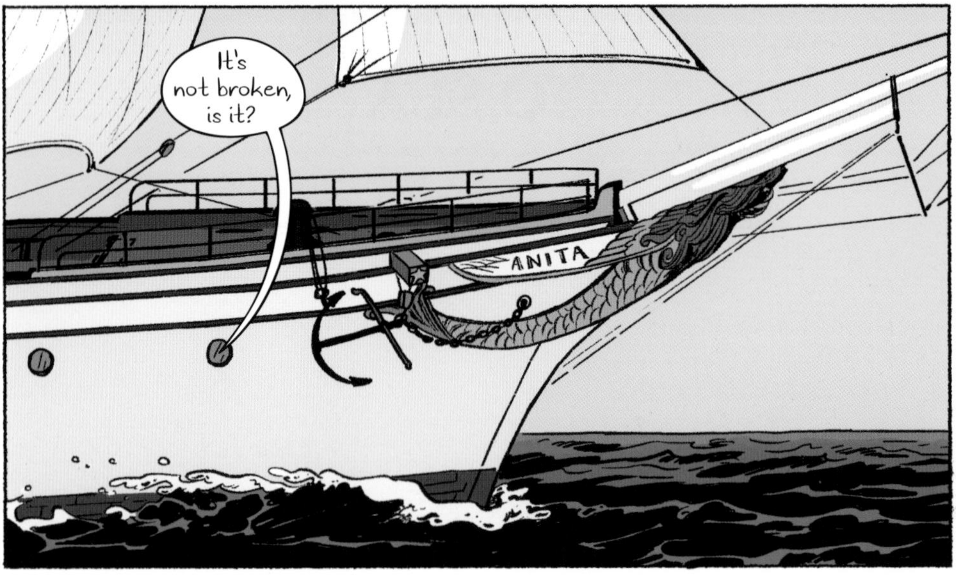
It's not broken, is it?
ANITA

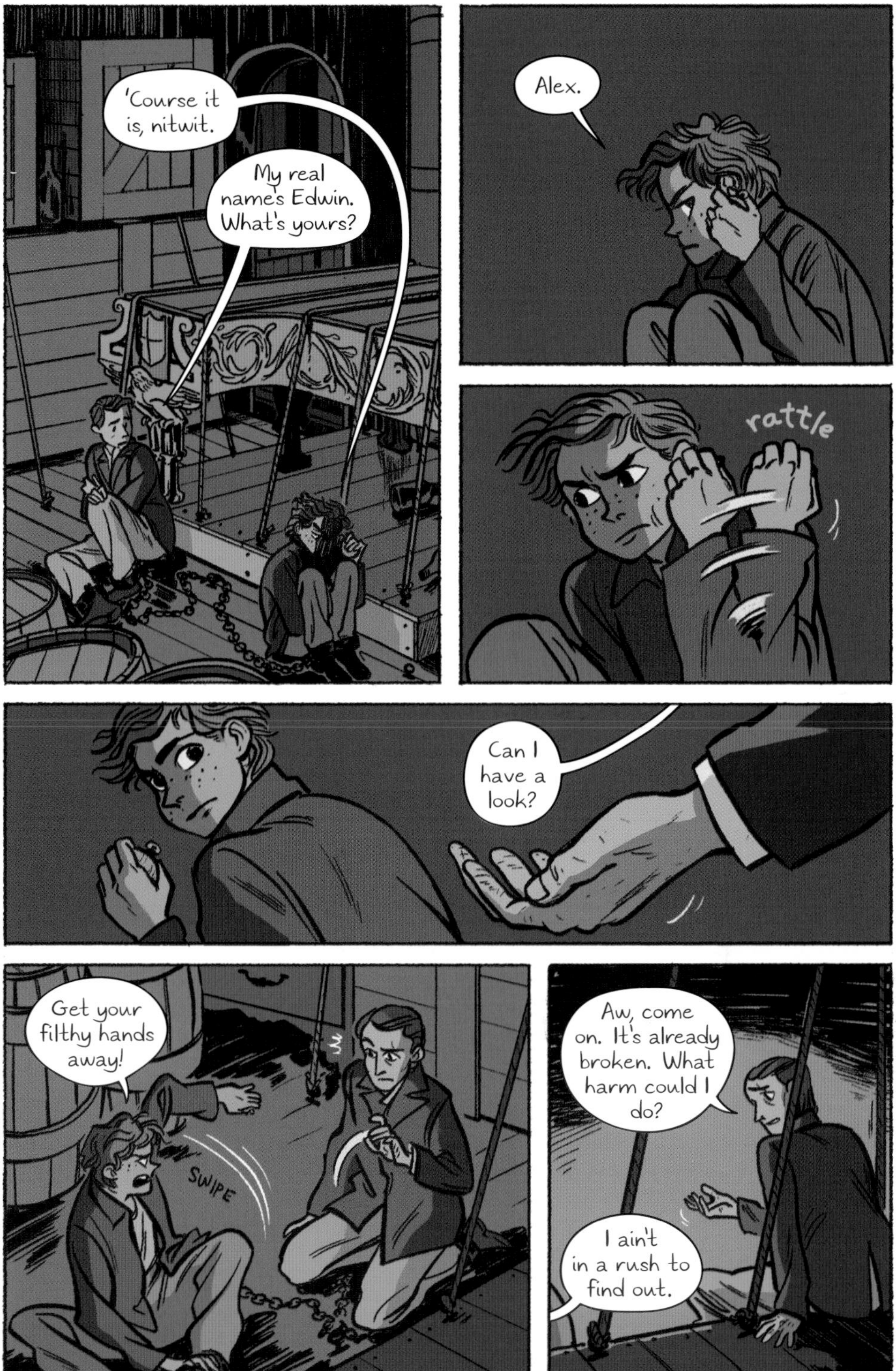
'Course it is, nitwit.
My real name's Edwin. What's yours?
Alex.
rattle
Can I have a look?
Get your filthy hands away!
SWIPE
Aw, come on. It's already broken. What harm could I do?
I ain't in a rush to find out.

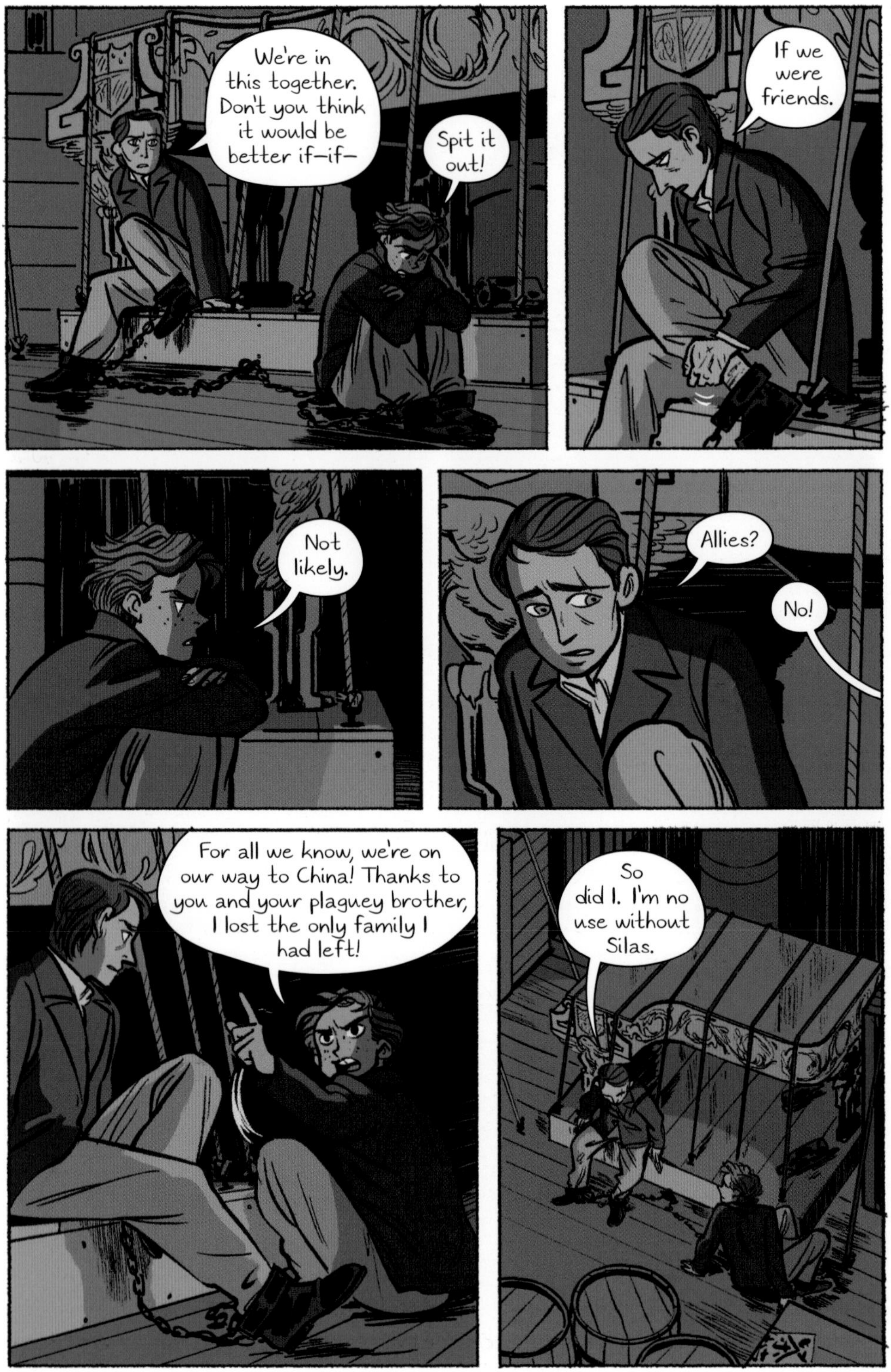
We're in this together. Don't you think it would be better if—if—
Spit it out!
If we were friends.
Not likely.
Allies?
No!
For all we know, we're on our way to China! Thanks to you and your plaguey brother, I lost the only family I had left!
So did I. I'm no use without Silas.

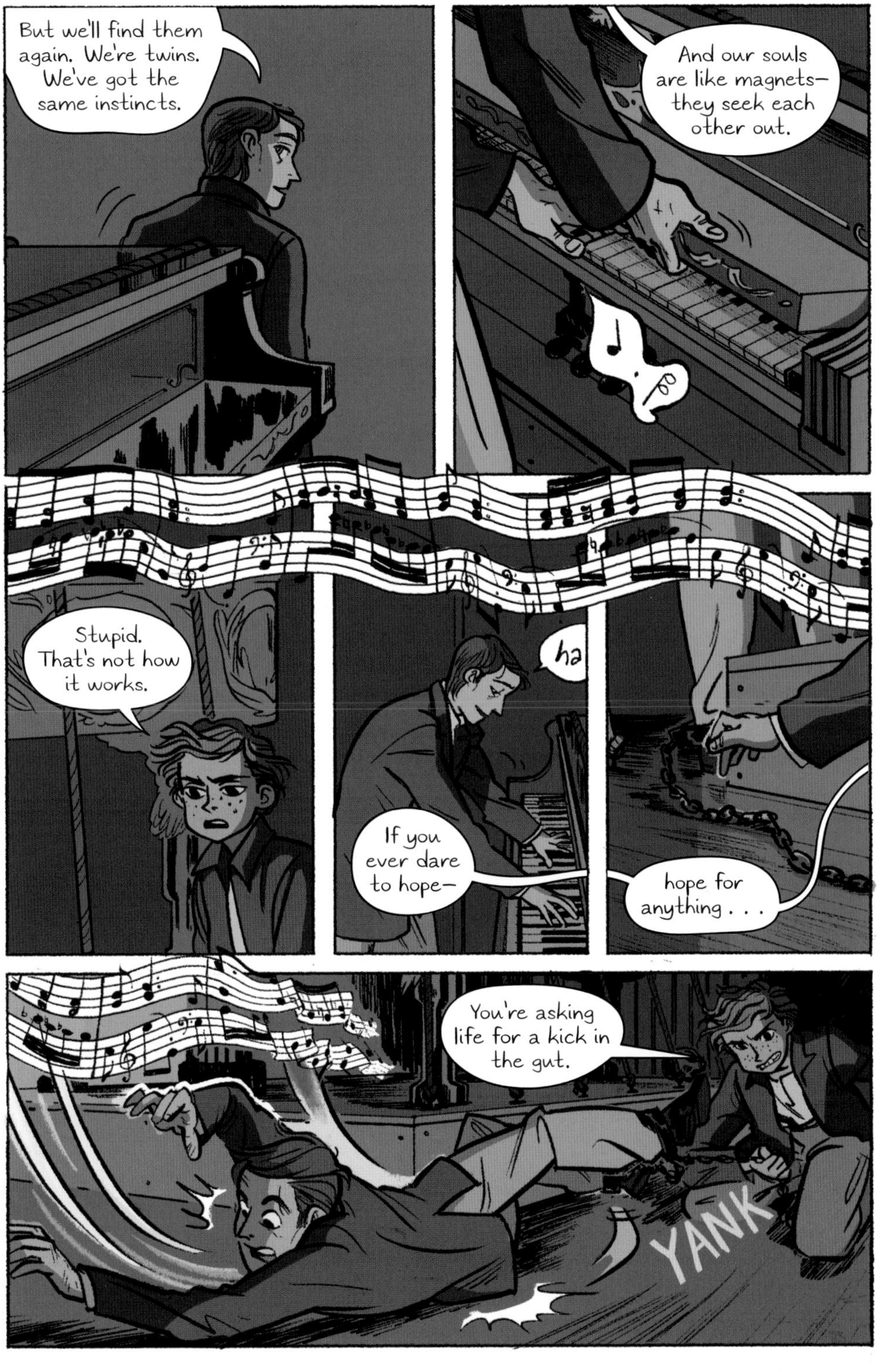
But we'll find them again. We're twins. We've got the same instincts.
And our souls are like magnets— they seek each other out.
Stupid. That's not how it works.
ha
If you ever dare to hope—
hope for anything . . .
You're asking life for a kick in the gut.
YANK

*SOUVENIR DE PORTO RICO BY GOTTSCHALK

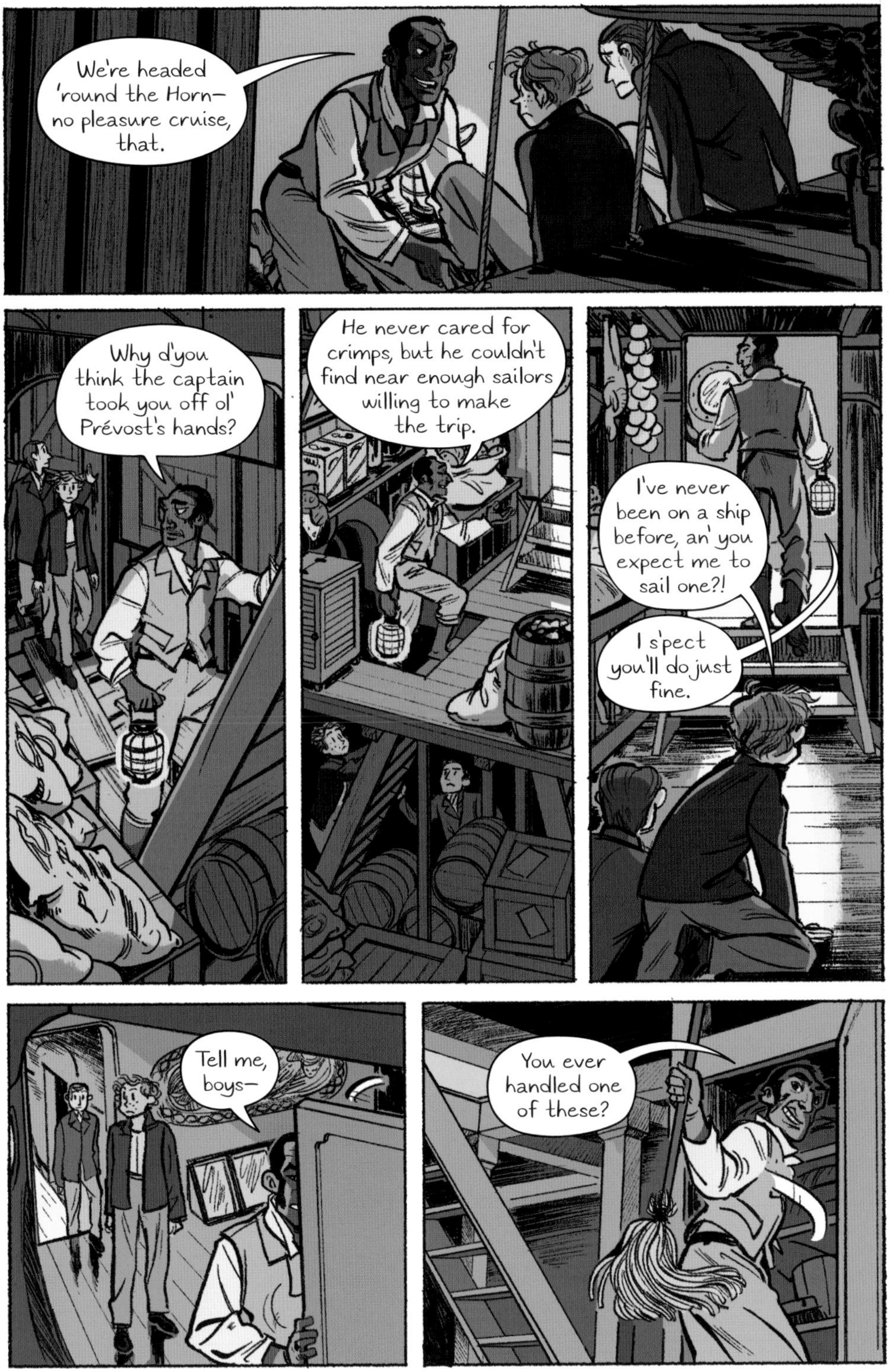
We're headed 'round the Horn— no pleasure cruise, that.
Why d'you think the captain took you off ol' Prévost's hands?
He never cared for crimps, but he couldn't find near enough sailors willing to make the trip.
I've never been on a ship before, an' you expect me to sail one?!
I s'pect you'll do just fine.
Tell me, boys—
You ever handled one of these?

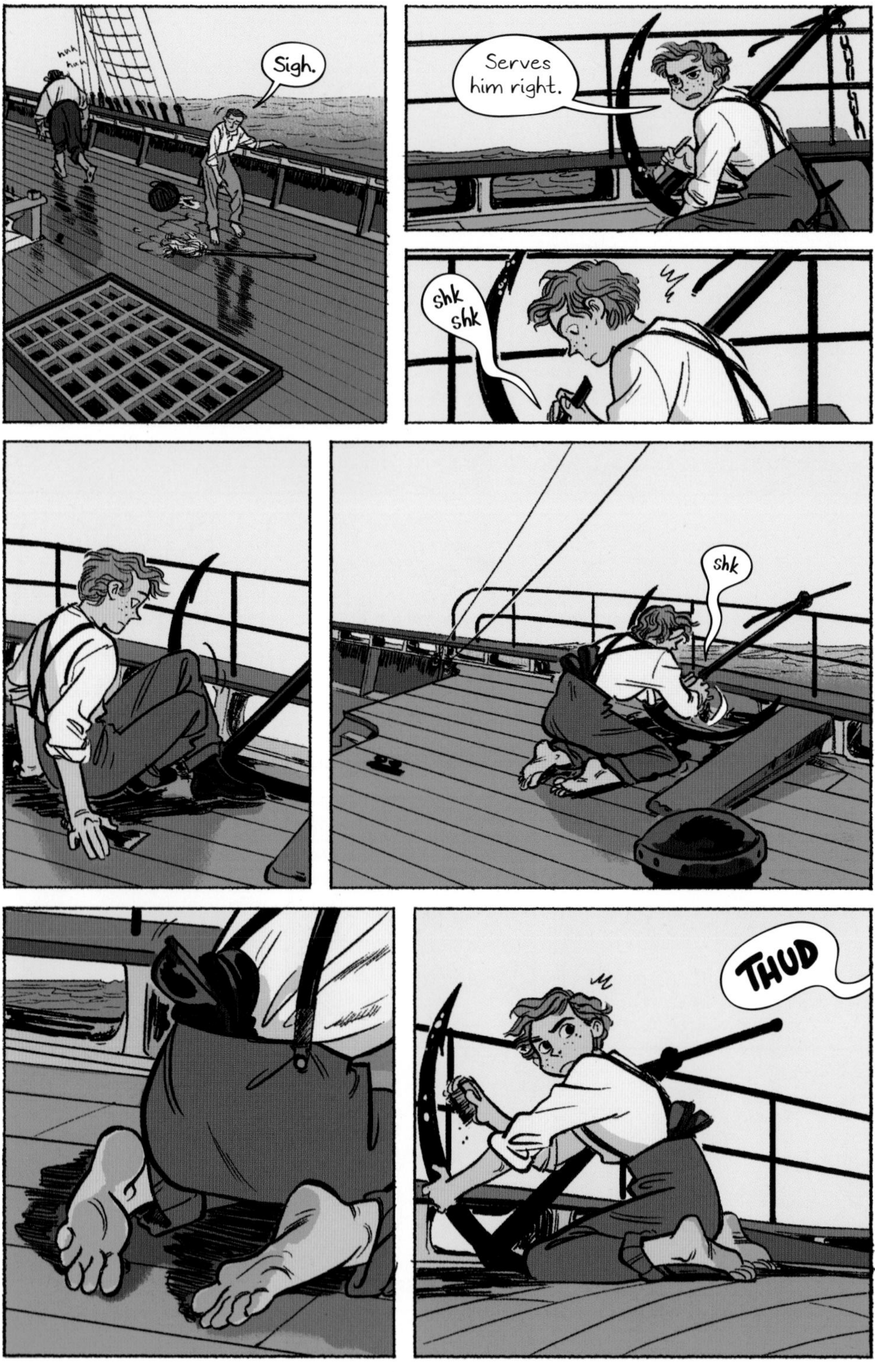
Sigh.
Serves him right.
shk shk
shk
THUD

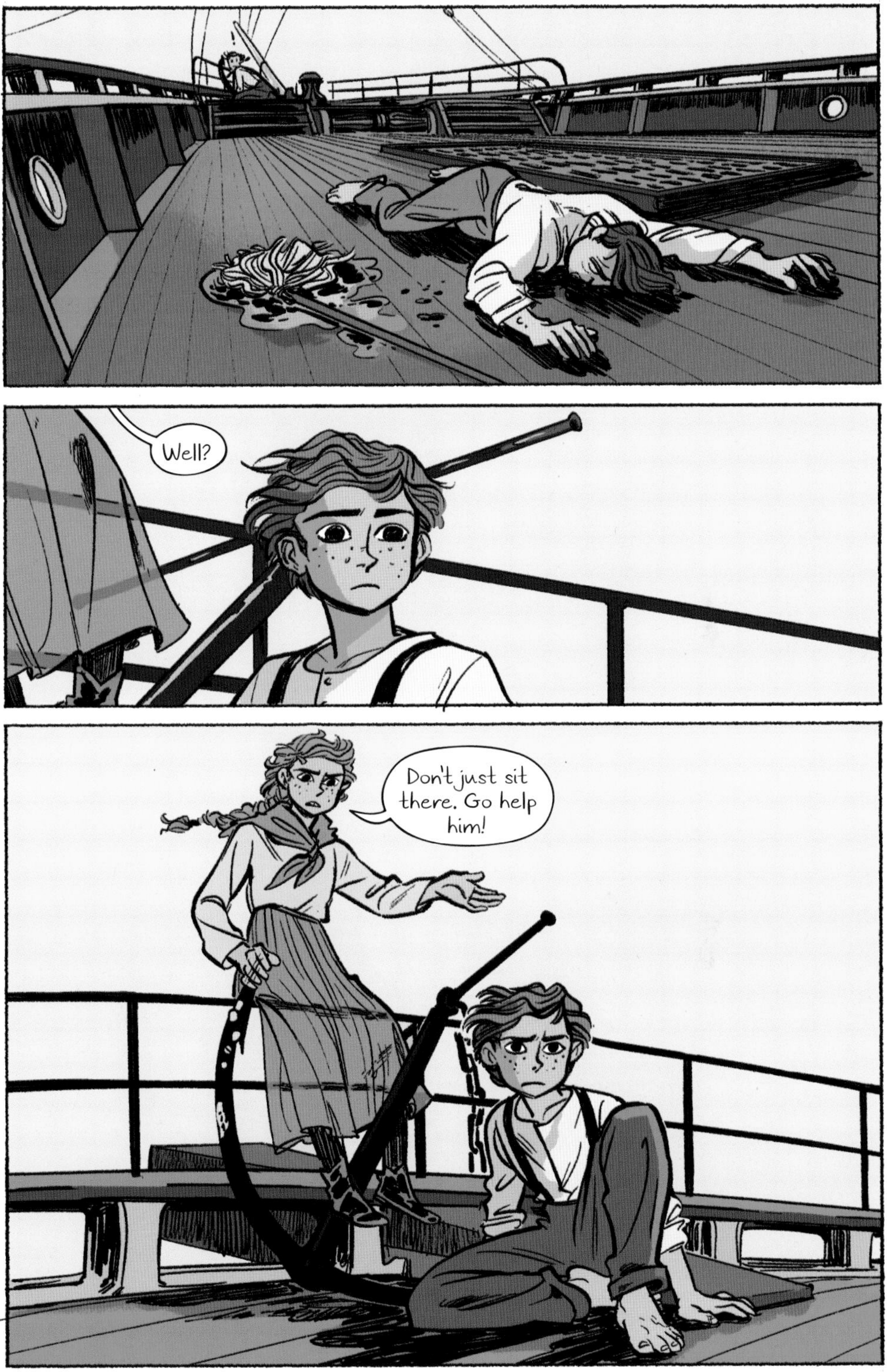
Well?
Don't just sit there. Go help him!

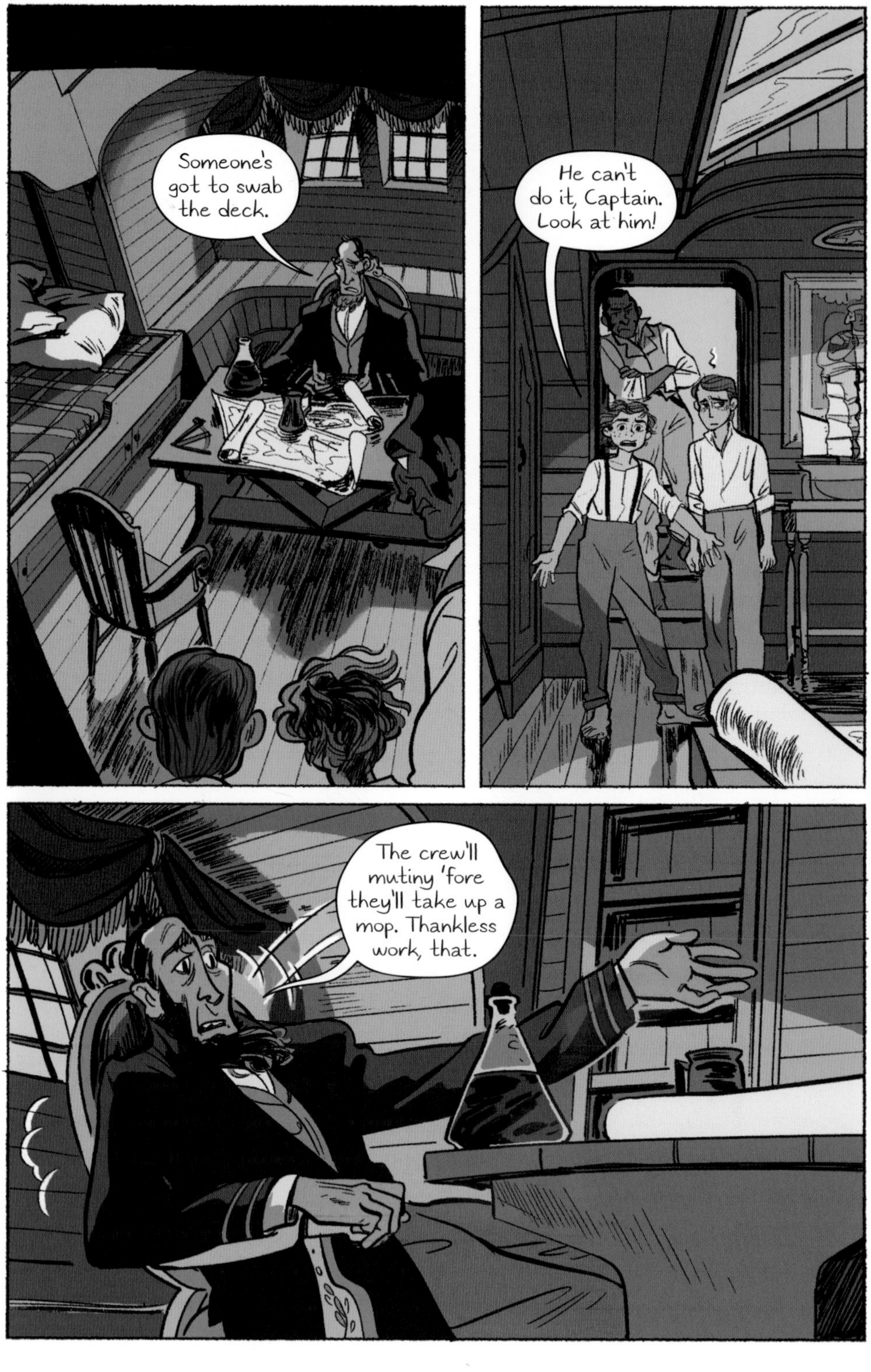
Someone's got to swab the deck.
He can't do it, Captain. Look at him!
The crew'll mutiny 'fore they'll take up a mop. Thankless work, that.

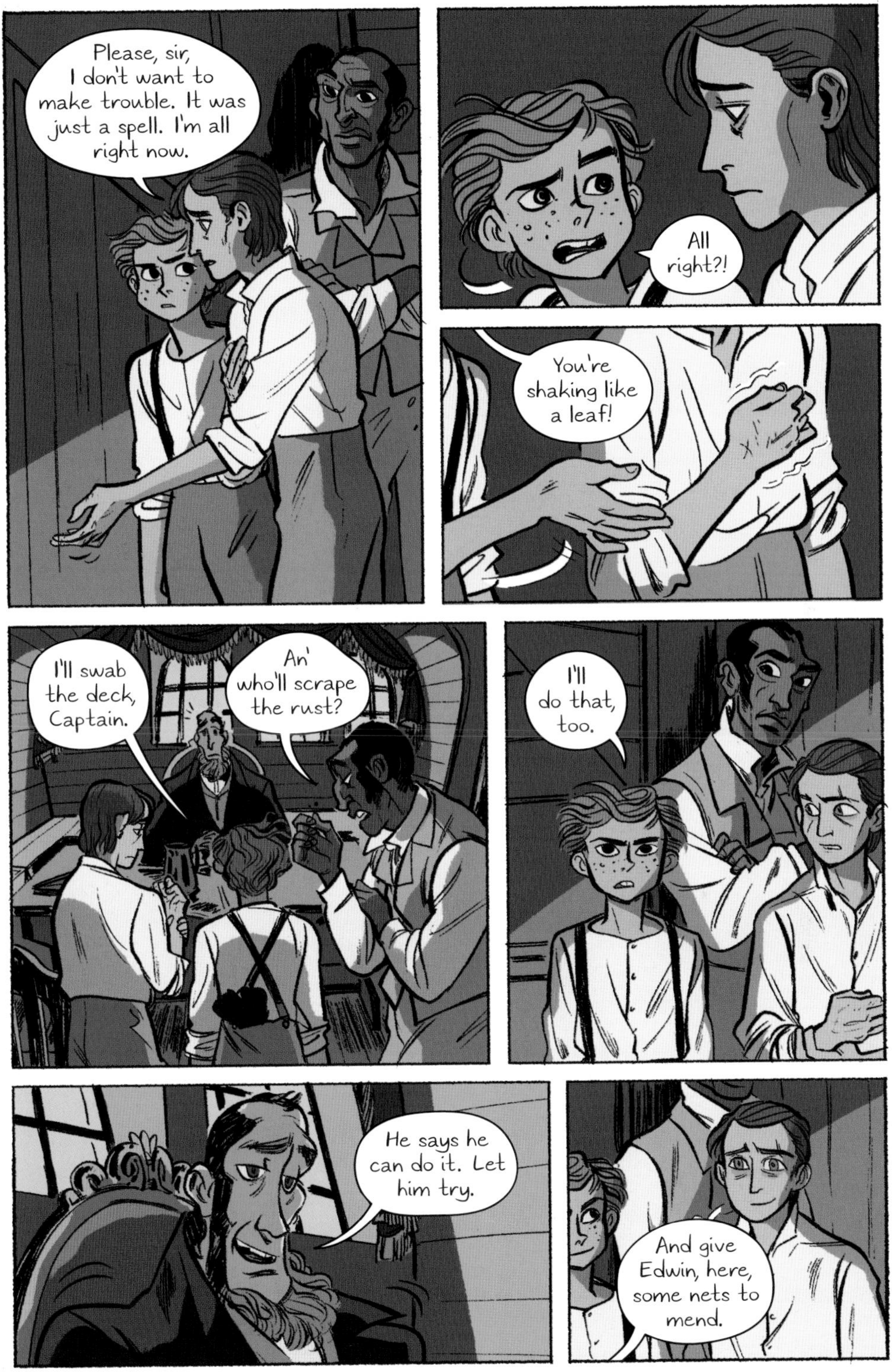
Please, sir, I don't want to make trouble. It was just a spell. I'm all right now.
All right?!
You're shaking like a leaf!
I'll swab the deck, Captain.
An' who'll scrape the rust?
I'll do that, too.
He says he can do it. Let him try.
And give Edwin, here, some nets to mend.

CHAPTER FOUR

# THE BREAKER
# AND THE BOILER

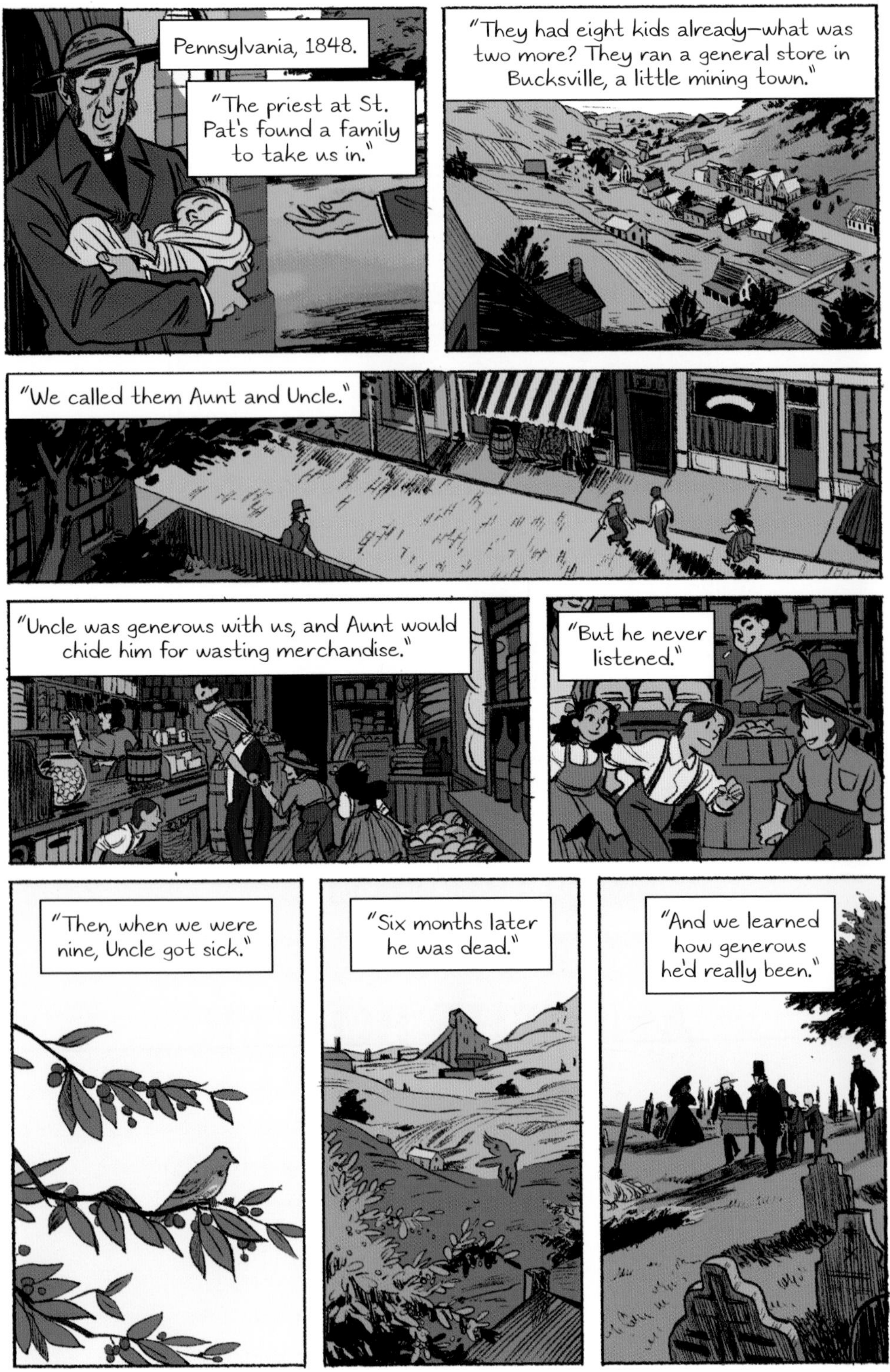
Pennsylvania, 1848.
"The priest at St. Pat's found a family to take us in."
"They had eight kids already—what was two more? They ran a general store in Bucksville, a little mining town."
"We called them Aunt and Uncle."
"Uncle was generous with us, and Aunt would chide him for wasting merchandise."
"But he never listened."
"Then, when we were nine, Uncle got sick."
"Six months later he was dead."
"And we learned how generous he'd really been."

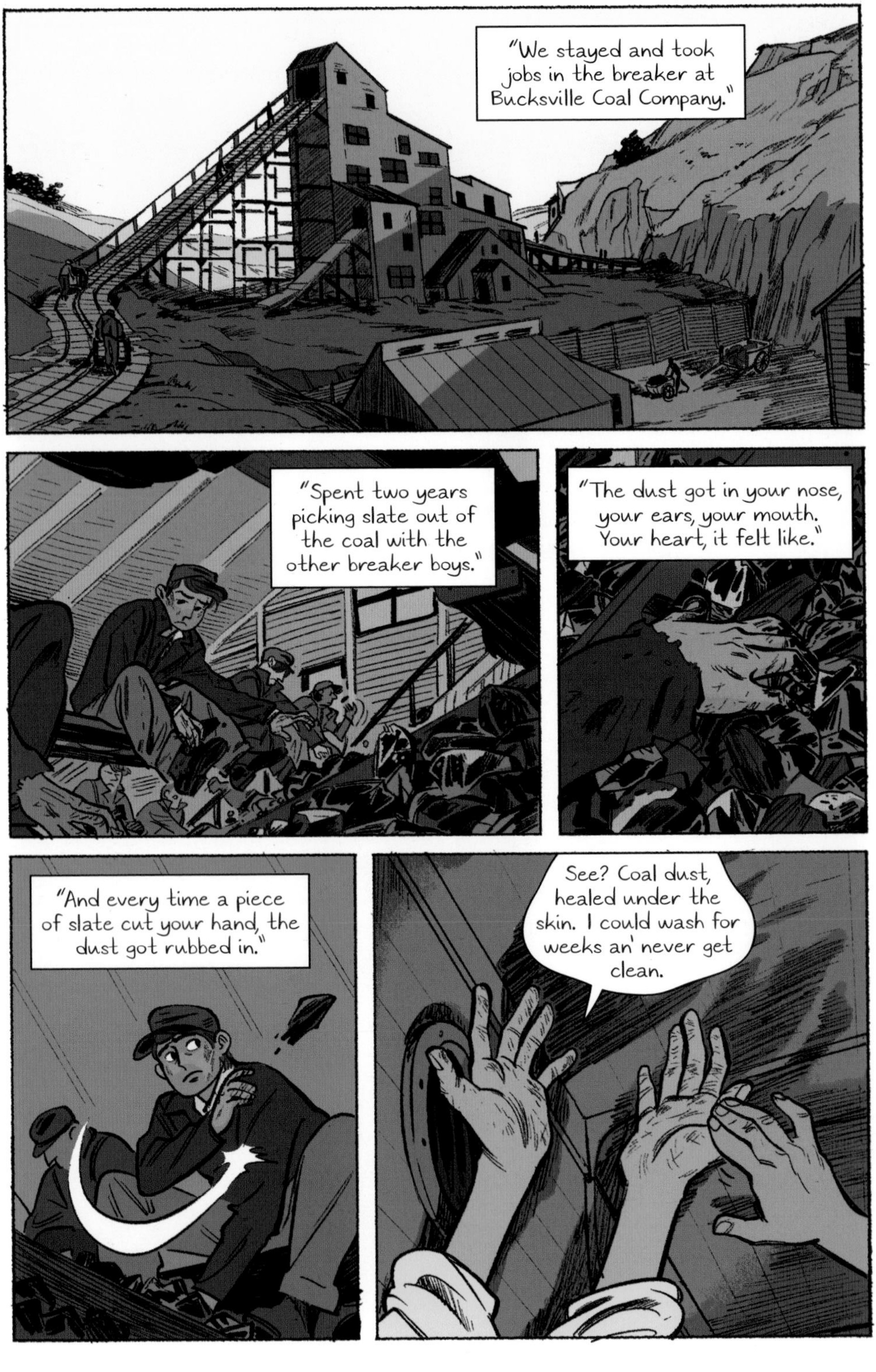
"We stayed and took jobs in the breaker at Bucksville Coal Company."
"Spent two years picking slate out of the coal with the other breaker boys."
"The dust got in your nose, your ears, your mouth. Your heart, it felt like."
"And every time a piece of slate cut your hand, the dust got rubbed in."
See? Coal dust, healed under the skin. I could wash for weeks an' never get clean.

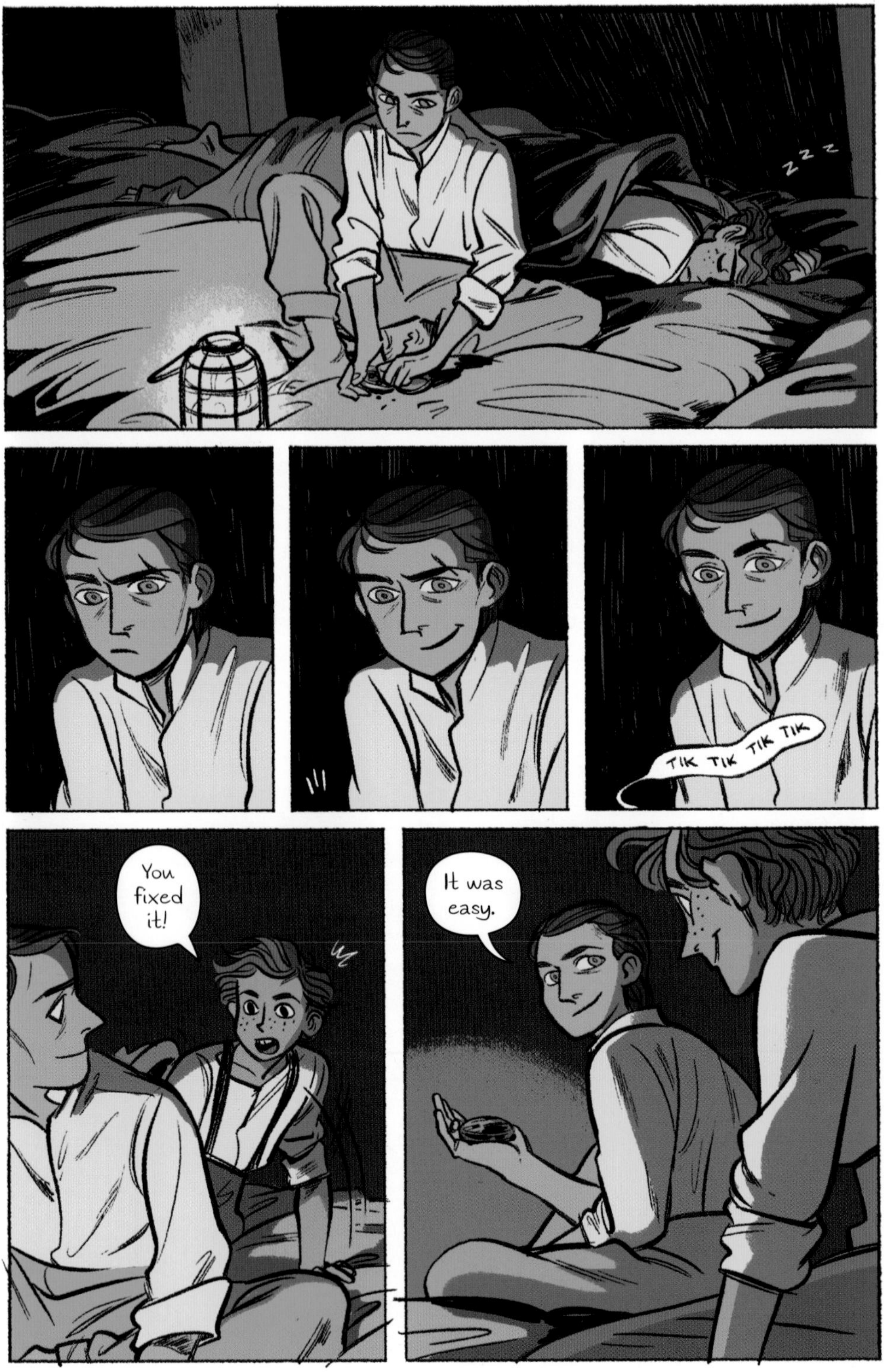
Z Z Z
TIK TIK TIK TIK
You fixed it!
It was easy.

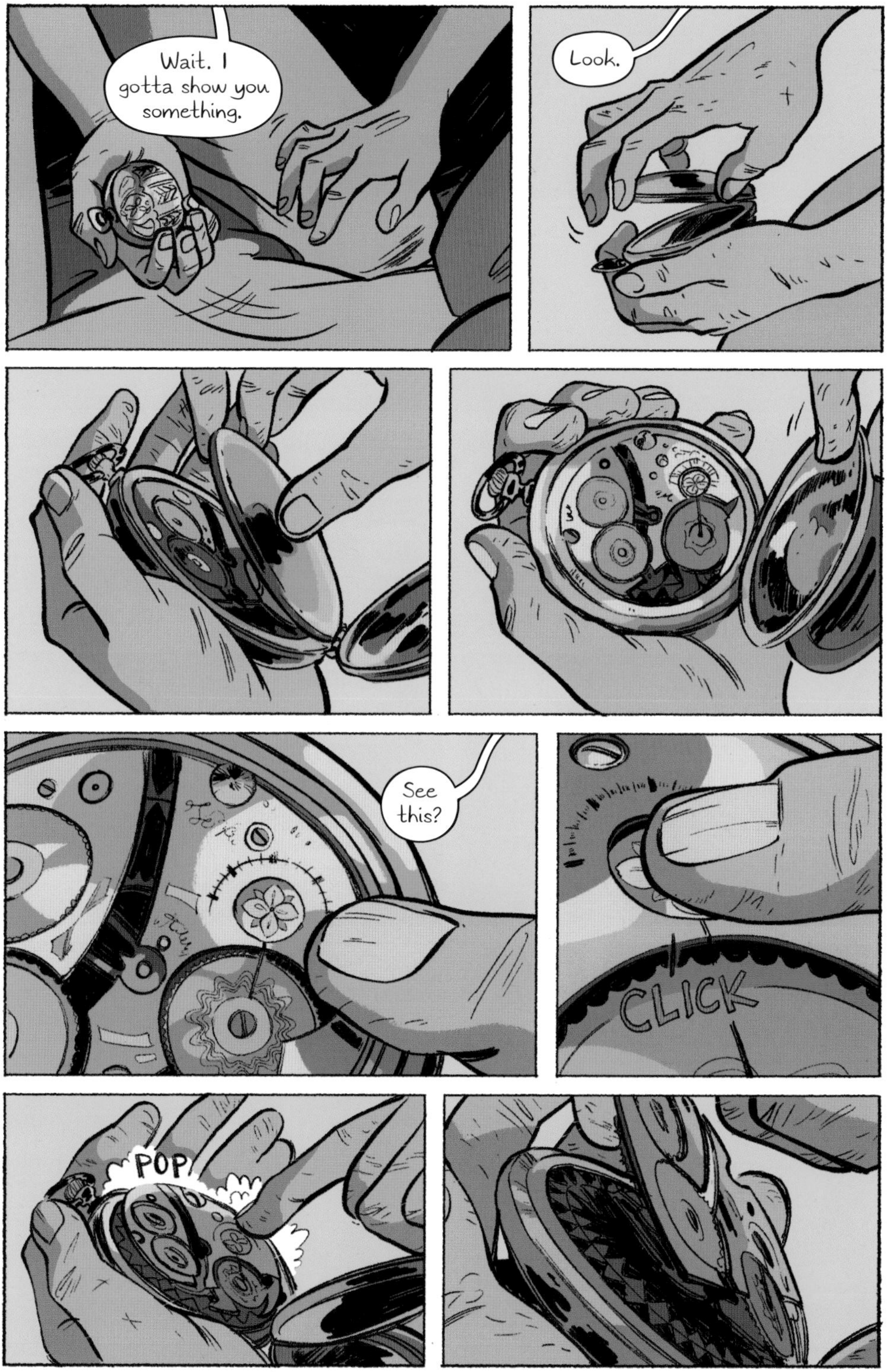
Wait. I gotta show you something.
Look.
See this?
CLICK
POP

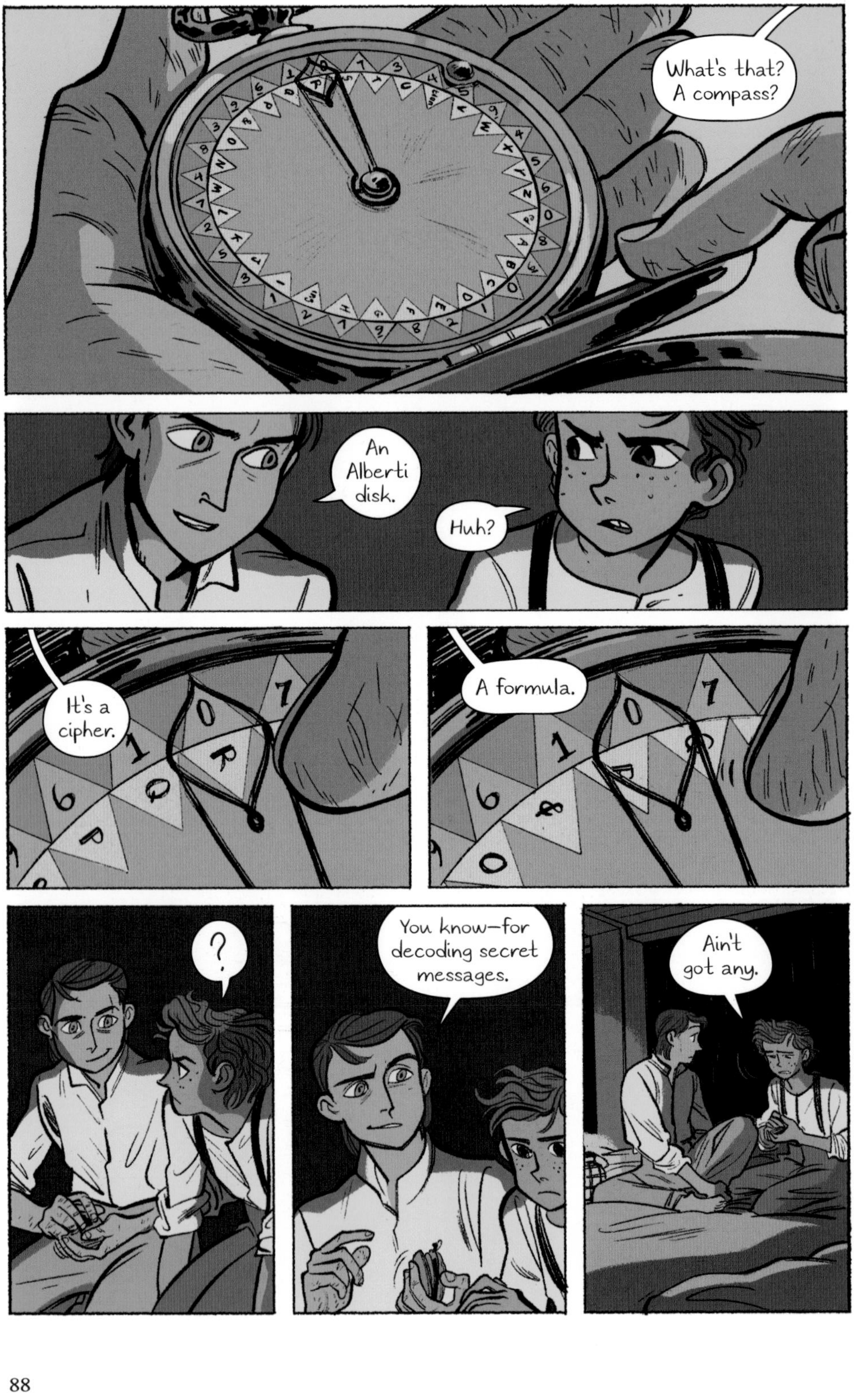
What's that? A compass?
An Alberti disk.
Huh?
It's a cipher.
A formula.
?
You know—for decoding secret messages.
Ain't got any.

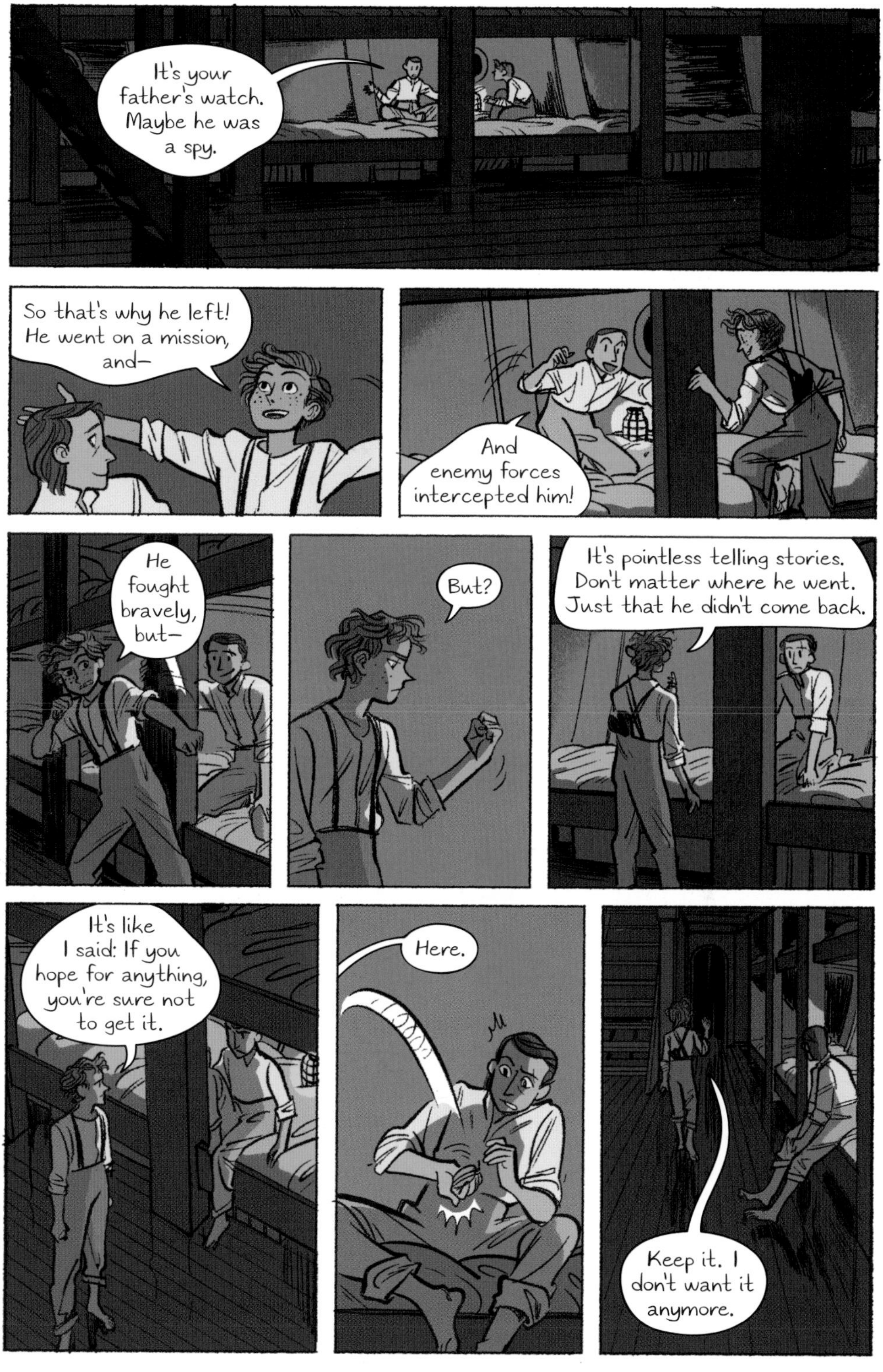
It's your father's watch. Maybe he was a spy.
So that's why he left! He went on a mission, and—
And enemy forces intercepted him!
He fought bravely, but—
But?
It's pointless telling stories. Don't matter where he went. Just that he didn't come back.
It's like I said: If you hope for anything, you're sure not to get it.
Here.
Keep it. I don't want it anymore.

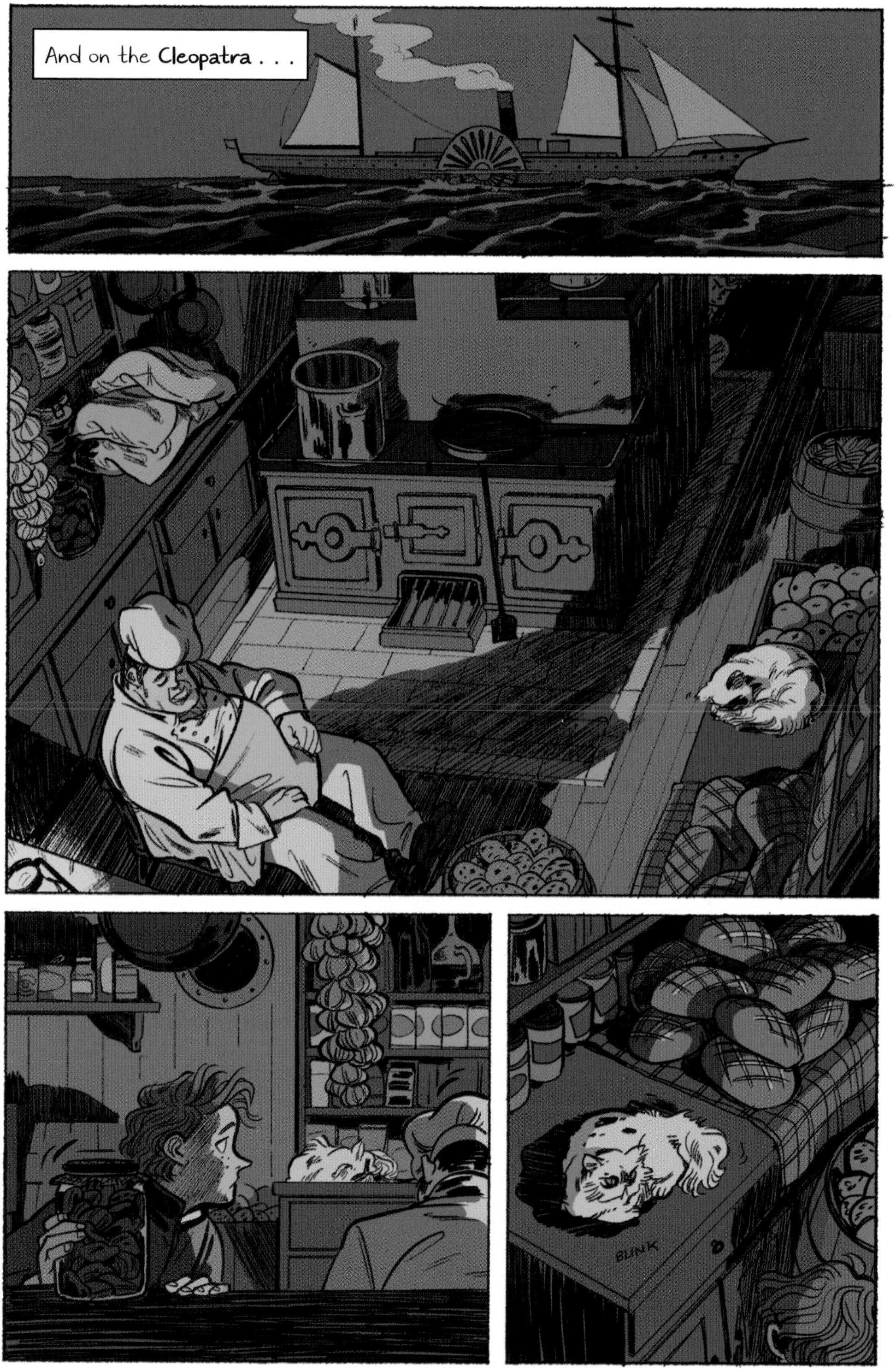
And on the **Cleopatra** . . .
BLINK

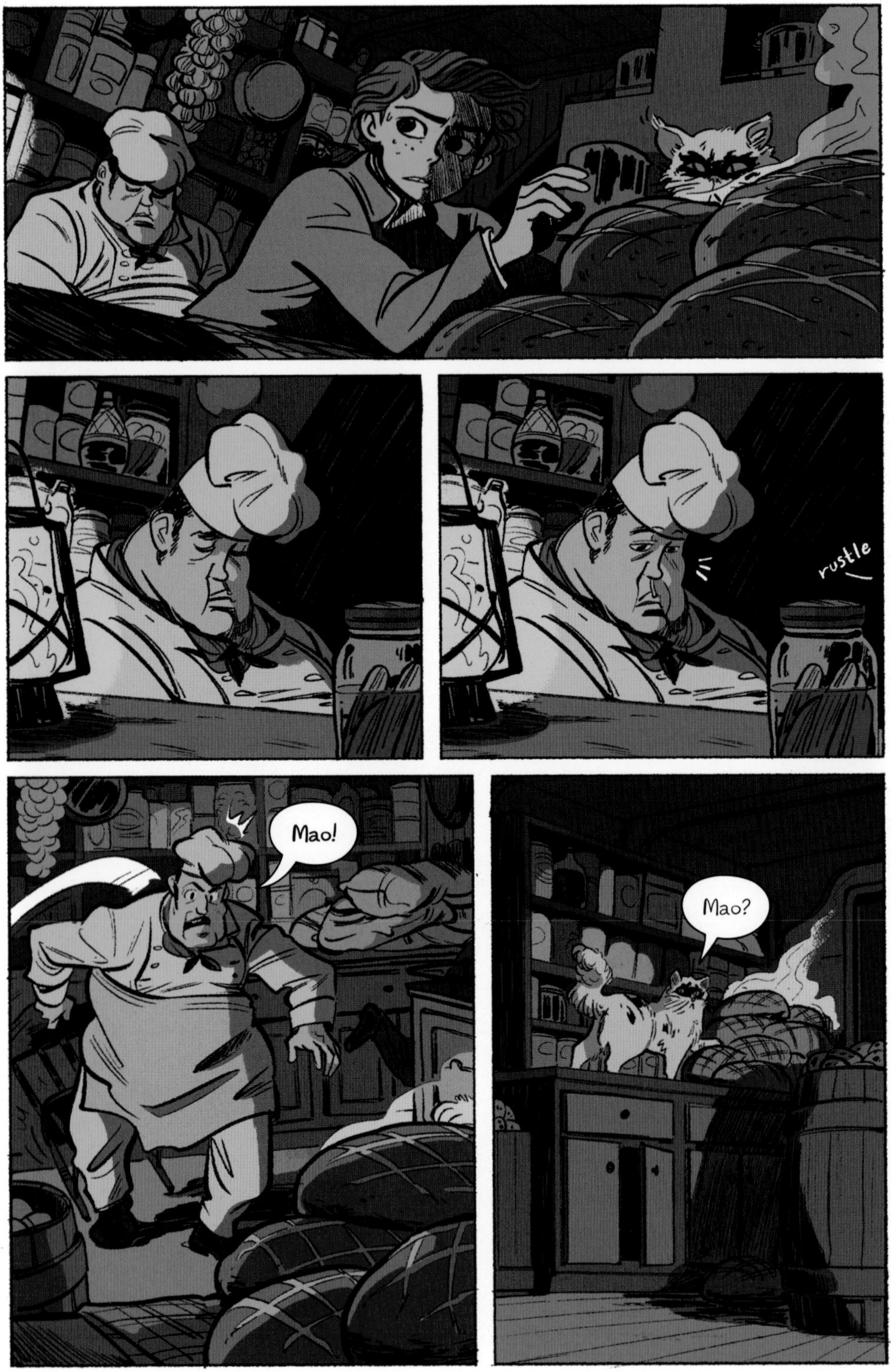
rustle
Mao!
Mao?

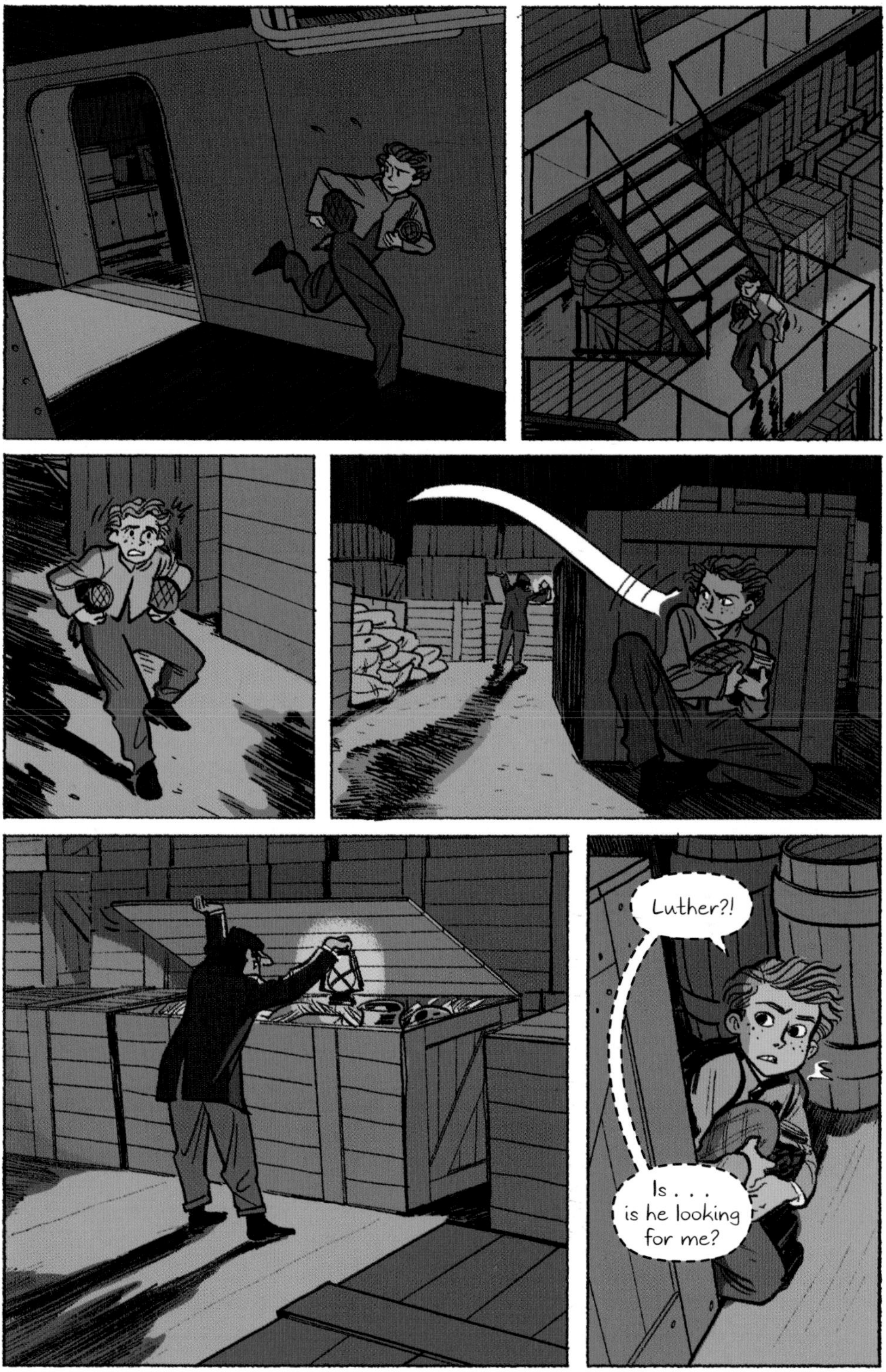
Luther?!
Is . . . is he looking for me?

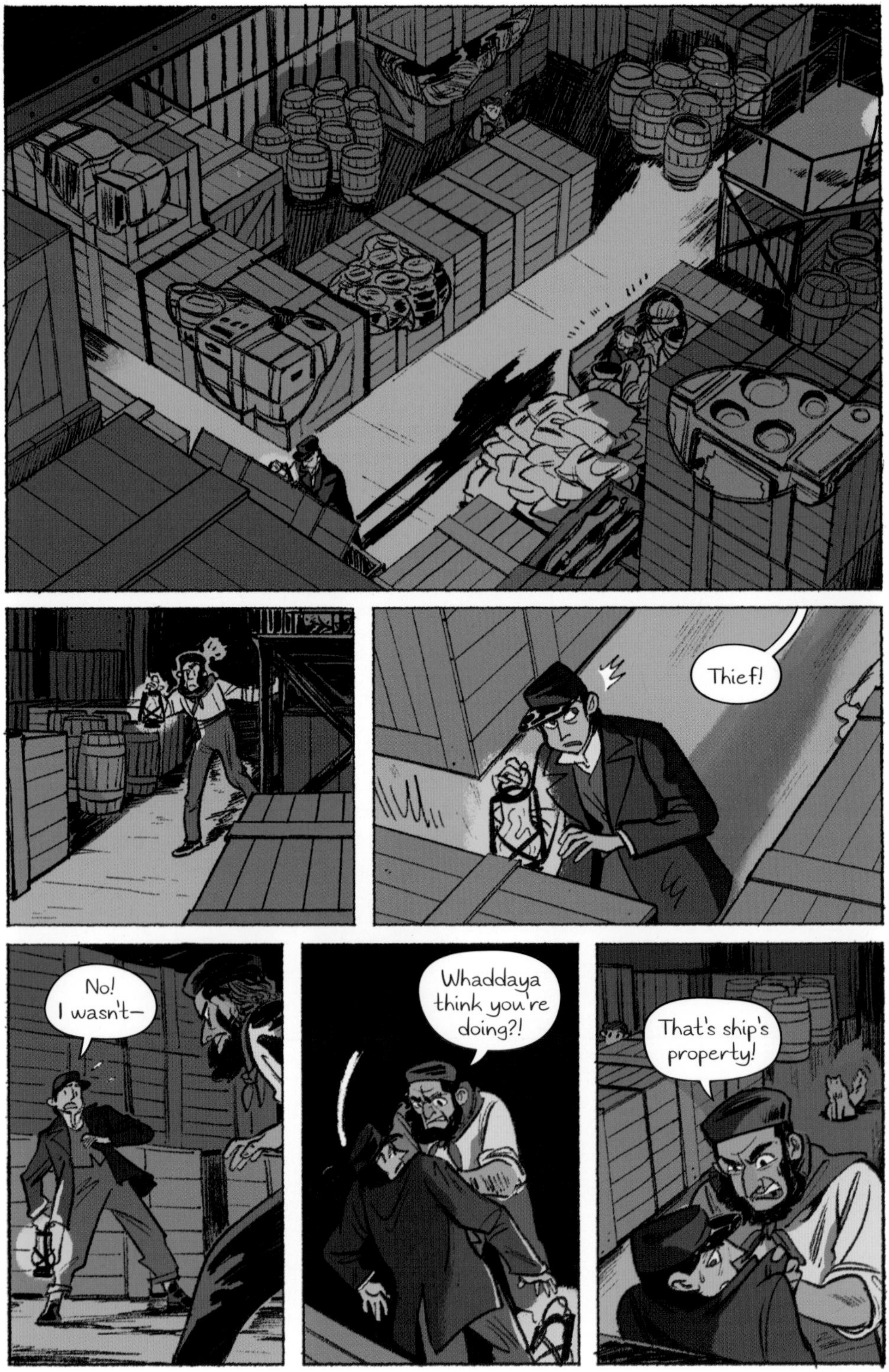
Thief!
No! I wasn't—
Whaddaya think you're doing?!
That's ship's property!

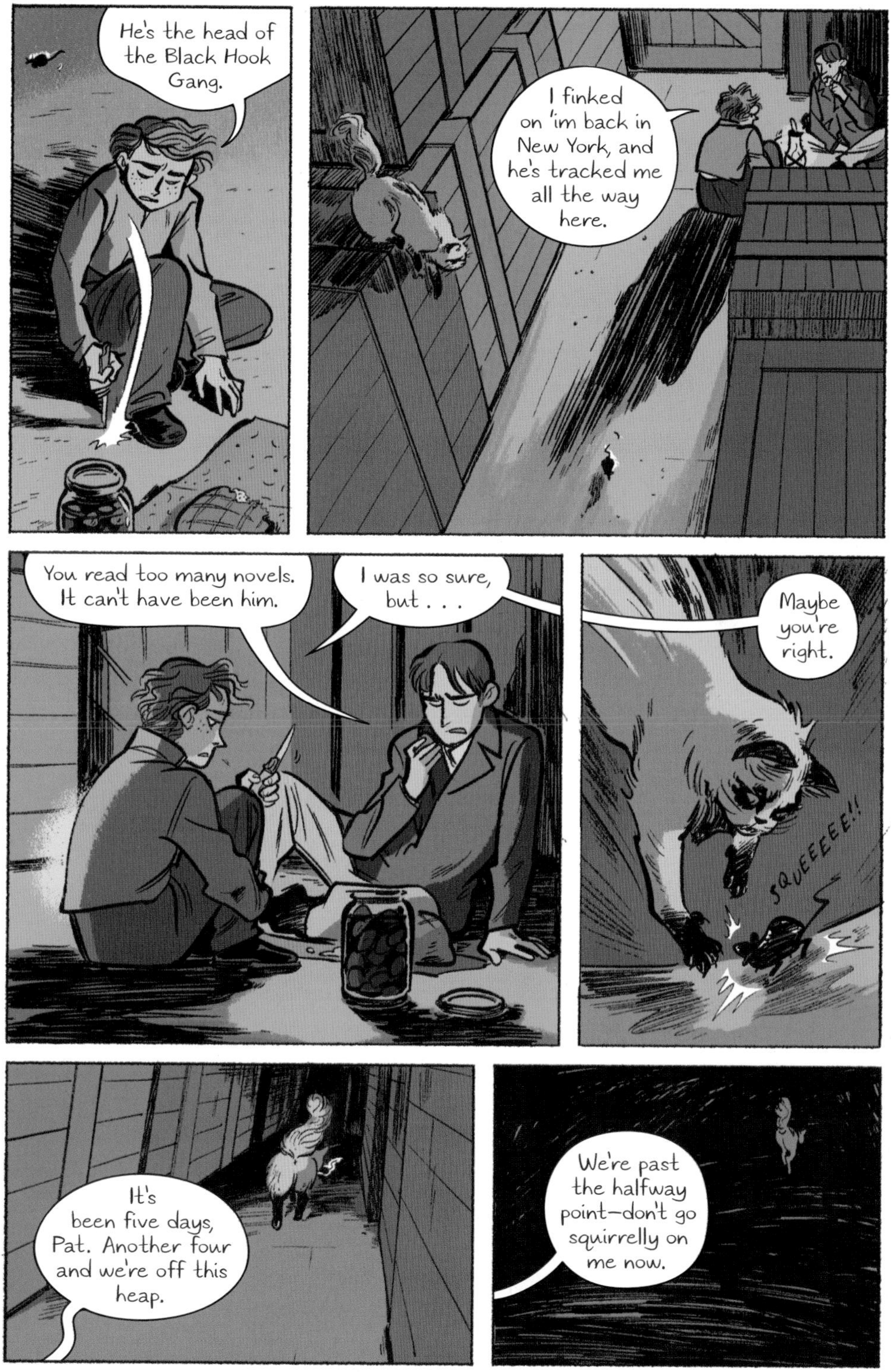
He's the head of the Black Hook Gang.
I finked on 'im back in New York, and he's tracked me all the way here.
You read too many novels. It can't have been him.
I was so sure, but . . .
Maybe you're right.
SQUEEEEE!!
It's been five days, Pat. Another four and we're off this heap.
We're past the halfway point—don't go squirrelly on me now.

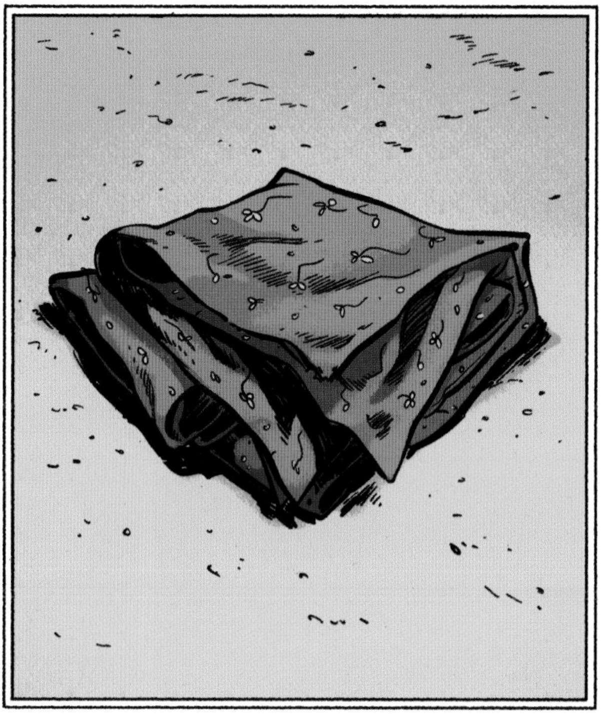

CHAPTER FIVE

# THE POCKETKNIFE

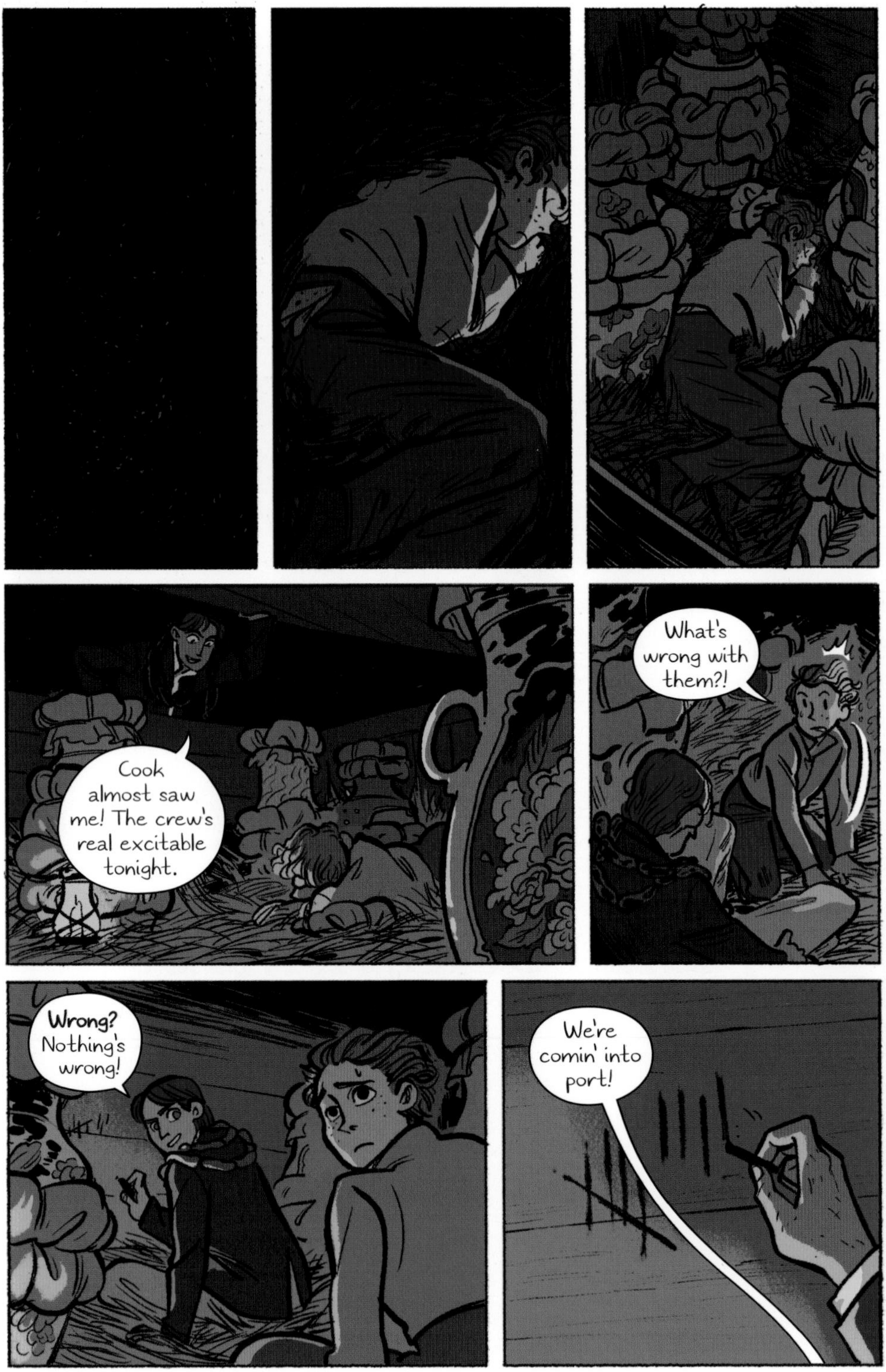
Cook almost saw me! The crew's real excitable tonight.
What's wrong with them?!
Wrong? Nothing's wrong!
We're comin' into port!

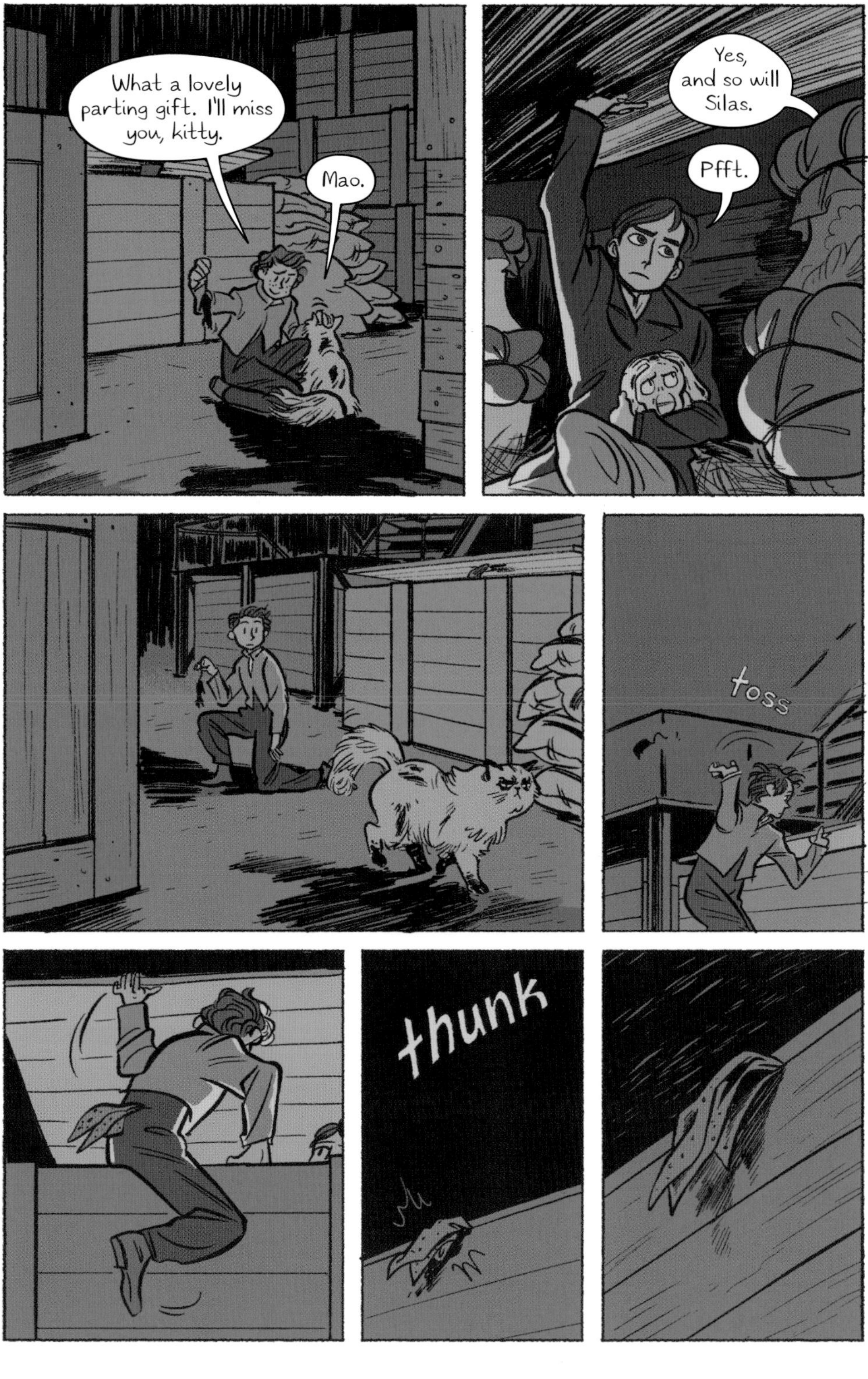
What a lovely parting gift. I'll miss you, kitty.
Mao.
Yes, and so will Silas.
Pfft.
toss
thunk

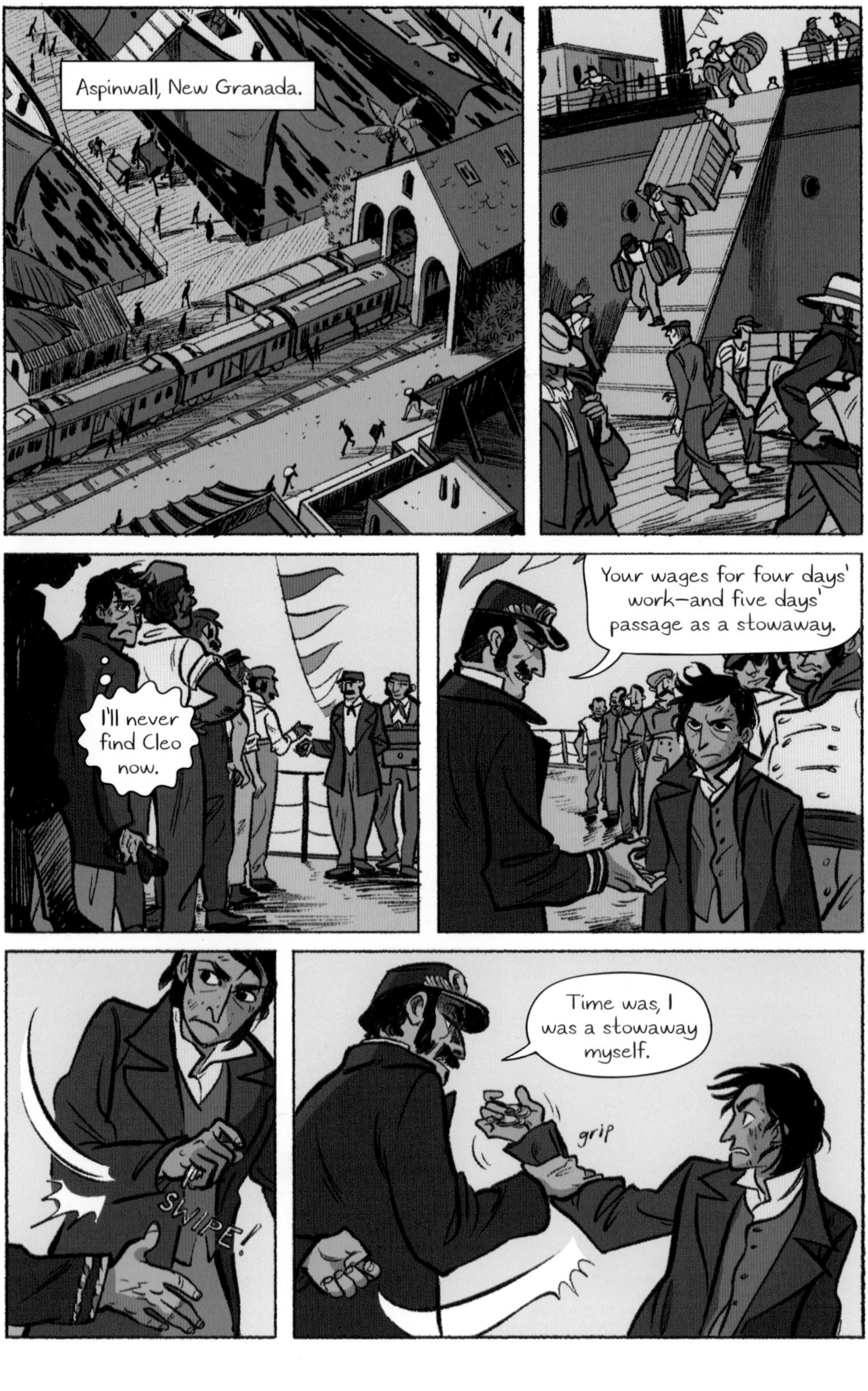
Aspinwall, New Granada.
I'll never find Cleo now.
Your wages for four days' work—and five days' passage as a stowaway.
SWIPE!
Time was, I was a stowaway myself.
grip

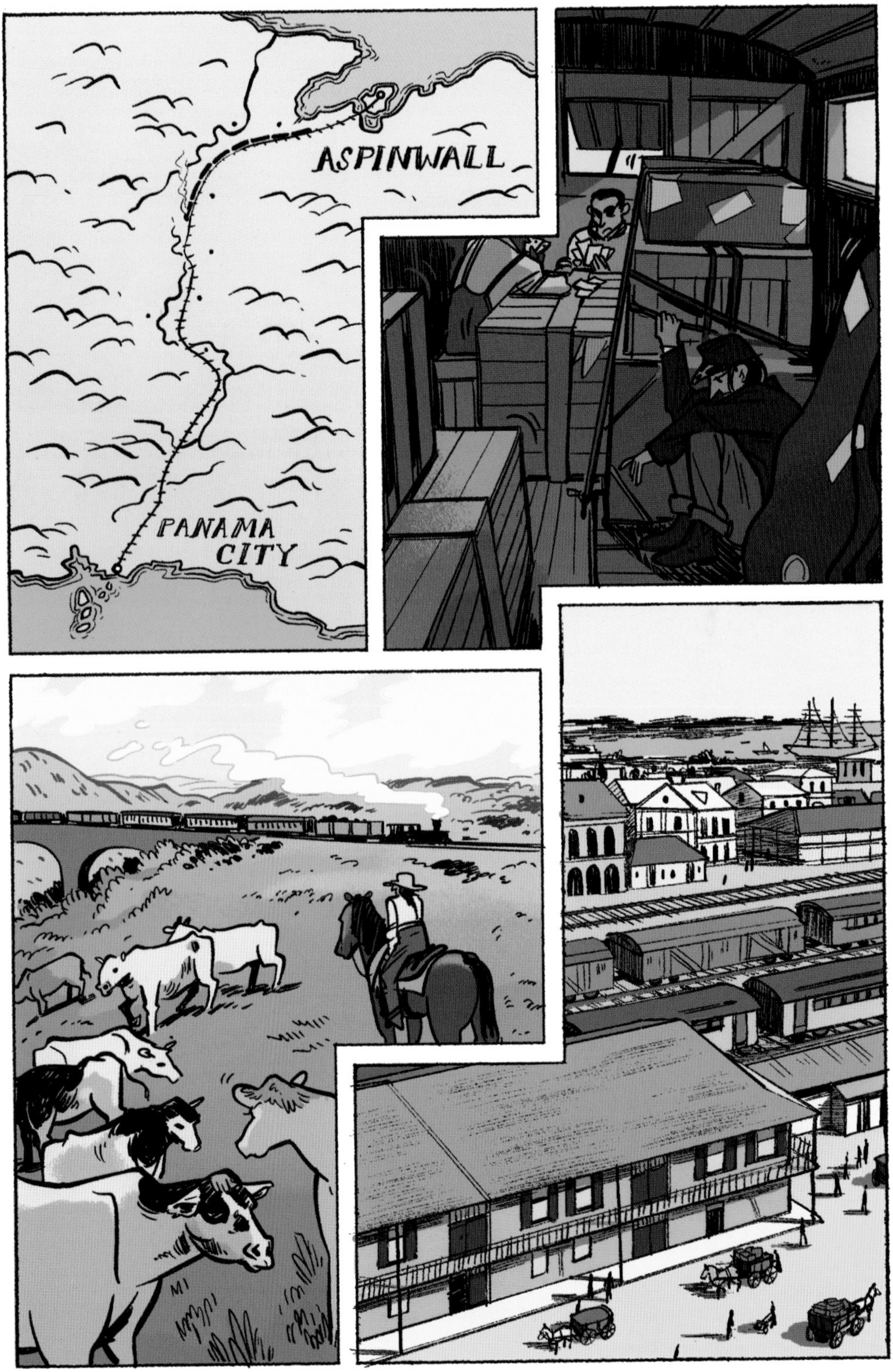
ASPINWALL
PANAMA CITY

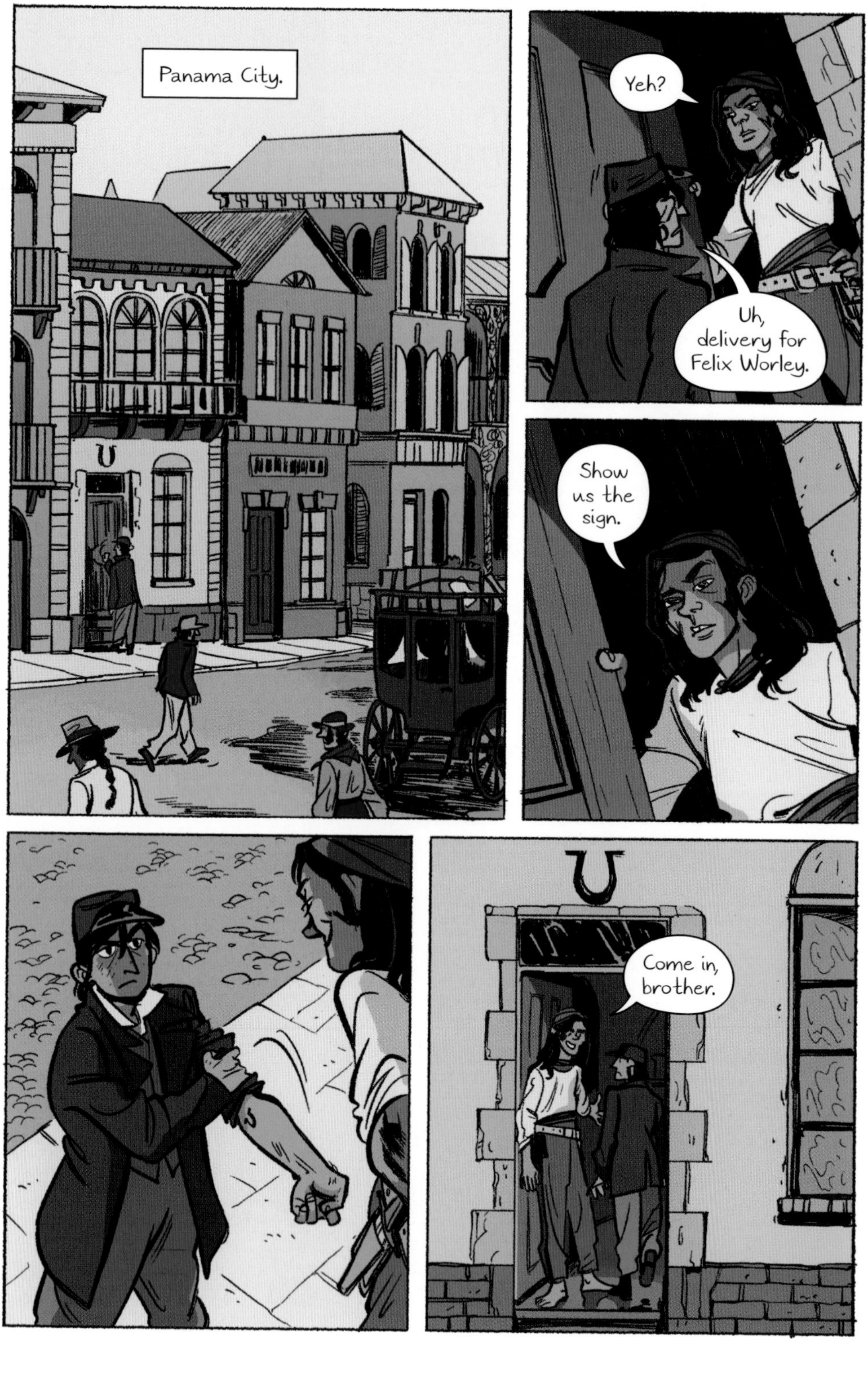
Panama City.
Yeh?
Uh, delivery for Felix Worley.
Show us the sign.
Come in, brother.

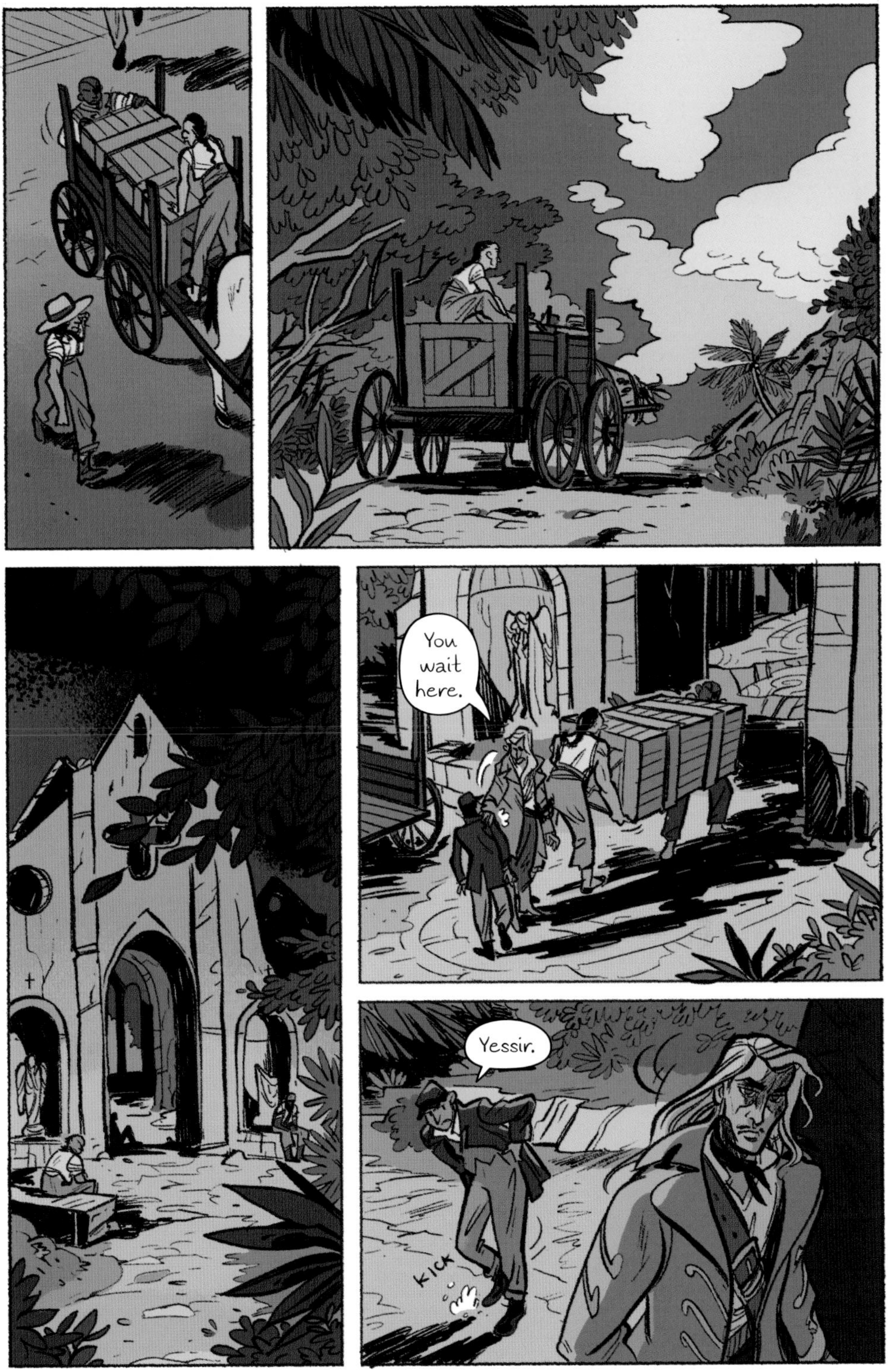
You wait here.
Yessir.
KICK

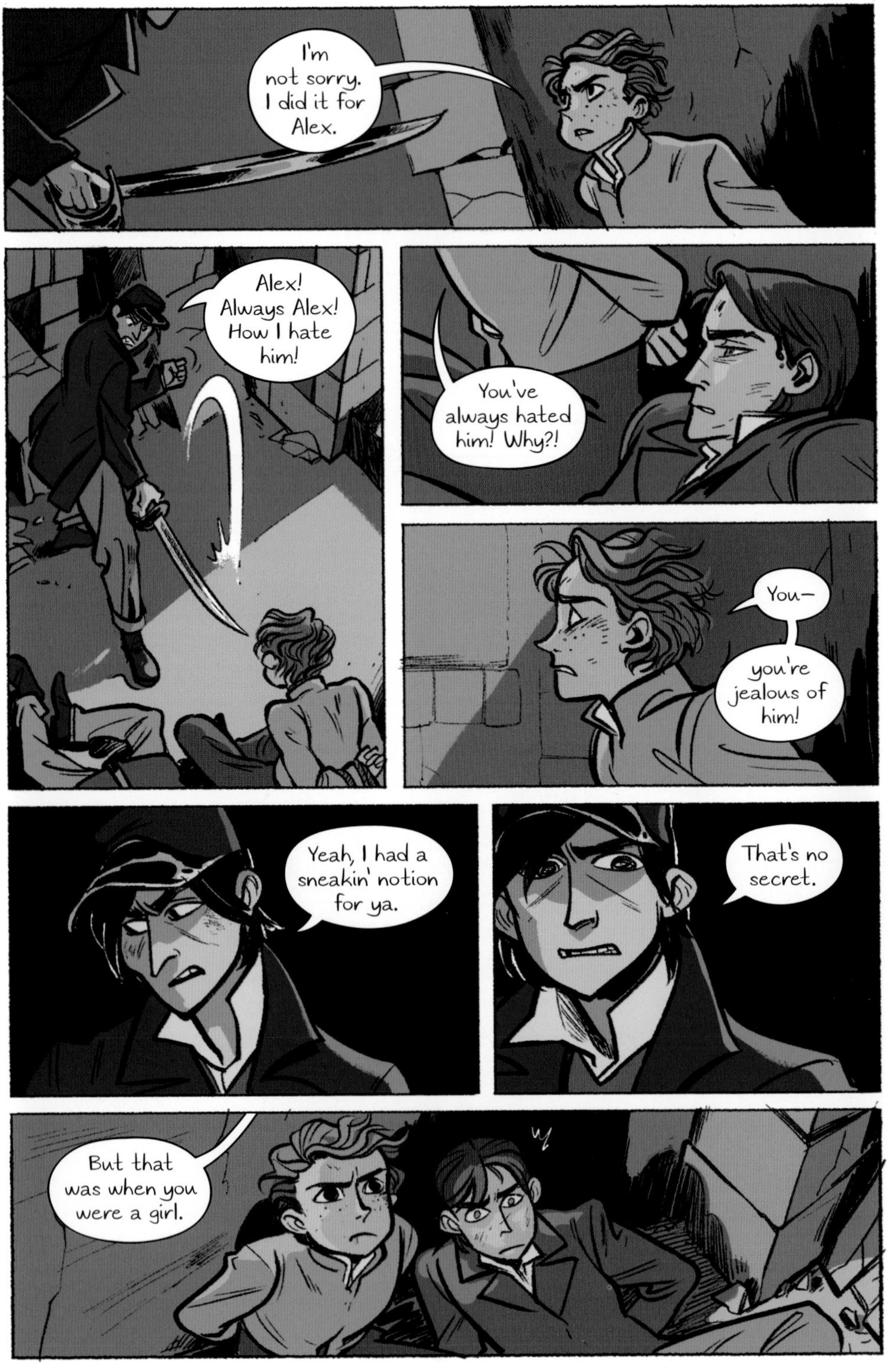
I'm not sorry. I did it for Alex.
Alex! Always Alex! How I hate him!
You've always hated him! Why?!
You—
you're jealous of him!
Yeah, I had a sneakin' notion for ya.
That's no secret.
But that was when you were a girl.

115

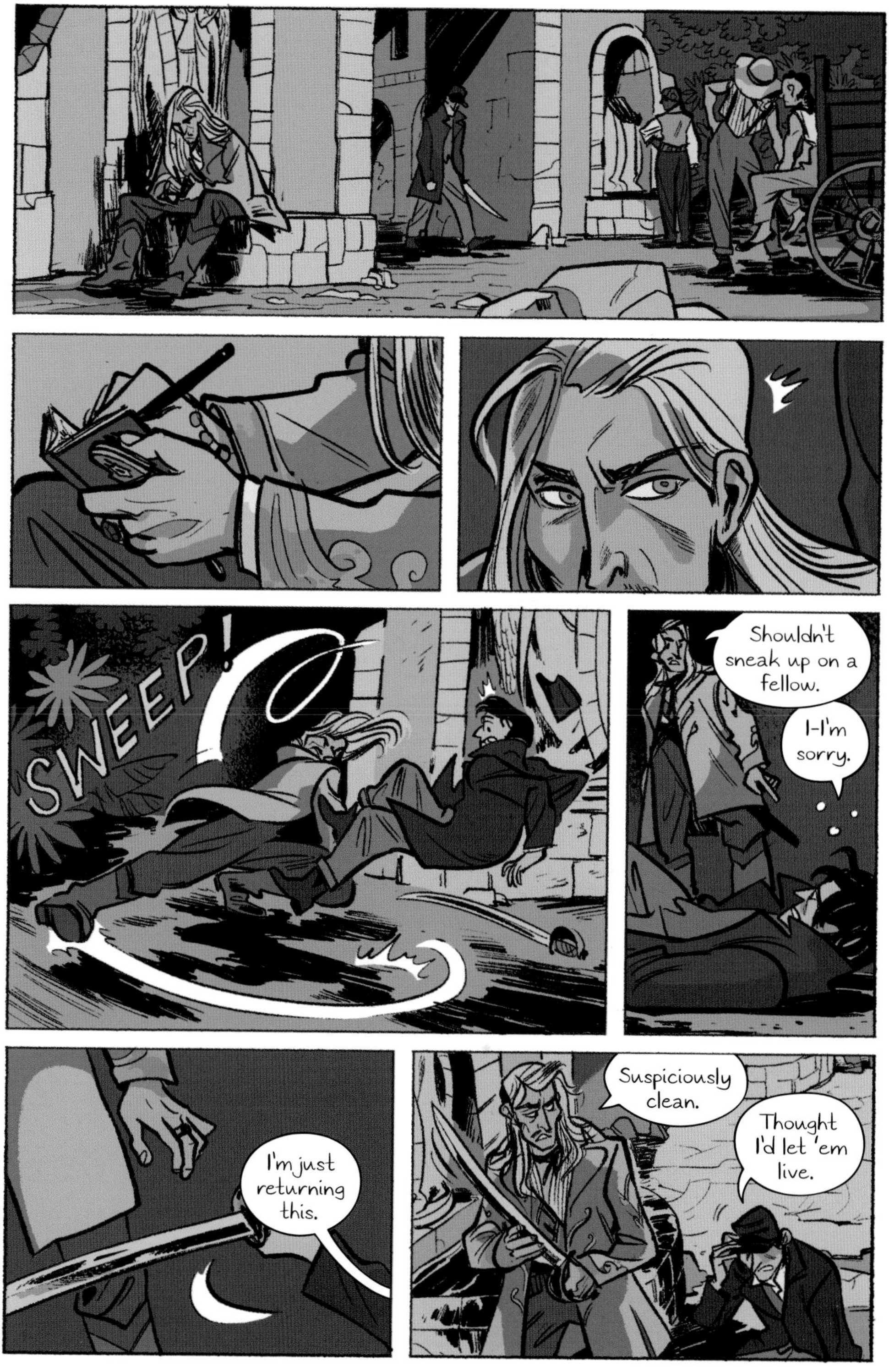
SWEEP!
Shouldn't sneak up on a fellow.
I-I'm sorry.
I'm just returning this.
Suspiciously clean.
Thought I'd let 'em live.

## CHAPTER SIX
# CAPE HORN

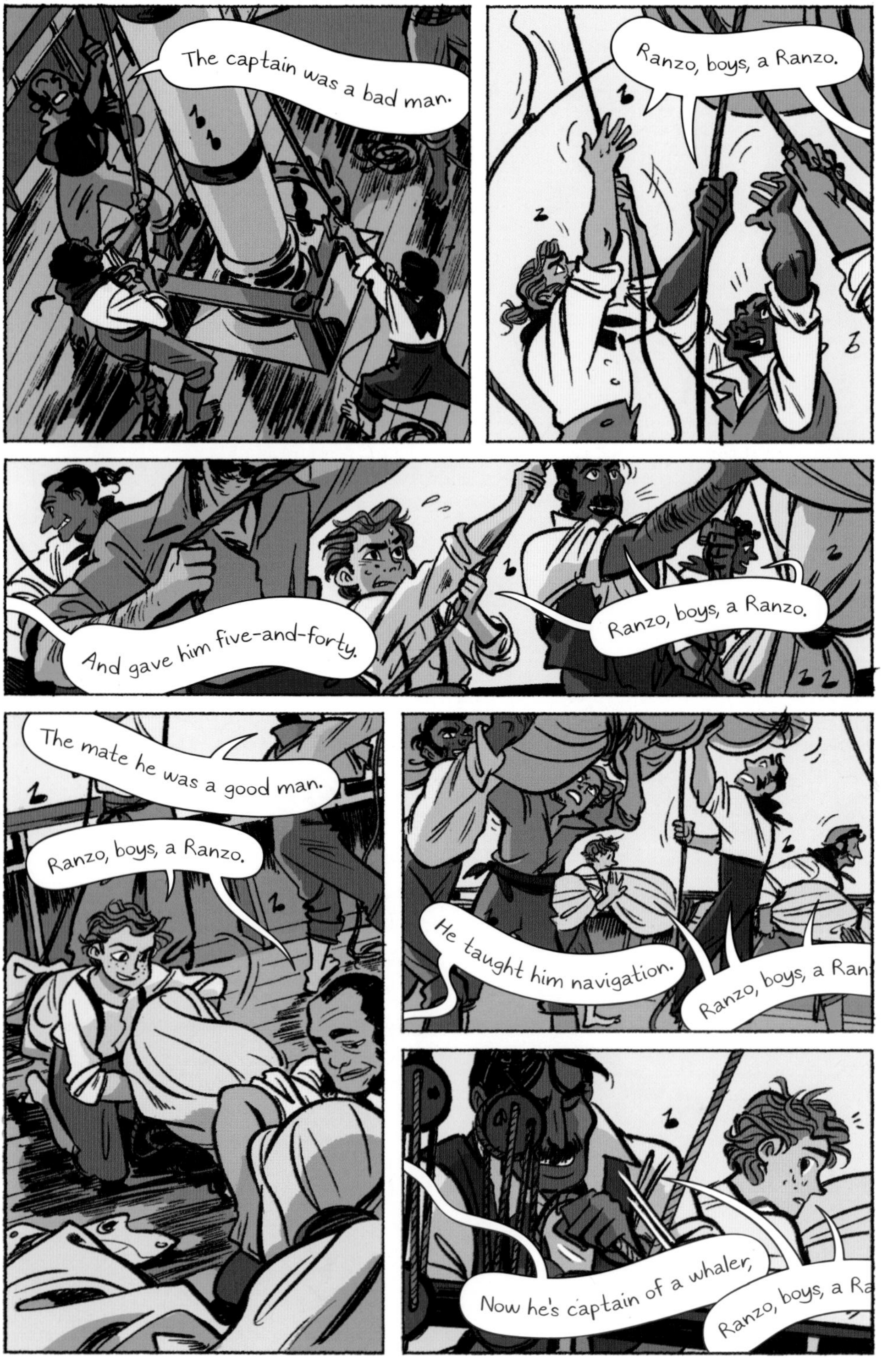
The captain was a bad man.
Ranzo, boys, a Ranzo.
And gave him five-and-forty.
Ranzo, boys, a Ranzo.
The mate he was a good man.
Ranzo, boys, a Ranzo.
He taught him navigation.
Now he's captain of a whaler,

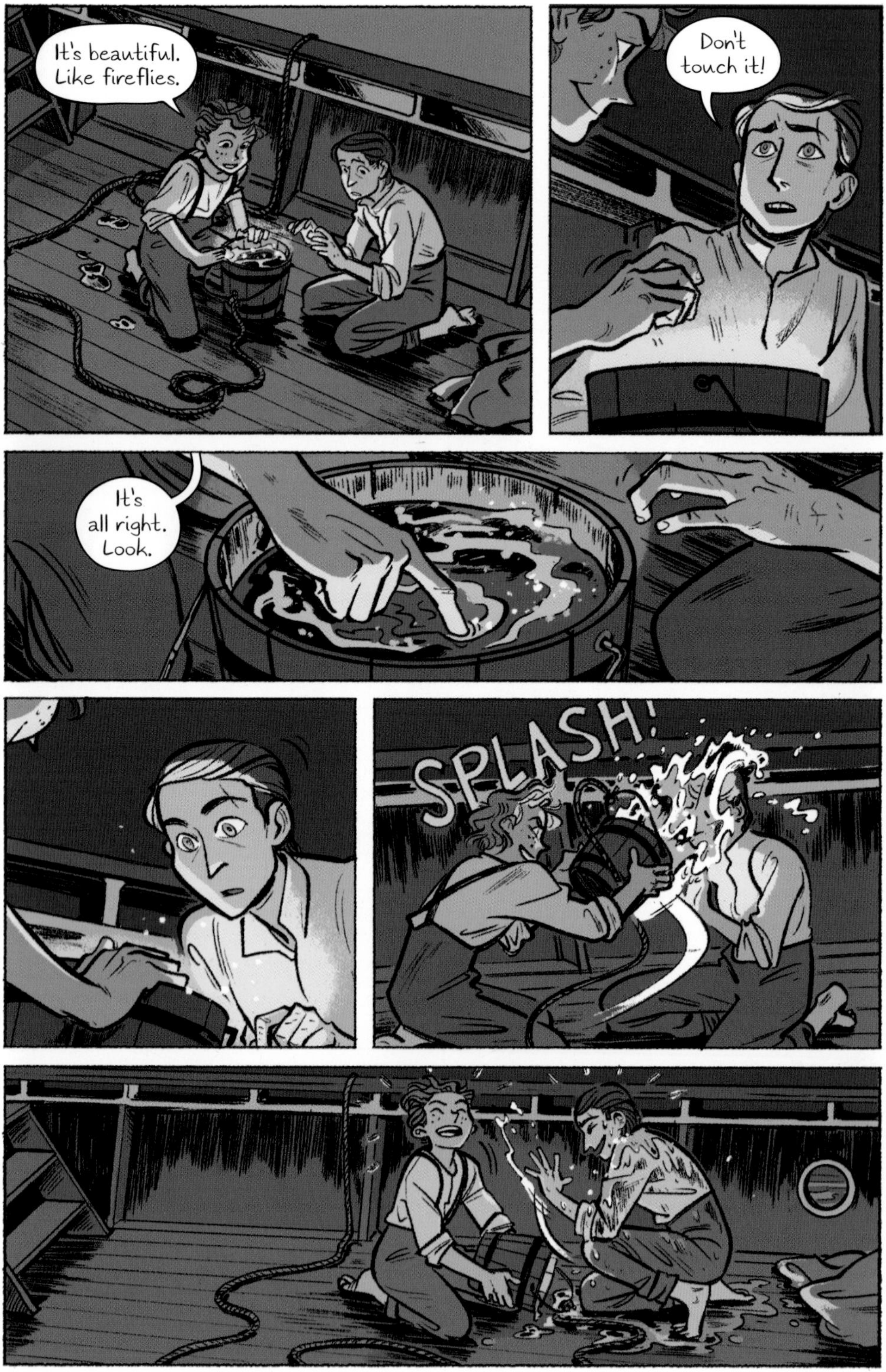
It's beautiful. Like fireflies.
Don't touch it!
It's all right. Look.
SPLASH!

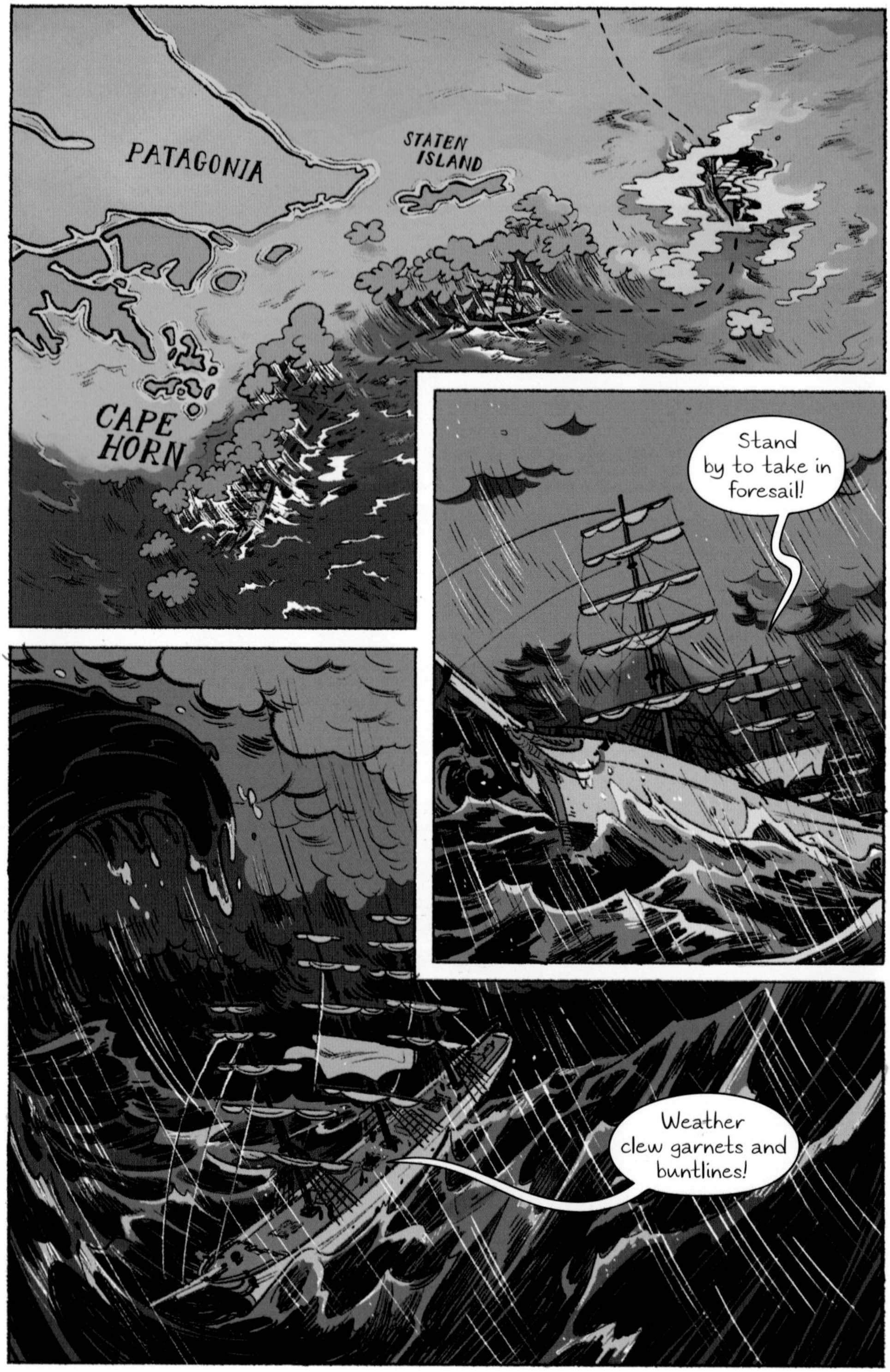
PATAGONIA
STATEN ISLAND
CAPE HORN
Stand by to take in foresail!
Weather clew garnets and buntlines!

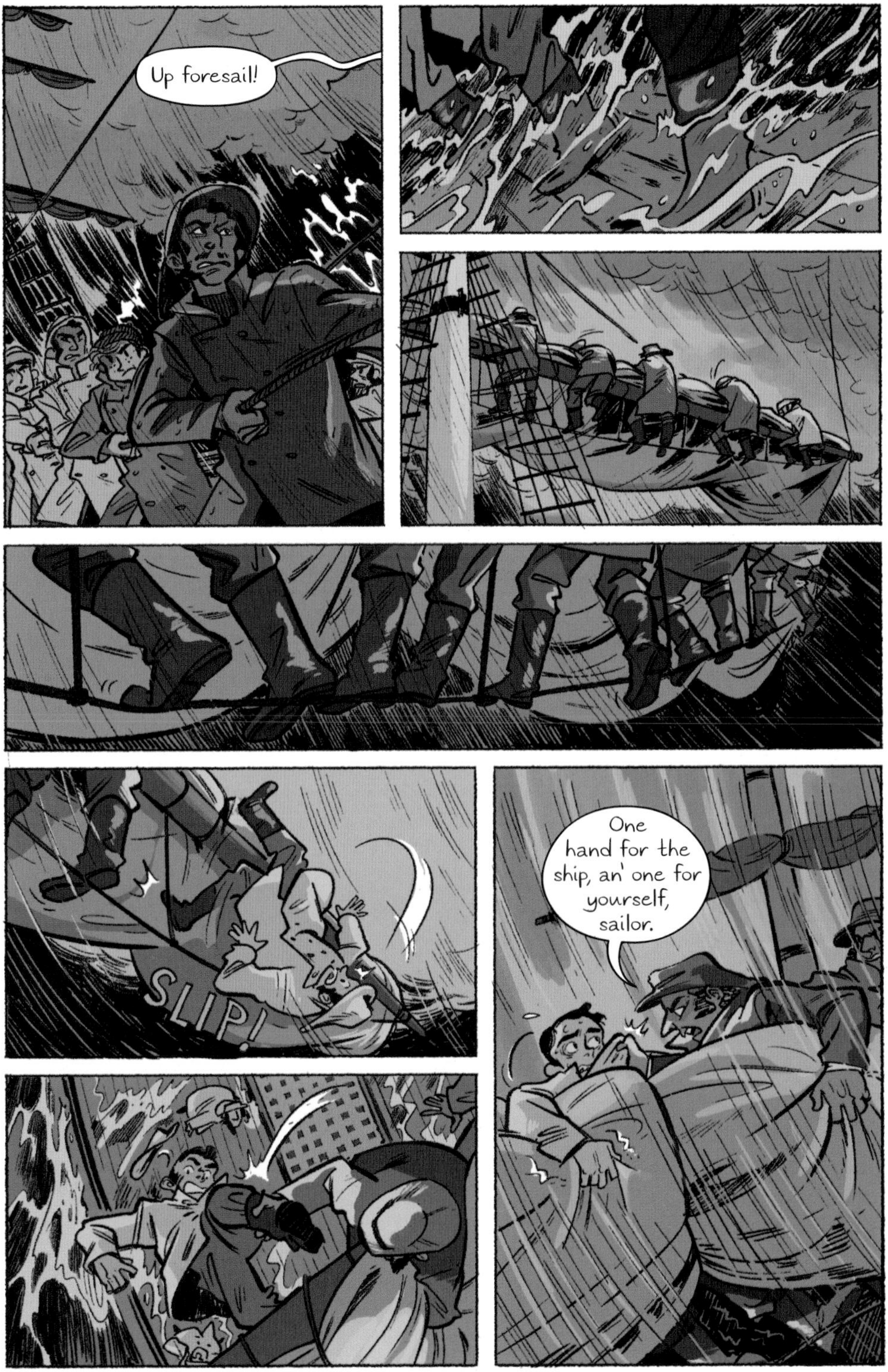
Up foresail!
SLIP!
One hand for the ship, an' one for yourself, sailor.

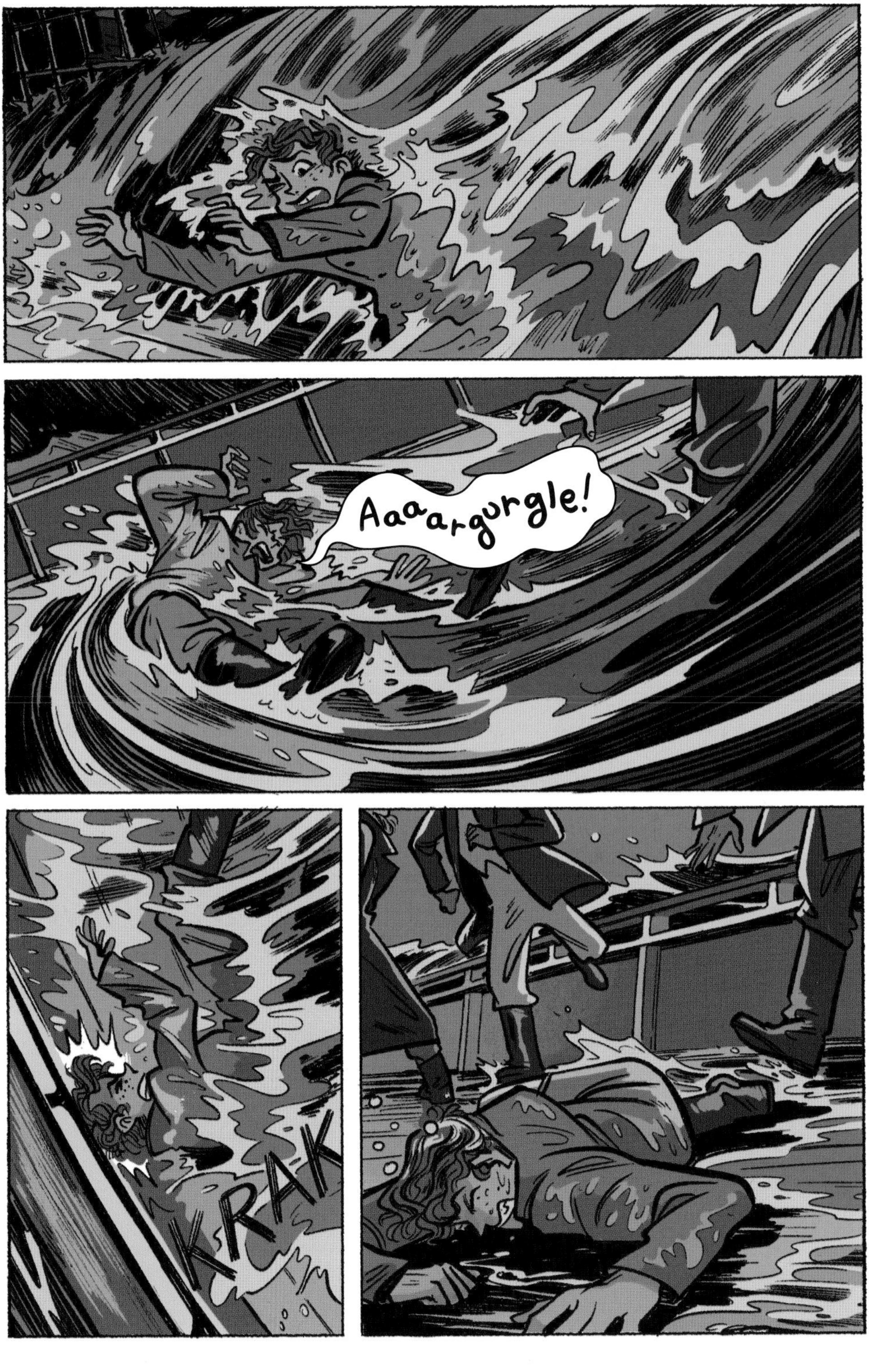
Aaaargurgle!
KRAK

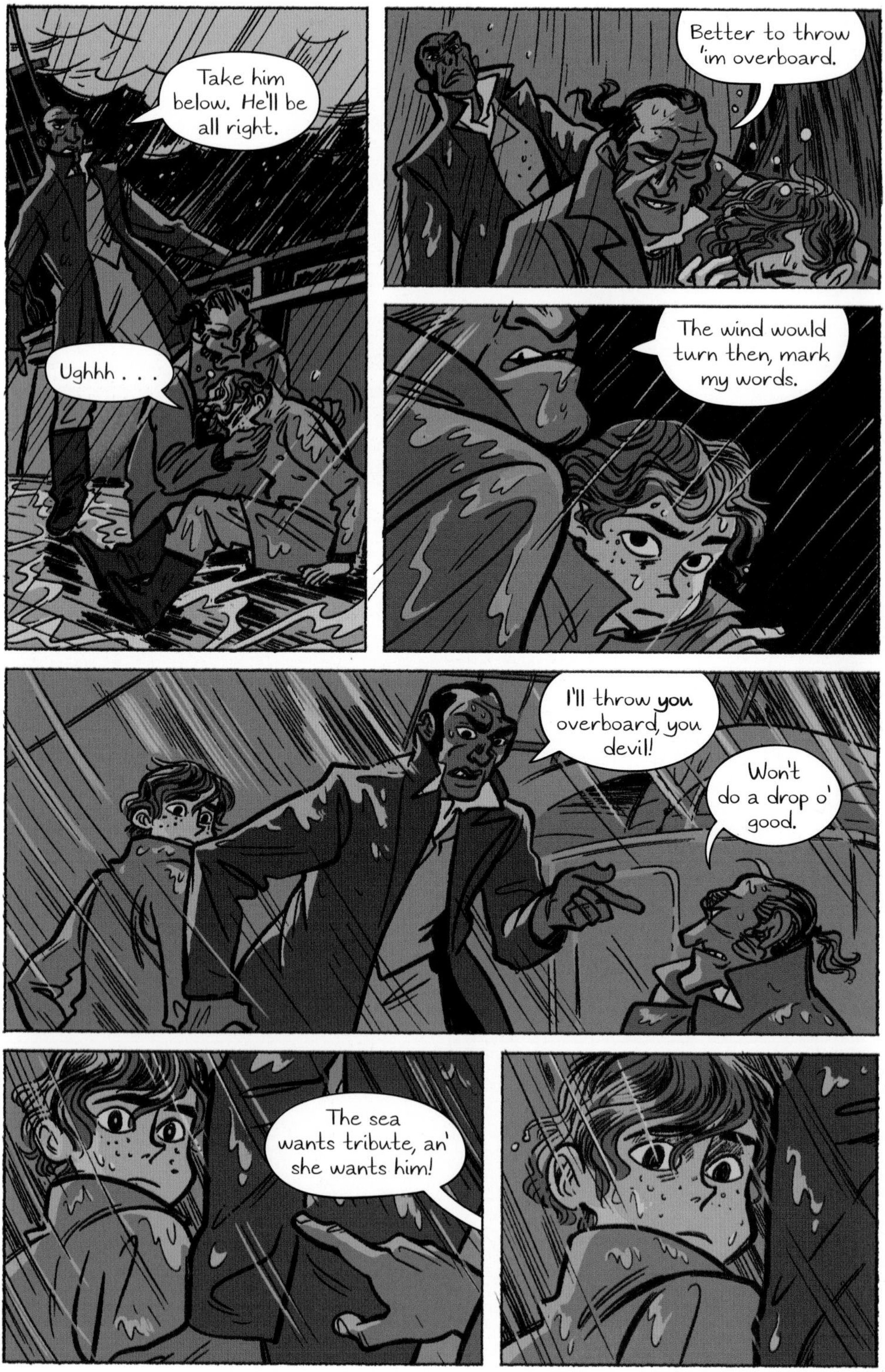
Take him below. He'll be all right.
Ughhh . . .
Better to throw 'im overboard.
The wind would turn then, mark my words.
I'll throw **you** overboard, you devil!
Won't do a drop o' good.
The sea wants tribute, an' she wants him!

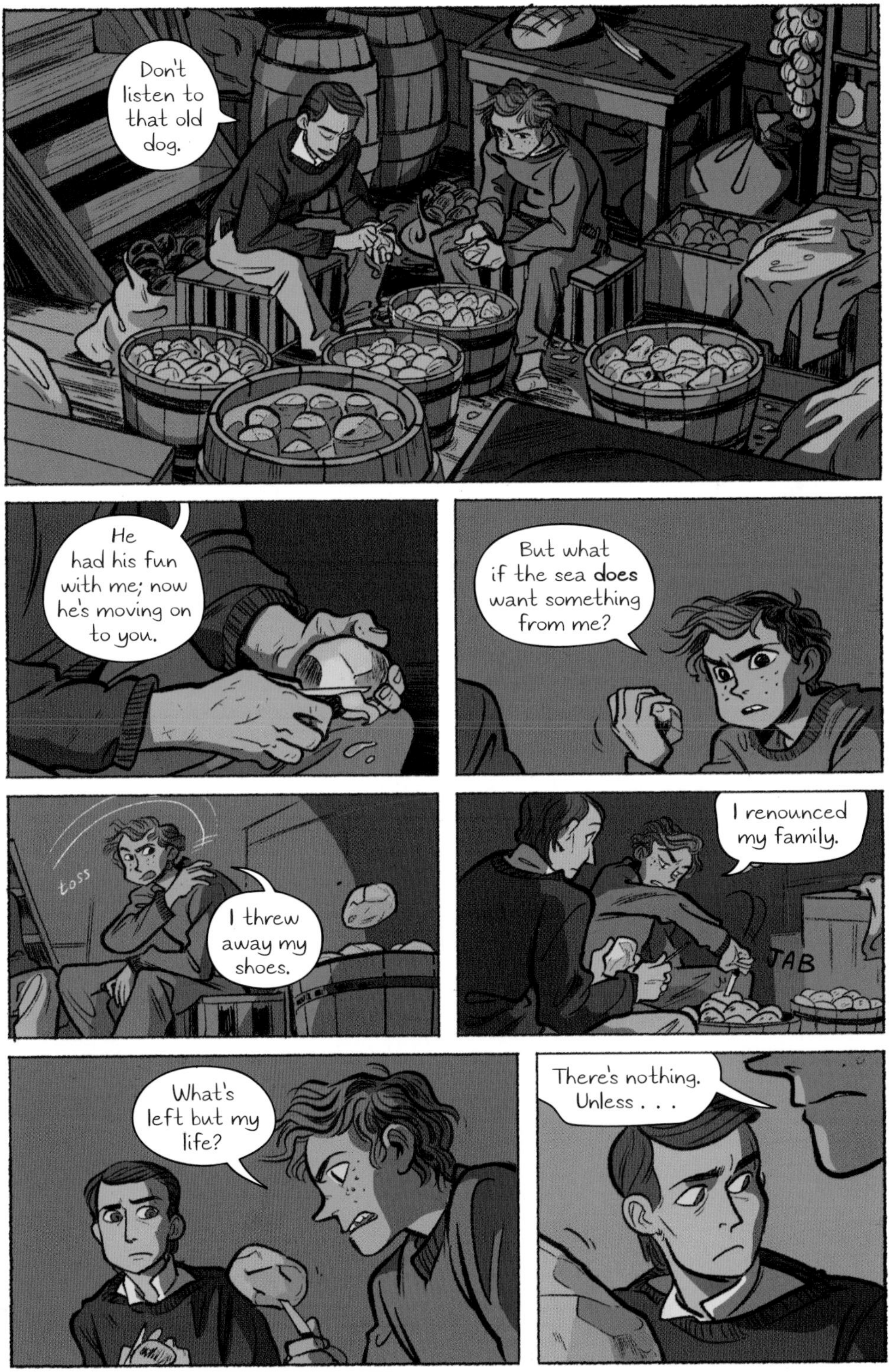
Don't listen to that old dog.
He had his fun with me; now he's moving on to you.
But what if the sea **does** want something from me?
toss
I threw away my shoes.
I renounced my family.
JAB
What's left but my life?
There's nothing. Unless . . .

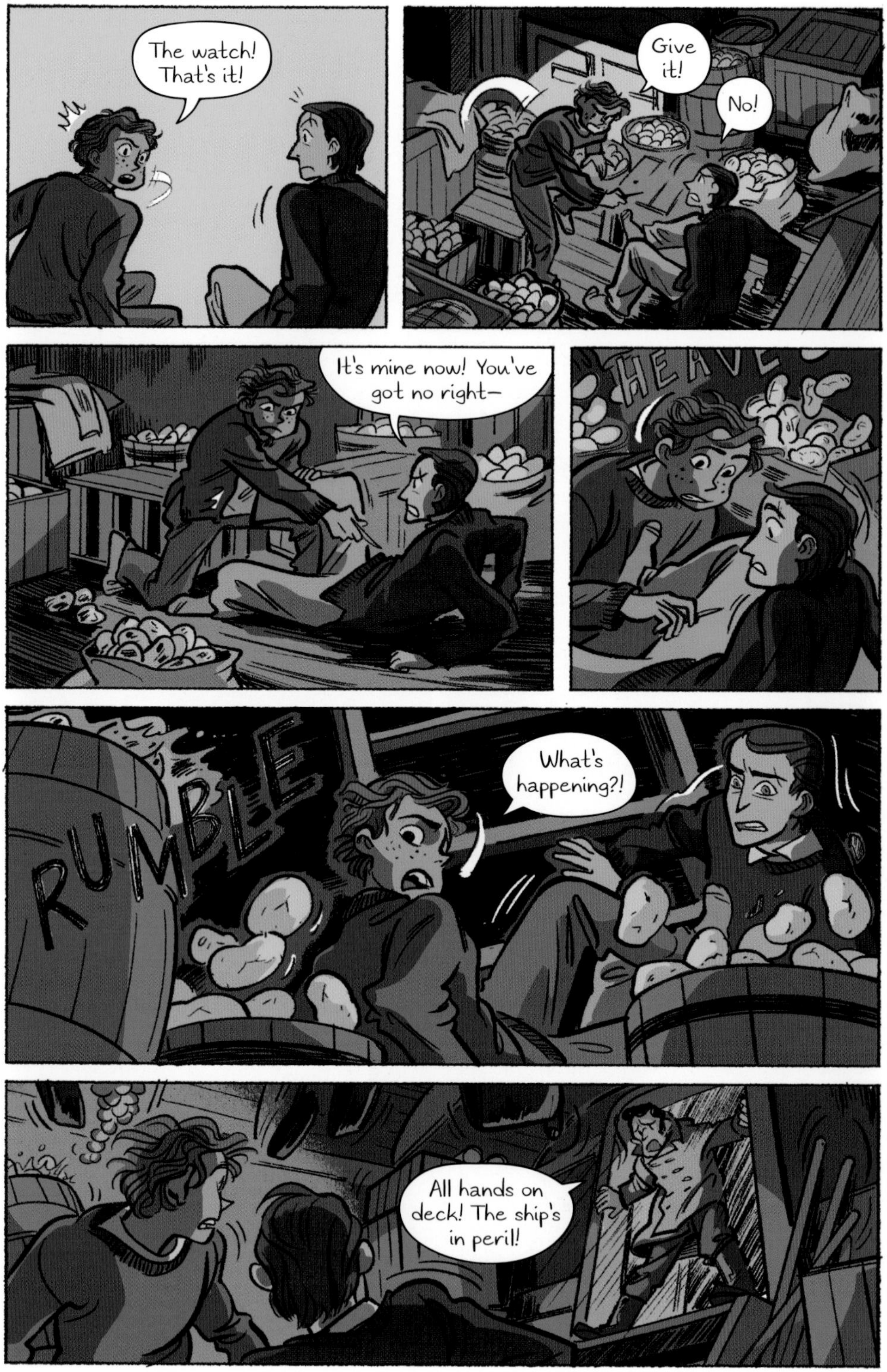
The watch! That's it!
Give it!
No!
It's mine now! You've got no right—
HEAVE
RUMBLE
What's happening?!
All hands on deck! The ship's in peril!

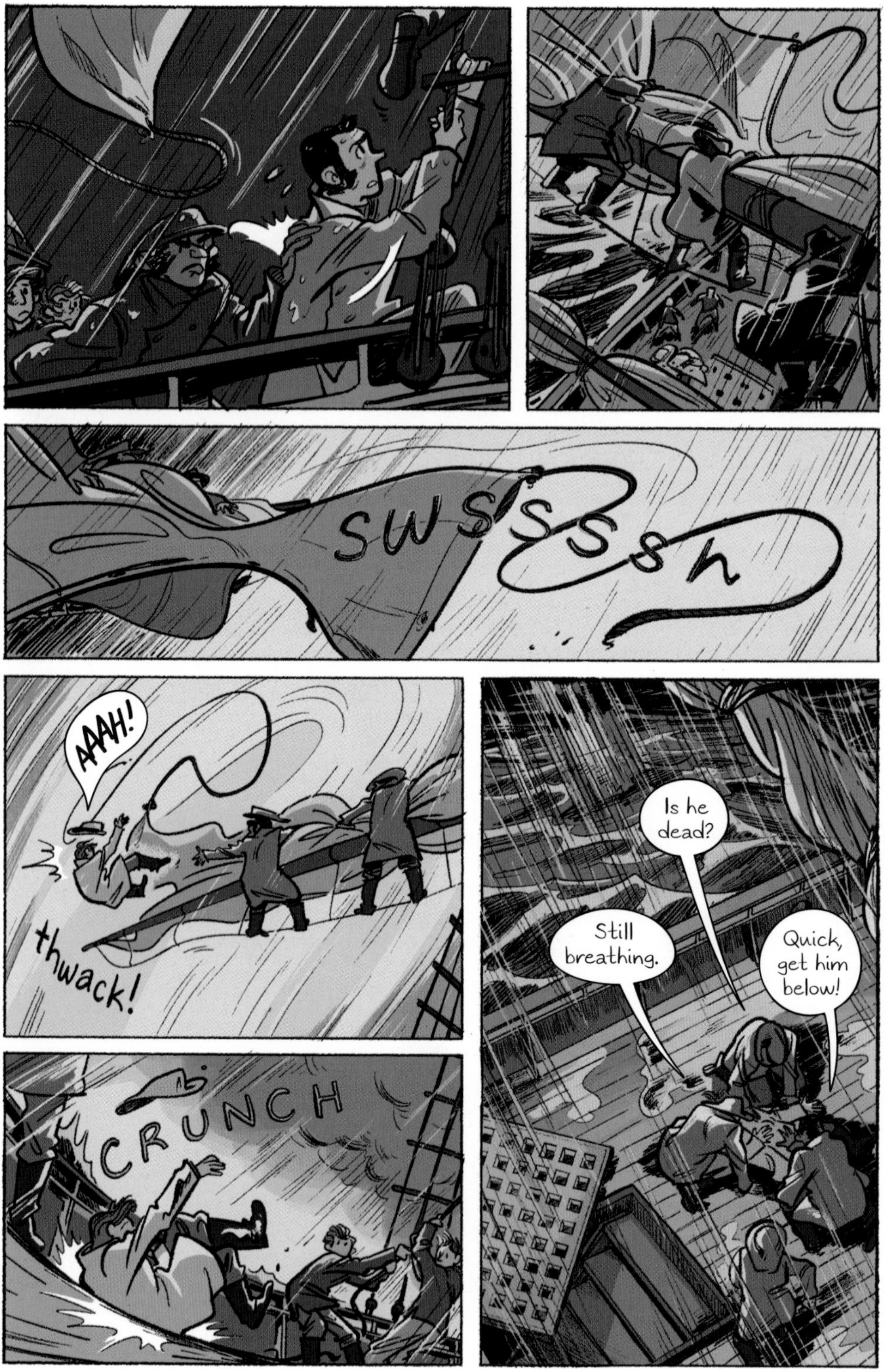
SWSSSSh
AAAH!
thwack!
CRUNCH
Is he dead?
Still breathing.
Quick, get him below!

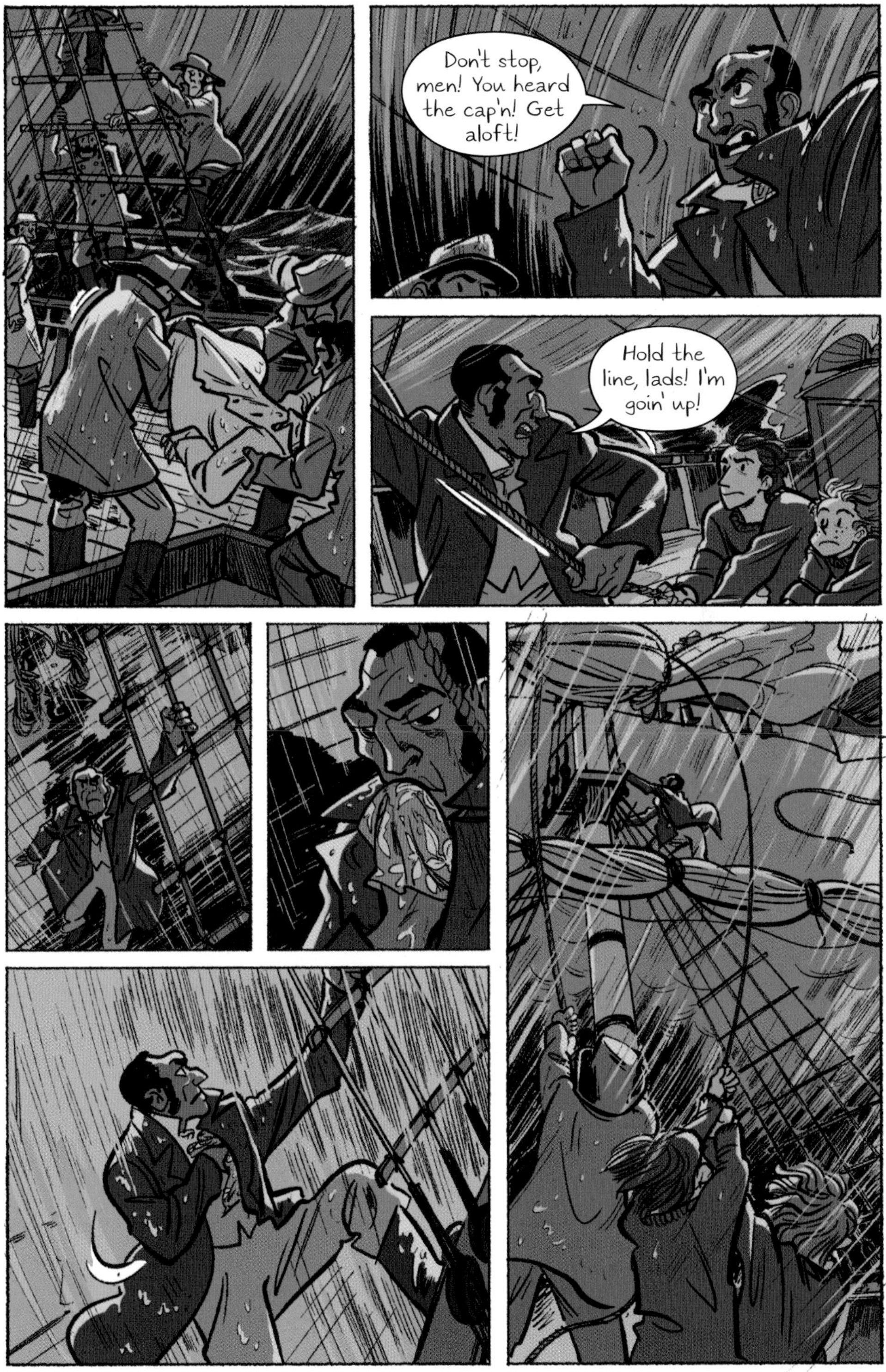
Don't stop, men! You heard the cap'n! Get aloft!
Hold the line, lads! I'm goin' up!

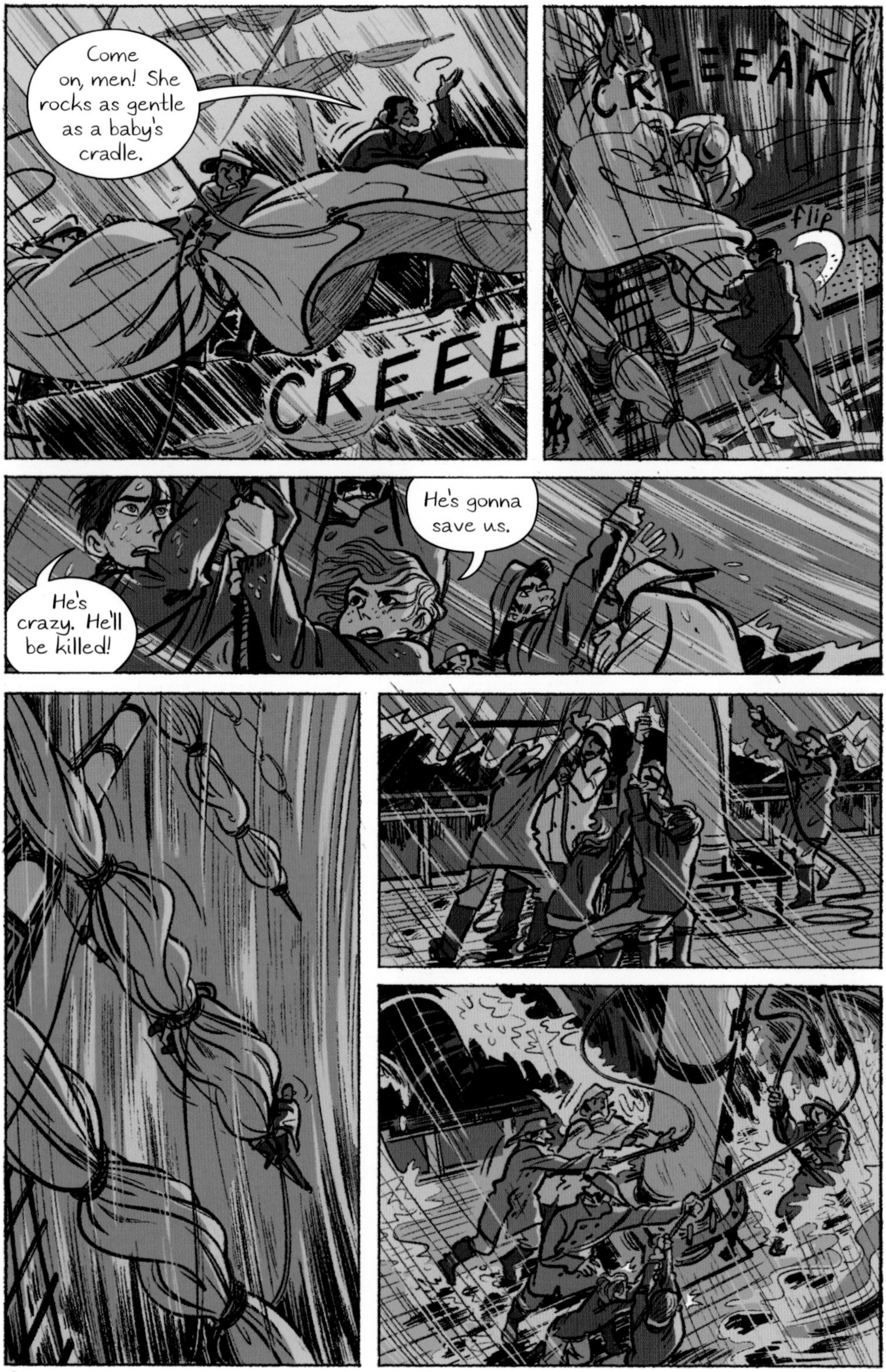
Come on, men! She rocks as gentle as a baby's cradle.
CREEE
CREEEAK
flip
He's crazy. He'll be killed!
He's gonna save us.

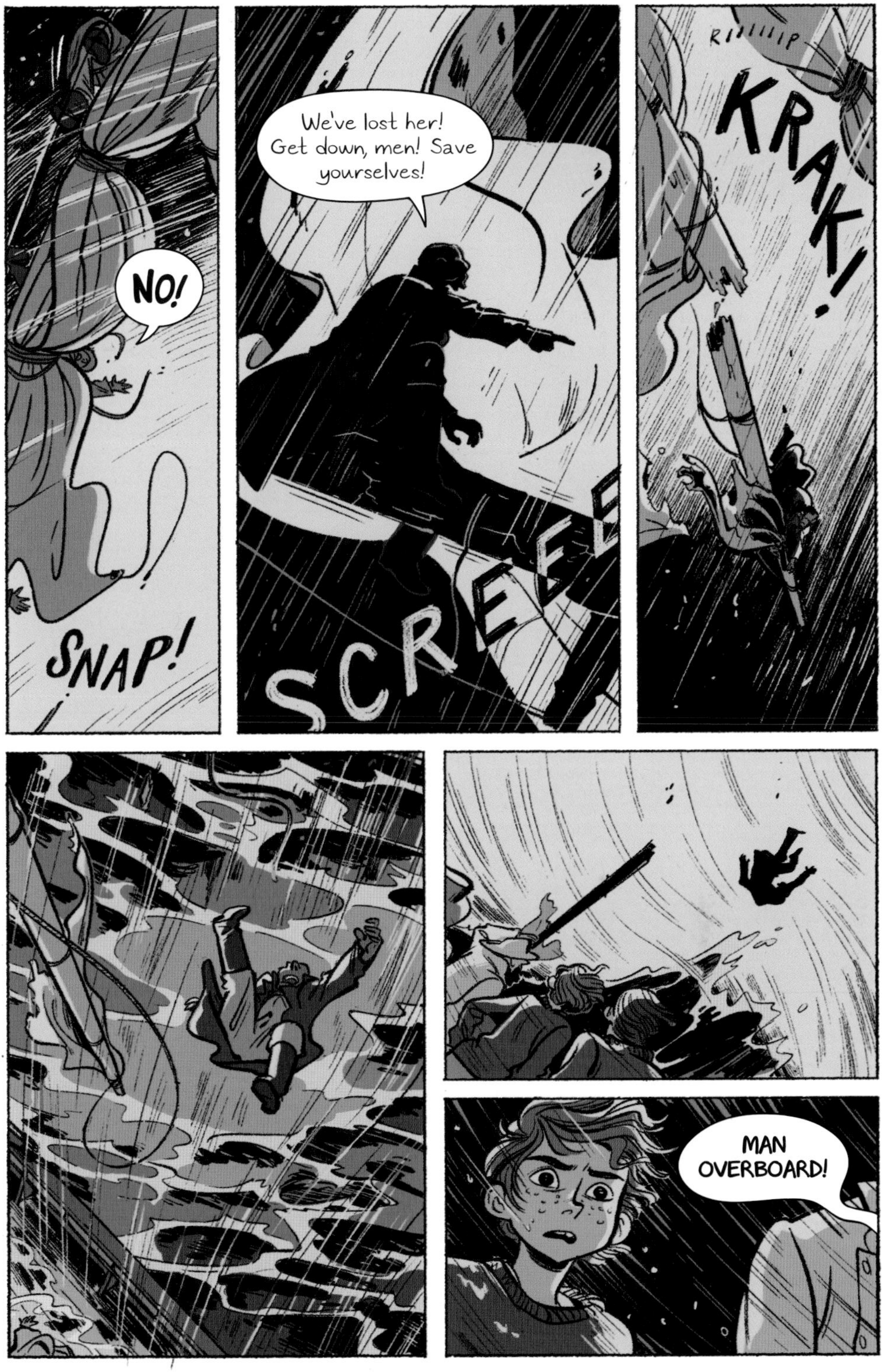
NO!
SNAP!
We've lost her! Get down, men! Save yourselves!
SCREEE
RIIIIIP
KRAK!
MAN OVERBOARD!

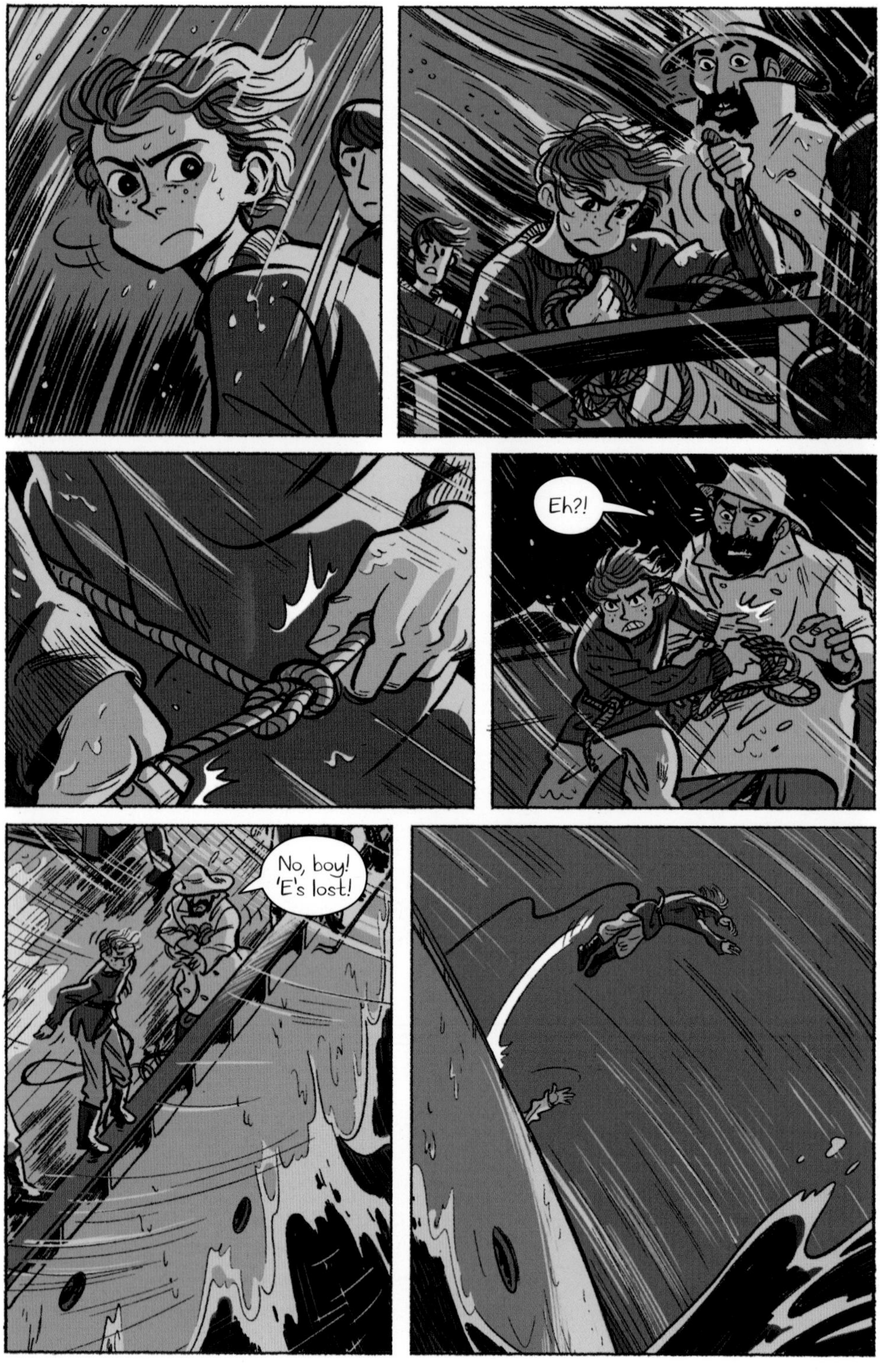
Eh?!
No, boy! 'E's lost!

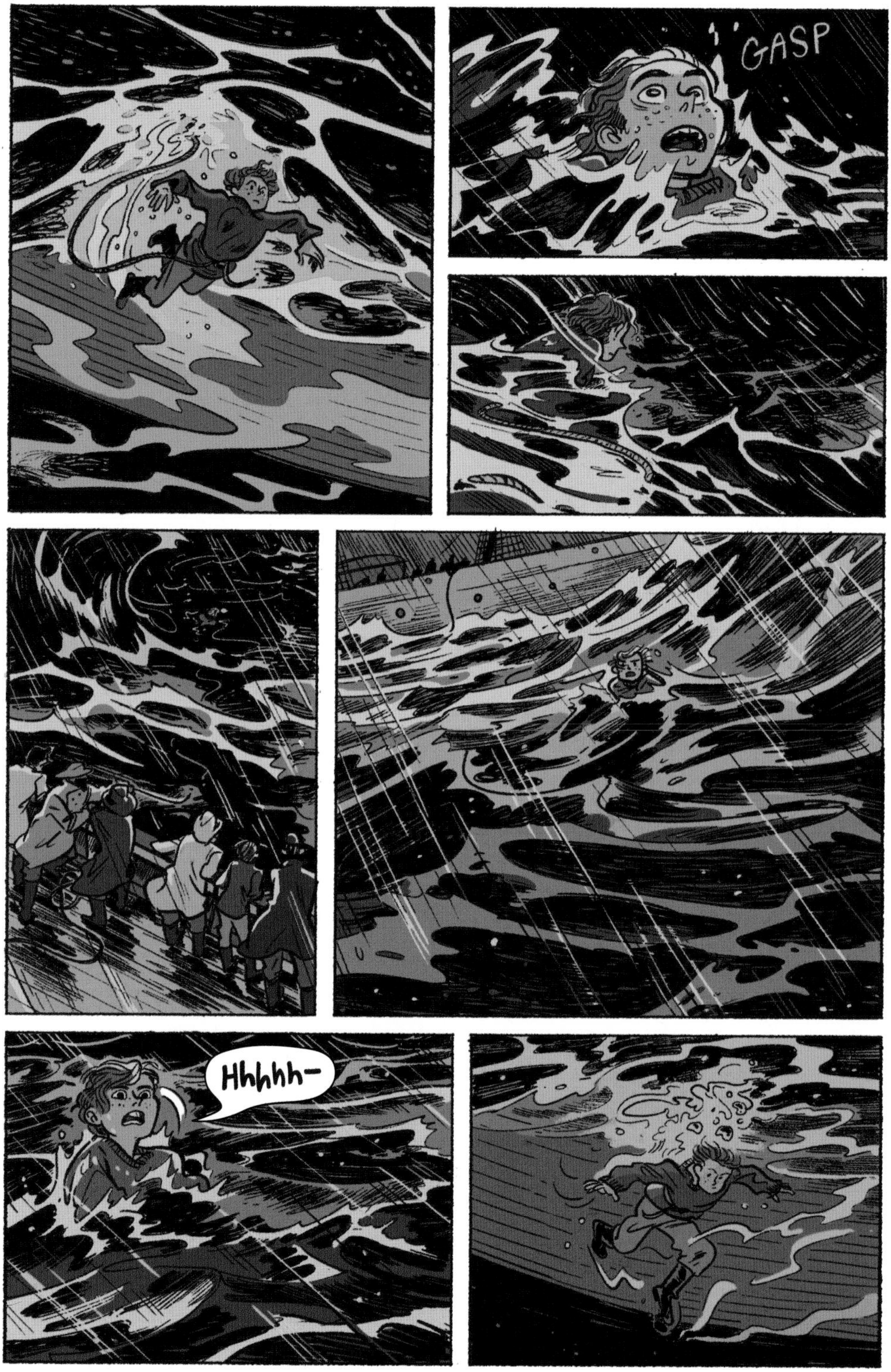
GASP
Hhhhh-

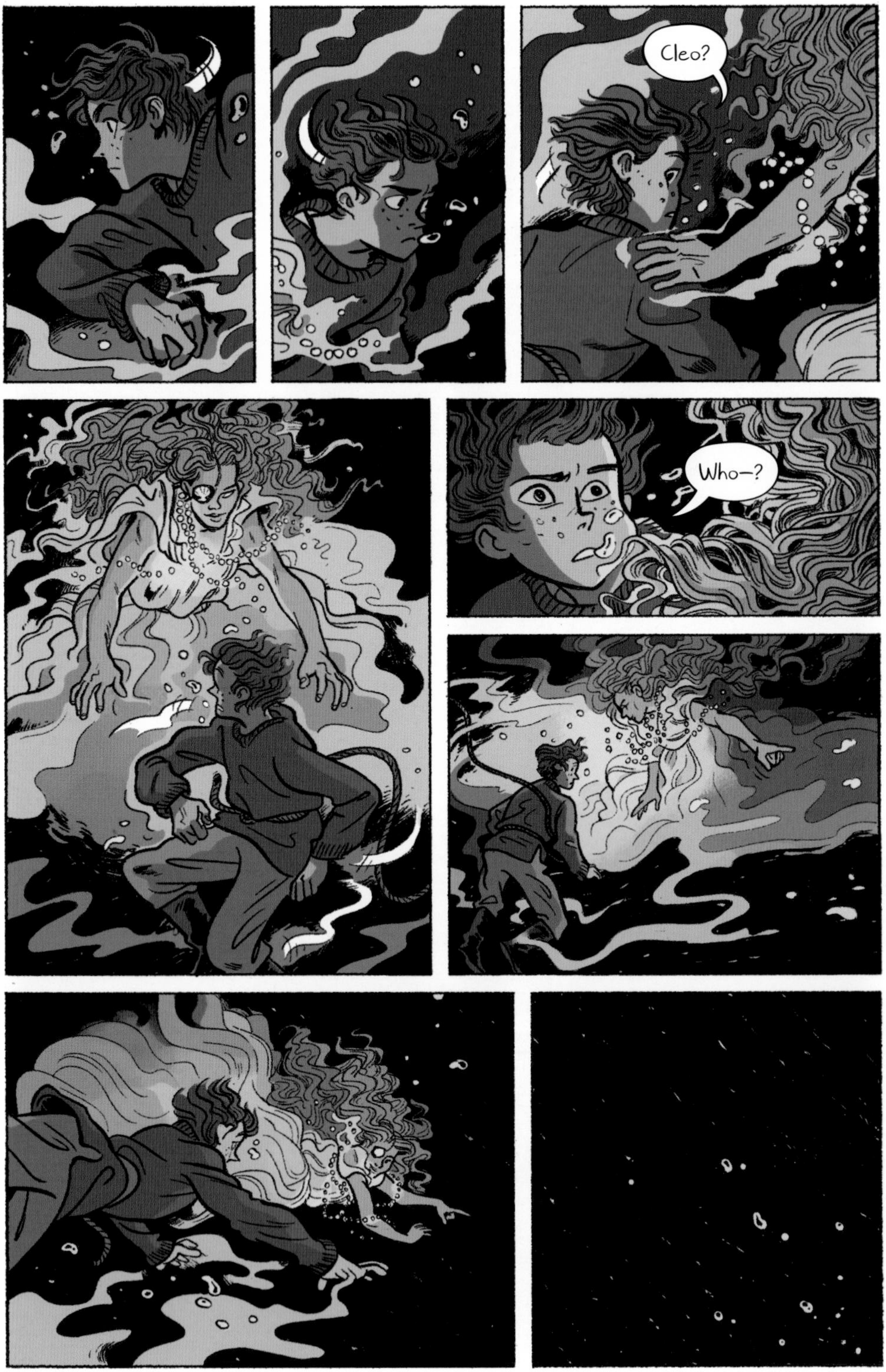
Cleo?
Who–?

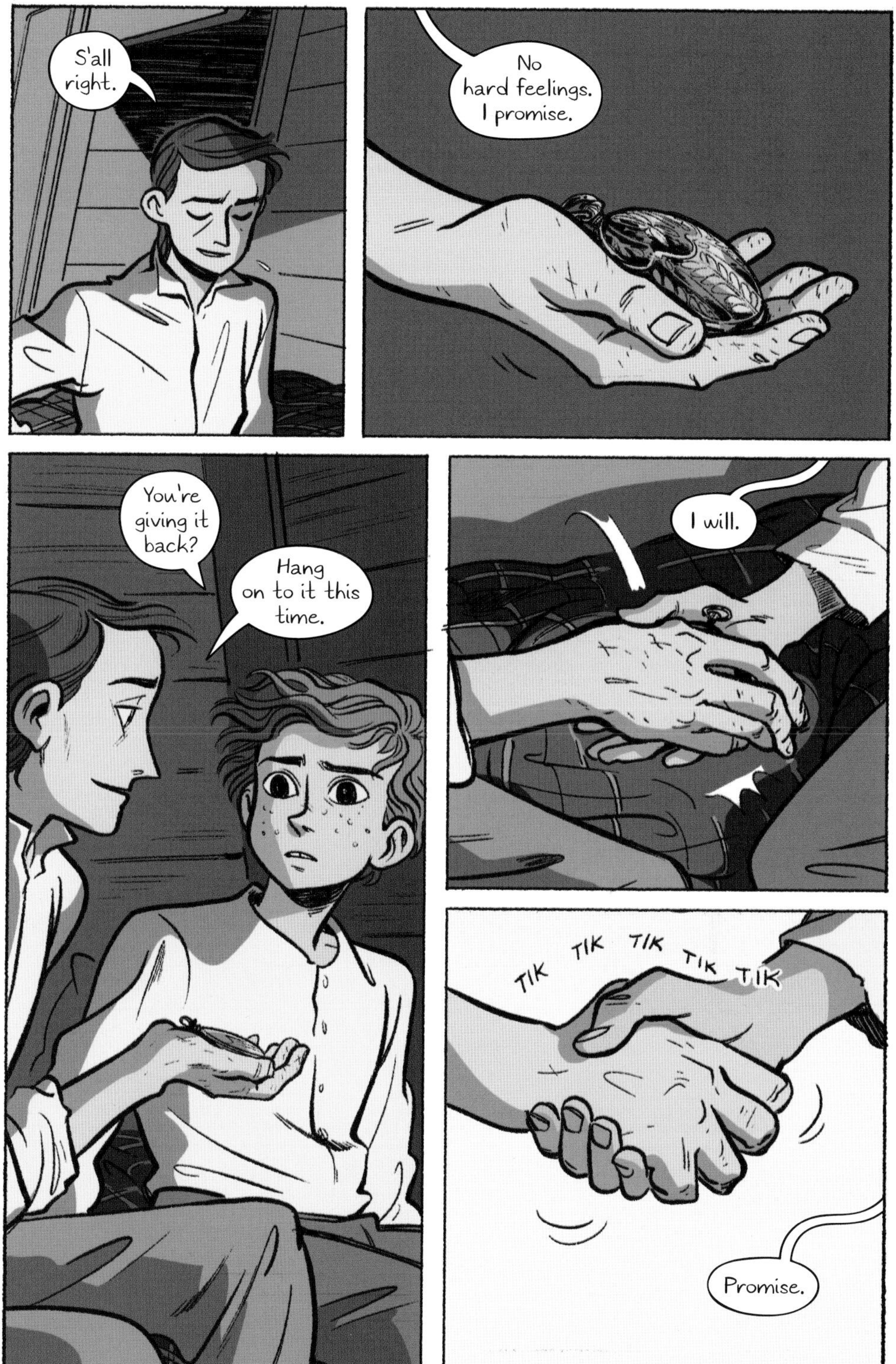
S'all right.
No hard feelings. I promise.
You're giving it back?
Hang on to it this time.
I will.
TIK TIK TIK TIK TIK
Promise.

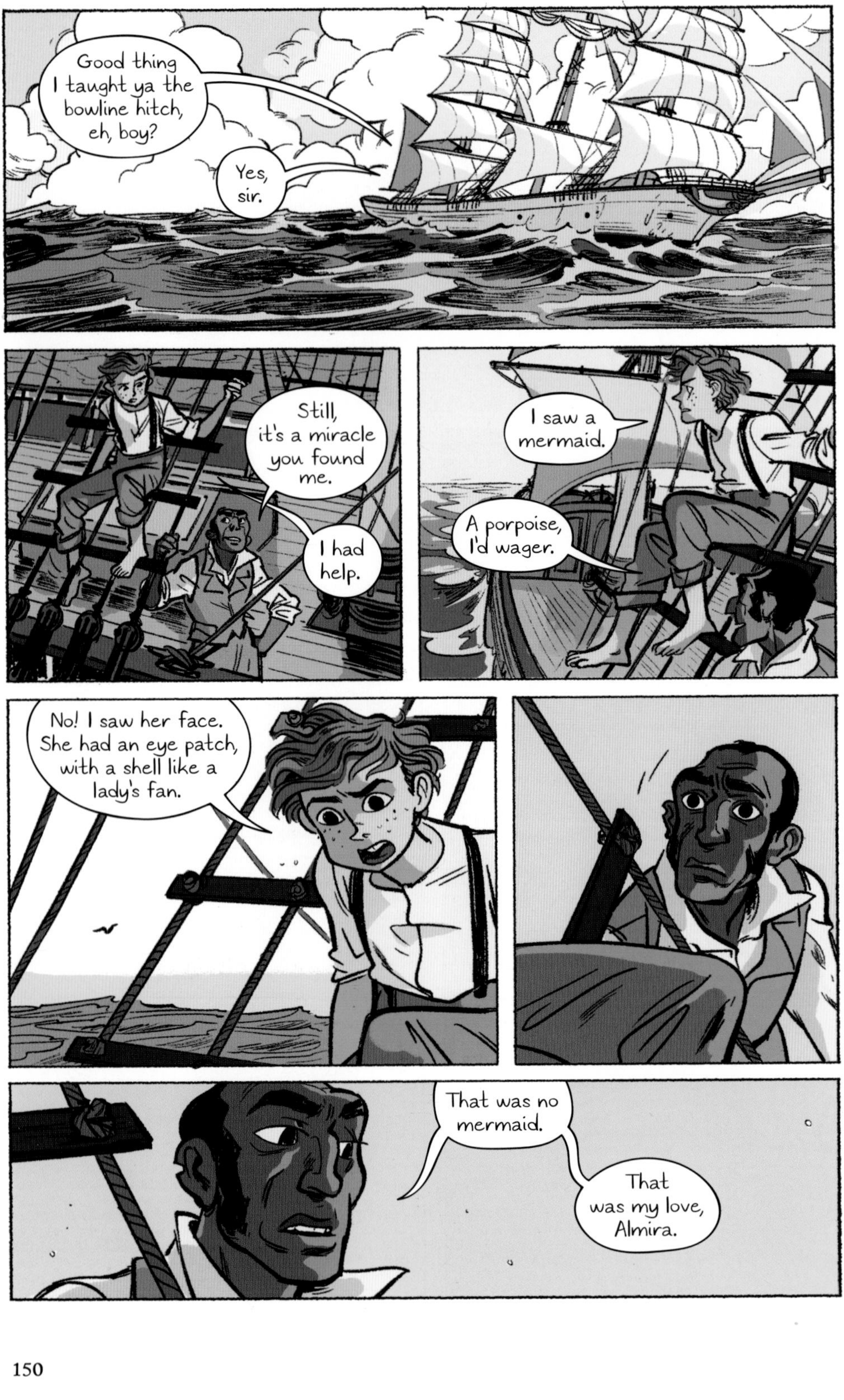
Good thing I taught ya the bowline hitch, eh, boy?
Yes, sir.
Still, it's a miracle you found me.
I had help.
I saw a mermaid.
A porpoise, I'd wager.
No! I saw her face. She had an eye patch, with a shell like a lady's fan.
That was no mermaid.
That was my love, Almira.

## CHAPTER SEVEN
# TOOTH AND NAIL

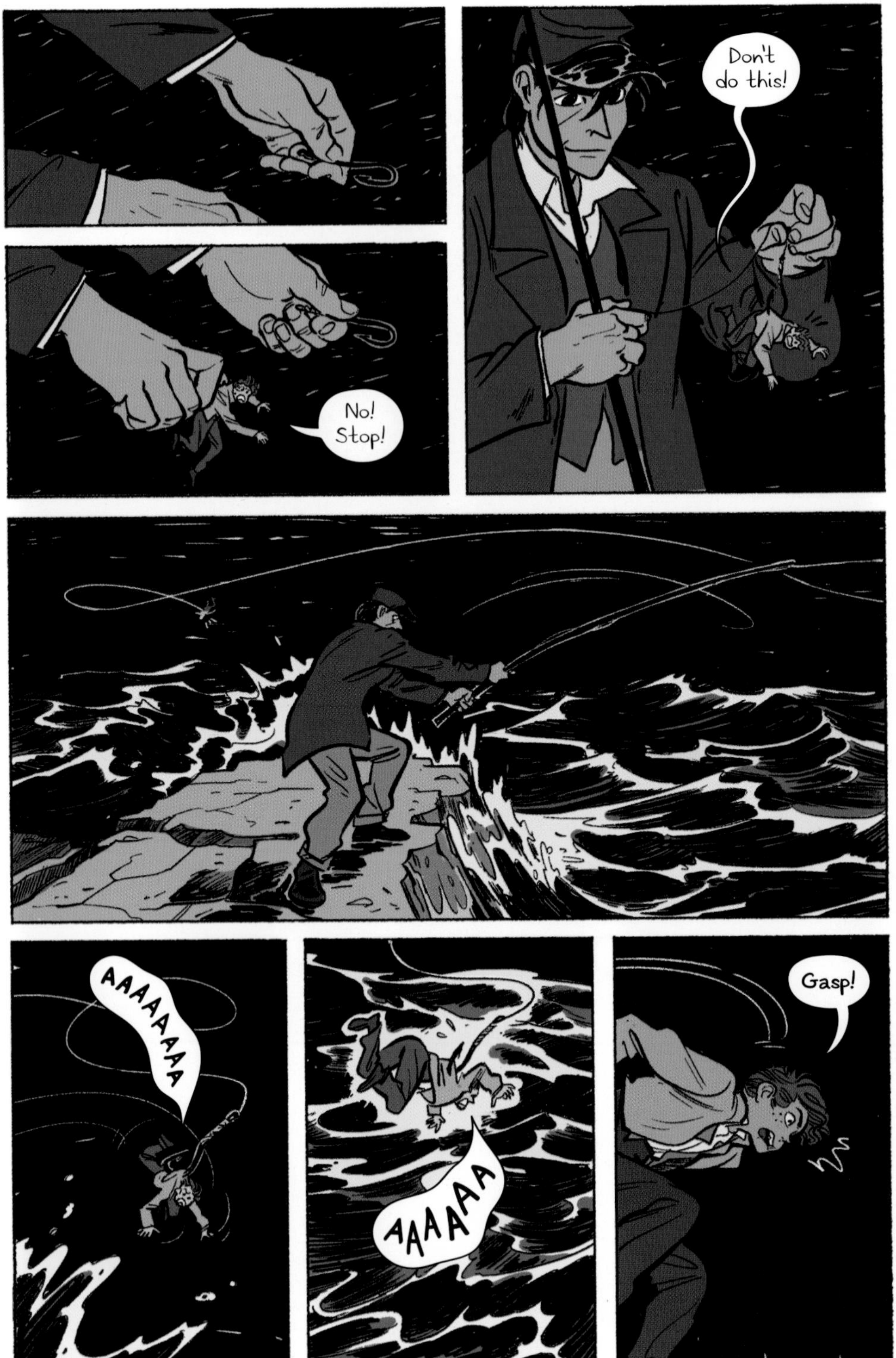
No! Stop!
Don't do this!
AAAAAAAA
AAAAA
Gasp!

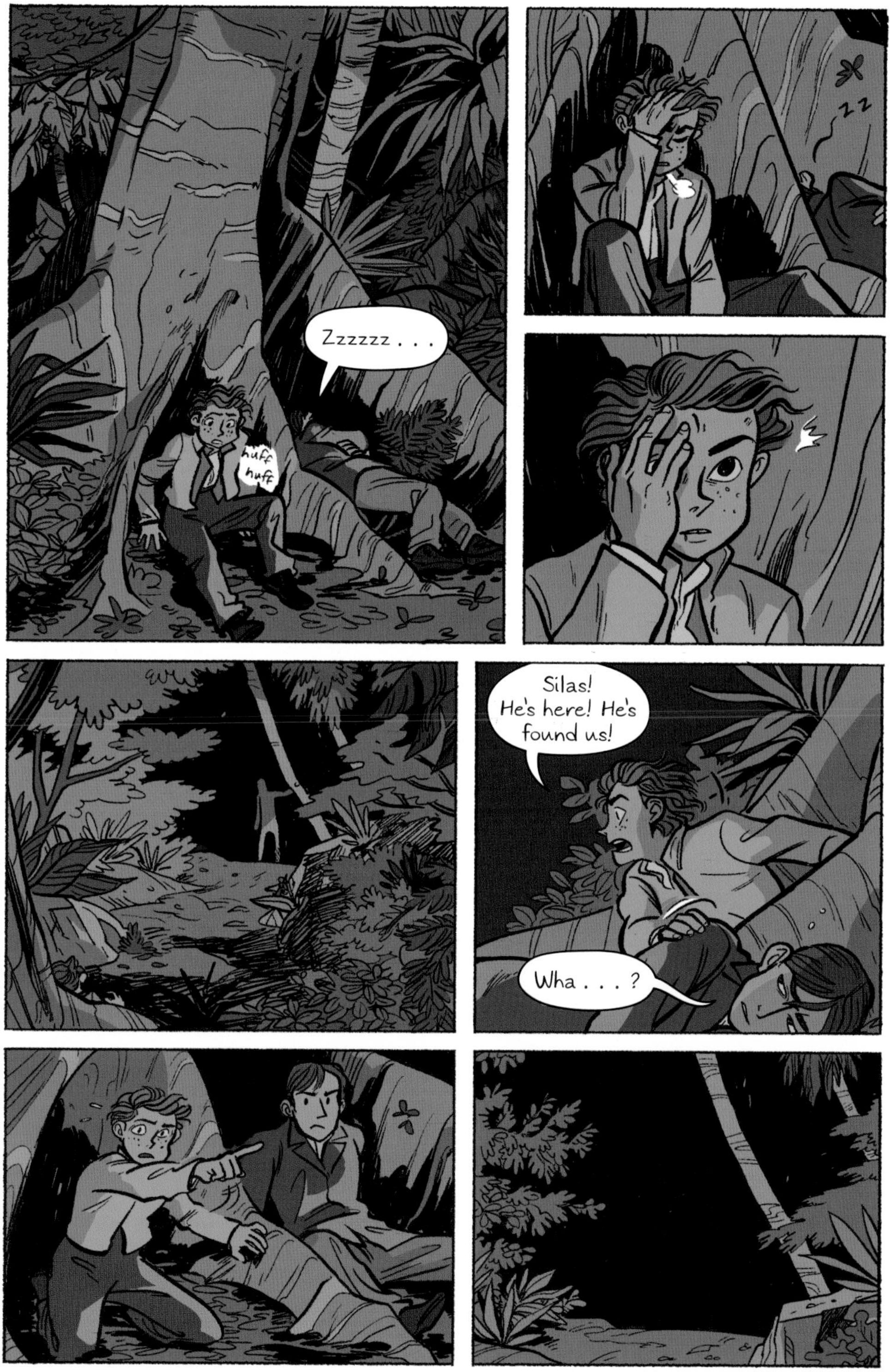
Zzzzzz . . .
huff huff
Silas! He's here! He's found us!
Wha . . . ?

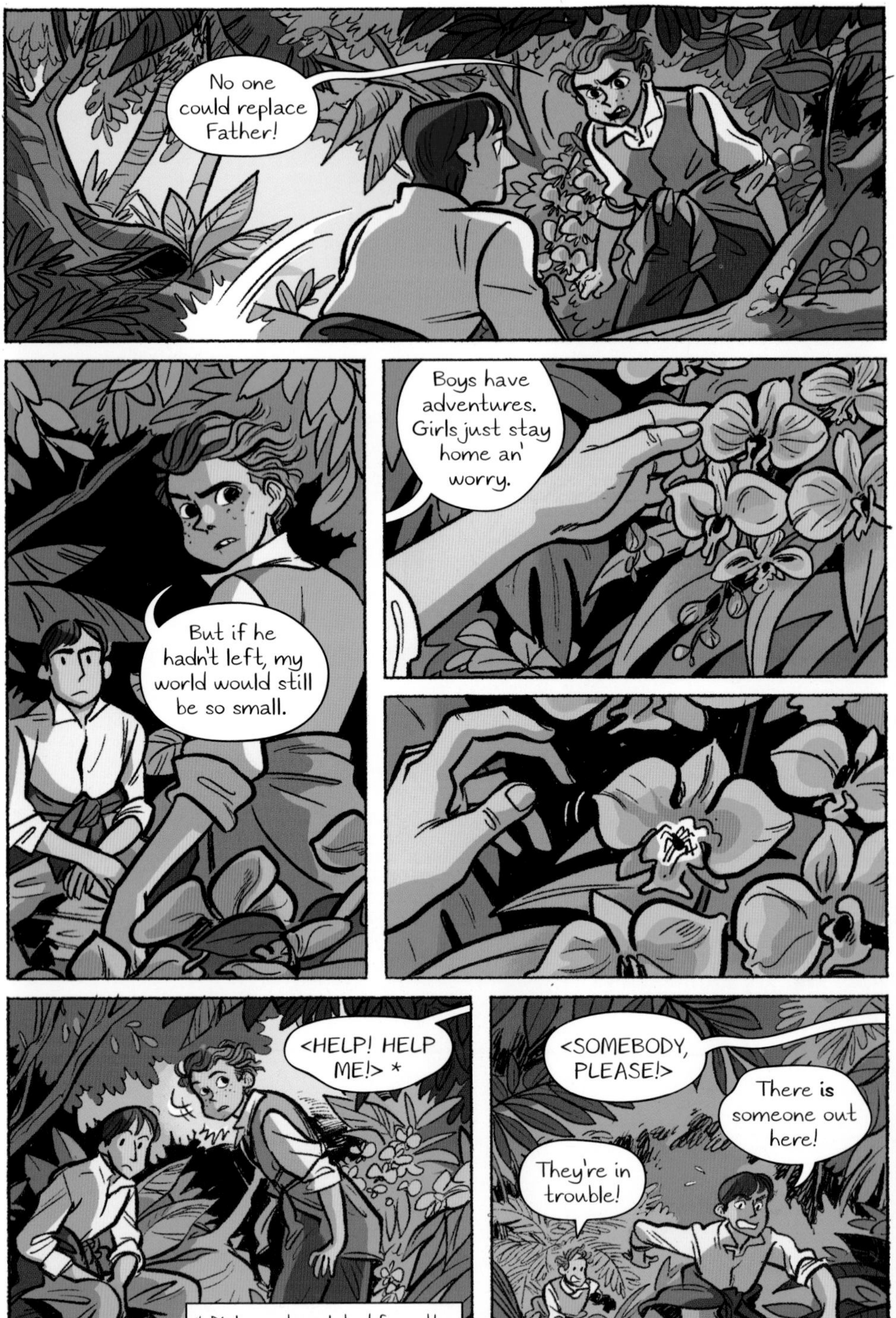
No one could replace Father!
Boys have adventures. Girls just stay home an' worry.
But if he hadn't left, my world would still be so small.
<HELP! HELP ME!> *
* Dialogue translated from the language of the Bribri tribe.
<SOMEBODY, PLEASE!>
There is someone out here!
They're in trouble!

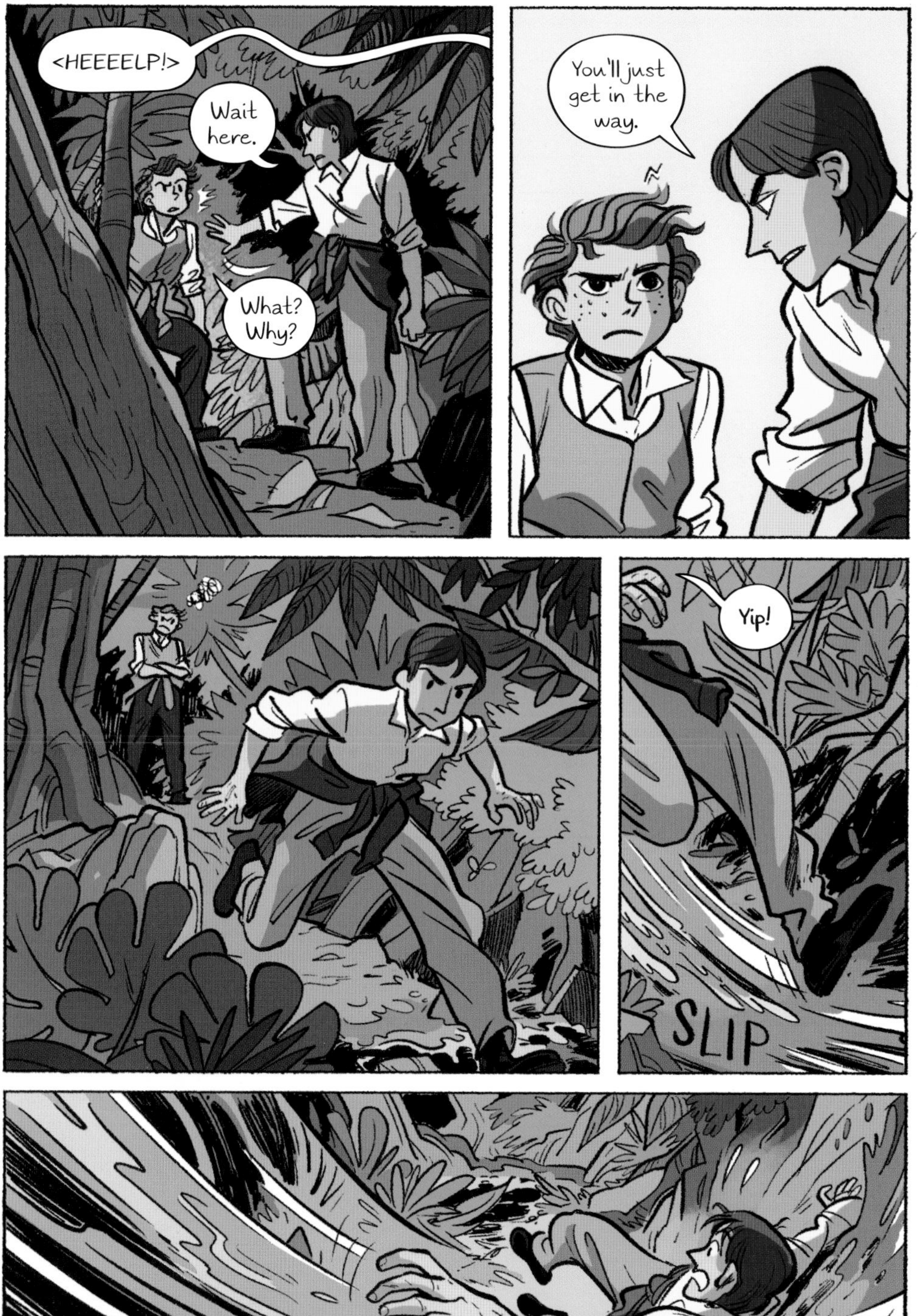
<HEEEELP!>
Wait here.
What? Why?
You'll just get in the way.
Yip!
SLIP

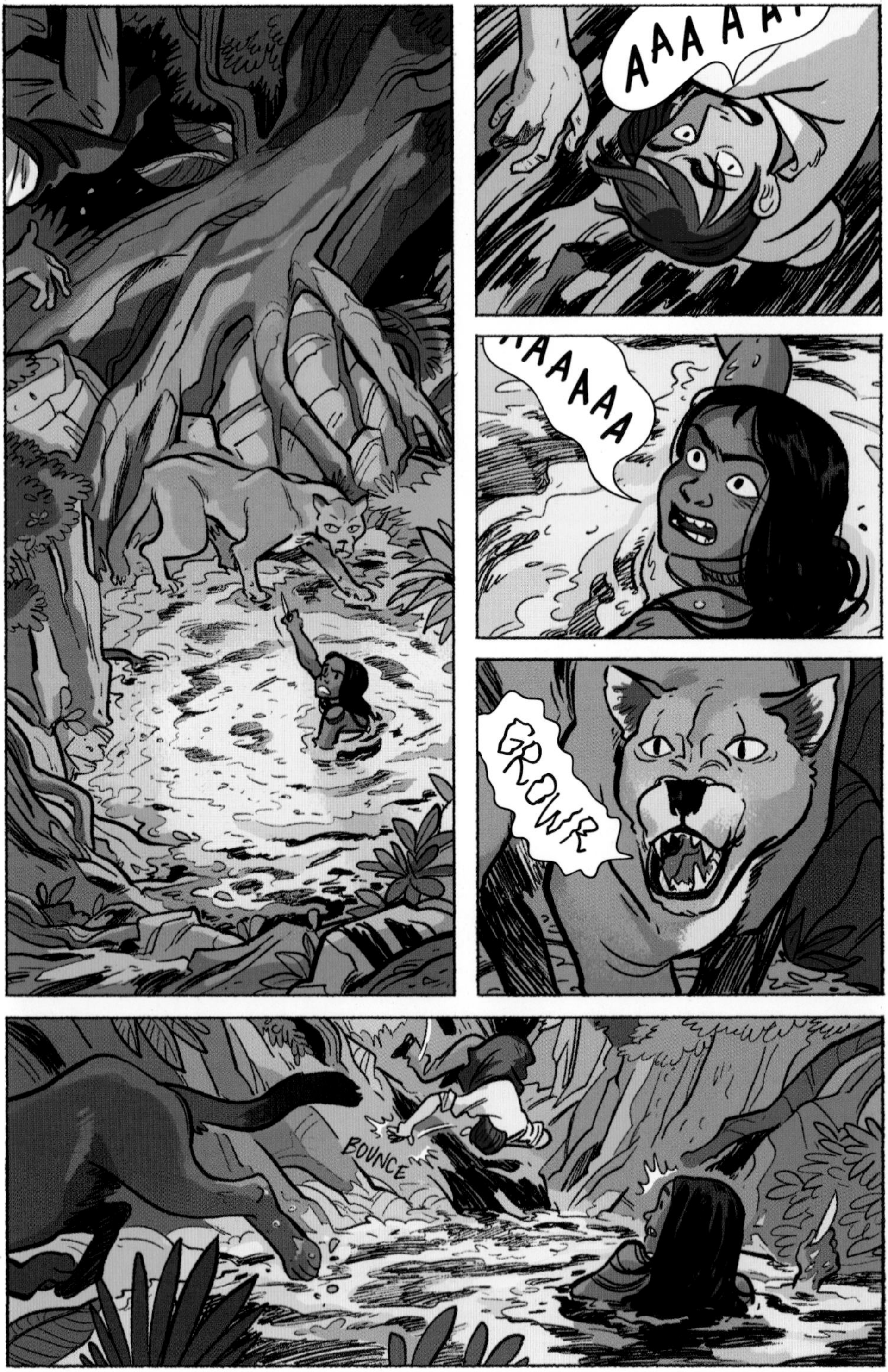
AAAAA
AAAAAA
GROWR
BOUNCE

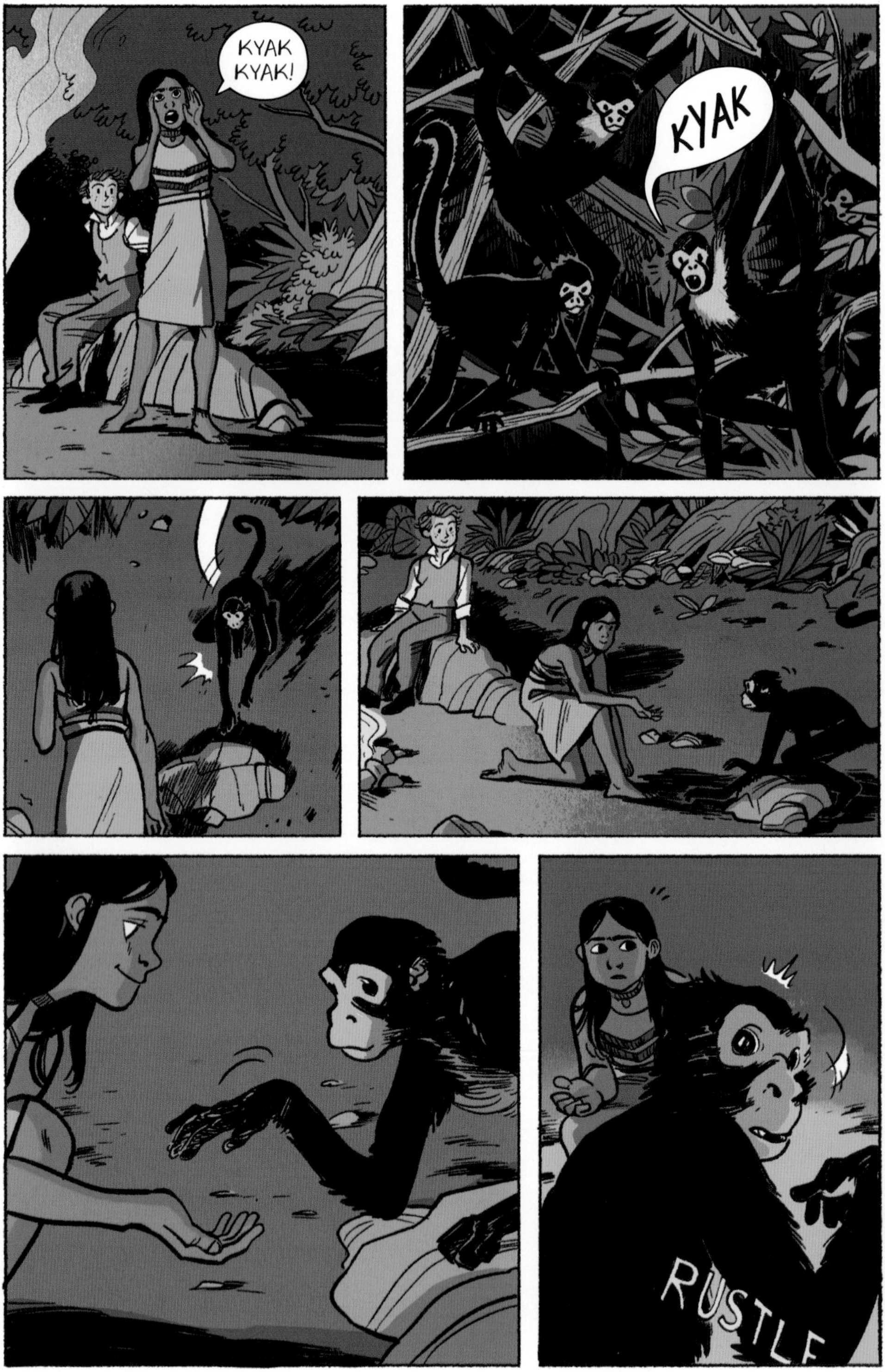
KYAK
KYAK!
KYAK
RUSTLE

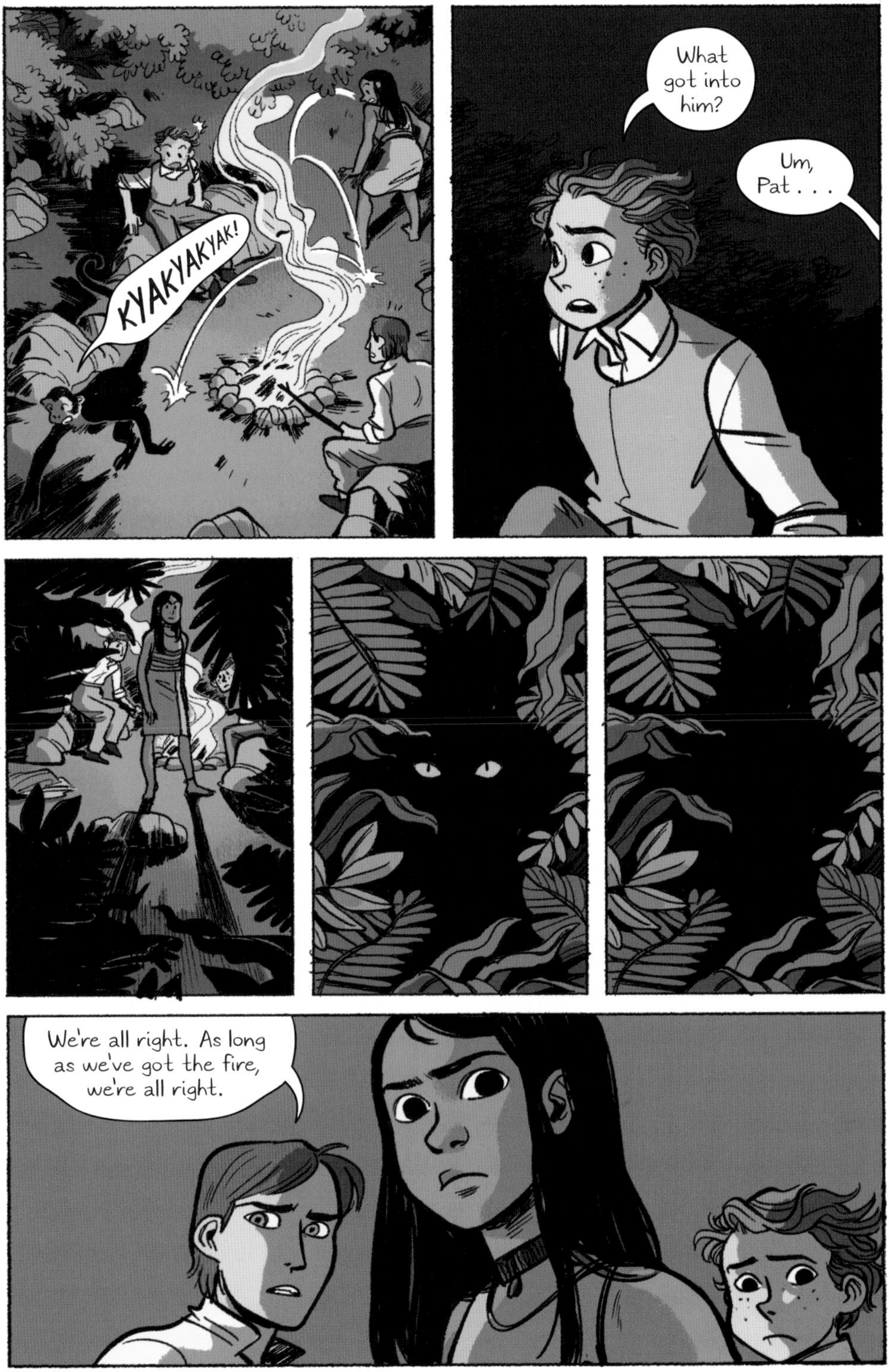
KYAKYAKYAK!
What got into him?
Um, Pat . . .
We're all right. As long as we've got the fire, we're all right.

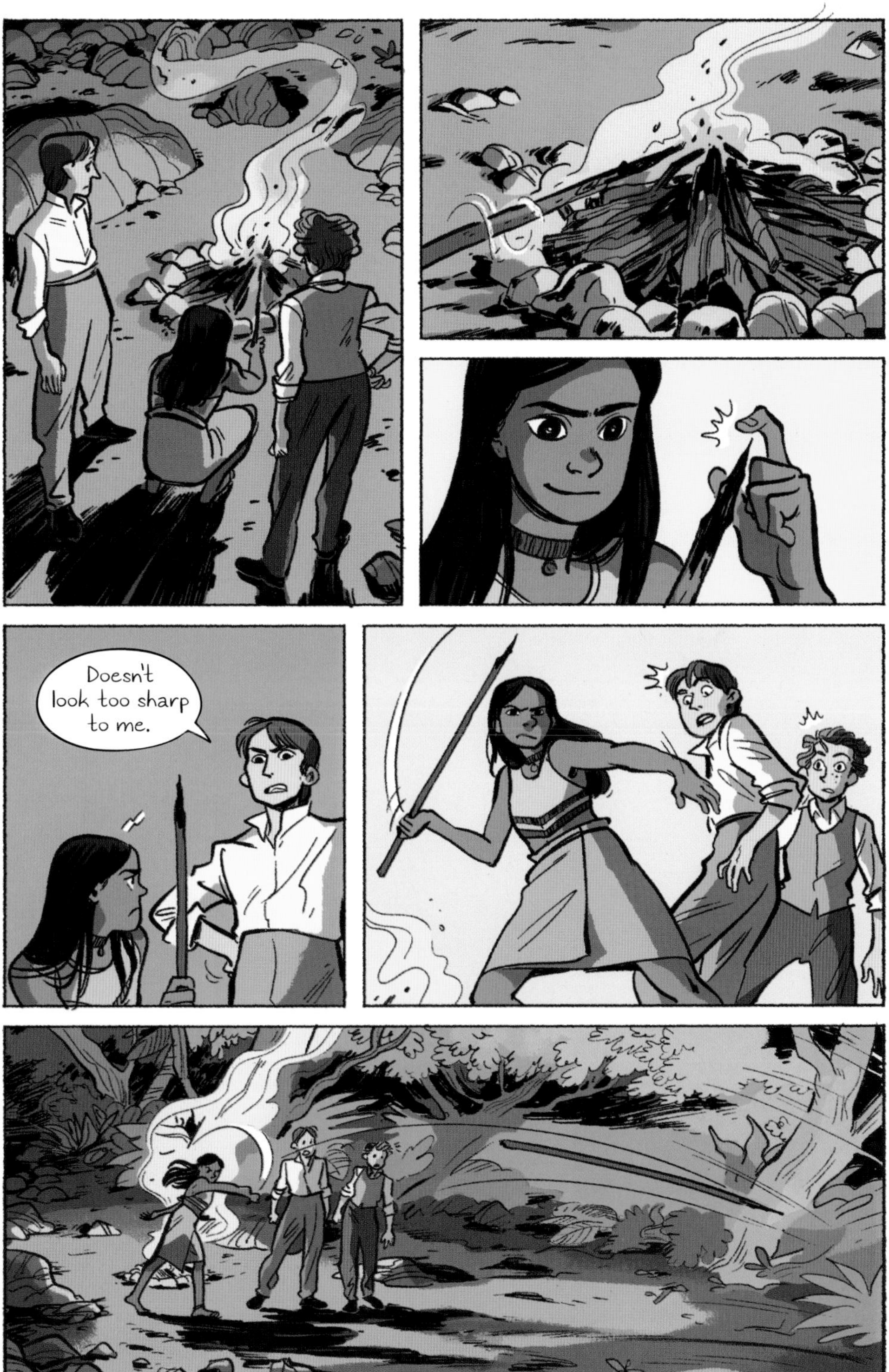
Doesn't
look too sharp
to me.

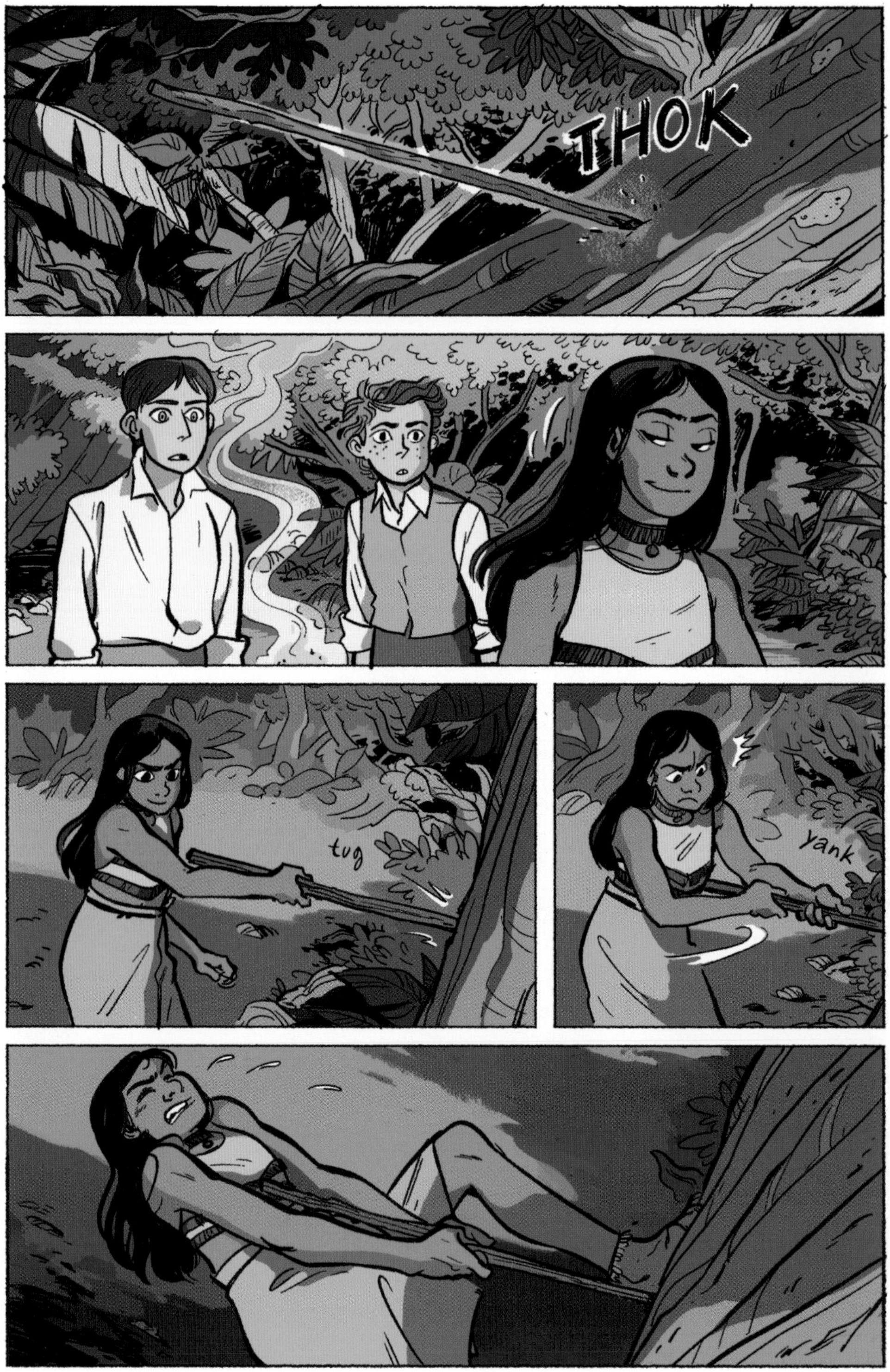
THOK
tug
yank

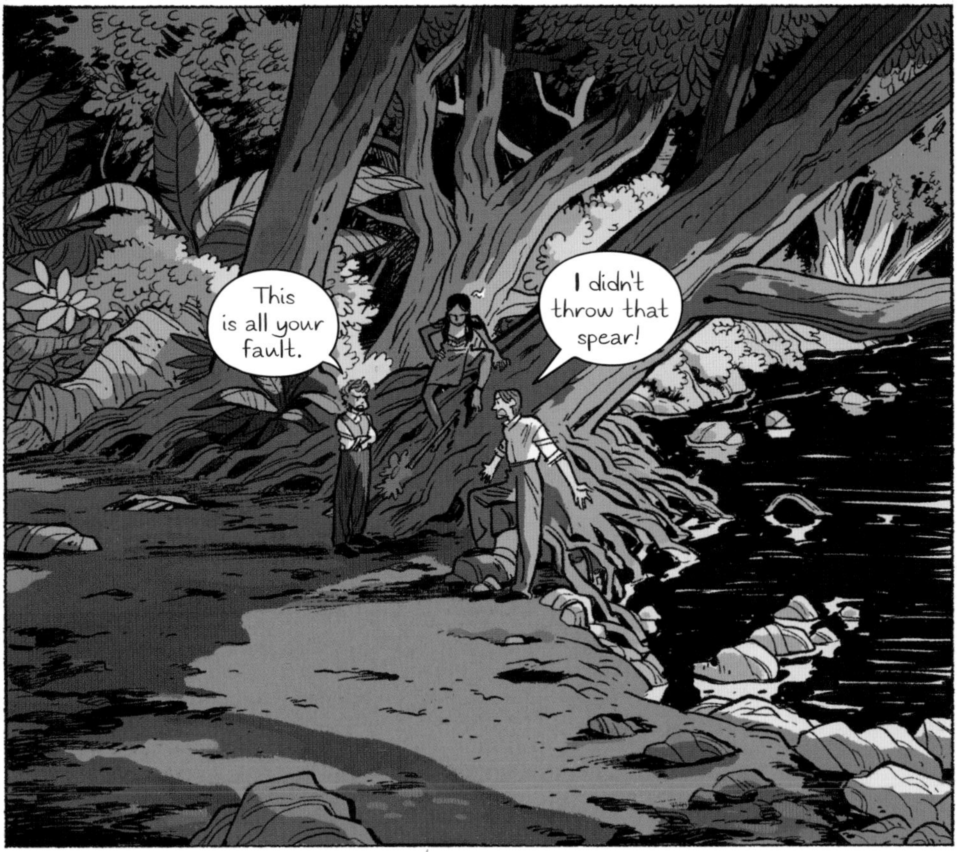
This is all your fault.
I didn't throw that spear!

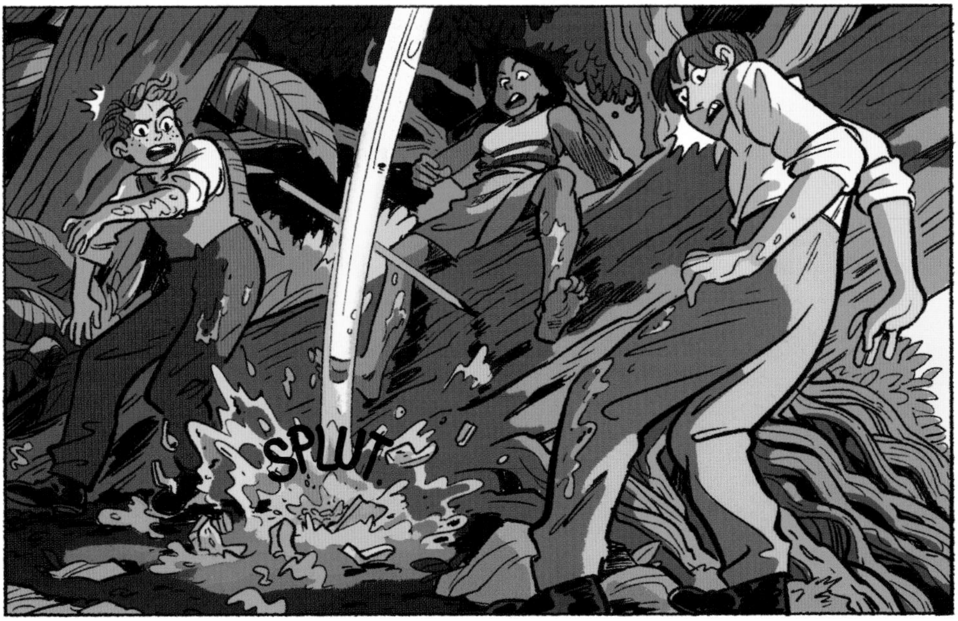
SPLUT

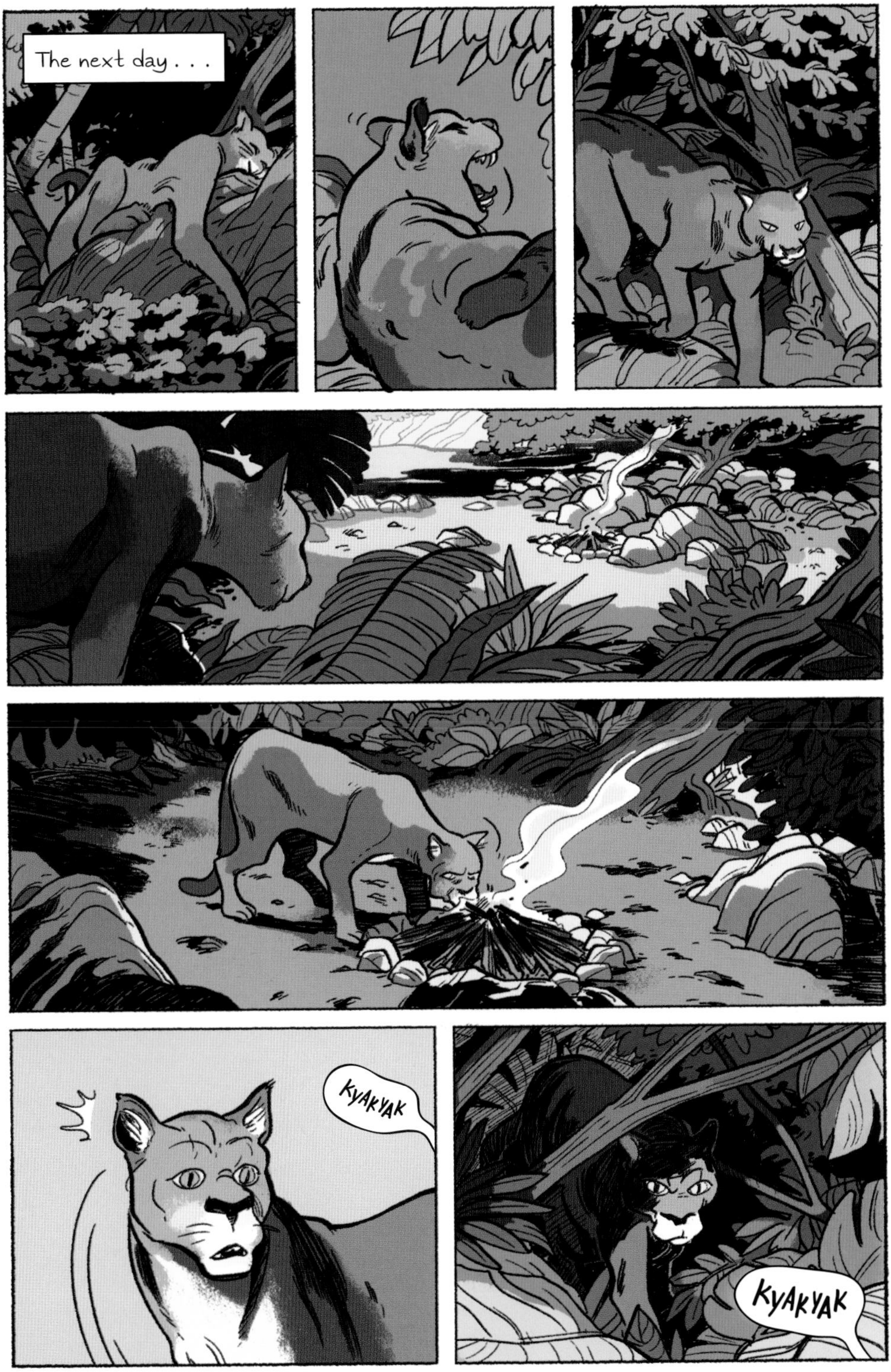
The next day . . .
KYAKYAK
KYAKYAK

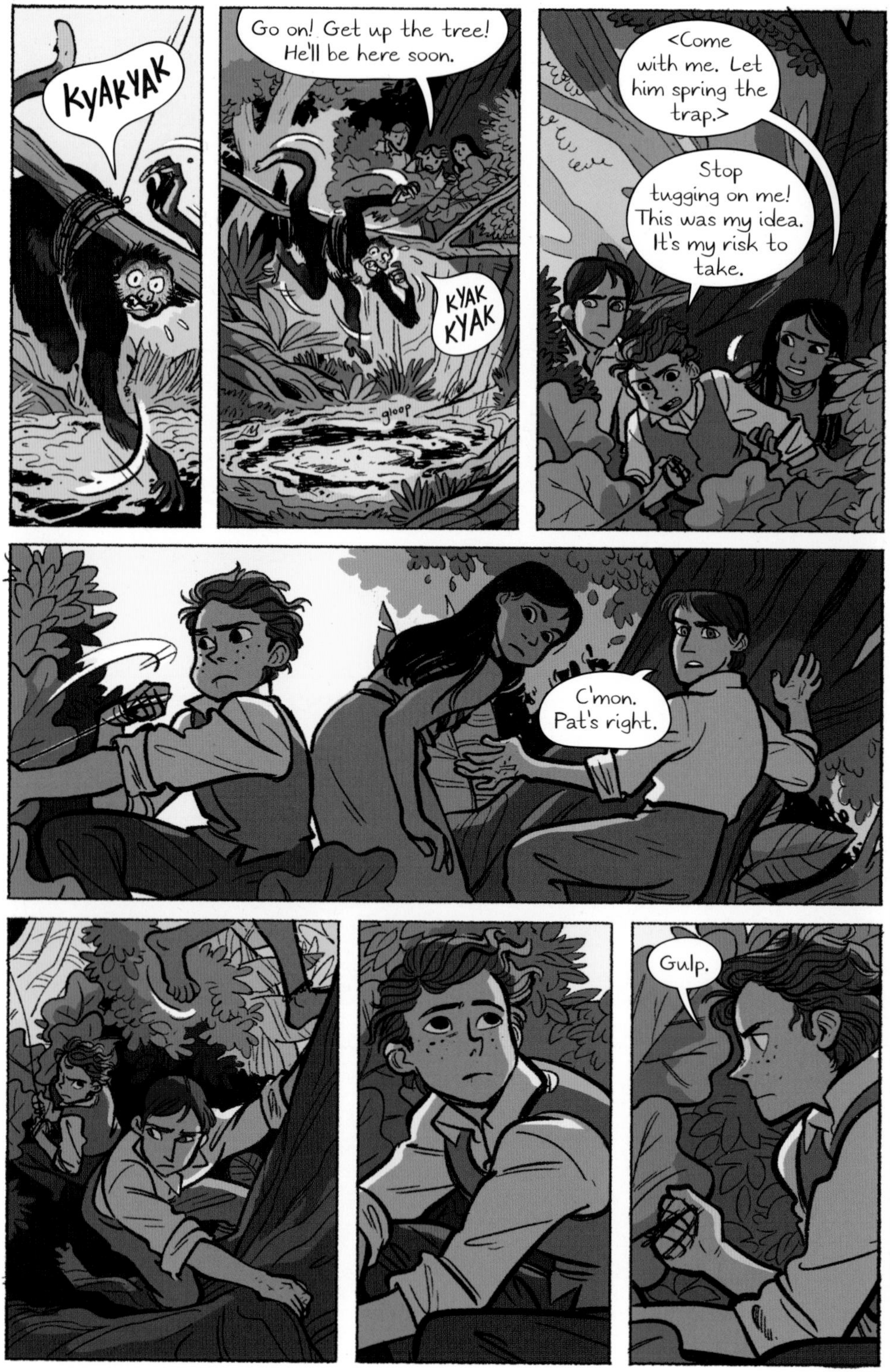
KYAKYAK
Go on! Get up the tree! He'll be here soon.
KYAK KYAK
gloop
<Come with me. Let him spring the trap.>
Stop tugging on me! This was my idea. It's my risk to take.
C'mon. Pat's right.
Gulp.

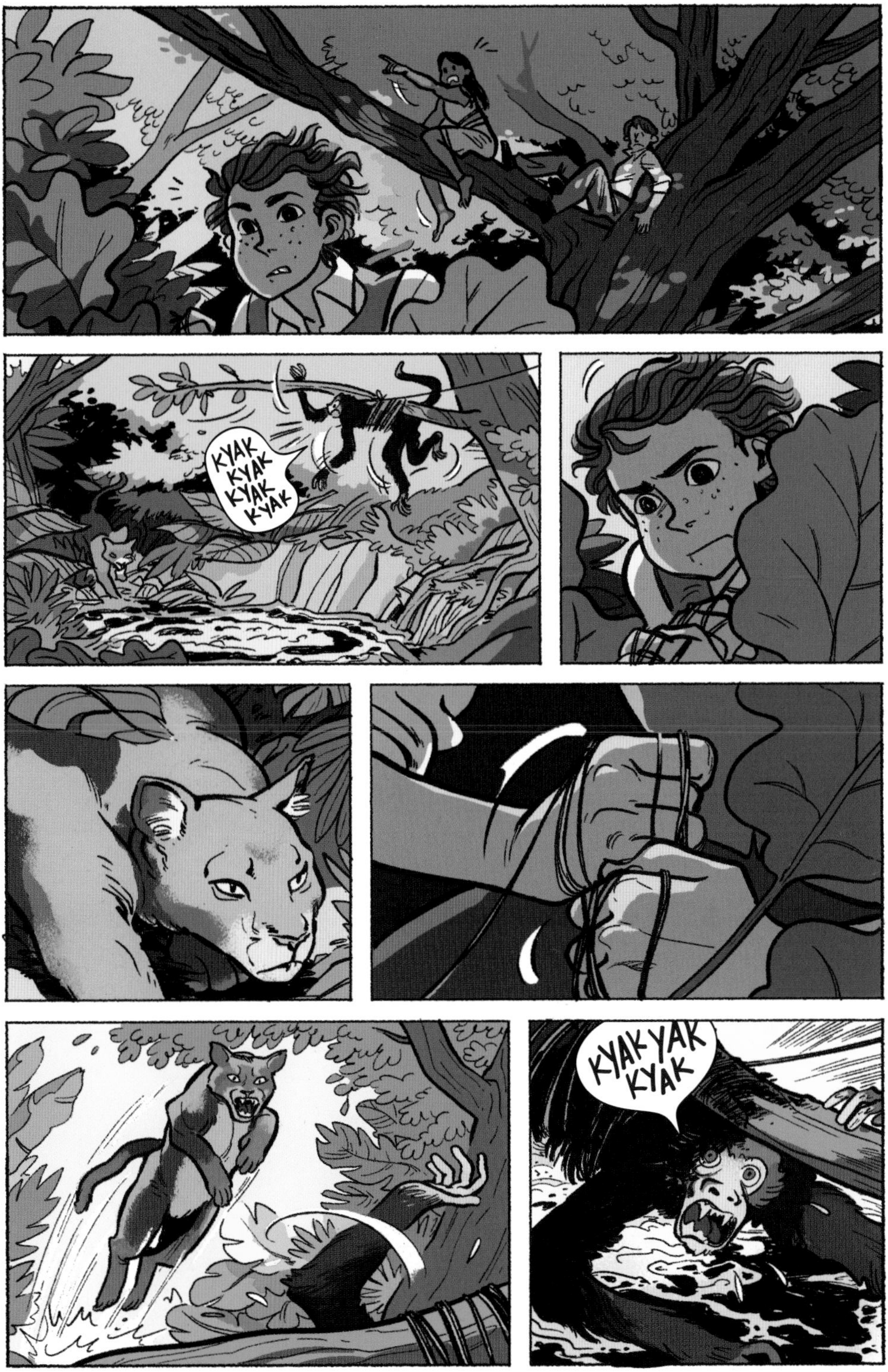
KYAK KYAK KYAK KYAK
KYAK YAK KYAK

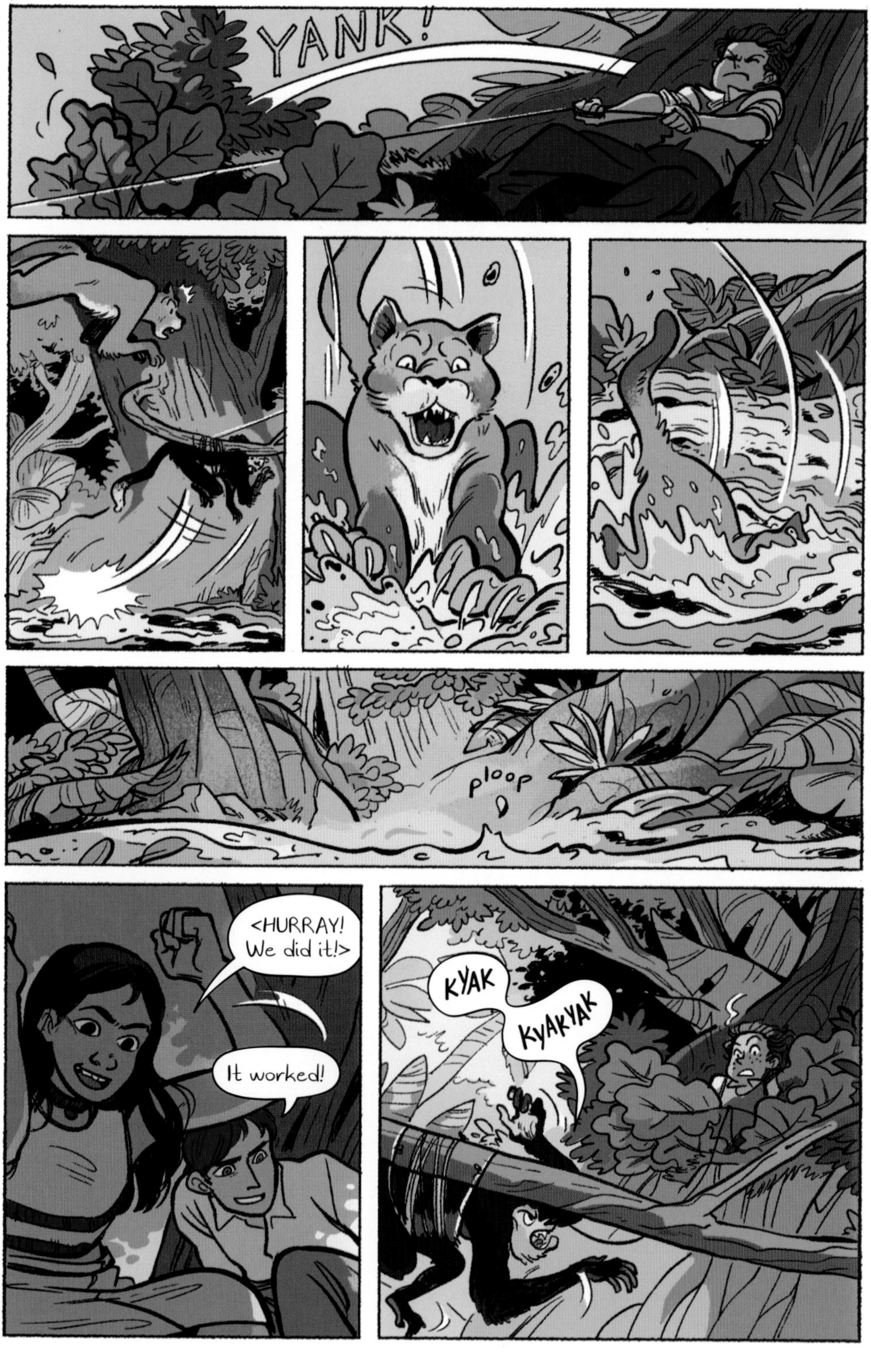
YANK!
ploop
<HURRAY! We did it!>
It worked!
KYAK
KYAKYAK

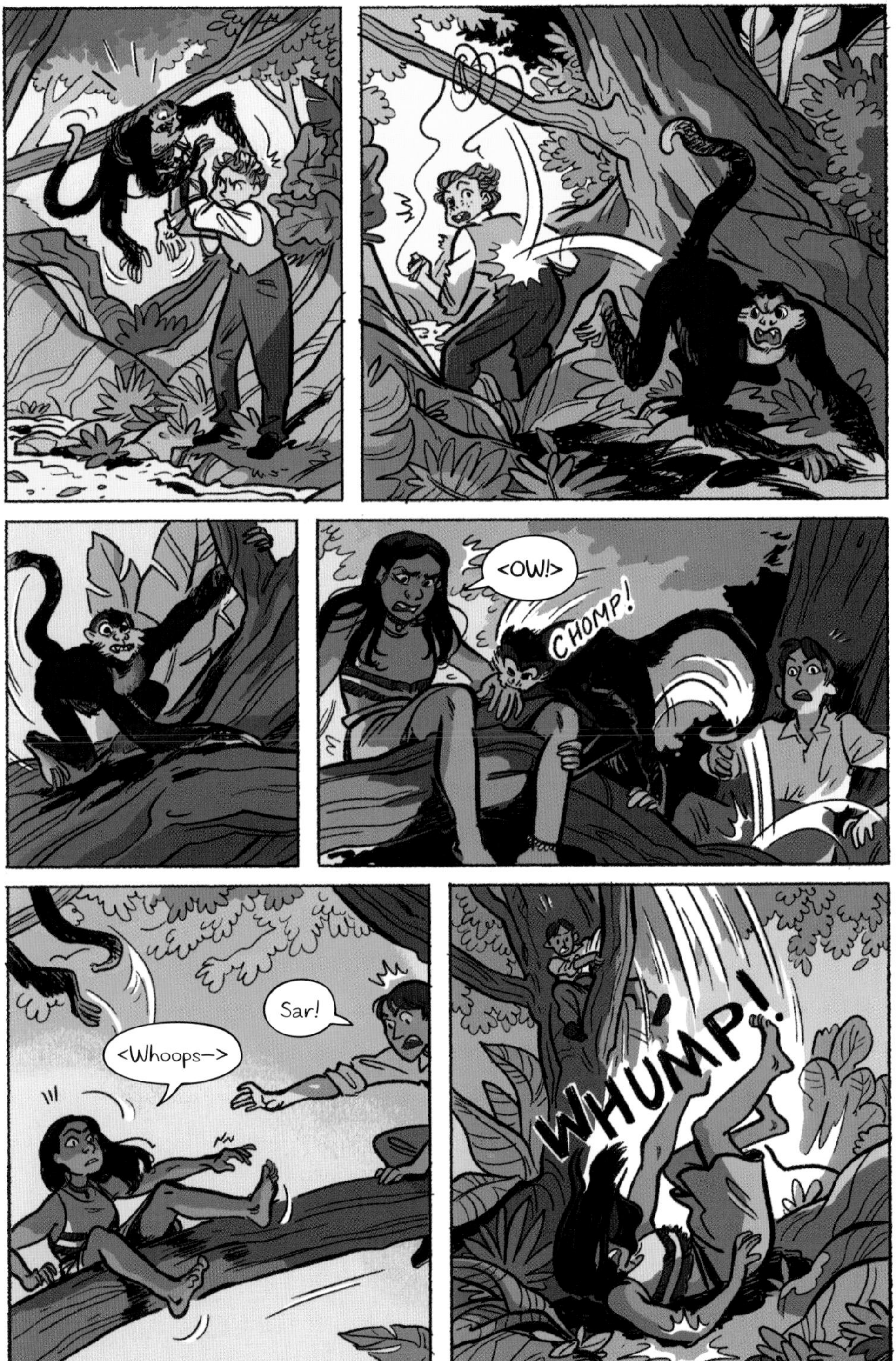
<OW!>
CHOMP!
Sar!
<Whoops—>
WHUMP!

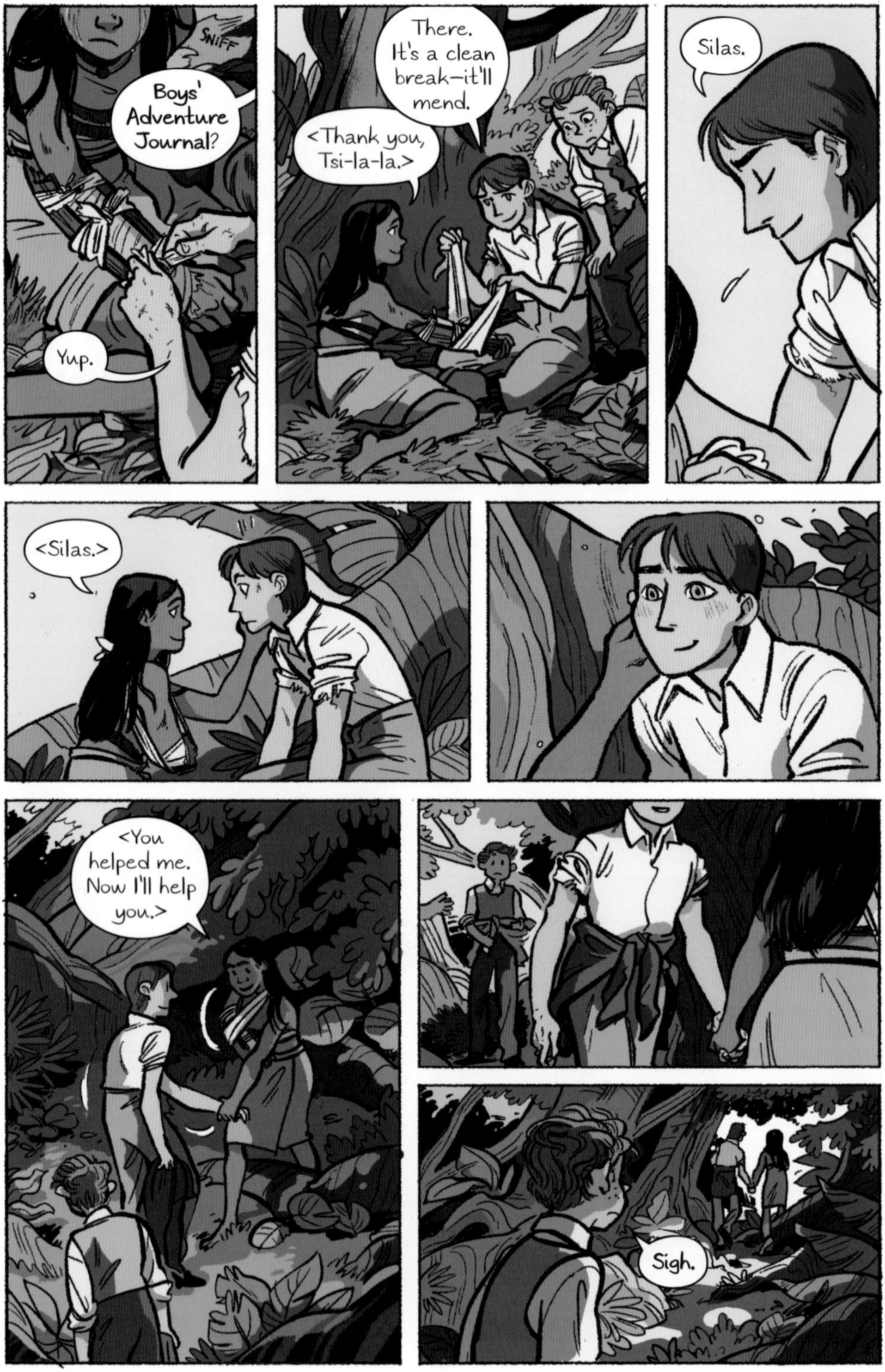
SNIFF
Boys' Adventure Journal?
Yup.
There. It's a clean break—it'll mend.
<Thank you, Tsi-la-la.>
Silas.
<Silas.>
<You helped me. Now I'll help you.>
Sigh.

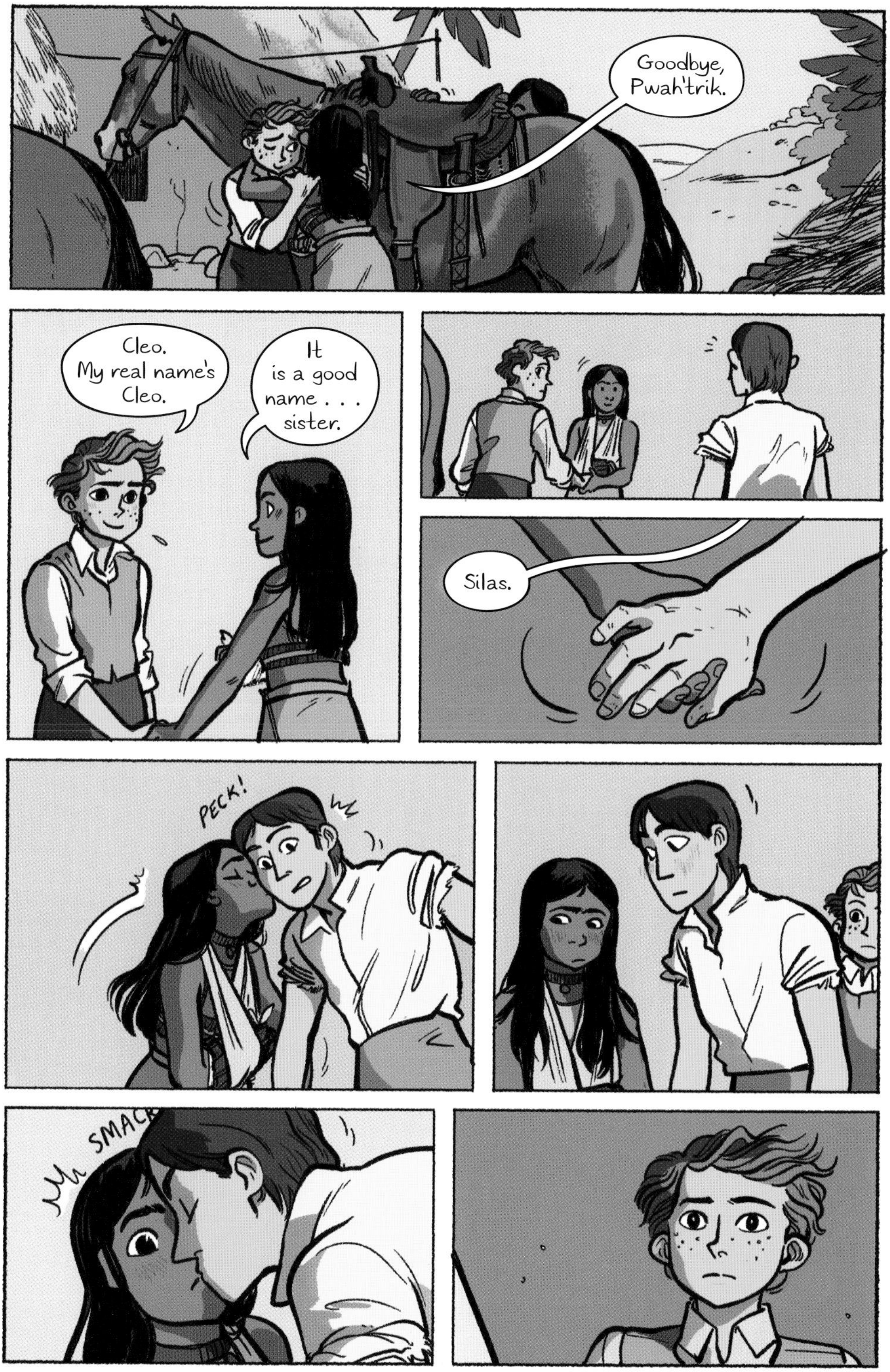
Goodbye, Pwah'trik.
Cleo. My real name's Cleo.
It is a good name . . . sister.
Silas.
PECK!
SMACK

180

# CHAPTER EIGHT
# *EL CALEUCHE*

185

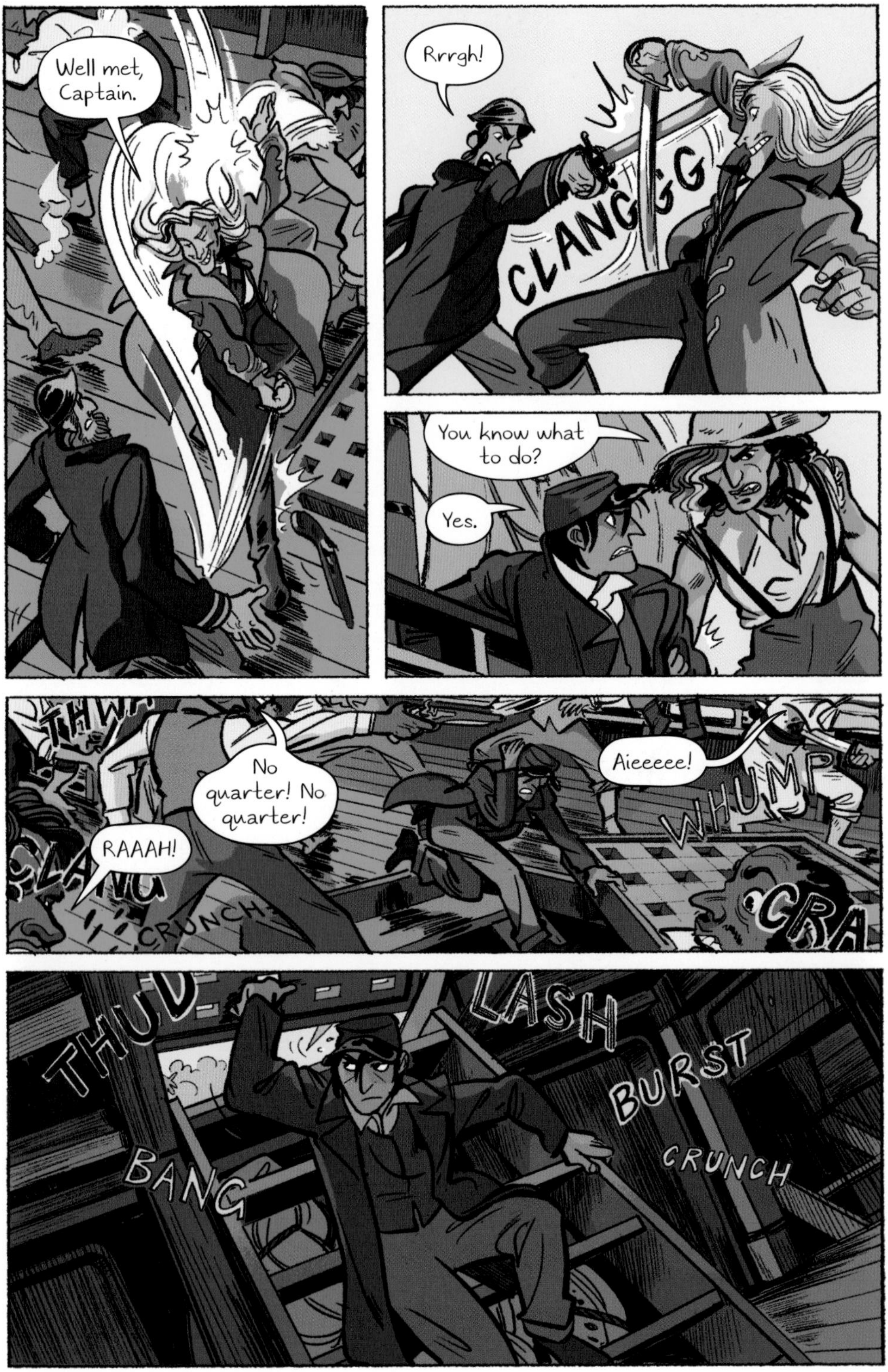
Well met, Captain.
Rrrgh!
CLANGGG
You know what to do?
Yes.
THWA
No quarter! No quarter!
Aieeeee!
WHUMP
RAAAH!
CLANG
CRUNCH
CRA
THUD
LASH
BURST
BANG
CRUNCH

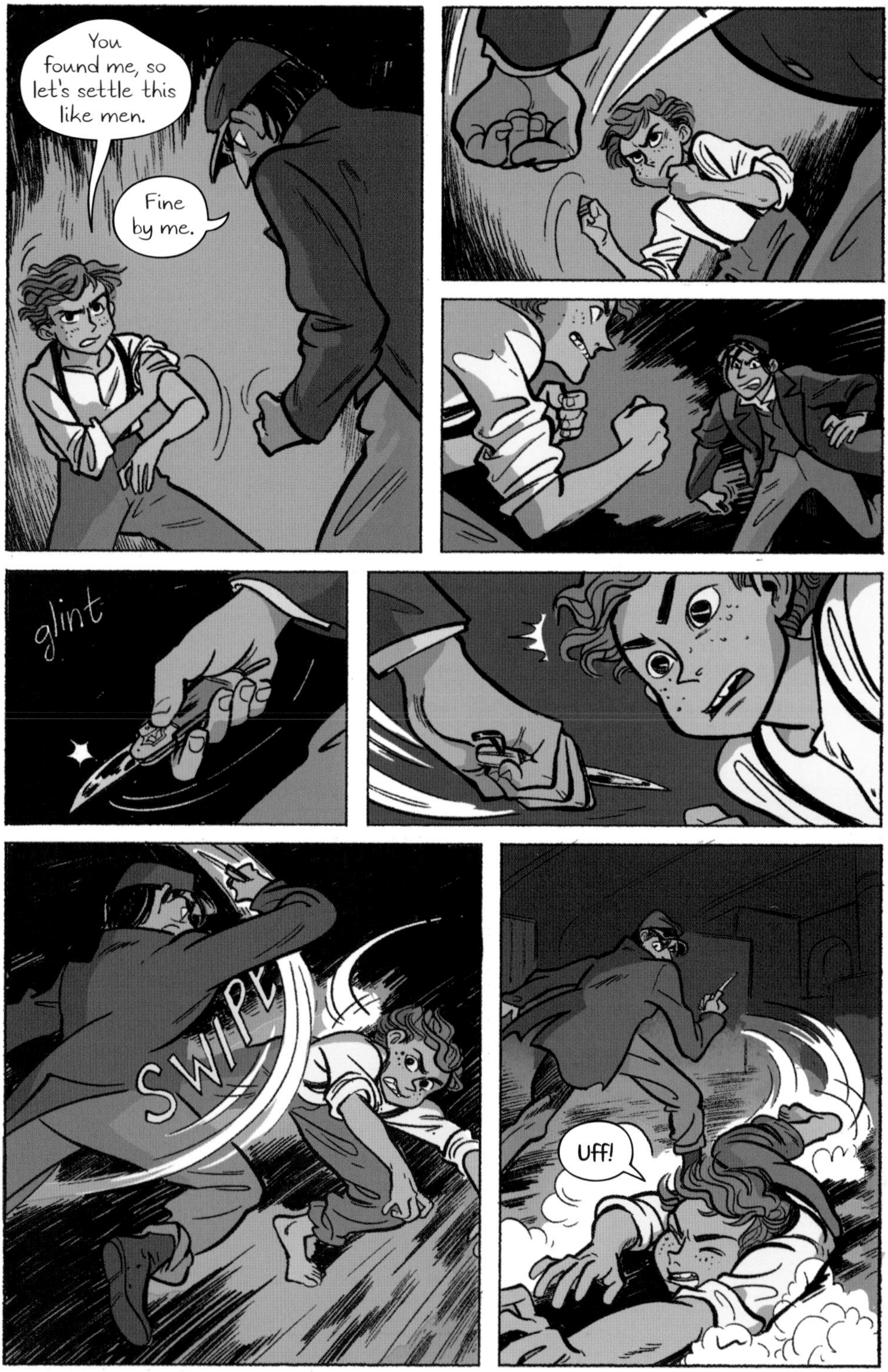
You found me, so let's settle this like men.
Fine by me.
glint
SWIPE
Uff!

192

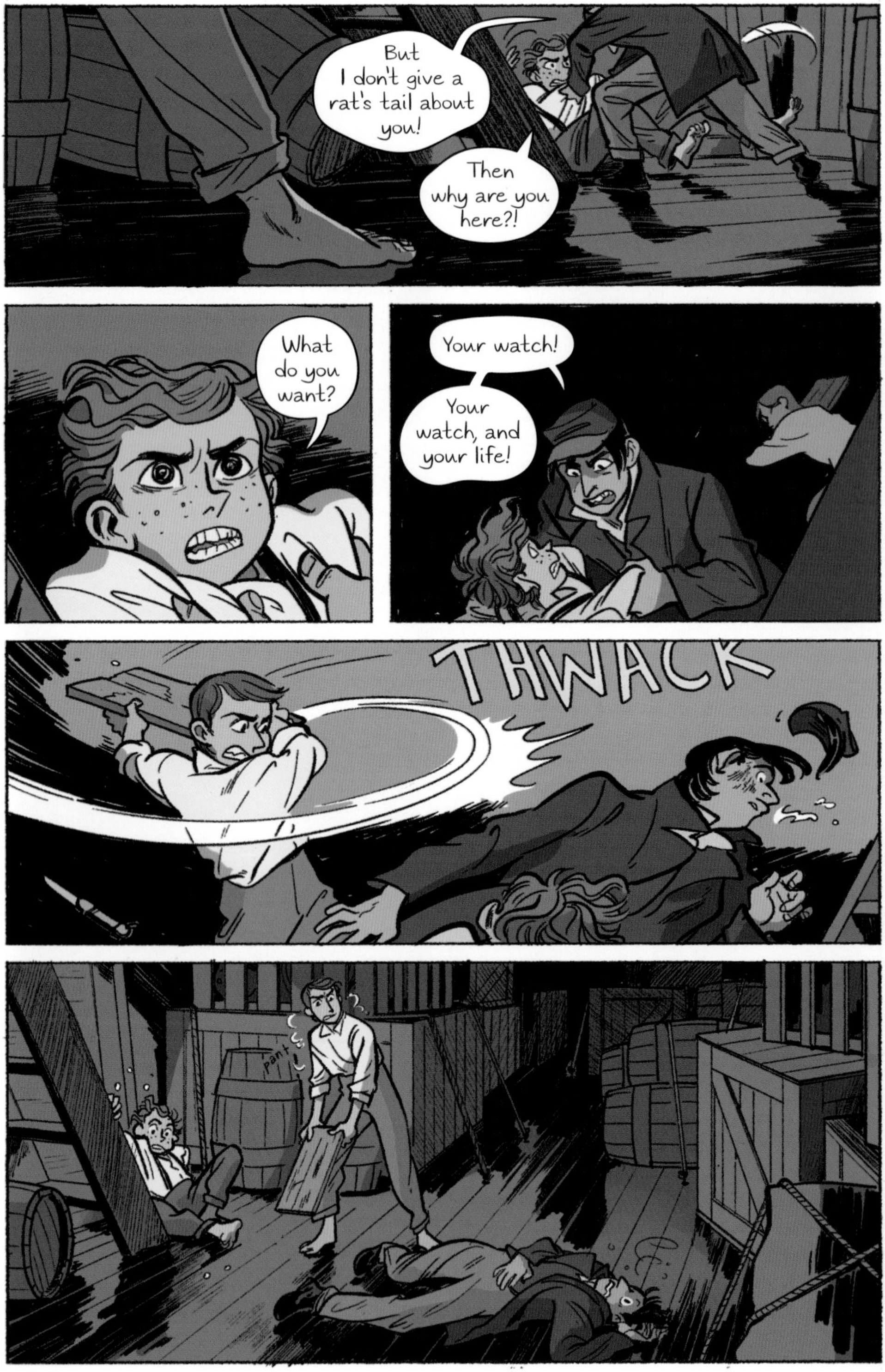
But I don't give a rat's tail about you!
Then why are you here?!
What do you want?
Your watch!
Your watch, and your life!
THWACK
pant

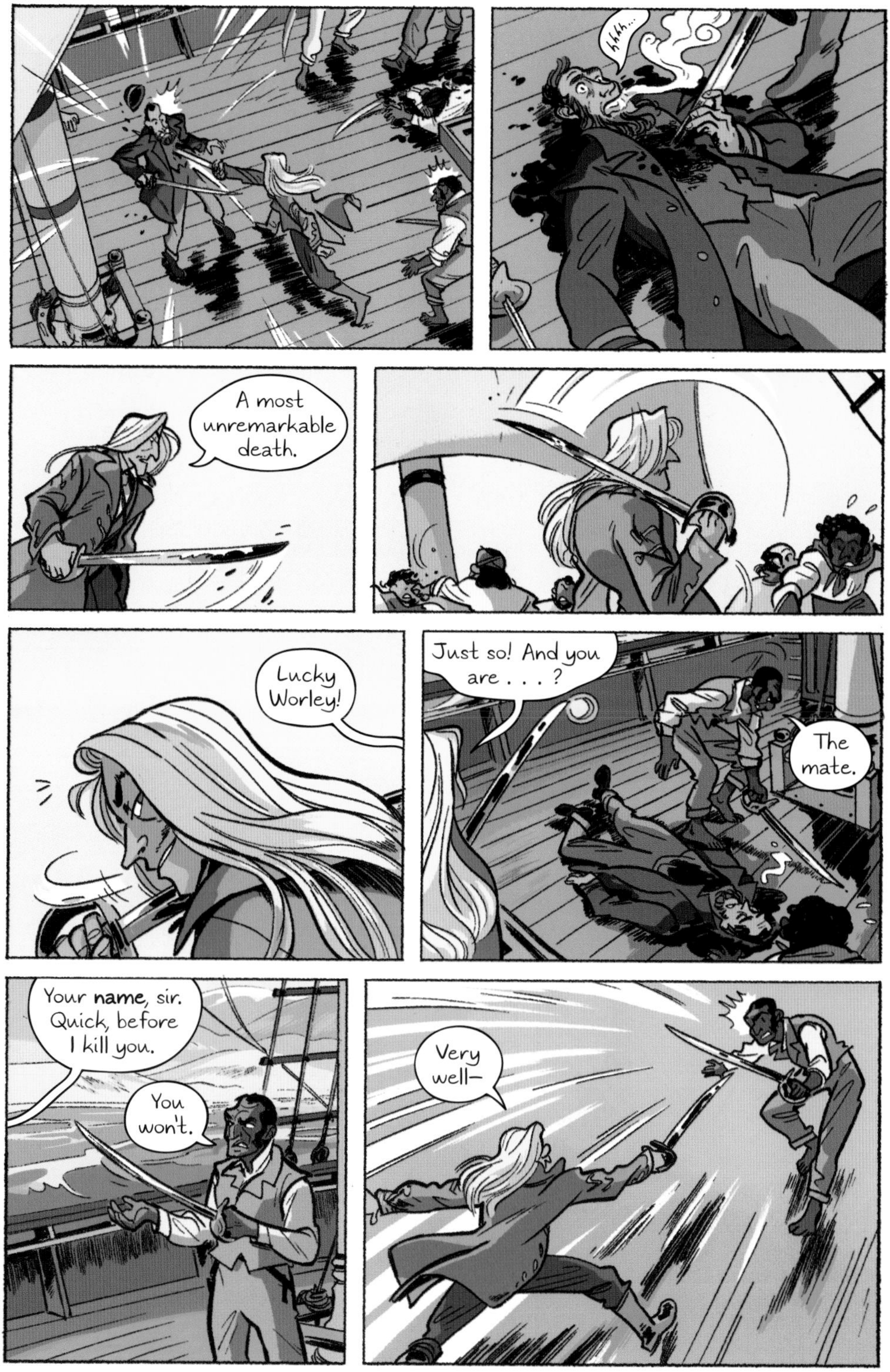
hhh...
A most unremarkable death.
Lucky Worley!
Just so! And you are . . . ?
The mate.
Your **name**, sir. Quick, before I kill you.
You won't.
Very well—

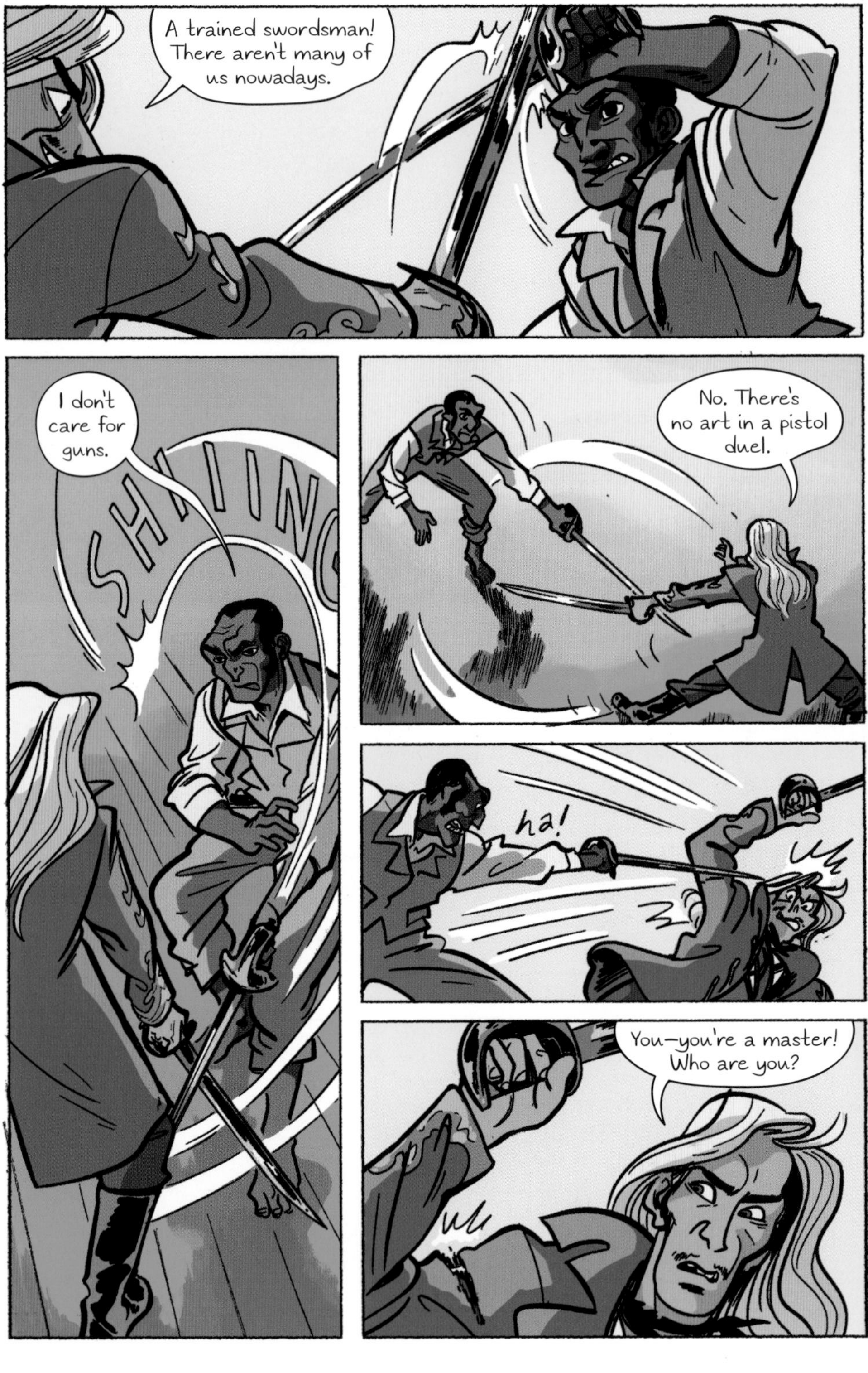
A trained swordsman! There aren't many of us nowadays.
I don't care for guns.
SHIIING
No. There's no art in a pistol duel.
ha!
You—you're a master! Who are you?

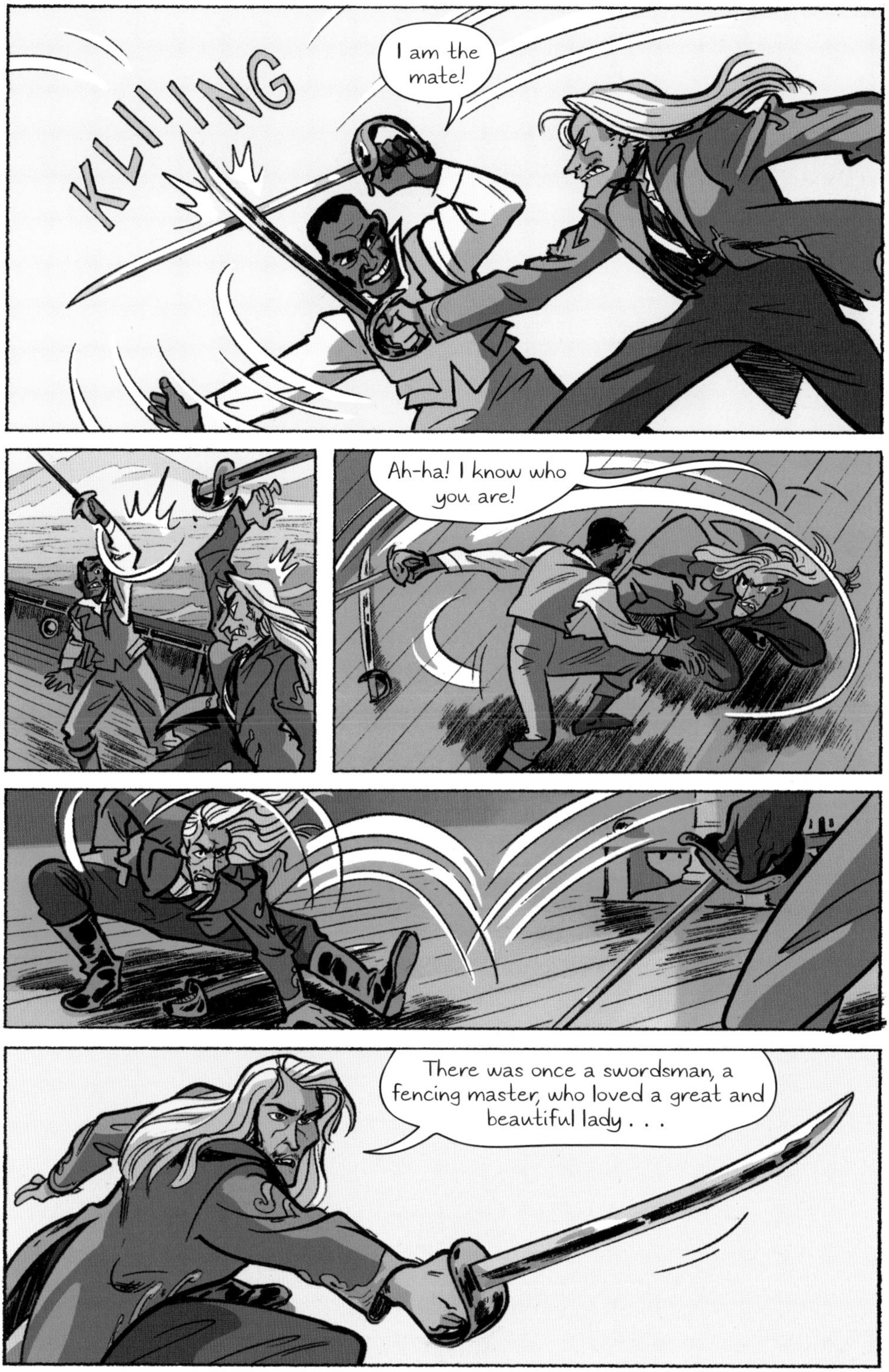
KLIIING
I am the mate!
Ah-ha! I know who you are!
There was once a swordsman, a fencing master, who loved a great and beautiful lady . . .

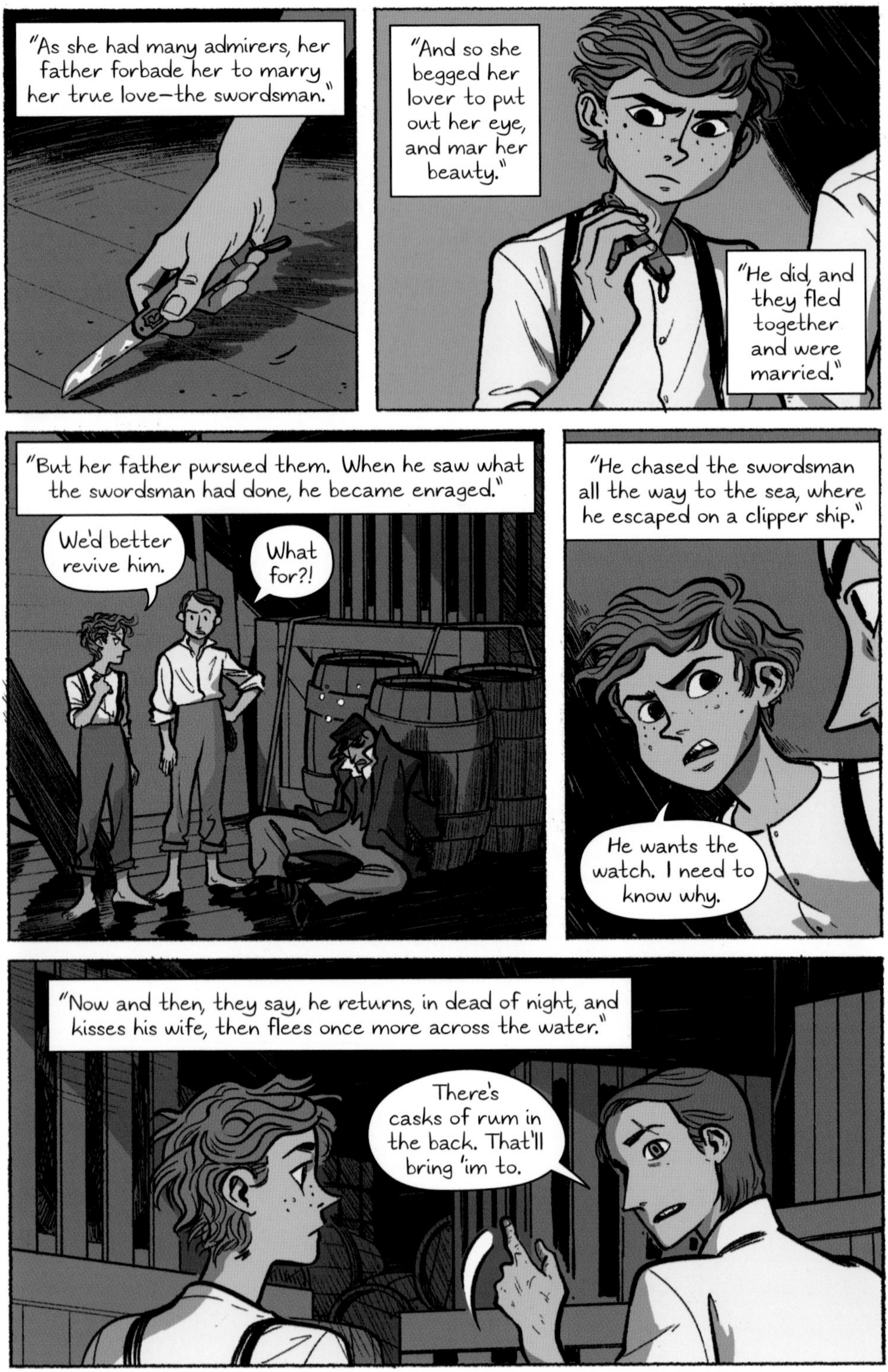
"As she had many admirers, her father forbade her to marry her true love—the swordsman."
"And so she begged her lover to put out her eye, and mar her beauty."
"He did, and they fled together and were married."
"But her father pursued them. When he saw what the swordsman had done, he became enraged."
We'd better revive him.
What for?!
"He chased the swordsman all the way to the sea, where he escaped on a clipper ship."
He wants the watch. I need to know why.
"Now and then, they say, he returns, in dead of night, and kisses his wife, then flees once more across the water."
There's casks of rum in the back. That'll bring 'im to.

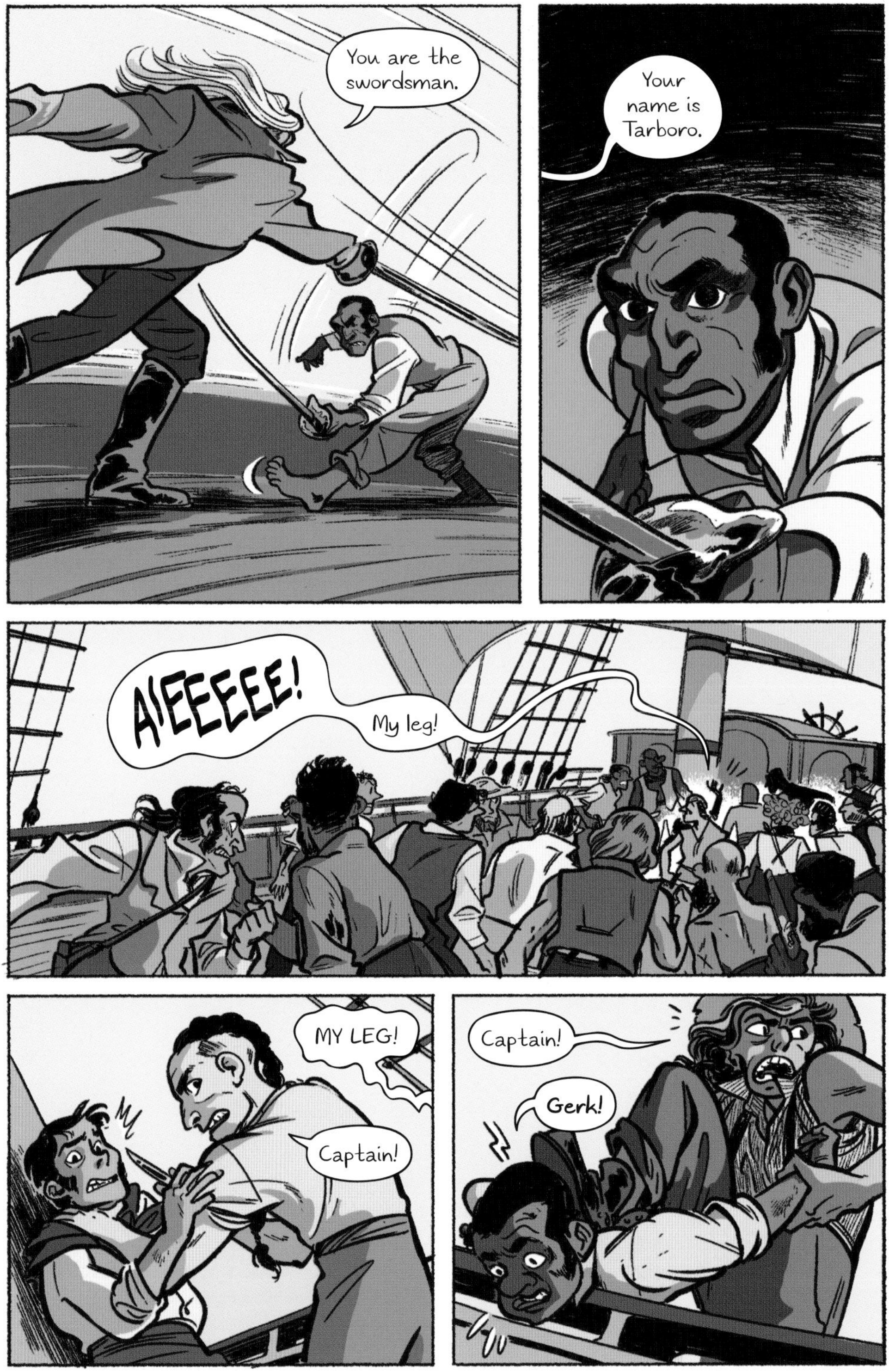
You are the swordsman.
Your name is Tarboro.
AIEEEEE!
My leg!
MY LEG!
Captain!
Captain!
Gerk!

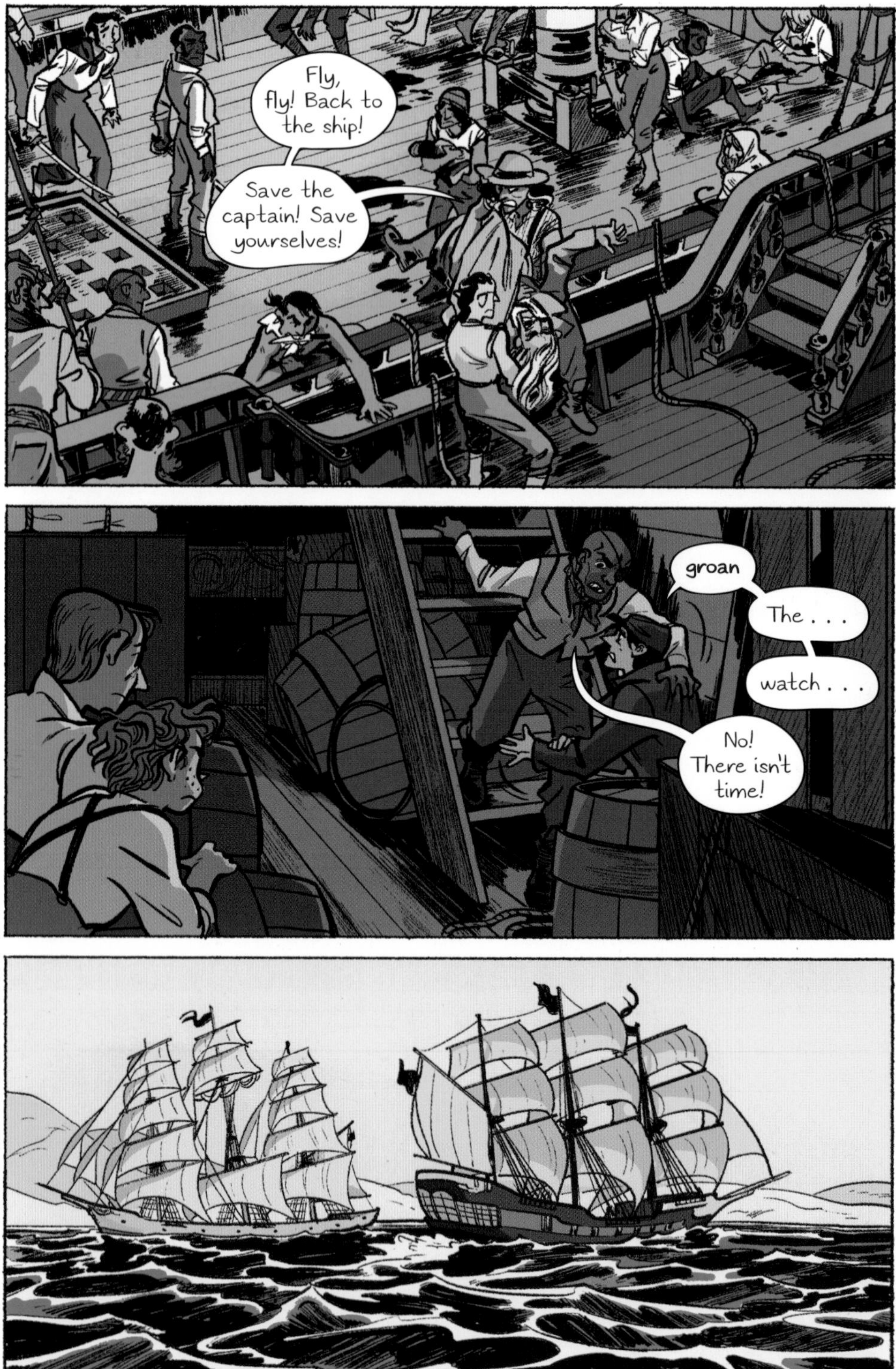
Fly, fly! Back to the ship!
Save the captain! Save yourselves!
groan
The . . .
watch . . .
No! There isn't time!

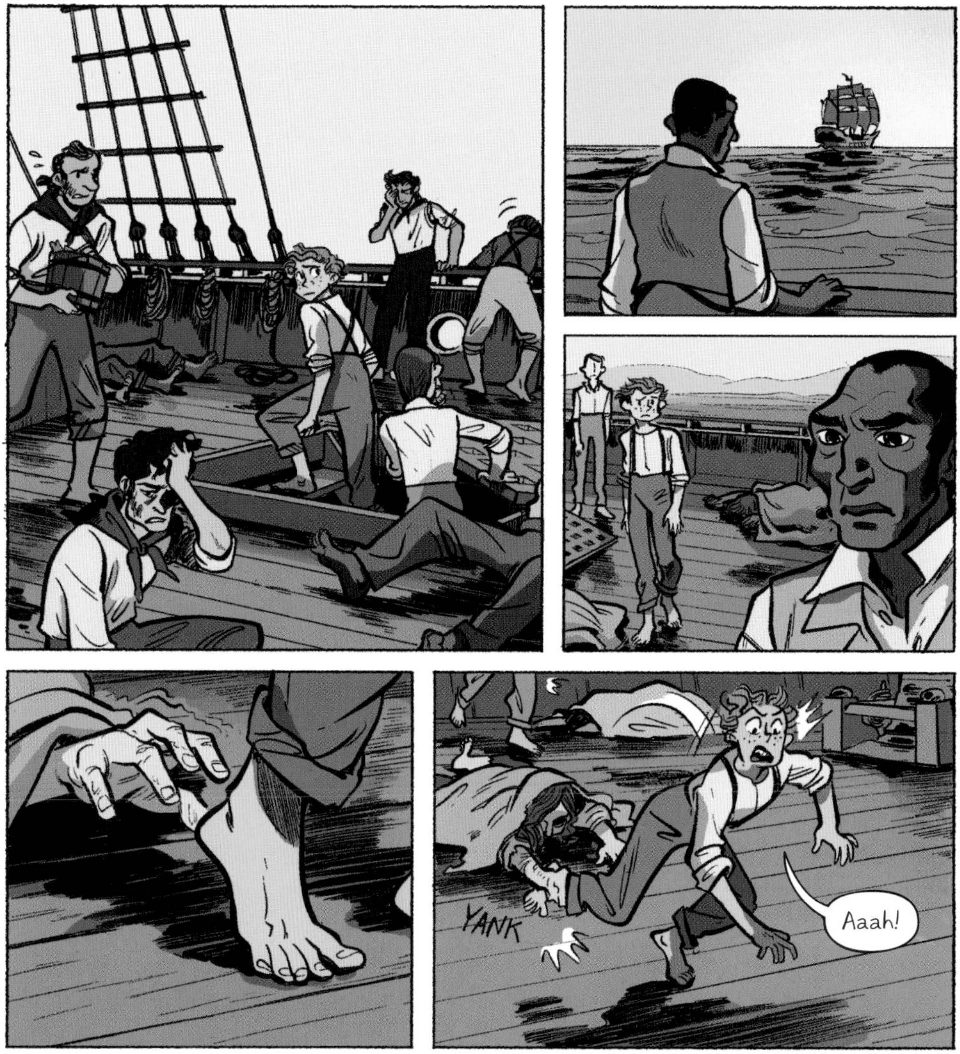
YANK
Aaah!
AAAAAAH!

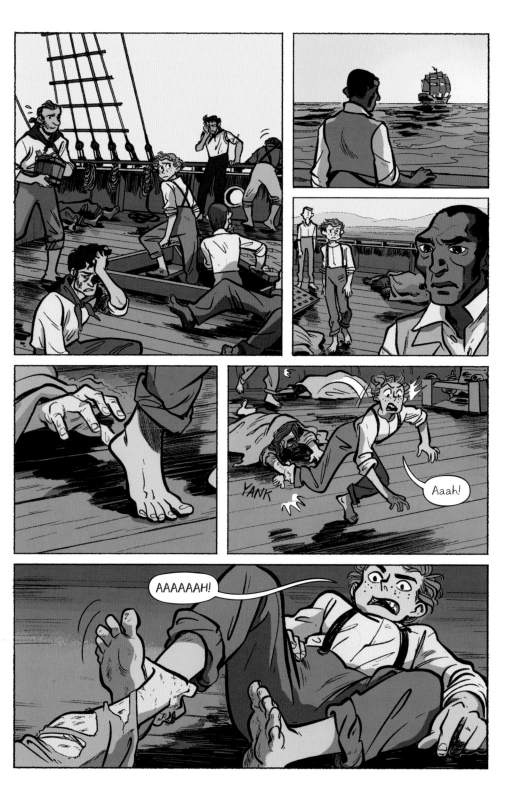

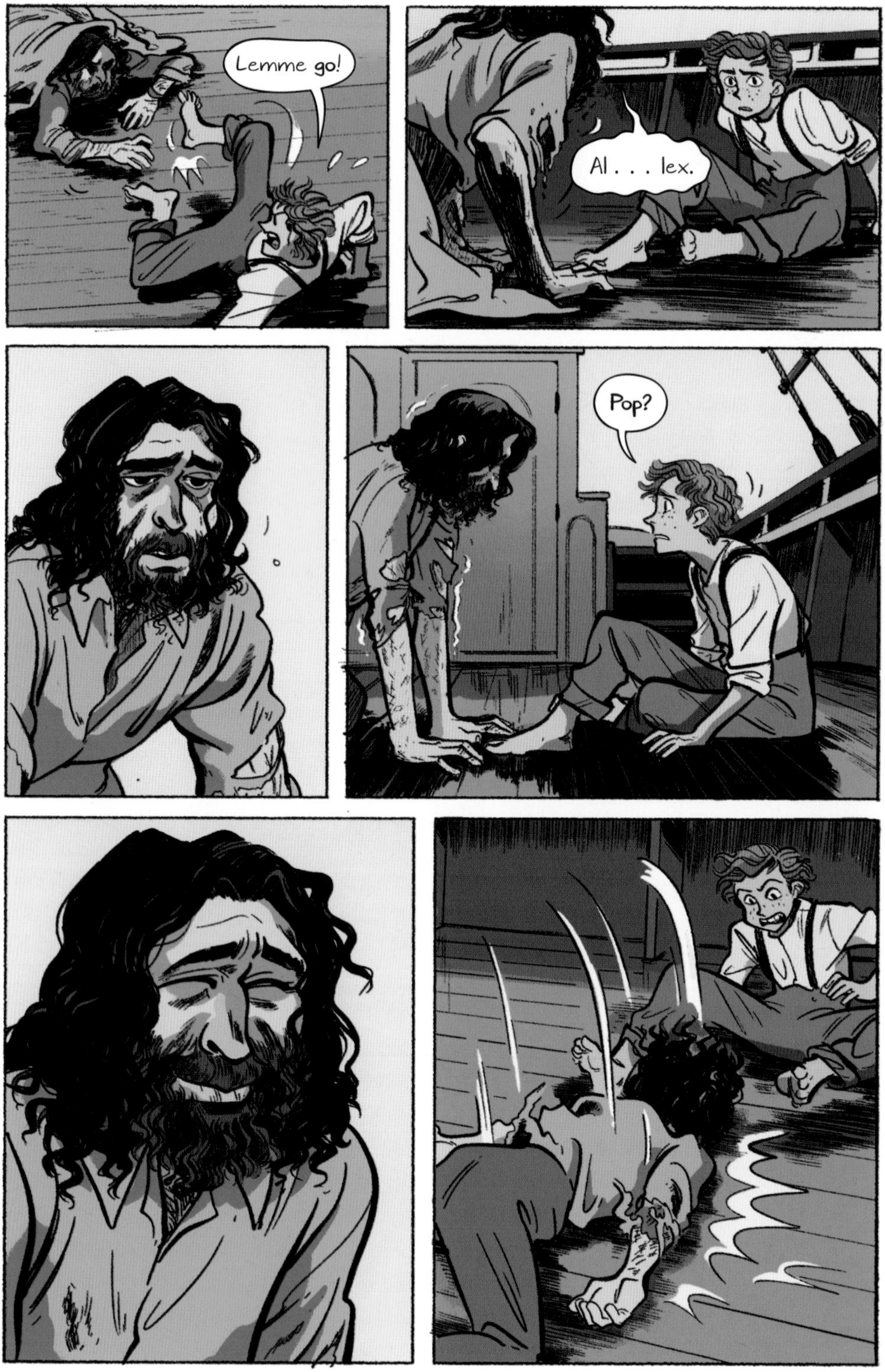

Lemme go!
Al . . . lex.
Pop?

## CHAPTER NINE
# CITY IN A CLOUD

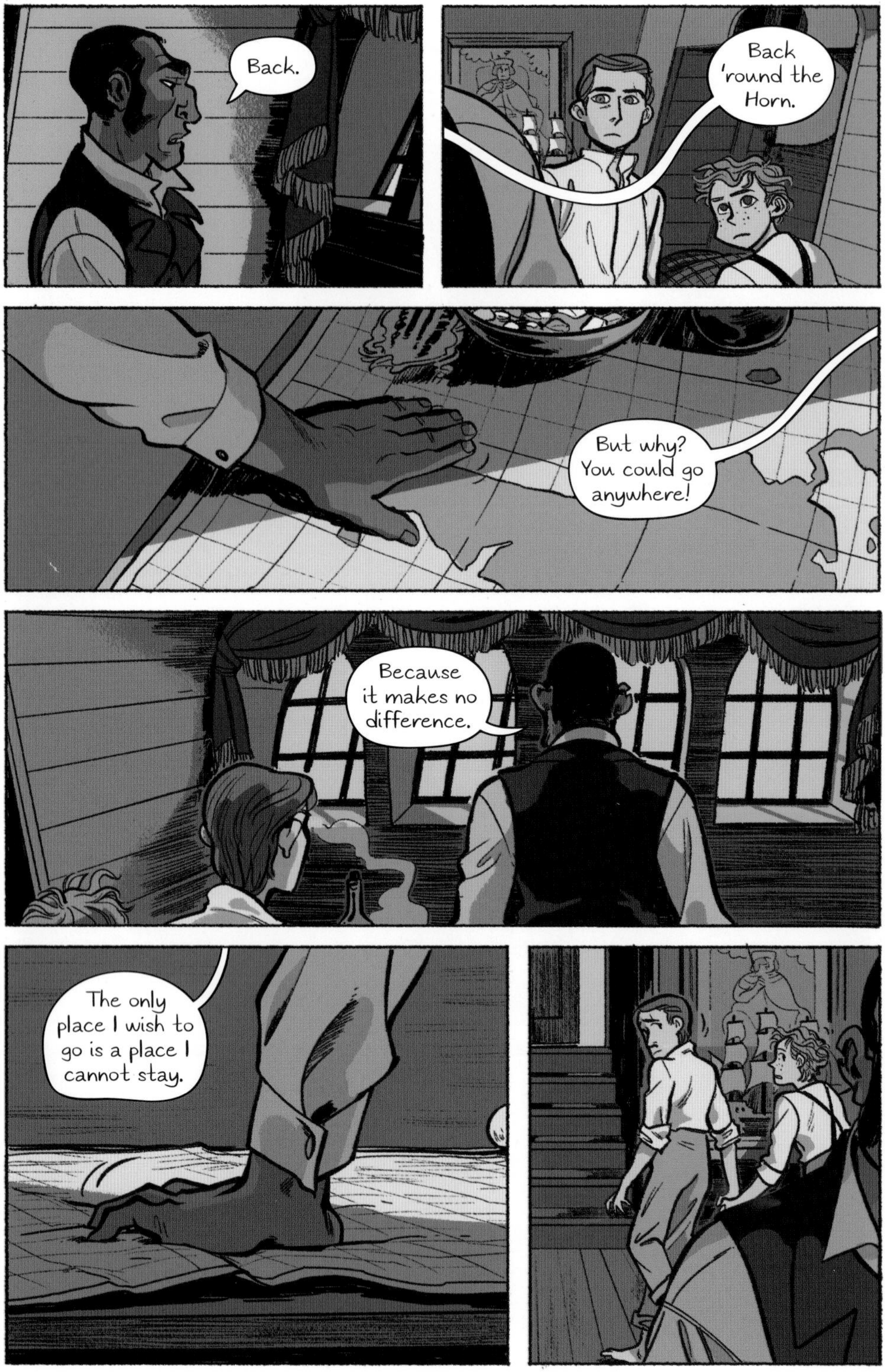
Back.
Back 'round the Horn.
But why? You could go anywhere!
Because it makes no difference.
The only place I wish to go is a place I cannot stay.

207

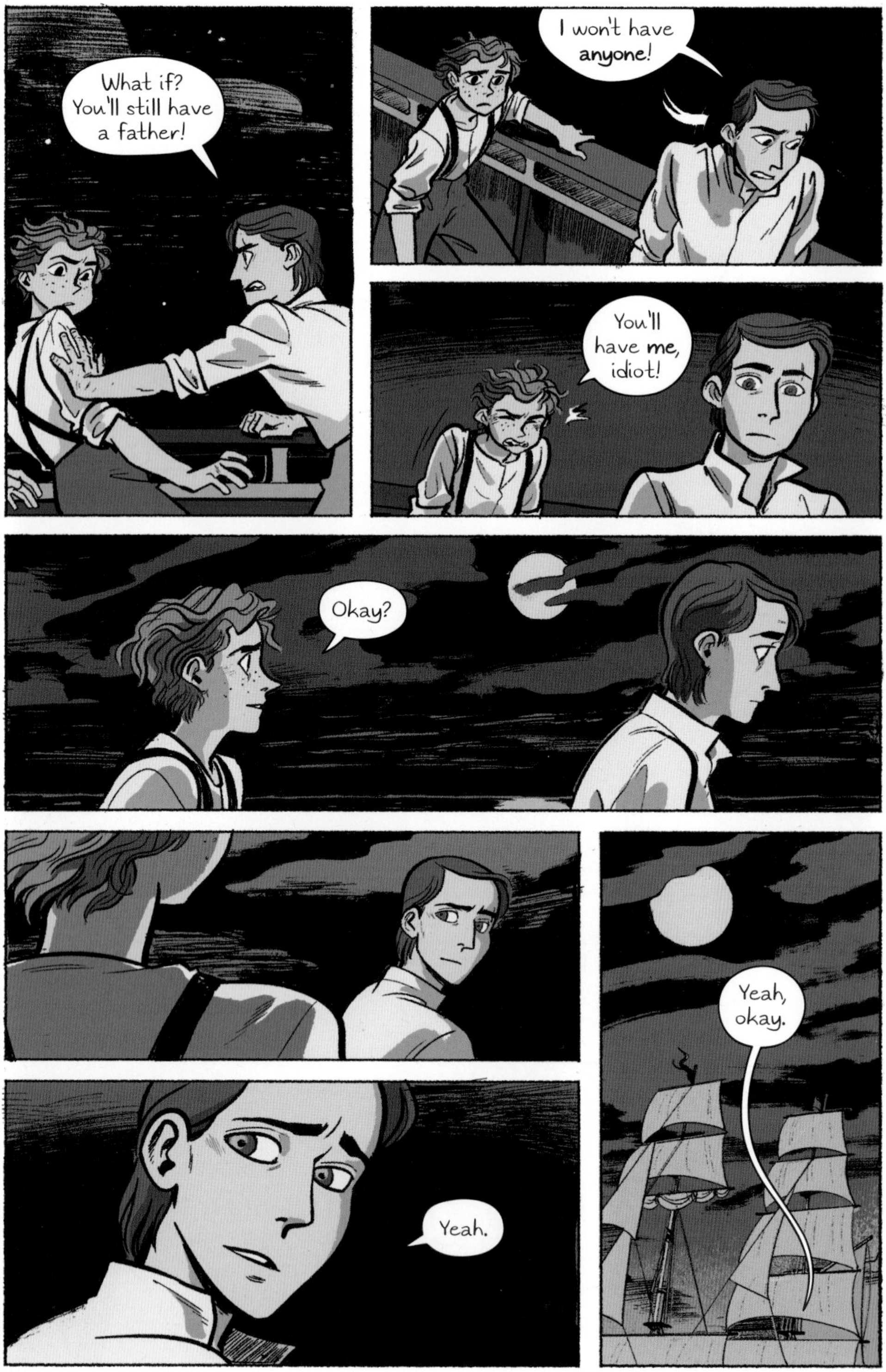
What if? You'll still have a father!
I won't have anyone!
You'll have me, idiot!
Okay?
Yeah.
Yeah, okay.

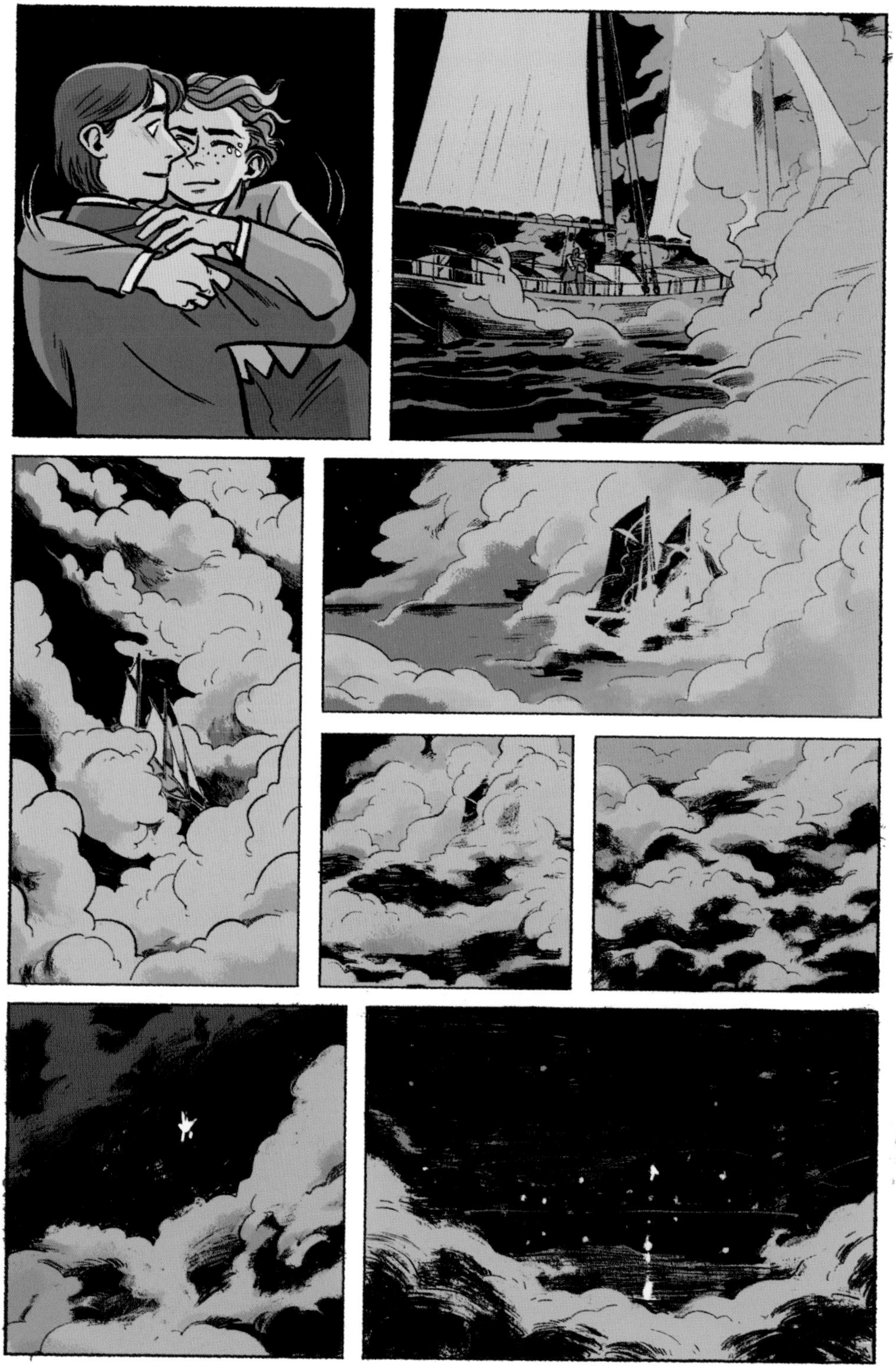

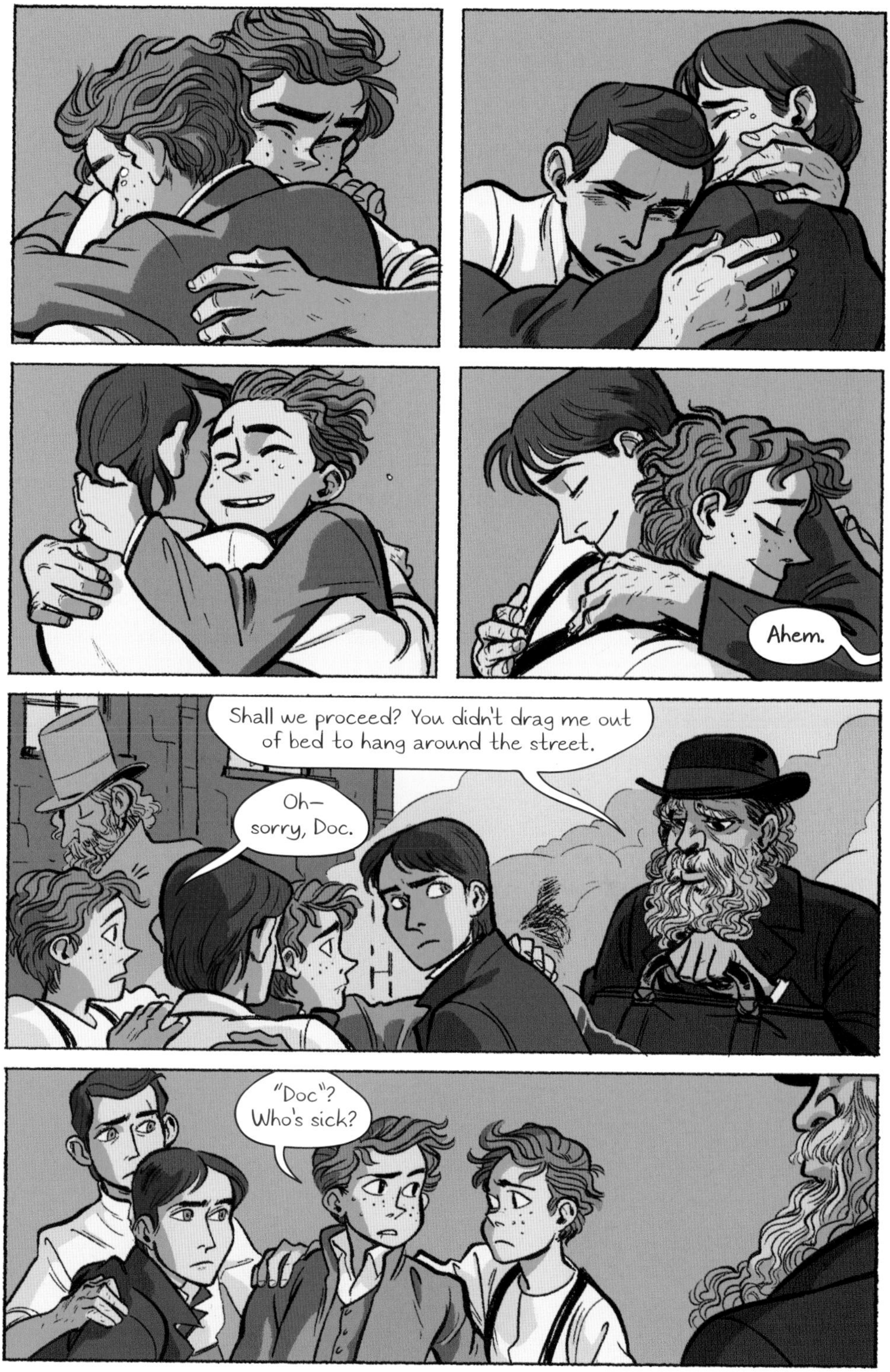
Ahem.
Shall we proceed? You didn't drag me out of bed to hang around the street.
Oh— sorry, Doc.
"Doc"? Who's sick?

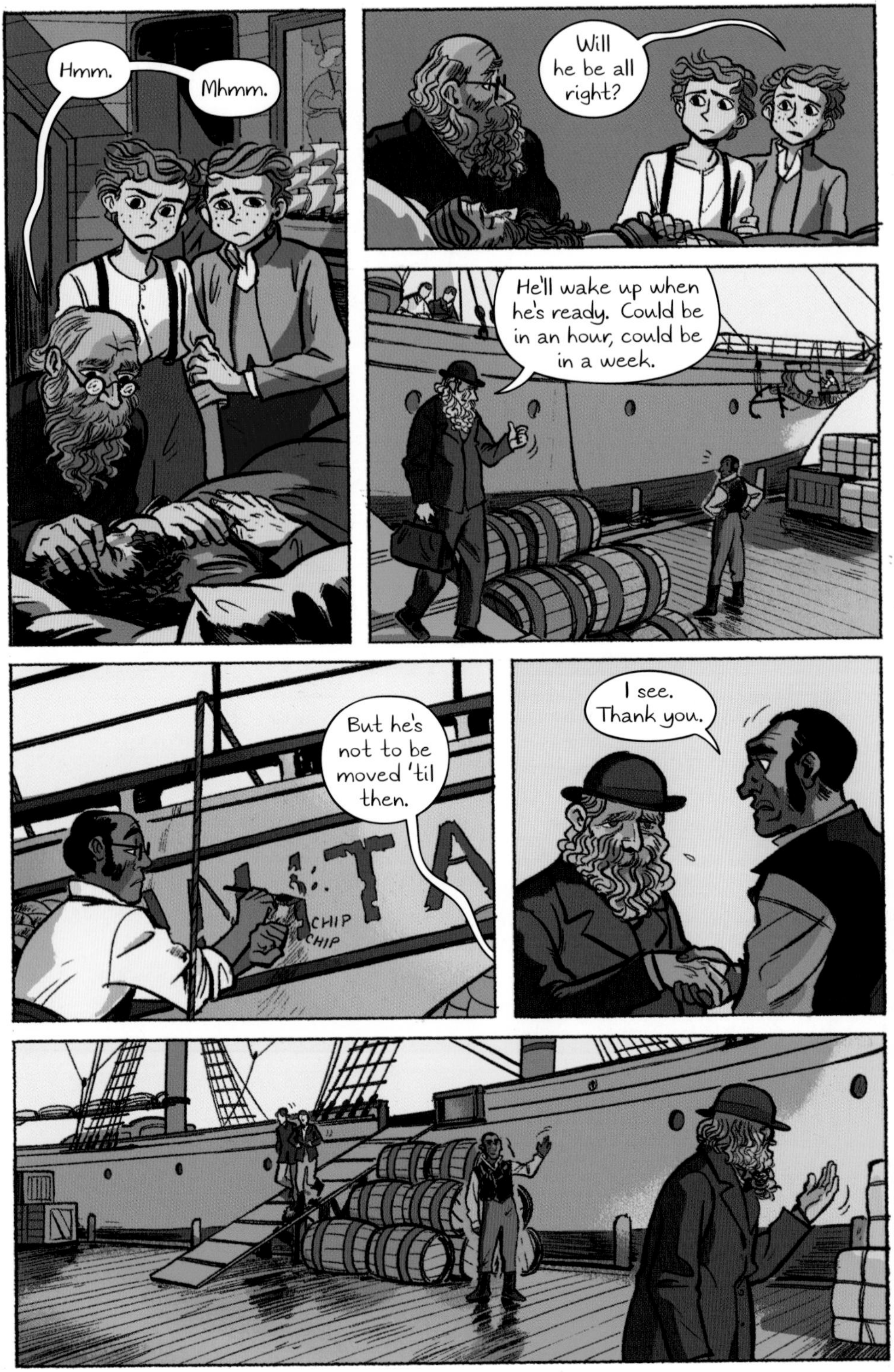
Hmm.
Mhmm.
Will he be all right?
He'll wake up when he's ready. Could be in an hour, could be in a week.
But he's not to be moved 'til then.
CHIP
CHIP
I see. Thank you.

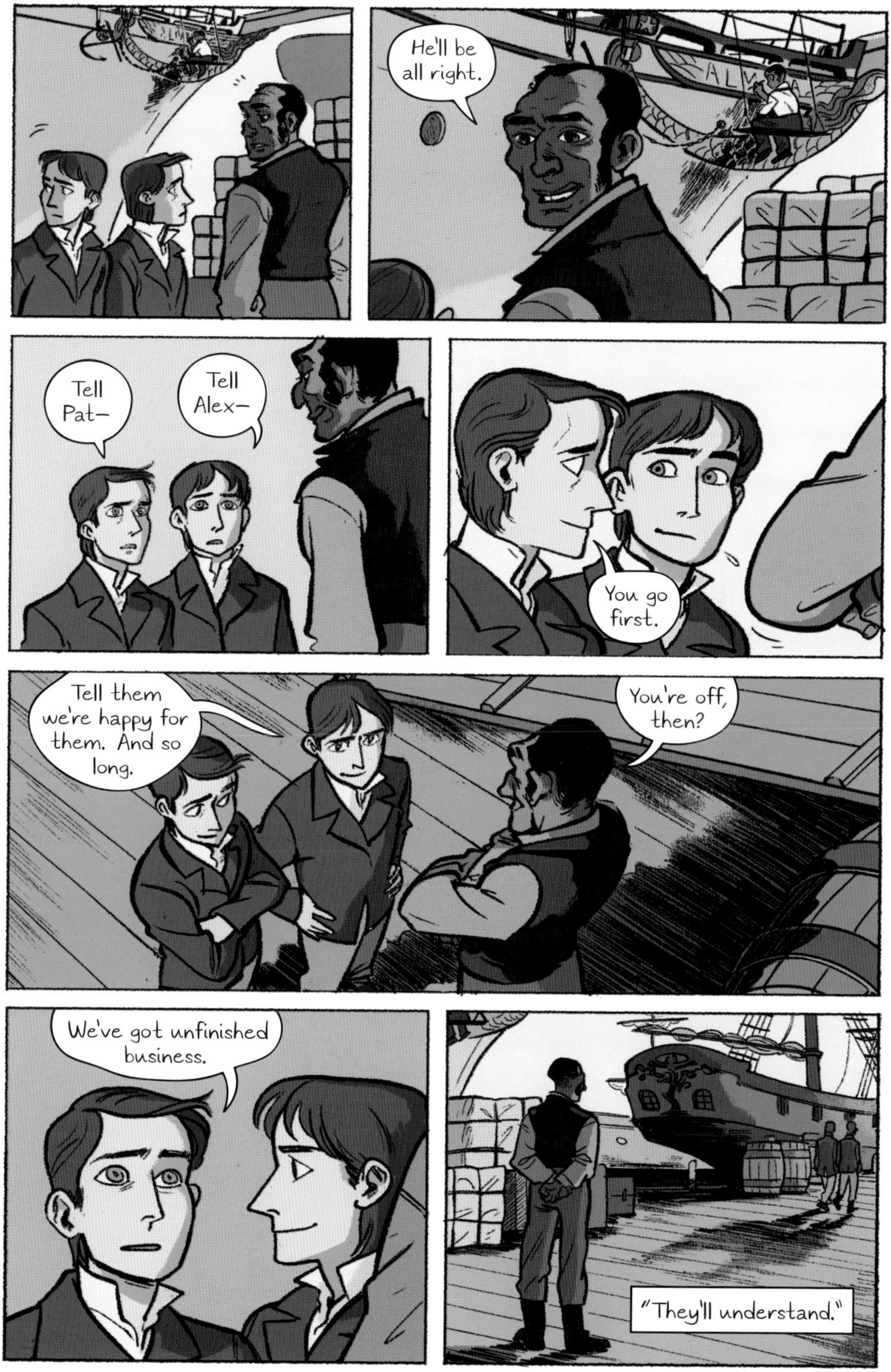
He'll be all right.
Tell Pat—
Tell Alex—
You go first.
Tell them we're happy for them. And so long.
You're off, then?
We've got unfinished business.
"They'll understand."

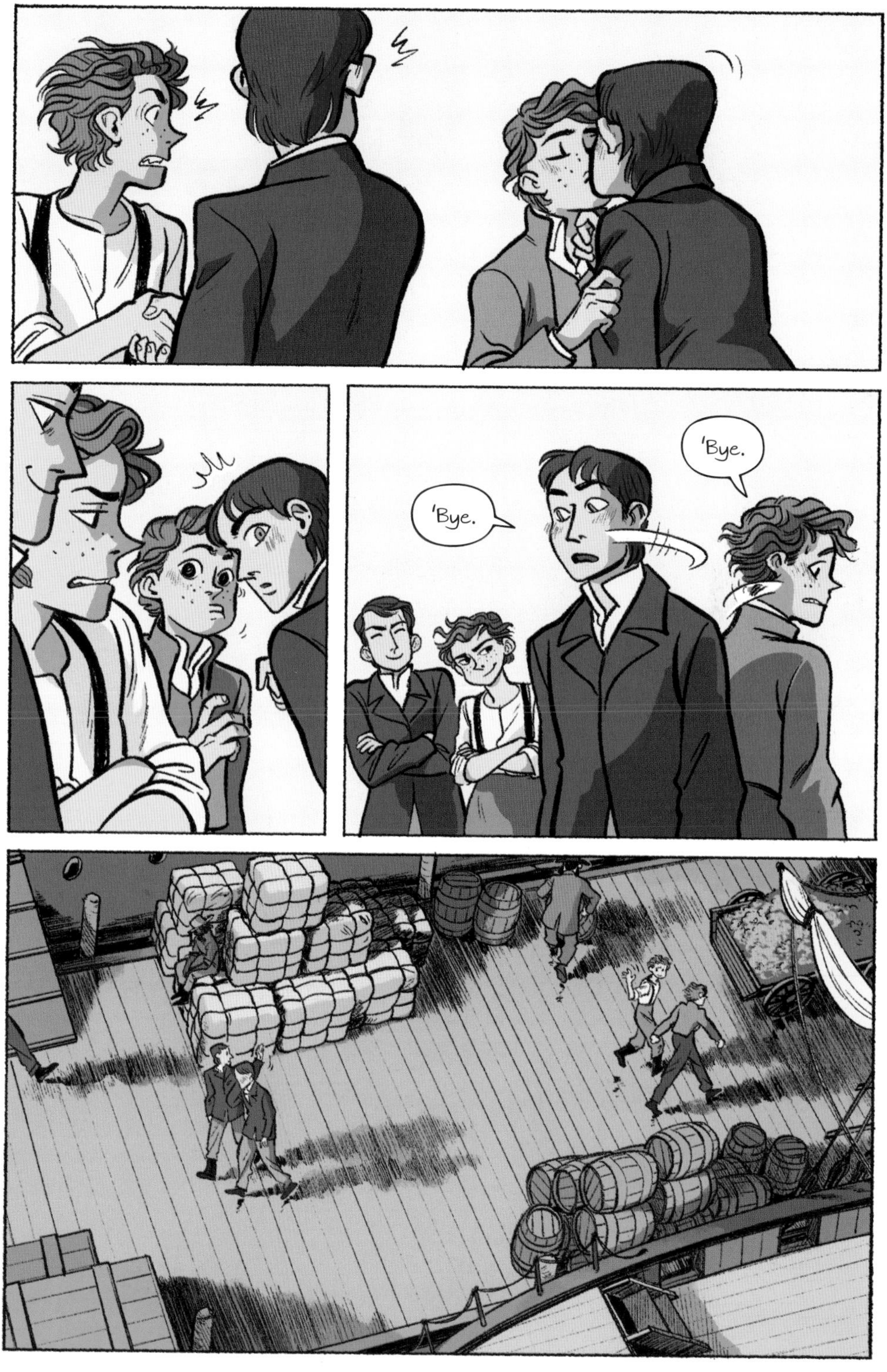
'Bye.
'Bye.

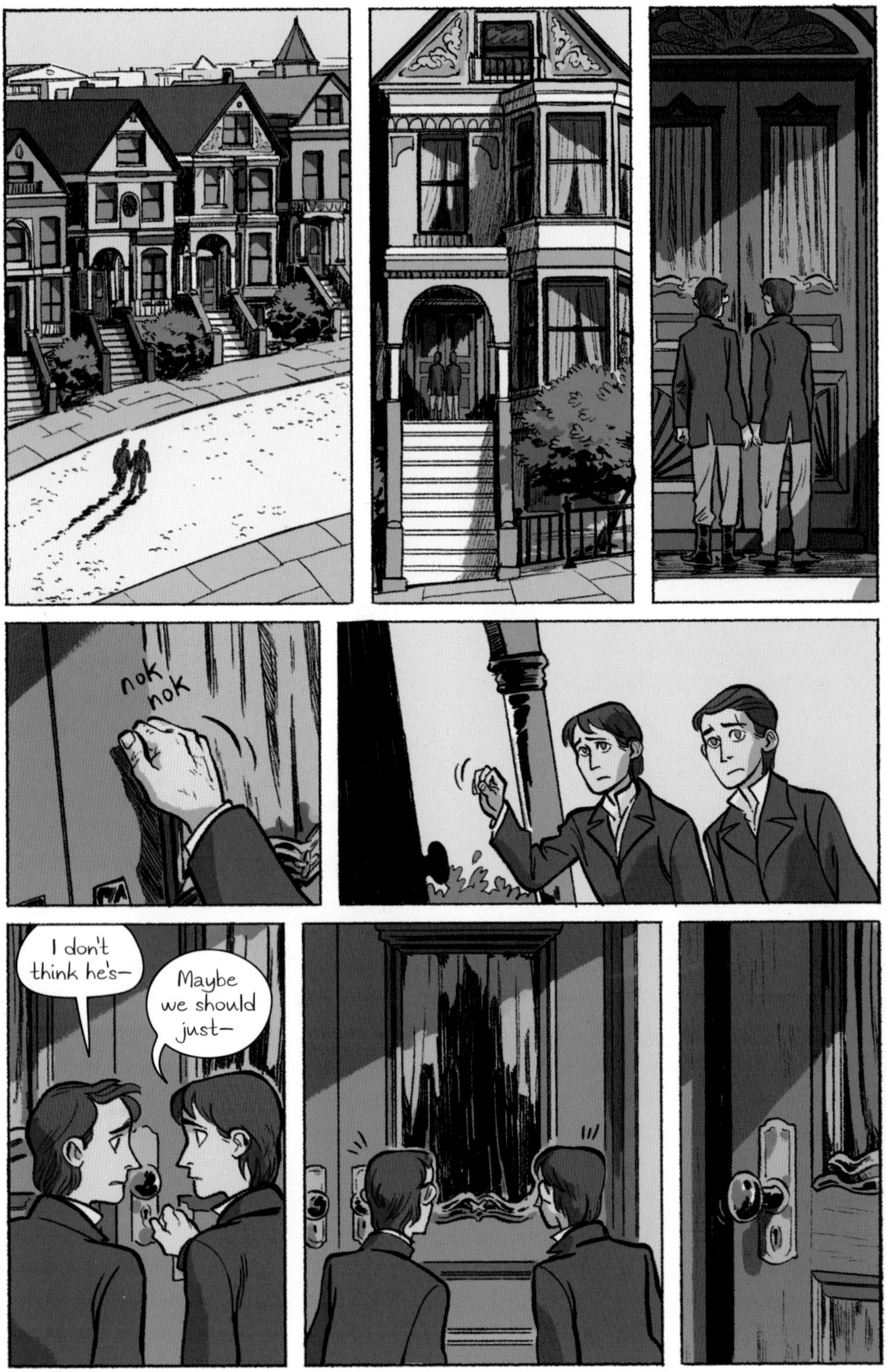
nok nok
I don't think he's—
Maybe we should just—

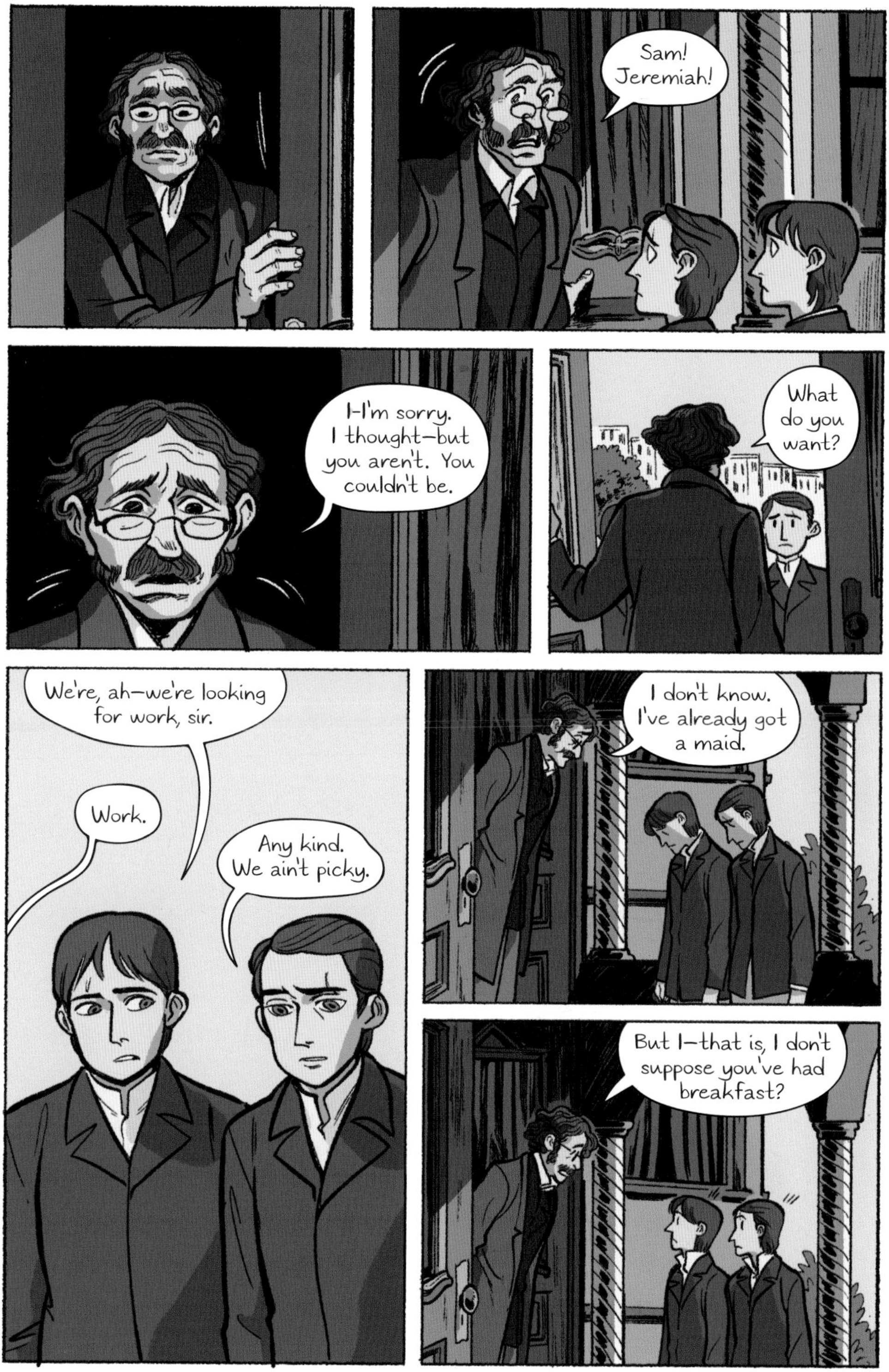
Sam!
Jeremiah!
I-I'm sorry. I thought—but you aren't. You couldn't be.
What do you want?
We're, ah—we're looking for work, sir.
Work.
Any kind. We ain't picky.
I don't know. I've already got a maid.
But I—that is, I don't suppose you've had breakfast?

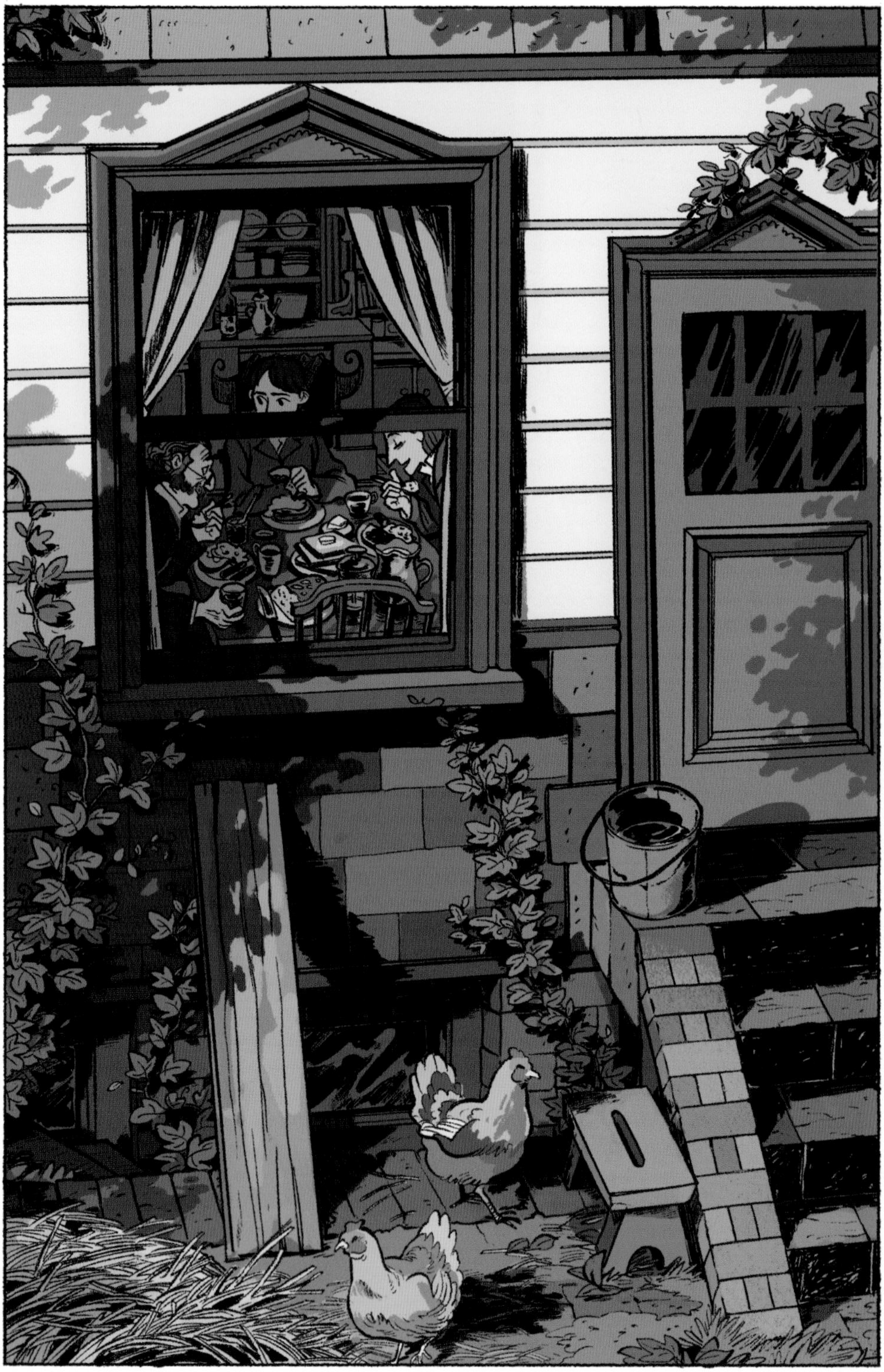

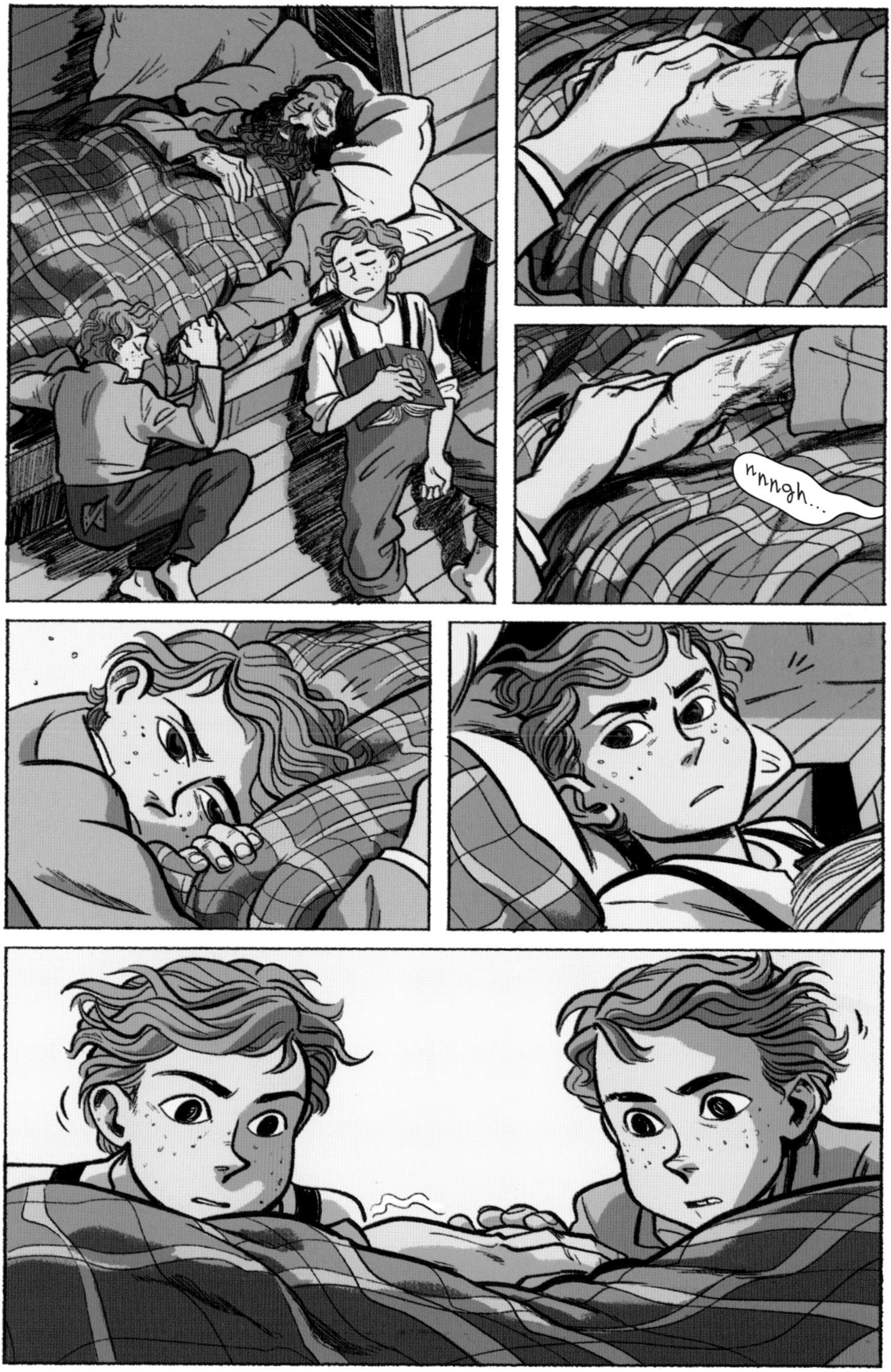
nnngh...

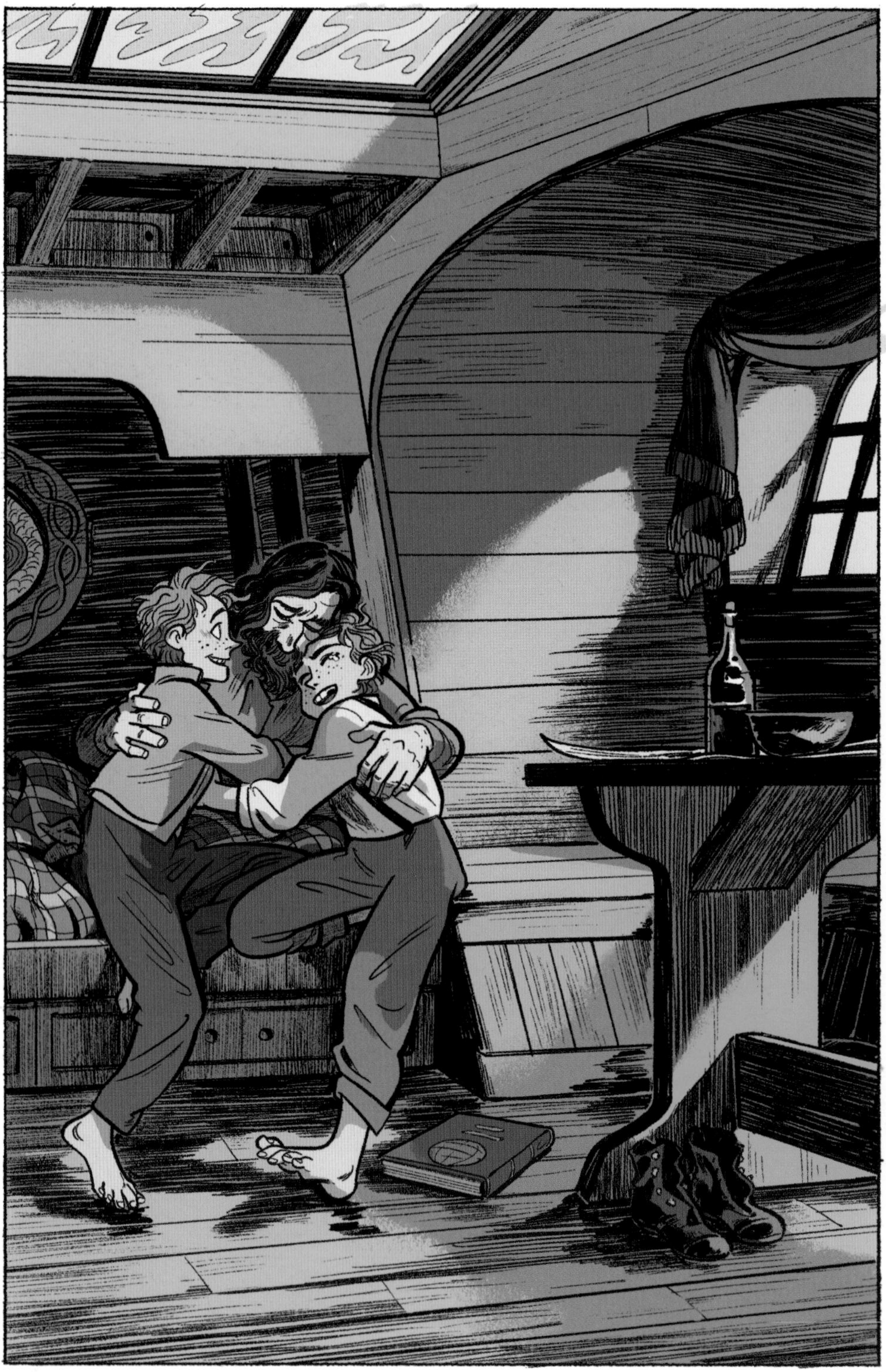